FLYAWAY VACAT SWEEPSTAKES!

W9-BMV-866

This month's destination:

Exciting ORLANDO, FLORIDA!

Are you the lucky person who will win a free trip to Orlando? Imagine how much fun it would be to visit Walt Disney World**, Universal Studios**, Cape Canaveral and the other sights and attractions in this area! The Next page contains tow Official Entry Coupons, as does each of the other books you received this shipment. Complete and return *all* the entry coupons—**the more times you enter, the better your chances of winning!**

Then keep your fingers crossed, because you'll find out by October 15, 1995 if you're the winner! If you are, here's what you'll get:

• Round-trip airfare for two to Orlando!

• 4 days/3 nights at a first-class resort hotel!

• $500.00 pocket money for meals and sightseeing!

Remember: The more times you enter, the better your chances of winning!*

*NO PURCHASE OR OBLIGATION TO CONTINUE BEING A SUBSCRIBER NECESSARY TO ENTER. SEE BACK PAGE FOR ALTERNATIVE MEANS OF ENTRY AND RULES.

**THE PROPRIETORS OF THE TRADEMARKS ARE NOT ASSOCIATED WITH THIS PROMOTION.

VOR KAL

FLYAWAY VACATION
SWEEPSTAKES

OFFICIAL ENTRY COUPON

This entry must be received by: SEPTEMBER 30, 1995
This month's winner will be notified by: OCTOBER 15, 1995
Trip must be taken between: NOVEMBER 30, 1995-NOVEMBER 30, 1996

YES, I want to win the vacation for two to Orlando, Florida. I understand the prize includes round-trip airfare, first-class hotel and $500.00 spending money. Please let me know if I'm the winner!

Name_____

Address _____ Apt. _____

City   State/Prov.   Zip/Postal Code

Account #_____

Return entry with invoice in reply envelope.

© 1995 HARLEQUIN ENTERPRISES LTD.   COR KAL

Cecilia sputtered at his manhandling,

but Jake no longer cared what she thought, or how angry she became. Her being there was making him nervous.

As he deposited her on the first step, she pulled away and whirled on him. "You, you brute!" she spat angrily.

"Brute?" Jake asked, feigning wonder. He puffed out his chest and tugged at his vest in mock pride. "No one's ever called me that before. I rather like it."

What a horrid man! Cecilia thought. And to think that even last night she had toyed with the idea—ludicrous now—that he was actually rather attractive.

"You stay out of my way," she warned.

"Out of your way? Just yesterday you indicated you were going to be my shadow. Perhaps you should take your own advice."

Her blue eyes flashed with ire. "That wasn't advice, Pendergast. It was a warning…!"

Dear Reader,

With this month's WOMEN OF THE WEST selection, *Cecilia and the Stranger*, contemporary author Liz Ireland makes her historical debut. This talented writer won the *Romantic Times* Award for Best Silhouette Romance of the Year for her first book, *Man Trap*, and we are delighted to welcome her to the historical genre. Don't miss this charming story of a schoolteacher who is not all he seems, and the rancher's daughter who is bent on finding out just who he really is.

Also this month, gifted author Deborah Simmons returns to Medieval times with her new book, *Taming the Wolf*, the amusing tale of a baron who is determined to fulfill his duty and return an heiress to her legal guardian, until the young lady convinces him that to do so would put her in the gravest danger.

Ever since the release of her first book, *Snow Angel*, Susan Amarillas has been delighting readers with her western tales of love and laughter. This month's *Scanlin's Law* is the story of a jaded U.S. Marshal and the woman who's waited eight years for him to return. And for those of you who like adventure with your romance, don't miss *Desert Rogue*, by the writing team of Erin Yorke. It's the story of an English socialite and the rough-hewn American soldier of fortune who rescues her.

Whatever your taste in historical reading, we hope you'll keep a lookout for all four titles, available wherever Harlequin Historicals are sold.

Sincerely,

Tracy Farrell

Senior Editor

Please address questions and book requests to:
Harlequin Reader Service
U.S.: 3010 Walden Ave., P.O. Box 1325, Buffalo, NY 14269
Canadian: P.O. Box 609, Fort Erie, Ont. L2A 5X3

LIZ IRELAND

CECILIA AND THE STRANGER

Harlequin Books

TORONTO • NEW YORK • LONDON
AMSTERDAM • PARIS • SYDNEY • HAMBURG
STOCKHOLM • ATHENS • TOKYO • MILAN
MADRID • WARSAW • BUDAPEST • AUCKLAND

ISBN 0-373-28886-7

CECILIA AND THE STRANGER

Copyright © 1995 by Elizabeth Bass.

This edition published by arrangement with Harlequin Books S.A.

® and TM are trademarks of the publisher. Trademarks indicated with
® are registered in the United States Patent and Trademark Office, the
Canadian Trade Marks Office and in other countries.

Printed in U.S.A.

LIZ IRELAND

grew up spinning yarns in rural East Texas, an area she believes supplied her with a never-ending supply of colorful characters for stories. Also an author of contemporary romances, she devotes most of her days to writing, but still finds time for reading history, watching old movies and taking care of a dachshund and two fat cats.

For Suzie, also known as Budro—equestrian, geneology freak and master of slang and hyperbole.

Prologue

Guthrie, Texas
1886

The man raised his head off the greasy bar just long enough to lift a sagging eyelid and make one last definitive statement.

"I ain't going," he announced with his strange Philadelphia cowpoke inflection just before his head again hit the wooden surface with a thud.

"You said that already, schoolteacher," Jake Reed said.

"Don' call me sh-shoolteacher," the man slurred. "The name's Pendergast. Eugene W."

Jake tried not to weave on his bar stool as he looked at the slumped form. The Yankee's newly bought Western duds, twill work pants and a plain cotton shirt, which had appeared comically pressed and new to Jake before, now seemed to have been worn just from hours of sitting in this smoky, smelly, dusty place. Even the black leather traveling bag at the man's feet now had a fine layer of grime coating it.

Was he that drunk? Jake wondered. He hoped not. The sun was finally peeking in through the windows now. He couldn't afford to let his guard down.

What he needed to sober up was another drink. He poured himself a generous slug from the sticky, near-empty whiskey bottle he and the other man had been sharing. "Well, *aren't* you a schoolteacher, Pendergast?"

"Not in this godforsaken place!" the man hollered, so loud that it echoed through the empty barroom, almost rousing the snoring bartender in the corner. "I ain't going to proceed to Annsboro, or any other destination in this whole damn hot, dried-up, uncivilized state. Soon as I can get my money back on these clothes, I ain't goin' anywhere but back to Philadelphia."

No doubt the heat wave they'd been having had colored the Yankee's opinion. Amused, Jake quirked an eyebrow. "Do all teachers in Philadelphia talk like you do?"

"Huh?" Pendergast regarded him through half-open bloodshot eyes. A curly black lock of hair fell lazily across his forehead. "Oh, you mean the cussing," he said, reaching for the splash of liquid left in the glass Jake had just poured. "I learned to talk this-a-way from my books. Nobody says ain't or cusses in Philadelphia. Everything's perfect in Philadelphia."

A beatific smile played across his whiskey-numbed lips as his head once more descended to the bar. He was out. Jake took off his hat and laid it across the man's head. A person deserved some privacy while he slept, after all. Shortly thereafter, a gentle rumble emanated from Pendergast's still curved mouth.

Philadelphia. The City of Brotherly Love. Maybe that's where he should be headed, Jake thought. He tried and failed to remember where he was now; Annsboro was the only name he could come up with. He'd never heard of the place before meeting up with Pendergast sometime after three in the morning. The schoolteacher had spent the hours since then alternating between romanticizing the little town he'd not yet seen and grouching about what he had viewed of Texas so far. Now Jake knew more than he ever wanted to about what sounded like just another little Western town the railroad had missed.

Annsboro probably had a lot in common with Redwood, where he'd grown up and been deputy for a short time. He had thought he'd found his calling when Sheriff Burnet Dobbs pinned that little piece of metal on his chest. It wasn't much of a job, really, in a sleepy place, but it had given him the opportunity to get what he'd most wanted in life since the age of ten—revenge on Otis Darby, the rich-as-Croesus rancher who muscled Jake's family off their land, and in so doing killed his father.

Jake frowned bitterly at the memory. Some revenge. After years of trying to get something on Darby, he had discovered that the man and his son-in-law had been stealing horses. The two had been found guilty, but some fool judge let them out of jail after only two years. Even though Jake had given up the lawman's life by that time and was working as a ranch foreman in the next county, Darby and Gunter were out to get him.

Jake had been dodging the man and his crazy son-in-law ever since. It seemed as if all he'd done was run for over a year now. But never fast enough. Otis Darby would always send his henchman Gunter to find him, and Jake would hit the road two steps ahead. They had harassed employers he worked for by burning their buildings, or killing livestock, although Jake could never prove it. He just knew, like a sixth sense—just as he knew what would happen if he dared to pursue his own dream of trying to start up his own ranch. The place would be burned to a crisp within a week.

Once upon a time he could have gone to the law. Maybe Burnet Dobbs would have helped him out, but in the beginning Jake hadn't wanted to drag his old friend into the mess. Jake fought his own battles. Sometimes he thought he might as well get it over with and face Gunter and Darby down; then, at least, he would have evidence of what they were doing. Of course, the proof would probably be his own carcass.

His mouth a grim line, Jake took another slug of the rot-gut in front of him and ruminated as it burned its way down his gullet. They would find him here, too, in this tiny little railroad whistle-stop town, and the chase would start all over again.

Maybe in a place like Philadelphia he could get lost. He wouldn't mind melting into a crowd and becoming somebody else, someone who wasn't always either running or looking over his shoulder, or both. As long as he could become somebody Otis Darby wasn't looking for.

A short sharp crack rang through the air, followed by the sound of glass breaking in the window. Reflexively, Jake collapsed to the ground—surprised, really, that he had any reflexes left. He scooted around the corner of the bar for cover. As his knees hit the floor, the large bar mirror and several bottles above his head shattered. For a split second it rained alcohol and shards of splintery glass.

"What's going on!" the roused barkeep cried.

"Get down, you fool!" Jake hollered, not stopping to watch as the man dived behind the bar.

Damn, damn, damn! The timing was all wrong. Belatedly, Jake reached for the gun that hadn't left his hip in what seemed like a lifetime. Another shot sounded.

"Who the hell's out there?" the bartender yelled.

Sweat broke out across Jake's brow, and he mopped his sleeve across his forehead. He knew who was out there. It was Will Gunter, Otis Darby's son-in-law, although Jake had heard the daughter had died while her father and husband were in prison. Seeing a flash of white-blond hair through the window before a third shot rang out confirmed it.

A familiar venom surged through him, the anger of the trapped animal ready to make yet another last stand. He focused on the window, lifted his Colt revolver and took aim. This time he would kill the man. At the very least, he would wound him, leaving a souvenir of their encounter that would be proof of the man's guilt later on.

His eyes narrowed on the small opening in the glass. His finger itched as he waited for just a glimpse, just a hint of movement. But there was only silence.

And then he heard hoofbeats. Retreating hoofbeats. Gunter had fled.

Jake's legs straightened cautiously. Something was not right. Thirty seconds had passed, if that much. Three shots. Jake hadn't fired. It wasn't like Gunter to hightail it just when he had his target cornered.

Shouts sounded on the street as Jake's eyes alit on a disturbing sight. Pendergast. In the few moments of excitement, Jake had forgotten about the sleeping schoolteacher. His stomach clenched. A dark crimson patch was spreading across the side of the man's shirt. On the other side of him, a pool of blood was gathering on the floor from another wound. Pendergast wasn't sleeping anymore.

"They got him!"

Jake glanced over at the now-standing bartender, whose face was filled with curious revulsion.

"I reckon it was some sort of vendetta," the man continued breathlessly, wiping his hands anxiously on the apron at his waist. "Man said he'd been a deputy!"

Jake froze as the man's words sank in. Slowly, he turned back to Pendergast and saw his own hat still perched on the dead man's head. There wasn't much difference in their sizes, or even their clothes for that matter, if one didn't stop to consider the newly bought appearance of the dead man's. Gunter had made a mistake. A fatal one for Pendergast.

Three men burst through the door of the saloon. "Lou! What the hell happened!" one of them cried.

A skinny, grizzled old fellow with a tarnished star stuck on the breast pocket of his work shirt pushed through the others to look at Pendergast's slumped form. His eyes bugged. "This man's dead!" he pronounced, shocked. "We ain't had but one dead person in town all year!"

"That's so," another man said. "And old Mrs. Grizwald was ninety-three."

"This here looks like murder to me!" the sheriff announced.

The men remained congregated around the dead man while the bartender recounted what had happened. As Jake shuffled closer he just barely heard the words *deputy* and *vendetta*. The bartender had been asleep since the small hours, so it was no wonder he'd gotten his facts confounded.

Jake's head was swimming. Gunter thought he'd killed him, that Jake Reed was dead. After five years of dreaming about it, and nearly two years of actively trying, the snake probably felt triumphant. More than likely, he was on his way back to Redwood right now to tell Darby the good news.

"I'd better find out the name of the deceased," the sheriff said, beginning his official investigation.

Jake's head snapped up. Four pairs of eyes were peering at him anxiously. He opened his mouth to speak, but hesitated, glancing down at the suitcase at his feet. *Why not?* Darby and Gunter would stop looking for him now. Becoming someone else would make him free—free to hunt *them* when their guards were down.

"Reed," Jake said, surprised at how easily the lie came to his lips once he'd made up his mind. "Jacob Reed, I think he said his name was." If he was going to be buried, he wanted the formality of his full Christian name.

The men shook their heads. "Guess we oughtn't even to call Doc," one of them said.

"No, it's like Arnie here says. This man's dead."

The sheriff shot glances at both Jake and the bartender. "Don't reckon either of you recalls where Reed came from."

Jake shook his head. "Nope," he said.

"You didn't see who was shooting, did you?" the old man asked.

"Nope."

"He was tight-lipped, that one," the bartender piped up, nodding at Pendergast, the man who had talked until he'd passed out. "I had the feeling he was running from something."

"That's it, then," said the sheriff, wiping his brow tiredly. "Maybe somebody around here saw something, but I doubt it." In the sheriff's mind, apparently, the investigation was now officially closed.

The bartender looked up as Jake picked up Pendergast's suitcase and slammed some money on the bar. "Good luck to you, mister. Sure sorry this had to happen, with you from the East and all."

"Could have happened anywhere." For all he knew. This sad excuse for a town was as far east as he'd ever been.

"Where'd you say you were going?"

Jake stopped for a moment. He'd need to lie low for a while, and Pendergast had given him the perfect opportunity. "Annsboro," he said.

The men nodded, then turned back to the more interesting matter at hand.

Annsboro. He didn't know where it was, but he'd heard enough about it. Lucky town, really. Pendergast had been on his way back to Philadelphia. Now it looked as though Annsboro would have a new schoolmaster, after all.

Chapter One

Even in late September, Annsboro was cloaked in a dry haze. What few patches of buffalo grass there were in the town itself had long since withered and yellowed, their scorched leftovers, as well as the occasional scrubby mesquite or cedar, lending the place its only landscaping.

Jake pulled one of Pendergast's white starchy handkerchiefs from his coat pocket. No wonder the schoolteacher had picked up new clothes, Jake thought as he raked the stiff cotton across his brow. The wool suit he had found in Pendergast's suitcase, which was a snugger fit than Jake had first thought it would be, was so hot it felt like he was walking around with a brick oven on his back.

"If you'll look to your left, you'll see not only Annsboro's mercantile, but also the sight of our future drug emporium."

Lysander Beasley, Jake's self-appointed guide to this wretched place, gestured grandly toward a squat brick building and the empty lot next to it. On a large wooden sign above the store, the word *Beasley's* was spelled out in red curlicued letters.

"Owned and run by yours truly." Beasley pinched proudly at one end of his pointy mustache. His neatly greased hair, parted down the center, created a pulled-back curtain effect, as though his forehead were a stage. The loud check print of his expensive-looking suit was showy, too—

a flashy display of wealth, like his shiny new gold watch chain that glinted in the sun. Pudgy, florid and fatuous, Lysander Beasley appeared every inch the prosperous model citizen—the kind Jake remembered from his deputy days who would rave for hours about law and order. Then, when one of their own, like Otis Darby, happened to land in jail, they would discover compassion.

But even putting his own feelings aside, Jake couldn't see much to be smug about in Annsboro, although one glance down the town's dusty main street confirmed that the mercantile was probably the town's most successful enterprise, except perhaps for what looked like a saloon clear over on the other end of town. That would make sense. If Jake lived here, he was sure he'd want to do more drinking than buying.

You do live here, fool, he thought, shaking his head in disbelief.

Incredibly, Lysander Beasley mistook his discouraged amazement for awe. "Oh, it's a fine little town, all right. Why, I'd bet that in two years we'll have a courthouse!"

"You don't say," Jake said, striking what he hoped was the appropriate note of wonder. He was rewarded with a hacking chuckle from his companion.

"But I'm sure you're more interested in the schoolhouse than in buildings that don't even exist yet." Beasley guffawed again. "This way, Mr. Pendergast."

Jake was staring at a dilapidated brick building directly across the dirt road from the mercantile. The place proclaimed itself to be a blacksmith's, but the windows were boarded up. And other than some scattered houses, that was it as far as the town went.

"Mr. Pendergast?"

Startled, he looked at Beasley and they continued walking. If he didn't get used to answering to the name of Pendergast, he might find himself with a heap of explaining to do.

The schoolhouse, set down a rutted road from the rest of the town, was in considerably better shape than the other buildings. A new coat of paint made the white wood-frame structure a standout against the dusty terrain.

"On Sundays Parson Gibbons comes in and holds services in the school. Other than that, the school will be quite your domain," Beasley explained. "Cecilia Summertree has been overseeing the children since our last schoolteacher left us. Wonderful girl, Miss Summertree."

But his disdainful tone conveyed the fact that he meant just the opposite. "Her father's quite a cattleman. The Summertree ranch is one of the biggest in the region."

So Jake had heard. It was impossible to have passed through this part of Texas without having heard something of Summertree and his vast spread. Jake had dreamed of having a ranch that would be even a fraction as successful. He couldn't imagine why a daughter of such a man would want to teach school in this barren place, though. "She's a local girl?" he asked.

"Oh, yes. She's not a professional academician like yourself, Mr. Pendergast. Mercy, she doesn't even have a certificate. Sometimes out here we're forced to bend all these new regulations, you know. She did spend five months at a school for young ladies in New Orleans this year." Beasley stopped and raised a speculative eyebrow. "She was *supposed* to have been gone for a full year . . ." He left the sentence dangling tremulously between them.

Kid probably got homesick, was Jake's first reaction . . . if a body could get homesick for this patch of dust. But what he thought wasn't at issue. "Hmm," he murmured suspiciously for Beasley's benefit, knowing the man probably expected his Philadelphia schoolteacher to be loaded with moral superiority.

"Precisely," Beasley said, pleased to have indoctrinated the new teacher in one of his own personal prejudices. He continued walking. "Now I wanted to tell you about my daughter, Beatrice. She's quite the little student."

As they approached the school, Jake only half listened to the litany of Beatrice Beasley's accomplishments. Undoubtedly any child of Lysander Beasley, formerly of Louisville, Kentucky, would be nothing less than a prodigy. Jake was more interested in the laughter and periodic high-pitched whoops coming from the schoolhouse. It was late afternoon already—just finding the town had taken Jake the better part of a day after disembarking the train in Abilene that morning—and school was definitely out.

Noticing his companion's distraction, Beasley broke off and cocked his head to the side, listening. "Hmm. Sounds as if Miss Summertree's in her usual high spirits today."

"It would seem so," Jake answered, injecting a hint of disapproval into his voice.

"I might add that my daughter's true genius would seem to lie in the area of literature," Beasley droned on. "Her dear mother, God rest her soul, started her early. Why, Beatrice could recite Shakespeare by the age of three!"

Jake nodded at this impressive tidbit, but at that moment, his attention was completely derailed. Through a window, he saw a young man—a cowboy—and woman cavorting around the teacher's desk. The woman, a pretty blond creature, let out a laughing cry and hopped nimbly on the high desk, revealing a glimpse of shapely leg.

"C'mon, Cici," Jake heard the man saying. "You know you want to."

"Not if you were the only man in Texas, Buck!" The woman's bright blue eyes sparked with a mix of amusement and annoyance.

"But I am the only man for you, sweetheart."

"You crazy—"

The cowboy reached for the woman's waist. She attempted to back away, but was thrown off-balance and regained equilibrium only by allowing herself to be hoisted high in the air. She rolled her eyes in distress, and as she did, caught sight of movement outside.

As her eyes alit on Beasley, dread crossed her face. Then when she glanced over to Jake, her expression changed to one of complete mortification.

Jake couldn't help it. He smiled.

Even caught slack-jawed with surprise, this Cecilia Summertree gave him hope for his short stay in Annsboro. Her figure, so easily held aloft by the rustic youth, appeared lithe and sturdy at once. It was encased in a blue muslin frock of practical design, but she wore the gown with a dash that would have made the cowboy's forwardness with her person humorous, had not her own reaction to seeing a stranger peeping in the window—and catching sight of such a spectacle—been comical in itself.

After the initial shock passed, Cecilia Summertree's eyes swept over him with feminine curiosity, making Jake groan at the memory of his ill-fitting brown suit. Not that he was normally a lady-killer... well, maybe he *had* made a few pulses flutter in his day. He instinctively tugged down his tight herringbone vest.

But the smirk that crossed the young woman's face halted him in mid-preen. Obviously, she found nothing heart-stopping about his appearance. And she couldn't even see that his pants nearly reached his shins! Jake silently cursed his suit as he watched her expression change yet again—to guarded anticipation.

"Put me down, fool!" the woman whispered urgently to her companion.

Beasley, beyond the sightlines of the window and therefore ignorant of the drama awaiting them inside, hurried his straggling companion into the building with a wave. Jake sobered his expression and eagerly stepped over the threshold ahead of Beasley, into a small hallway that held a coatrack. Suddenly, the subject of Miss Summertree's early return from finishing school, or anything else about the woman, fascinated him.

Before he could step through the door, the man named Buck had set her down, and she was giving the bodice of her dress a firm straightening jerk. When their gazes met again, her brilliant blue eyes were narrowed on him suspiciously.

Jake was irked that he wasn't able to make more of an impression. Not that what this woman thought made any difference, he reminded himself. He was just here to lie low, not to spark the local schoolteacher. Ex-schoolteacher.

"Mr. Beasley," she said in a high feminine voice whose energy enchanted him immediately. "What did you bring me?"

"Looks too old for a student," the cowboy joked, eyeing Jake with genial curiosity.

"Good heavens!" Beasley said sharply, as if the offhand comment had done grave insult to their guest. "This is Mr. Eugene Pendergast. Mr. Pendergast, this is Miss Summertree, who I was telling you about. And this is . . ."

"Buck McDeere," Cecilia supplied. That Beasley wouldn't know the cowboy's name came as no surprise to Jake, or apparently, to Cecilia.

"Mr. Pendergast is our new schoolteacher, just arrived from Philadelphia."

At the word *schoolteacher* Cecilia Summertree's mouth dropped open. Once again her blue eyes assessed his person, this time without mirth. She stiffened her spine and jutted her jaw forward. "Philadelphia, you say?" she said disbelievingly.

Jake bit back a laugh. No curtsy, no how-do-you-do. Just a question about his origins and another scathing once-over. Maybe Miss Summertree expected men from Philadelphia to have better tailors.

In spite of the cool reception, he bowed politely. Trying to think of a way to respond, Jake remembered his uncle Thelmer, from St. Louis. The one time Thelmer had visited his relatives in Texas, it was clear he had considered himself to be hands-down more civilized than his poor relations. And to give the man his due, the ladies had been impressed.

"Pleased to make your acquaintance, Miss Summertree," he said now in his best impression of Uncle Thelmer's sophistication.

Cecilia Summertree pursed her lips. "You sure took your time getting here. We'd begun to think you weren't coming."

"I'm afraid I was detained."

"Detained where?" Cecilia demanded sweetly.

"Now, now, Cecilia," Beasley interjected, agitated by the girl's curiosity. "It's true, Mr. Pendergast, we'd expected you last week. Nevertheless, we're simply glad that you had a safe trip."

Jake breathed a sigh of relief at Beasley's interruption. He hadn't expected to meet with such skepticism. Obviously Miss Summertree wasn't happy giving up her post to a stranger. He managed a weak smile. It helped to remember the reason he was late—the real Pendergast had apparently been on a week-long toot. What would Beasley have said to that?

"I'm certainly glad to be here."

Cecilia's eyes narrowed to fiery little slits. "He doesn't sound like a Yankee."

"Cecilia!"

"My parents were from Alabama," Jake retorted sharply. The woman was beginning to make him nervous. Besides, his parents *were* from Alabama.

"There now," Beasley said, as if Pendergast's parentage settled everything. "I expect you'll be a marvelous help getting Mr. Pendergast acclimated to his new surroundings, Cecilia. But all that's left for you to do today is to hand over the building key."

Cecilia crossed her arms. The young woman was at least a foot shorter than Jake, but that didn't seem to intimidate her any. Nor, apparently, did the fact that Beasley was going to stand by him. Jake took in her honey blond hair and bright blue eyes with admiration and annoyance. She didn't look as if she would be much help.

"I suppose you went to college," she said sharply.

Jake grinned. "Of course." Pendergast had looked like the college type. Soft, sheltered.

"Where?" she pressed, surprising him.

Jake's smile froze. "You want to know where?" he asked inanely, fingering the hat he held in his hand with stiff, sweaty fingers.

"The University of Pennsylvania!" Beasley cried, angered by Cecilia's inquisitiveness.

Jake's gaze shot to the obnoxious man in gratitude. "Yes, that's right." He grinned broadly at Cecilia.

"Same as Watkins," Beasley added.

"Yes, Watkins," Jake agreed. Who was Watkins? "Good old Watkins."

Beasley chuckled anxiously. "There. Now that's settled..." He held out his hand toward Cecilia. "The key?"

"The key is on the desk," she said proudly, nodding toward it. Then, impulsively, she glared at Jake and added, "But I wouldn't trust it to this—this fraud!"

Jake felt the blood drain from his face as her accusation hit its mark. Yet fraud though he was, he hadn't narrowly escaped death to let his future be snatched away by an ornery little rich girl. He clenched his fists at his sides and prepared to speak in his own defense.

But this time, chiming right in with Beasley's shout of outrage was a mumbled warning from Buck. "Cici, I'd watch my words..."

"But it's true!" she cried. "This man isn't a schoolteacher any more than I'm a...a—"

"Lady?" Jake couldn't resist drawling.

Her blue eyes flew open in shock. "How dare you!"

"Hey, now..." Buck said, as if he'd never heard a man speak unkindly to a woman before.

"He couldn't even tell you what college he went to," Cecilia argued.

"The University of Pennsylvania!" Beasley again cried out in exasperation.

"Like I said," Jake said, smiling at her smugly.

Cecilia pushed past Buck and came forward menacingly, in spite of Beasley's ineffectual sputtering. Before setting foot in this little classroom, Jake hadn't given much thought to the difficulties of assuming another person's identity. Having spent two years one step ahead of an assassin, he couldn't imagine much danger in pretending to be a school-teacher.

He was wrong.

When Cecilia spoke, she punctuated her sharp words by jabbing a slender pointy-nailed finger toward his chest. "I'll be watching you, Pendergast, and following you like a shadow. You might be able to fool the likes of the Bucks and Beasleys of this town, but you can't fool me."

By the time she finished, mere inches separated them. Jake had to give her points for bravery, as well as keen insight. Nevertheless, he smiled. This little performance of hers had Beasley so distressed that the storekeeper would probably stand by him even if it turned out that he was Sam Bass resurrected.

Even so, if he didn't try to settle this now, this little slip of a woman would try to harass him right out of town. Keeping in mind that he was a mild-mannered schoolteacher, Jake took a slight step forward and looked straight into Cecilia's eyes.

"If a beautiful flower such as yourself cares to stay close to me, how could I be anything but thrilled at the prospect?"

In a gesture that would have done Uncle Thelmer proud, Jake clasped her hand and gallantly hoisted it to his lips. Letting loose a startled gasp, she attempted to yank it back all the while, so that when he did suddenly let go, the loss of resistance propelled her backward.

"Oh!" she cried, colliding with a desk. Her eyes were wide pools of blue as she stared at him, a furious blush rising in her cheeks. Jake was prepared to be slapped, spat upon or shouted at, but Cecilia remained immobile, for the first time—blessedly—at a loss for words.

Beasley quickly stepped between them. "How nice! Now that you two have settled your little differences, I'm sure that I won't have to mention your unfriendliness to your father the next time I see him, Cecilia."

"My father?" Cecilia pivoted toward Beasley.

The man grinned again in that smug way that made Jake's skin crawl. "Cooperation, you know," Beasley blustered, "it's what makes little communities like ours flourish." He obviously thought he had her over a barrel.

And apparently he did. Cecilia aimed one last glare at Jake, then turned with a flounce and stomped toward the door. Before crossing the threshold, she sent Jake a final warning. "Don't forget—I'll be watching. Come on, Buck." Her companion mumbled something to the two men, then shuffled after her.

When the door closed behind them, Beasley smiled stiffly. "Like I said, a wonderful girl. So...wealthy," he added, as if this explained exactly what made her wonderful. Most likely to Beasley it did.

"I see."

Beasley wasted no time in launching into another monologue, this one mostly about the moral standards expected of the schoolteacher by the community. Once he realized Beasley was one of those blowhards who was only interested in the big picture and not in details that might actually prove helpful, Jake only half listened. Instead, through the window he watched Cecilia Summertree's slim, alluring figure in retreat.

She was beautiful. Strange, Jake thought, that it seemed like years since he'd noticed a woman. Of course, never before had a woman demanded his attention in such a way. But he liked that about her, too. Cecilia Summertree was the most tenacious, forthright woman he'd ever met. He had no doubt that if she set her mind to do something, she'd do it.

Like run him out of town on a rail.

Jake frowned. That woman could mean trouble. Big trouble.

Cecilia barreled toward Dolly Hudspeth's boarding-house as fast as the heat would allow. But it wasn't only the temperature that caused her to flush red. She couldn't wait to ensconce herself in the privacy of her spacious room and start plotting her revenge. That slimy hand-kissing Alabama Yankee wasn't going to get the best of her.

"Cecilia, wait up!"

At the sound of Buck's voice Cecilia stopped and turned, her arms akimbo. "Buck, why are you following me?"

He came up short a few feet away, his face a mask of confusion. "You told me to."

That's right, she did—but then, she hadn't been thinking clearly at the time. With a limp wave, she attempted to shoo him away. "Well, never mind. Go home. And don't you dare whisper a word of this to my father!"

A wide smile broke across Buck's face. It was a handsome face, bronzed from the sun. His hair was colored a light brown and his blue eyes were open and friendly. Too friendly, Cecilia thought. The man hadn't stopped pestering her since she'd come home from New Orleans in disgrace.

"Don't you think it's time you came back to the ranch, Cici?" he asked. "Not much keeping you in town now."

Not much, Cecilia agreed, except the thinnest thread of civilization, which incidentally meant everything to her, although she couldn't expect the heathens she was surrounded by to understand. There was no way she was going back to that ranch. She'd go out of her mind with boredom, and the tension there between her and her father was thick enough to cut with a knife. No, thank you. That house had seen too much sadness.

Cecilia had watched her poor delicate mother languish for years on that blasted ranch, fretful and depressed. Not that her father had cared. He'd allowed his wife to return to her people in Memphis for visits to her family, but she'd inevitably come back ahead of schedule, unable to stay away from that mournful place. When she'd finally died of scarlet fever, her parting words to Cecilia had been instructions on where not to live, and Cecilia had taken the advice to heart.

Even so, before Evelyn Summertree's eyes had closed that last time, she'd been watching out the window, waiting, her eyes scanning the hated barren landscape.

"I'm staying in town," Cecilia said firmly, fighting against a familiar ache in her heart that came with thoughts of her mother.

Buck ambled closer, one thumb looped at his belt. "Aw, c'mon, Cici. You don't really believe the man's not a schoolteacher, do you?"

"Didn't you hear him call me a beautiful flower? What kind of snake-oil salesman talks like that?"

"But you are," Buck responded with a grin that made Cecilia puff in exasperation. "Besides, he looked just like a regular fella to me."

"That's just the trouble, Buck. Everyone looks nice to you."

"Especially you, sweetheart."

She ignored the flirtatious comment. "Besides, he looked *too* much like a regular fellow—not a teacher. He was staring around the place as if he hadn't been in a classroom before!"

"Maybe it looked different than the ones up North."

Cecilia bit her lip thoughtfully. No, there was something else....

Before she could finish her thought, Buck took another troubling step forward and then pulled her to his chest. Cecilia freed herself with one firm shove.

"Buck, go home," she repeated. "I'm staying here."

He crossed his arms, growing petulant. "How are you going to pay for your room?" he asked. "Your father won't give you money for that."

"Leave my father out of this. As far as you're concerned, the new schoolteacher still hasn't arrived. I'll figure out a way to pay Dolly."

"Your father's going to find out sooner or later, you know," Buck warned sensibly, "and he's going to be madder than a hornet when he finds out you didn't come back to the ranch first thing."

"I know, I know." First she was kicked out of Miss Brubeck's, now this little deception. When he found out, her father would probably lock her in her room till the turn of the century. Well, she'd cross that tedious little bridge when she came to it. At least locked in her room she wouldn't have to deal with randy ranch hands.

"Let me worry about my father," she said with finality. "If nothing else I'll tell him that I still have work at the school. You heard what Beasley said about helping Pendergast get settled." As if anyone would need help running that ragtag little school—and as if she would actually do it!

Buck looked away, trying to think of an argument to dissuade her. Not surprisingly, nothing came to him. "It's your funeral," he said at last. Smashing his hat more firmly on his head, he turned and ambled away. Toward Grady's saloon, no doubt.

Freed from that appendage, if not from her worries, Cecilia continued full steam toward Dolly's. Oh, she had known it would be hard to give up her teaching job—though during the past week, when the man failed to show up, she was beginning to hold out hope that he would never arrive. Now his breezing into town late made losing her position all the more agonizing.

Eugene Pendergast! She didn't know why he struck such a chord in her, but something about the man wasn't right. He didn't look right. He didn't talk right. His clothes fit funny.

Damnation! This temporary teaching job had been such a godsend. After being sent home from New Orleans in disgrace, she'd desperately needed a way to get out from under her father's disapproving glare. She and her father had clashed ever since she'd been old enough to wear long skirts. He thought her only purpose in life was to get married, preferably to a rich rancher, and since her mother had died when she was twelve, there was no one to take her side.

No, it was always Cecilia against the world. Convincing her father to send her to New Orleans had seemed such a coup, so freeing. Then, due to her own stupidity, she'd been sent home for "rowdy behavior." Just because she sneaked out one night—just that once! But what was the point of being in New Orleans, she'd insisted, if you could only see a tiny, well-manicured portion of it, and then only during the daytime with a fussy old chaperone?

Her father had been livid. She'd jumped at the opportunity to move into town and serve as schoolteacher until the real one came along. A room of her own in Dolly Hudspeth's boardinghouse wasn't like living in New Orleans, but it was as close to it as she was going to get in the foreseeable future. Now the schoolteacher *had* arrived—supposedly— disrupting her life yet again....

But she wasn't willing to admit defeat yet.

Cecilia marched up the dirt path to Dolly's, the only two-story house in town. Dolly's husband, Jubal, had been the first blacksmith in the area, so they had been prosperous before his untimely death. Now Dolly made do by renting out the extra rooms in the generous house her husband had built for her.

Grateful to finally have some privacy to think through her troubles, Cecilia headed straight for the stairs. Maybe she'd prepare herself a bath, she thought. No, that was too much trouble. Her imagination settled for a quick wash, then a leisurely afternoon nap on her soft mattress.

"Cecilia, is that you?" Dolly's head poked out from the parlor.

"Hello, Dolly," Cecilia said, only slowing as she single-mindedly headed for her haven of a room. "I'm bushed. Will you call me for dinner?"

"Oh, dear..."

Cecilia heard a rustling of skirts behind her and stopped. Dolly Hudspeth was still a young woman, not yet thirty, and the closest thing to a confidante Cecilia had. Her light brown hair was swept back from her face and pulled into her usual economical bun. As she caught up with Cecilia, she looked as put-together as always, except that her high forehead was wrinkled in dismay and her bow-shaped mouth puckered into a frown.

"Is something wrong?" Cecilia asked, continuing up the stairs. Dolly was always in a snit about something.

"Oh, I do wish I'd had some warning!" Dolly said, keeping one pace behind her friend.

"Warning about what?" Cecilia asked.

"I'm sure we could have handled this better."

Confused, Cecilia walked to her door and turned the knob. "For heaven's sake, Dolly, you're not making any sense. What is the matter?"

She threw wide the door and saw immediately what was wrong—her things were gone!

"What happened!" she cried, surging forward. Her trunk, her clothes, even her silver comb set that had been on the washbasin stand—all were gone.

"Now, Cecilia," Dolly began. "You know that this is my best room. It's always been reserved for the town's schoolteacher. Always, even when Jubal was alive."

Cecilia's gaze narrowed in on the black leather valise on the floor next to the bed. It belonged to Pendergast, that snake. He'd usurped her job, and now her room.

But not for long, she vowed.

Taking a deep breath to compose herself, she turned to Dolly with a warm smile. "Of course," she said, even managing a gay little laugh as if she didn't care a fig about losing her prized accommodations. "How stupid of me to forget. Just tell me, Dolly, where *are* my things?"

Dolly looked at her anxiously, not quite trusting Cecilia's sudden change of mood. "Well, I stowed them downstairs.

I imagined you'd probably ask Buck to give you a ride home this evening."

"Home?" Cecilia asked, blinking innocently. "With Buck? Whatever for?"

Dolly put her hands on her hips. "Cecilia," she said sternly. "Now, you know how things are. I have three rooms to let. One to the schoolteacher, and Miss Fanny's been here since you were in school yourself. And I couldn't put Jubal's cousin Lucinda out. He'd come back to haunt me for sure."

Panic began to seize Cecilia. Home. She was being sent home, back to the ranch, when she had so much to do right here in Annsboro. If no one would believe her suspicions about Pendergast—who she was willing to bet money wasn't a schoolteacher at all—then she needed to stay close by and gather her own evidence. In the end, the town, even Beasley, would thank her for her pains.

But there was no way to stay if Dolly didn't help her. She wouldn't be able to spy on Pendergast. She'd never get her job back, or her independence. She'd be trapped on the ranch to wither away until she finally gave in and married some rancher who would take her off to another patch of dirt. And then she'd still wither away, just like her poor mother.

She practically threw herself at the older woman's feet. "Oh, Dolly, you must have a place for me somewhere! Anywhere!"

Dolly shook her head worriedly. "I can't think of a thing. The house only has four bedrooms, Cecilia, apart from the tiny room off the kitchen for my laundry girl, and that's no bigger than a cupboard."

Laundry girl? Cecilia remembered Lupe, the young woman who'd been doing laundry before she'd married one of the poor farmers in the area. Her heart surged with hope. "Cupboard?" she asked excitedly. "I can sleep in a cupboard, I don't mind!"

Dolly's face fell. "Oh, no, Cecilia."

"I could even have some of my things sent home—I'll tell Buck to take my trunk this very evening!"

"Absolutely not," Dolly said, shaking her head. "That room is for the laundry girl. I've always done the wash for my boarders. And if I pay the girl room and board, I don't have to come up with as much cash money."

She was right, Cecilia realized, her spirits plummeting fast. About the only thing to hope for now was that Buck hadn't left the saloon yet. What a miserable day this was turning out to be!

Dolly giggled.

Annoyed by the other woman's laugh, Cecilia lifted her head slowly and caught her doing it again. "I fail to see anything amusing about this situation," she snapped.

Dolly shook her head and then laughed outright. "I'm sorry, Cecilia," she said, breathing hard to hold back a chuckle, "it's just..." A rumbling laugh exploded from her chest, cutting off her words. "Oh, it's too silly!"

Cecilia bit her lower lip and waited for Dolly's laughter to subside. "What is?" she asked impatiently.

The other woman wiped a tear from her eye. "Oh, Cecilia, I just had this picture in my head of you leaning over a washboard."

Cecilia laughed along heartlessly for a moment—until she was struck, rather violently, by the obvious. She snapped her fingers and turned joyfully to Dolly. "That's it!" she cried, circling the older woman in a playful little jig. "Dolly, you're a genius! When can I start?"

Dolly wasn't laughing anymore. "Oh, no, Cecilia, I was just joking you."

"Joke or not, I'll take the job."

"But I can't offer it to you," Dolly countered firmly. "Your father would have my hide, not to mention yours, if I hired you to do the wash. Do you even know how to do wash? The idea!"

"What's wrong with my doing a little work? Father didn't mind me teaching!"

Dolly sent her a wry look that made it clear she wasn't buying into that line of thinking for one second. "There's a whopping difference between teaching and being a washer-woman." She laughed again. "Imagine if your father found out you were rinsing out my boarders' underclothes for a living!"

"He won't find out," Cecilia said, her usually merry voice dropping an octave. Having seized on this improbable solution, she was not about to budge.

Sensing that she was moments away from hiring the Summertree heiress into a position of manual labor, Dolly's eyes widened in alarm. "There are no secrets in Annsboro, Cecilia."

"I know," Cecilia said, more brightly. "But Daddy doesn't live in Annsboro, does he?"

Chapter Two

Because her new quarters lacked the generous wardrobe of the teacher's room, during the next few hours Cecilia weeded out what essential items she would need for the next weeks, packing the rest to send home with Buck, who was under a strict oath of secrecy. Once Pendergast was gone, and it was her intention to make sure his departure was close at hand, she would send for her things again and be comfortably reinstated into her old room.

Dolly filled her in on her other duties; apparently, the "laundry girl" was also the cook's helper, maid and woodcutter. But Cecilia didn't mind hard work—not that she'd had much experience in that area—as long as it had some reward. In this case, the prize was her little room behind the kitchen.

The room, which had originally been built as a pantry, consisted of a tiny bed, a table for a washbasin and a half window overlooking the privy. Despite the heat, Cecilia immediately shut the window. So much for fresh air.

By the time dinner was served, she also discovered that the situation of her room actually put her in a double bind. The kitchen's wood stove was not ten feet away, which, without the window for ventilation, turned her bedroom into something like an oven itself. After taking only ten minutes to freshen up for the meal, Cecilia felt a kindred spirit to the baked chicken lying on the center of the table.

When all was ready, Dolly looked proudly at her spread. She'd used her best china, which had been her mother's, and had put little cordial glasses by each plate. "For after dinner," Dolly explained in a prim low voice. "I thought we should welcome Mr. Pendergast properly."

"Everything looks fine," Cecilia said without enthusiasm. Greeting this particular guest properly, to her mind, would have entailed meeting him at the door with both barrels loaded.

Steps sounded on the staircase, as well as the *ker-thlump* footfall of Fanny Baker and her cane coming from the parlor, where the elderly widow spent most of her days. Jubal's spinster cousin, Lucinda, quietly made her way in, her nose wrinkling nervously at the sight of the china. Lucinda was shy.

At the sound of approaching heavy footsteps, Cecilia hastily straightened her clothing and ran a smoothing palm over her hair, which she'd pulled in a high bun, much like Dolly's, away from her neck. If only it wasn't so hot! She would have felt much more confident meeting her adversary if she wasn't half-wilted.

When Pendergast finally appeared, she was glad to note that he was wilted, too. Dust still showed on his brown suit, although it was obvious he'd made an effort to brush it off, and his hair was damp with sweat. He'd changed his shirt underneath that awful herringbone vest, which served to work Cecilia up to the proper level of annoyance.

More laundry.

"What a beautiful table, Mrs. Hudspeth," Pendergast said with a gusto that surprised Cecilia. "I had no idea you were planning a feast for this evening."

In Dolly's modest parlor, Eugene Pendergast appeared much taller than Cecilia had remembered, and as much as she hated to admit it, he was nearly handsome. His thick brown hair had a rakish curl at the brow, if the word *rakish* could be used in context of the schoolmaster. Not only that, but his build was much more impressive than Cecilia had noticed before. This made her more suspicious still. A person didn't develop muscles like that by reading books!

But more than anything else, his dark eyes captured her attention, eyes as dark as two glistening coals. Their gaze was intense, wary...and very much interested. A little shiver of awareness worked its way down her spine, but Cecilia wasn't so overcome that she overlooked the tiny lines in the man's weathered face, especially around those dark, fascinating eyes. Up close, it was clear the man had spent a great deal of his life in the outdoors.

In a dither over her big dinner, Dolly blushed and smiled and showed Mr. Pendergast his place as Fanny Baker entered the room and went directly to hers. Cecilia stood behind her own chair, anticipating the moment when her foe would address her. They awaited Mr. Walters, who, other than working at Beasley's store and taking his meals at Dolly's, was rumored to be something of a recluse. This label never failed to confuse Cecilia, since practically all of the man's waking hours were accounted for and spent in public.

"I suppose you don't think much of our town, Mr. Pendergast," Cecilia said, irritated further that the man had yet to greet her.

"Ah, Miss Summertree." He looked upon her as though she was an annoying little gnat that had landed behind a place setting. "I had thought you would be back on the ranch by now." Pendergast kept his expression veiled, but his words made it clear that he had hoped not to see her.

She smiled in triumph. It was obvious he'd assumed he had turned her out. Good. "Not at all. You see, Mr. Pendergast, I'm very resourceful."

"Then how lucky for myself and all of Annsboro to be graced with your lovely presence for...how long, did you say?"

Cecilia looked at him squarely. "Indefinitely."

The word went down like a bitter pill. It took all the fortitude Jake could muster not to let out a weary sigh. He'd finally guessed that the man named Watkins, Pendergast's old school chum, didn't live in Annsboro. At least the man hadn't made an appearance, and no one else had mentioned his name again. Maybe he was the old schoolteacher. Jake had hoped that Cecilia Summertree wouldn't live in Annsboro much longer, either.

"So you see," Cecilia said, smiling wickedly, "I'll be able to help you along, just as Lysander Beasley instructed."

He knew that nothing would have pleased Cecilia more than seeing him squirm, so Jake kept his disappointment to himself. The woman had him up a tree, but maybe it was for the best. As long as she was around, his guard would be up. Her presence reminded him that he couldn't afford to lapse into his old self. Not for a while, at least, until he was no longer a stranger in town, or even better, when he actually left Annsboro.

Already he was praying for that day.

Uncomfortable chitchat followed until Walters finally arrived. The balding man nodded mutely when presented to Pendergast, and finally the company sat down to devour the chicken, snap beans and rolls that Dolly had prepared. Jake was happy to eat the tasty meal in silence, although he should have known such good fortune couldn't last.

"I wish you'd tell us about your home," Cecilia said, not two minutes into the meal. She primly wiped her lips with her napkin. "I'm sure Annsboro is a far cry from Pittsburgh."

"Philadelphia," he corrected.

"That's right." She smiled, though Jake could have sworn she looked disappointed that he actually remembered the city he'd supposedly come from. "Still, it must be a far cry from here."

Even without having come within a thousand miles of Philadelphia, Jake knew her words to be an absurd understatement. Annsboro was a far cry from any town he'd ever been in.

Pleasant, you have to be pleasant. Buying time, he cleared his throat and swallowed. "The chicken is wonderful, Mrs. Hudspeth," he said, enjoying both Dolly's warm smile and Cecilia's expectant fidgeting across the table. Before she could pounce on him for not answering, he said, "All I can say about Annsboro is that it seems a . . . one-of-a-kind sort of town."

Dolly nodded eagerly. "You wouldn't believe how much development we've seen here, Mr. Pendergast."

No, he wouldn't have believed it. "I heard Beasley's building a drugstore."

"And just in time, too," Dolly said enthusiastically. "We have nearly thirty families in Annsboro now." She darted a glance toward Cecilia, who couldn't keep a frown off her face at the blatant lie. "Well, in the environs, anyway," Dolly explained.

"Dirt farmers," Fanny Baker said flatly. Fanny had been among the first ranching families to settle the area over a decade before, and although the Bakers had since lost their land, she still retained her rancher's snobbery toward the late-arriving farmers. "Most of them probably won't last through the winter, but there will be more to replace them when they leave. Everyone wants their own land, even if it's just a parcel of dust. Only the really large ranchers, ones whose lands encompass enough water, can survive out here."

"I suppose that includes the Summertree ranch." Jake couldn't quite keep all the sarcasm out of his tone as he turned on Cecilia. He'd known big ranchers, and worked for them. He'd also sent one to jail, and was paying highly for it.

"Yes, but that doesn't mean that some of us don't sympathize with the smaller farmer," Cecilia said, bristling. How dare he attempt to insult her! What did this man from Philadelphia, if he truly was from there, know about this world?

Now more than ever, she hoped to make short work of getting this man out of town.

Dolly laughed nervously in an attempt to calm her feuding diners. "I'm afraid we're all very opinionated here, Mr. Pendergast." She frowned at her young friend. "Even the women."

Jake smiled warmly. "It's a very interesting town. I'd like to learn more about it someday." Once again, he raised the false hope that he would be able to eat in peace.

But before he'd managed another bite, Cecilia piped up. "Well, maybe we should tell him about the Indian massacre, then."

"Oh, Cecilia!" Dolly's hand flew to her mouth. "Not at the table, please!"

Jake bit back a smile. Cecilia had gotten his attention, and he could tell by the way her eyes danced mischievously that she was pleased with herself. He almost enjoyed putting on an anxious Pendergast frown for the company's benefit. It wouldn't do to have a Philadelphia man hear about Indians without quivering in his too-tight boots. "Indian massacre?" he asked nervously.

Mr. Walters put down his fork, as did the other boarders, as if one couldn't eat and hear about Indians at the same time. Bowing to local custom, Jake also put his fork down. Lucinda and Mrs. Baker shook their heads sadly in unison.

"This was Comanche country," Cecilia began.

"Oh, Cecilia!" Dolly moaned. "Must you?"

"Comanches are Indians," Cecilia explained to Pendergast, ignoring her friend. Painful as the tale was, it would be worth the telling if only she could scare the man back to Philadelphia.

"Comanches? I believe I've heard of them," Jake said, straining to sustain a fretful expression.

"Right after the first ranchers came here the Comanches tried to run them off. They attacked in the morning, while the people were about their chores. Three people died, slaughtered, and several of the women had been set upon by the savages.''

Jake translated the delicate phrase to mean that the women were raped. Lucinda nearly swooned.

"One girl, twelve years old at the time, was taken captive and has never been seen again."

"Oh, my," Jake breathed. The scenario was all too familiar, but still chilling.

"Cecilia, enough," Dolly entreated.

Cecilia was flushed from reliving the tale, which had always fascinated and horrified her in equal measure. "The settlers decided to name the town after the little girl, so that if she ever managed to escape, she might find her way home."

For a long moment, the diners simply sat, staring at their plates without expression. Clearly, the girl named Ann hadn't yet returned. Jake knew that the Indians hadn't been banished from this land long enough for the pain and fear of raids to have subsided completely, and especially not with such a wound as Annsboro had left open. Comanche raids were brutal. Those lucky enough to live through them rarely forgot. Or forgave.

"Such a sweet girl," Fanny Baker announced, clucking her tongue before lapsing back into silence.

"What a terrible story!" Dolly exclaimed. "Cecilia, you should be ashamed for bringing that up. Mr. Pendergast will get the wrong impression of our town!"

Suddenly, Jake remembered who he was supposed to be. Across the table, Cecilia sent him a flat, humorless smile. "I hope I didn't frighten you, Mr. Pendergast."

"Oh, my," he said, rewarding her storytelling with a fretful cough. "There aren't any more of these Comanches around, are there?"

Before Cecilia could speak, Dolly exclaimed, "Not in years! It's been seven years since we've had real Indian trouble around here."

"Thank heavens for that."

"I still lock my doors at night." Cecilia looked him square in the eye with a deadly earnest gaze, and strangely, although he knew she was only trying to scare him, Jake believed her. If Eugene Pendergast hadn't been gunned down in a bar the week before, he would certainly have died right here at this dinner table, of fright. Cecilia's strategy couldn't have been better, but unfortunately, she had the wrong target.

After a pause, Jake gave his plate a little shove forward. "I'm afraid my appetite for this lovely food has disappeared."

Dolly let out an exasperated sigh. "See what you've done, Cecilia?"

Her big blue eyes widened innocently. "But Mr. Pendergast said he wanted to know a little bit of our history."

Their gazes met and held for just an instant. In that moment, Jake understood that Cecilia meant what she said about being resourceful. There was defiance in those innocent eyes, too, aimed just at him. No matter how long it took, no matter how many people she offended, she was determined to have his job.

Damn. Why, of all the schoolteaching jobs in all the world, did Cecilia Summertree have to covet the one measly position he needed? He had to stay put for at least a few weeks, until Gunter and Darby were assured he was good and dead. Unfortunately, during those weeks he was apparently going to be harassed by this tenacious blond vixen.

Jake never denied having as many frailties as the next man, but he'd never considered women to be high on his list of weaknesses. Now he wasn't so sure. Mesmerized as he was by those alluring blue eyes, he could well imagine Cecilia Summertree being his downfall, his own Delilah. He would have to be very, very careful.

"Goodness, I'm full," Dolly said with a giggle, trying to shrug off the disturbing tension at the table. "Let's try the blackberry wine, shall we?" She walked over to get a bottle that was on the small side table in the corner. "I put this up year before last."

The people around the table perked up a bit as she poured the dark liquid into their small crystal glasses, which even Fanny Baker, who'd been with Dolly the longest, had only seen once before.

"You sure can get high tone when you want to, Dolly," the older woman said.

Dolly raised her glass. "To our town's newest citizen, all the way from Philadelphia."

Even in a room full of immigrants from other parts of the country, Philadelphia sounded impressively far. Jake bowed, and the rest of the table smiled before swigging down their unfortunately modest portions of wine. The beverage was fruity, not at all unpleasant, and had a definite kick to it.

Jake licked his lips in appreciation. "Very flavorful, Mrs. Hudspeth," he said.

Dolly acknowledged his compliment with a blush and a smile. "Do have another glass," she said, offering him the crystal decanter.

Cecilia looked at the schoolteacher sharply as he poured himself a hefty drink. "Are you a wine connoisseur, Mr. Pendergast?"

Jake managed not to smile too openly. What she really wanted to know was whether he was a lush. "Everyone enjoys a fine glass of wine every now and then, don't you agree?" he answered evasively. When Cecilia's lips turned down in the frustrated pout he'd expected, he downed the liquid, bade everyone a good night and made his exit.

He just stopped himself from looking over his shoulder as he left the room. This morning it had seemed his troubles were coming to a close, but it looked as though he'd simply traded one enemy for another. Now Cecilia Summertree was gunning for him.

* * *

Upstairs, Jake cozied down into the bed. The pressed linens felt incredibly rich, making him realize how long it had been since he'd stayed in a real house, with a woman tending it. Dolly's cooking had provided him with the best meal he'd had in months, which was certain to be a benefit to his hopefully short stay in Annsboro. Mostly he didn't mind the independent life, but there were times when a woman's touch was refreshing.

The homey feeling reminded him of the small house his family had owned, before Otis Darby had gotten into his head that their tiny spread had a coal deposit. Always a speculator, and with the railroads expanding all the time, Darby had decided to get the Reed land by hook or by crook. Preferably by crook. Rather than making an offer, Darby attempted to trump up a charge that Jake's father had filed claim to the land illegally. The ensuing battle had killed Jake's father, and though Darby's accusations were proven false, Jake and his sick mother weren't able to manage the land on their own.

Jake frowned, swallowing back his bitterness. Darby got his land, all right—land that never turned up an ounce of coal or anything else. The bastard had probably forgotten all about it. But his trying to get that land had hastened the death of both of Jake's parents, and that was something Jake would never forget.

He took a breath and tried to think of something else. Something pleasant.

The room held the scent of a lingering perfume, which, now that he thought about it, probably was Cecilia's. She had lived here, slept in this bed. A vision of brilliant blue eyes and pouting pink lips danced in front of him, making him ache for another feminine touch he hadn't partaken of in a long time. But that was best not to think about right now, either.

He had some unhappy business to tend to—namely, the bundle of letters he'd found in Pendergast's things that he'd been avoiding reading for a whole week. Luckily, he'd also found some rather entertaining reading material—a stack of cheap flimsy books about sheriffs and outlaws and other infamous frontier characters.

The silly tales had probably been fodder for Pendergast's fantasies, fueling his disappointment with the true frontier. They surely explained the man's half Yankee half gunslinger way of talking. During the past few days, Jake had been thankful for the books, since reading the stories had allowed him to put off the inevitable.

He dreaded the thought of having to write the dead man's grieving wife, or sweetheart, or worse, his mama, and explain Pendergast's messy—not to mention confusing—death.

It was an easy guess that the letters were from a woman. The lilac stationery still had a trace of flowery smell to it, probably the scent favored by the sender, and the graceful handwriting across the envelopes could only belong to a female. Thankfully, all the letters were written by the same hand. There would be only one person to write to.

There weren't many letters, either, and as he opened them, he saw that the dates were all recent. He took the one with the oldest date and with a sigh began reading.

Dearest Brother... So it was his sister. That had been easy enough to figure out. *I wish you had not felt the need to leave us so soon, although I understand perfectly your restlessness. You would probably be shocked to know that I, your quiet older sister, also have dreams of travel. Though I would have chosen an area other than Texas, surely a wilder place than those of my fantasies. But you are a man, and younger...* Jake skimmed the remaining paragraphs to the signature. *Your loving sister, Rosalyn.*

All the remaining missives struck a similar chord. This Rosalyn was not one to dwell on the tedious details of everyday life, preferring a more philosophical tone. Fortunately, Jake was able to glean a few facts. First, that Rosalyn was still living in Philadelphia, where she gave lessons and lived in the home of a not-too-well-loved hypochondriac aunt, to whom she gave most of her earnings. Not a happy life, Jake gathered, and it had probably been stifling for a young man.

As for Pendergast, Jake discovered that he'd been gone for some months, choosing to travel to Texas at a snail's pace, visiting every relative and friend he had along the way. He didn't think he would return to Philadelphia, apparently, or ever make enough as a country schoolteacher to afford to travel again.

He'd been right on both counts.

The most disturbing aspect of the letters was Rosalyn's obvious intent to join Pendergast when he was settled—as if Pendergast would have lasted that long! Small chance, considering the fact that the man was already hotfooting it back to Pennsylvania when Jake ran into him. Nevertheless, Jake needed to nip this plan of hers in the bud, fast.

It was taking a risk, but Jake decided to simply tell her the truth—after a fashion. There was no reason the woman should know that the bullet her brother took was actually meant for him. Just that it was an unfortunate mix-up, and her brother had met a brave end.

What more would a woman want to know, after all? Jake would of course enclose the money he found in Pendergast's satchel, a tidy sum that she could squirrel away from her aunt. Probably the woman would write back, requesting Pendergast's things. He would just have to plead ignorance on that score. There was no way he could explain that he couldn't return them because he needed to wear them himself.

After that, she would probably be satisfied...or in any case, by that time his charade would be over. Then, with any luck, Jake would never have to hear the name Rosalyn Pendergast again.

Mr. Pendergast was written in large, neat letters across the top of the blackboard at the front of the classroom. The children were all in their seats, working busily. Pendergast himself was seated at the teacher's desk, helping twelve-year-old Wilbur Smith, normally the rowdiest one in the class, with a mathematics problem.

Cecilia, peeping around the corner at the back of the room, could have cried. Her hands were red and chapped from scalding water, and she still had the linens yet to do. She'd come over to the schoolhouse in hopes of buoying her spirits, but this was not the chaotic scene she had anticipated.

The eighteen pupils in the small room were all perfectly behaved, bent over their books and slates, their faces studies in concentration. Here and there a whisper would break out, only to be silenced moments later, voluntarily, by the offender. What on earth had the man done to these children, Cecilia fumed, mesmerized them?

They had never behaved so well for her!

Maybe he really was a teacher, and all her suspicions were just so much wishful thinking. If that was the case, then there was no point to her being in Annsboro, working her pruny scalded fingers to the bone. At least at home, even under the disapproving eye of her father, she had Clara, their wonderful housekeeper, to cook and wait on her.

Of course, Clara, who was concerned about Cecilia's motherless state and took it upon herself to warn her of the many pitfalls in life, especially when it came to men, was not the most scintillating companion. Mostly, she criticized Cecilia's penchant for trouble and handed out advice on how to behave around the male sex.

This time next week, she'd probably be up to her ears in platitudes....

As Cecilia began to back dejectedly toward the door, her boot heel scraped against a knot in the floorboard, throwing her off-balance. She pitched forward and grabbed onto the coatrack, grasping for dear life. Unable to get a steady handhold or regain her footing, Cecilia pawed frantically at the knobs holding a variety of caps, hats and bonnets. She did an awkward little dance downward with the stick of wood until her rump unceremoniously hit the floor.

Eighteen bodies swiveled in their seats, then jumped to attention. During her short tenure, she'd tried to teach the children to stand respectfully when an adult entered the room. Naturally, after a day under Pendergast's stewardship, they actually did it.

"Ah, Miss Summertree," Pendergast said, scurrying down the room's center aisle. "How nice of you to come for a visit." As he loomed over her, his dark eyes danced with speculation. Gallantly, he offered her his hand. "Although I could swear you looked as though you were spying on us."

"Spying? Spying?" Cecilia asked, unmoving. She felt the strings of a sunbonnet dangling by one of her ears. "Of course I wasn't spying!"

Muffled giggles broke out among the children who'd gathered around. Seeing their former schoolmistress literally brought low was obviously irresistible.

Jake wanted to laugh himself. He'd seen Cecilia nosing around and wondered if she was going to announce herself. Apparently, she'd hoped to find him completely inept, which of course he was. Fortunately, his dealings as a deputy had taught him about seedier ways of getting what you want—namely, through bribery. For his class's performance this day, he was nearly a dollar down in candy payments. Yet it was worth every penny to see the distress in his beautiful adversary's liquid blue eyes.

Cecilia ignored his outstretched arm and pushed herself up. "I just wanted to see if you were having any difficulties," she said hastily, dusting herself off. "I thought you might need some help on your first day."

"How thoughtful of you," Jake said, frowning distastefully as she swatted at her clothing, sending dust flying into the air. He pulled out a handkerchief and limply waved the cloud away.

She forced a smile. "But I can see you don't need my aid."

"Heavens, no," he said. "No more than you would need mine hanging out the laundry." He smiled back, a triumphant show of gleaming white teeth that let her know she hadn't fooled him about her real purpose for dropping by. "This is wash day, isn't it?" He couldn't resist rubbing salt in her wound.

Cecilia's smile dissolved, as did the thin veneer of politeness she'd been putting on for the children. She didn't savor the idea of being this man's servant, even indirectly. "Watch it, Pendergast, or you might find 'Ode to the West' on that blackboard one of these mornings."

Startled, he raised an eyebrow questioningly. What was she talking about?

Cecilia grinned mischievously. "The poem I· found in your shirt pocket, Mr. Pendergast."

Oh, hell! He should have expected that, after reading all those stupid books, Pendergast wouldn't have been able to resist the urge to put pen to paper. "Oh, that...that was probably something I just jotted down."

Cecilia crossed her arms and narrowed her eyes on him in a posture that he was beginning to find touchingly familiar. "I'd take more care to check my pockets if I were you. Or it might just get around town that—" She cleared her throat to prepare for her recitation. "'Your heart yearns to rest in the bosom of the old prair-ie.'"

Several titters came from behind them, and Cecilia warmed to her audience as she noted Pendergast's face reddening. Perfect. "Or how about this—'The sky 'tis like a lover's eye, it twinkles upon me nightly.'"

The children jeered openly now. "Give us some more, Cecilia!" Tommy Beck howled.

"Yeah, more bosoms!" shouted Wilbur.

Pendergast's surprisingly strong hand clamped down on her arm. Cecilia was momentarily thrown off by the buzz of excitement she felt at the contact, but recovered in time to dimple at him sweetly. "Why, Mr. Pendergast, your beautiful verse about caused me to swoon over my washtub." She batted her eyelashes dreamily at him, bringing whoops of laughter from her former students.

Damn Pendergast, damn, was all Jake could think. And damn Cecilia's pert little nose and saucy smile. She'd managed to throw the kids into a rowdy mood. It would probably cost him another dollar's worth of candy to quiet them all down again! He began propelling her toward the door.

"Thank you, Miss Summertree, for your little visit," he said stiffly, feeling hampered by the manners he was supposed to possess. If he wasn't supposed to be Pendergast, he would have let her know exactly what kind of a minx she was.

Having never been dismissed from anything but a girls' school and the houses of her snooty Memphis relatives, Cecilia couldn't quite comprehend what Pendergast was doing. Only that her performance was being received well. "I had no idea Philadelphia men were so brawny. You must spend your time lifting some heavy schoolbooks, Mr. Pendergast."

More jeers came from the pupils.

"Of course," Pendergast said, giving her a final little shove over the threshold. "How else could I toss out impertinent young women from my schoolroom?"

Tossed out? Was that what was going on here? Cecilia thought. But he had no right to do it! She didn't even want to go into who her daddy was and where her family came from. She was a person to be reckoned with in her own right...at least, in Annsboro, she was.

At least...until now.

She fought against the sagging sensation in her shoulders. Yesterday she'd been Cecilia Summertree, the town schoolteacher, with the best room in Dolly Hudspeth's boardinghouse. Now she was nothing but a washerwoman, Lupe Viega's replacement, with a squat room overlooking the biggest privy in town.

Her mind whirred, and then she caught sight of the many sets of eyes fastened on her. None of them seemed to truly appreciate the desperation of her plight. Not even Tommy, who moments before had spoken as her ally. Although, God bless him, the boy was still chewing mesquite gum against school rules.

Suddenly, she became self-conscious. This building, which she'd so recently considered her own, was no longer a welcoming place. Not while Pendergast ruled there.

Before she could voice a response, Jake stepped forward, locked on to her elbow and steered her down the steps. Cecilia sputtered at his manhandling, but he no longer cared what she thought or how angry she became. Her being there was making him nervous.

As he deposited her on the first step, she pulled away and whirled on him. "You—you brute!" she spat angrily.

"Brute?" Jake asked, feigning wonder. He puffed out his chest and tugged at his vest in mock pride. "No one's ever called me that before. I rather like it."

What a horrid man! Cecilia thought. And to think that even last night she had toyed with the idea—ludicrous now—that he was actually rather attractive.

"Stay out of my way, Pendergast," she warned.

"Out of your way? Just yesterday you indicated you were going to be my shadow. Perhaps you should take your own advice."

Her blue eyes flashed with ire. "That wasn't advice, Pendergast, it was a warning." After sending him a final glare, she spun and beat a hasty retreat.

Jake smiled lazily as he again watched Cecilia huff toward town, relieved to have survived the encounter so successfully. He was getting to her. Soon her better sense would prevail—Cecilia would tire of doing chores for Dolly Hudspeth and run back to Daddy's ranch, leaving him in peace.

But until that time, he would have to be very, very careful—and pray he had enough money to keep these students good and bribed till he was ready to beat it out of town.

Chapter Three

Eugene Pendergast would rue the day he came to Annsboro, Cecilia vowed. He'd actually humiliated her in front of her former students, dismissing her as if she was a—a nobody! Of course, she had to admit that she had behaved rather disgracefully herself, standing on the schoolhouse steps ranting about warnings—but he'd provoked her!

She clenched her fists at her sides as she marched down the dusty street, passing right by the turnoff to Dolly's house. With all the pent-up frustration inside her, she would probably be able to get the wash done in no time, but she couldn't face Dolly just yet. Her friend would sense something had happened, and Cecilia didn't want her to know that she had designs on Pendergast. Designs to get him fired, that is.

But how?

At her frantic pace, she'd nearly covered the entire length of the town when she spotted Buck reeling out of Grady's saloon. He was supposed to have taken her trunk full of clothes back to the ranch the night before, but by the looks of him the man hadn't made it home at all.

"Buck McDeere, get over here!" she bellowed.

Although the street was practically deserted save for the two of them, the slow-moving cowboy looked muzzily in her direction before appearing to focus on her. Woozily, he shaded his eyes with his hand and stumbled forward. God only knew what he'd done with his hat.

"Buck, have you been in that place since last night?" Cecilia demanded.

"Have not. Just since this morning."

"This morning?" That was strange. "Did Daddy send you into town for something?"

"Yep. You."

Cecilia gulped.

"He heard about the new teacher, Cici. He doesn't like the idea of you staying with Dolly now. 'Imposing' is how he put it."

"Damnation!"

"He's been stomping around all day, saying you think you're too good for the rest of us."

Cecilia puffed up with indignation. "That's a lie!"

"I know that, but your father's been bent out of shape ever since you left the ranch."

"He's been bent out of shape since I came back from New Orleans." Which is why she hadn't spent much time at home. Of course, she could understand him being mad about her being tossed out of school, but what did he care if she stayed cooped up on the ranch with him or not?

Buck hesitated, then told her, "He says you ought to get married and learn your place."

"Oh, for heaven's sake! Have you ever heard anything so infuriating?" Marriage!

"I knew you'd be mad." He clasped his hands in a pleading gesture. "Please, Cici. I'm just the messenger."

"Oh, bother." Some days it just seemed as if the whole world was plotting against her. Cecilia stamped her boot and held her breath against the dust she'd just kicked up. "I'll have to think of something. Meantime, Buck, you shouldn't have been so nervous that you had to spend the entire morning with a whiskey bottle. If you aren't careful, you'll end up like poor old Dooley Hodges."

Both of them shook their heads sadly. Dooley Hodges had been a crackerjack ranch hand before he'd had the misfortune to fall in love with a woman at Grady's. When the girl had said she wouldn't marry him, he'd decided to stand sentry at the bar, effectively cutting off her clientele. Unfortunately, the girl moved on and Dooley didn't. He became a permanent fixture on his bar stool, until finally he just collapsed in an alcoholic funk. His people, from Fort Worth, had come for him, and Dooley was never heard from again.

"Poor Dooley," Buck said, still shaking his head. "Bet he's working in a store, or some such." As if that was a fate worse than death.

"But of course, if his family hadn't come for him, the temperance ladies probably would have run him out."

Buck nodded. Some of the farmers' wives deeply resented the presence of the bar—not to mention brothel—in Annsboro. Their husbands barely scratched out a living anyway, so it was a small wonder women begrudged cash money going to the consumption of women and alcohol, when some of them couldn't afford to make decent winter clothes to send their children to school....

School!

A tantalizing vision of Eugene Pendergast being run out of town, with several large, outraged farm women on his heels, hurling rocks at his swiftly retreating back, flitted titillatingly through Cecilia's imagination. Her lips curled up in a wide smile. Could she manage it? she thought, wondering whether Lysander Beasley had given Pendergast the same pompous morality lesson he'd given her.

It just might work, she thought, her heart racing. All she needed was an accomplice. "Buck, listen to me. I promise I'll explain my extended stay to Daddy, in person, if you'll just do me one tiny little favor."

Buck regarded her through suspicious, bleary eyes. "Aw, Cici, why don't you just come on home?"

"Because my home is right here," she lectured sharply. "And if you liked me half as much as you're so fond of saying you do, you'd understand that."

"I do, but I don't understand—"

"I'm a lady, Buck. What's the point of being a lady if you're stuck where nobody ever sees you?"

Buck rubbed his chin thoughtfully. "Yeah, but your mother was a lady, and she lived out there."

"And died there," Cecilia snapped.

He winced at her piercing words and shrugged in obeisance. "Okay, okay. What am I supposed to do now?"

"I want you to get that new schoolteacher rip-roaring drunk."

Buck let out a sharp, surprised laugh. "No, really," he urged, then saw the earnest, withering look on her face. "You're not jokin' me?"

She paused a moment for effect. "I am not."

And while Buck was inebriating her nemesis, she would get to work on her own line of sabotage. And she knew just where to start. For years, Lysander Beasley had stumped around the county trying to raise money for new school readers—because, of course, his daughter at six could read better than most adults. Finally, with generous contributions from Cecilia's father and some others, he'd been able to purchase fifteen new Gibson readers. It would be too wonderful if anything happened to those precious books during Pendergast's short tenure.

Buck was having trouble accepting her orders. "But I don't even know the man. He might not be the kind to get liquored up."

"Last night I saw him gulp down two glasses of Dolly's potent blackberry wine like it was water. He drinks, all right."

"But—"

"No buts," Cecilia said in her firmest schoolmarm tone. "Buck McDeere, if you don't do this for me I'm going straight home tomorrow to tell Daddy I saw you reeling out of Grady's at half past eleven. Don't forget who Dooley Hodges worked for. Daddy's sensitive when it comes to workers and the bottle.''

"Aw, Cici, that's...that's—"

"Blackmail." Cecilia smiled. "Same as you've done to me since we were kids."

Buck shrugged helplessly and Cecilia knew she had him. Mentioning their long history never did any harm, since he considered that to be one of his best selling points as a suitor.

"All right," he said. "I guess I'll try."

In her triumph, Cecilia beamed a smile at him and reached over to squeeze his arm. "Buck, I'm sorry for thinking you're such a good-for-nothing."

Buck grinned back happily. Although he was a bit nervous about his mission and suspicious about Cici's motives, maybe she'd appreciate his efforts. He'd been trying to rush her for five years now and frankly, he was beginning to feel a little discouraged.

Pendergast took her hand and gazed deeply into her eyes. Cecilia remembered thinking that his dark eyes had a smoldering quality, and that was the word that came to her now. Lit by fire, they were, and desire for her alone.

They stood by the pond near her house, almost dry now since August. Still, the trees there provided shade, and a very promising privacy. With only a quick glance to confirm that they were alone, perfectly alone, he pulled her into his arms. Before Cecilia could react, his lips covered hers, warm and persuasive...

And then he started singing.

Cecilia bolted upright in bed, gasping for air. Pendergast had kissed her!

No, no, he hadn't. Fuzzily, as she attempted to gain her bearings in the dark, her mind began to make sense of what had happened. She'd been dreaming—but surely, it had been more like a nightmare! Her labored breathing certainly indicated that something traumatic had occurred.

And yet, as she strained to remember the dream, her recollections were not at all unpleasant. First she'd been captivated by his coal dark eyes, which had drawn her closer to him without his even touching her. But how could that have happened?

Of course, the answer was that it *hadn't* happened. But the scene was so vivid—his lips, his voice, singing...she could hear it even now. That truly was strange. She could make out the tune quite clearly. He was singing "Lorena"!

Cecilia pushed back her coverlet and hopped from the bed. Standing on tiptoe, she craned her neck out the window to hear the mournful ballad. Someone was singing down the street, but it didn't sound like Pendergast. It sounded more like...Buck!

A light breeze brought with it the ripe smell of the side yard, causing Cecilia to duck her head back inside. She groped through the darkened room for her robe, then remembered that it was one of the items she'd sent home. Letting out an exasperated breath as the singing neared the house, she left her room in her nightgown and bare feet to meet the roving minstrel.

The evening was unseasonably warm as she stepped outside through the front door, but she crossed her arms over her chest instinctively as the fresh air made contact with her scantily clothed body. Narrowing her eyes toward the road, she caught sight of Pendergast and Buck, draped over each other so that she could hardly tell where one ended and the other began. They weaved off the main road toward the house.

As they came closer and Cecilia's eyes adjusted to the moonlight, it became clear who was who. Buck, staggering and singing, was on the left, and Pendergast on the right, was practically dragging him along—cold sober!

She couldn't believe how miserably Buck had failed her. Her only comfort was that *she* had had a successful evening. After the boardinghouse residents had gone to bed, Cecilia had sneaked over to the schoolhouse, climbed through a window and tossed out the readers. Unfortunately, she had to toss herself out the window, too, and had done a belly flop in the dust. But in so doing, she had discovered the most ingenious hiding place for the books—on a ledge in the crawl space beneath the schoolhouse steps.

Which only proved that if you wanted something done right, you had to do it yourself.

Regardless of her state of dress or who might see her, Cecilia sped off the porch and sprinted across the dry grass of Dolly's yard to meet Pendergast and Buck. The sharp splintery blades poked at the soft pads of her feet.

"Buck, you idiot!" she said under her breath, coming to a quick stop in front of the pair. "Do you want to wake up the entire town?"

"And the next county."

Cecilia looked at Pendergast, who seemed none the worse for drink. How had he managed it? In fact, his eyes were clear, almost twinkly, as they regarded her state of undress.

"Buck wanted to see you," Pendergast said, grinning madly. "Said something about a man named Dooley Hodges and camping out on your porch until his relatives hauled him away."

"Oh, for heaven's sake!" Cecilia frowned. This was a terrible mess. "You shouldn't have brought him here."

"He insisted," Pendergast explained, and then his gaze again swept her from head to toe, making her feel nearly naked, which of course she was. "Now I can understand why."

A vision of her dream by the pond flashed through Cecilia's mind. She felt her face burn and was glad there was only a quarter moon's worth of light illuminating her embarrassment.

"What am I supposed to do with him?" she asked fretfully.

Seeing her distress, his expression softened. "Honestly, Cecilia, I couldn't send him off to your father's ranch. He'll stay in my room for the night."

Suddenly, Cecilia relaxed a bit. As much as she hated to admit it, this was her fault, and Pendergast was at least being decent about it. And he was right. She wouldn't want Buck to have attempted the ride home, or risked her father's wrath when he got there.

"All right," she agreed, then bent her head toward his companion. "But Buck, you've got to try not to wake up Dolly or Lucinda." Mrs. Baker slept like a rock.

"Dolly or Lucici—cinda," Buck slurred loudly.

Cecilia looked doubtfully at Pendergast. "I'll help you get him upstairs."

He nodded, and Cecilia ducked underneath Buck's other armpit. His crazily limp body was terribly unwieldy, and by the time they made it inside and to the stairs, bumping and thumping all the way, Cecilia had lost all hope of not waking the others.

"Shh," she entreated, and Pendergast nodded.

Backfired. She couldn't believe her little scheme had blown up in her face. What had she done to deserve this?

Oh, well. At least *she* had managed to set a trap for Pendergast. Beasley would stroke when those expensive books turned up missing, and Pendergast would bear the brunt of his wrath. She smiled already in anticipation.

"You know," Pendergast whispered seriously, "the man probably wouldn't be driven to drink if you didn't tease him so unmercifully."

"What?" Cecilia almost shrieked.

He ducked his head and pressed a finger to his mouth in warning. "Shh."

"Don't shush me, Pendergast," Cecilia said, spitting the words over Buck's practically unconscious head. "How dare you deign to tell me my business after spending all of three days in this town?"

"Fine," he answered. "I won't mention it again. I reckon it's none of my business if you choose to ruin this man's life."

Cecilia's eyebrow shot up in alert. "You *reckon?* Is that one of your Philadelphia words, Mr. Pendergast?"

"No, actually, I picked it up on the train."

"I'll just bet you did," she replied.

"You know, you ought to consider going to Philadelphia someday. Maybe you'd pick up some manners on the train."

"Oh!"

"Shh." This time, a smile touched his lips. "We don't want to wake the ladies, now, do we?"

If it wouldn't have meant dropping Buck on his head, she would have slapped the man. "Why Lysander Beasley had to look all the way across the country just to find a schoolteacher, I'll never know."

Jake had been wondering that himself. Yet, at this precise moment, he was enjoying teasing Cecilia too much to worry about it. Her honey blond hair appeared almost white in the faint light, and her blue eyes were two dark, flashing pools. For a moment, as his eyes fastened on her full lips, he regretted that they were adversaries.

Nevertheless, that's what they were.

"I should have thought that was obvious," he said at last. "Yankees are smarter."

Her mouth dropped open at his audacity, making Jake unable to hold back a chuckle. The lady wanted to belt him. Fortunately for him, they were approaching his door. Getting Buck in the room was going to take some fancy maneuvering.

Gingerly, he shifted his weight so that Buck was propped on his shoulder, which freed Jake's hand for the doorknob. The entrance was too narrow for three people abreast, so they shuffled through one at a time, swaying in a jerky little dance.

Finally, the trio arrived at the bed.

"Pull down the covers," Cecilia said.

"What for?"

She gaped at him as though she couldn't believe her ears. "We just can't throw him on the bed. Pull down the covers."

Only a woman, Jake thought, shaking his head. "That's crazy. But if keeping your sweetheart warm means so much to you, *you* pull them back."

"He's not my sweetheart!" she snapped. "Besides, you're closer."

A quick glance toward the bed confirmed she was right. But this was silly. "You can't hold him up by yourself."

It was the wrong argument to make. "Who says?"

Jake rolled his eyes. "Let's not bicker. If you insist, I'll turn down your damned covers."

"There's no need to resort to profanity, Mr. Pendergast," she said haughtily, "just because you're faced with ceding your meager but typical male show of strength to a woman."

Jake relinquished his hold on Buck and stepped away, watching Cecilia stagger under the sudden burden. "Is that what I'm doing?" he asked innocently.

She weaved and leaned precariously for a moment before getting Buck's bulk under control. "For heaven's sakes!" she cried. "I almost dropped him, thanks to you."

"Thanks to the loss of my meager strength, you mean?"

Cecilia rolled her eyes in exasperation. "Yes."

From Dolly's room across the hall, Jake heard stirring. He looked anxiously at Cecilia, who was glaring at him. Suddenly, an idea struck him.

Why not? he thought.

"Well," he said, in his primmest Pendergast tone, "I am glad to know that you'll thank me for something. And now I suggest you put this man to bed."

Cecilia frowned, but followed his very logical suggestion. Her bent frame was about to snap in two from Buck's weight. With Pendergast lifting not a finger to help, she shuffled closer to the bed.

"You need to turn the other way," he said, calculating.

Cecilia puffed out an exasperated breath. She should have just pulled back the damned covers and left Pendergast to do the lifting. "But that doesn't make sense," she said. "That would put me between him and the bed."

"Trust me," Pendergast said.

Foolishly, but just wanting to get this all over with, she did. Gathering her last vestiges of strength, she pivoted herself and Buck around so that the backs of her thighs were pinned against the mattress.

"I told you this was all wrong," she said.

Pendergast smiled, and behind him, Cecilia heard the opening of a door, then approaching footsteps. Dolly! "Oh, no!" she whispered, looking at him entreatingly. "Do something!"

He nodded obligingly, and then, with an evil little grin, put two fingers to Buck's back and gave him a gentle but firm shove. The slight pressure was enough to throw Cecilia completely off-balance, and she yelped helplessly as she felt herself falling, falling—and saw Buck poised to land right on top of her!

They hit the cotton batting and down mattress with a dull thud just as Dolly scurried into the room.

"What is happening!" she cried, trying to make sense of the mass of arms and legs entangled on the bed. Cecilia let out a winded moan, and Dolly's eyes widened.

"Don't, Mrs. Hudspeth," Jake urged, enjoying himself immensely as he took her arm to steer her toward the door. "Don't look on it."

Dolly dug in her heels. "But that's—that's Cecilia under that man!"

Cecilia let out a muffled cry and began to struggle to free herself.

"I've never witnessed such a scandal," Jake said in a low voice. "I never dreamed such things went on in respectable houses!"

Dolly's hand flew to her mouth, her friend forgotten momentarily at the mention of the word *scandal*. "They don't!" She looked at Cecilia, puzzled. "But who is that on top of her?"

"Dolly, for heaven's sake!" Cecilia yelled, poking her head free. "It's just Buck. Get me out of here!"

Jake's hopes faltered. If only he'd had time to think this through better...

Dolly paled. "Buck?" she asked, her voice almost a whisper. "Buck McDeere?"

"Yes!" Cecilia said. "What other Buck is there?"

Jake began to worry when Dolly swayed, high color returning to her cheeks in a sudden rush. The woman looked drunk herself! Tears appeared in her eyes, and her mouth twisted in an attempt to hold back a cry.

"Mrs. Hudspeth?" he said, concerned, grasping her arm more firmly.

She shook her head mutely, lifting her hand to her mouth. The tears she'd been attempting so valiantly to hold back gushed forth. Without a word, she pivoted on her slippers and ran from the room.

Jake looked after the woman in silence, wondering what on earth had happened.

Sputtering, Cecilia finally extricated herself and flew off the bed in a rage. "You planned that!" she accused sharply.

Jake crossed his arms and faced her squarely. "And you sent that man to try to get me drunk."

Her jaw dropped open, then popped closed. "You can't prove anything."

For his money, she might as well have admitted her guilt outright. Jake smiled. "All right," he said. "We neither of us have behaved very well tonight. I think we should call a truce."

She pressed her lips together and glared at him stubbornly. "Truce, my foot! My best friend is terribly upset, my reputation is on shaky ground, and I'll probably be sent home because of this."

To Jake, her words were like a balm.

"And as for you," she continued, "what do you have to complain about? You aren't even tipsy!"

Jake nodded toward Buck's sleeping form and shrugged. "Your friend was rather transparent in his designs."

Cecilia crossed her arms. "I should have known I needed to handle this problem myself."

"I don't think getting loaded up on hooch at Grady's would have done your reputation any good, either."

"Very funny," she said with a scowl.

Now that he had the upper hand, Jake was much more relaxed. Cecilia Summertree had learned her lesson; the woman would probably stop deviling him. Which led to another happy thought—they would no longer be adversaries, after all.

He took in her pretty, pouting mouth, the lips a luscious pink from where she had worried them with her teeth. Her arms were crossed over her chest. Although her nightgown came up to her neck and was perfectly proper, its snowy white folds, and the womanly curves they covered, were as inviting as a warm bed on a cold night.

Jake swallowed hard as he looked into her blue eyes. She appeared likewise mesmerized, her chest rising and falling rapidly, but no longer from anger. He reached out, and she stepped back.

"You're wrong, you know," he said, taking another step forward.

"About what?" Her voice came out in a wary, squeaky whisper.

"I do have something to complain about." He continued toward her, and she continued backing up until she backed right into a table.

"Wh-what?"

"No bed." He nodded lazily in the direction of Buck, never taking his eyes off her. "Where am I supposed to sleep?"

A little shiver tremored through Cecilia. She'd gone too far this time. Why hadn't she left as soon as she'd untangled herself from Buck? Innocuous words like *bed* and *sleep* sounded woefully intimate when you were alone with a man in his room. His dark room. Especially when your only champion was out cold.

Looking into his eyes had been the big mistake. She glanced at him, and then remembered that troublesome dream. Nightmare, she corrected. She'd remembered those smoldering eyes, and then that kiss, and . . . and then he'd started prowling toward her like a prairie wolf stalking a rabbit.

She was trapped, she thought, reaching back to steady herself. Her hands bumped against something hard and smooth. The washbasin! Heart beating rapidly, she felt around and found what she was looking for.

Jake smiled. Cecilia looked up at him, her eyes shy and a shade coy. She was beautiful. He understood why Buck was so smitten.

"Do you have any suggestions?" he asked, bending closer.

Her eyes widened when he touched her arm. "Oh, you mean to solve your little problem?"

"Uh-huh." He nibbled at the soft lobe of her right ear.

"Yes, yes, I think I do," she answered, gritting her teeth. She would never have taken the schoolteacher of yesterday, with his tight vest and floodwater pants, to be such a slimy lecher. But then, neither would she have guessed that she would find herself tempted by him in the least. Yet looking into those dark eyes, she could almost imagine allowing herself to find out if the man kissed as well in real life as he did in her dreams . . . .

Almost.

He pulled back to look into her eyes, and she broke out in a wide grin. "What is it?" he asked.

"Just this." Reaching from behind, she produced a white pitcher and flung half its contents in his face.

Jake let out a muttered curse as the water hit him, then dripped down his shirtfront. Reflexively, he stepped backward, shaking the water from his hands.

"I suggest you sleep on the floor," Cecilia said. Then, with a last disdainful glance, she turned and ran from the room.

Chapter Four

Cecilia swept the kitchen with long, energetic strokes. She had known Pendergast was going to be trouble, she'd just underestimated how much.

At breakfast this morning he'd been the soul of courtesy. The man hadn't cracked a smile or even looked at her funny, nothing to indicate he was the wolf who had cornered her in his bedroom the night before. The closest he'd come to communicating anything at all to her was to compliment her ironing!

After Pendergast left for school, she'd run up to his room to check on Buck, who was nowhere to be seen. Which was good, since he needed to get back to the ranch. Unfortunately she was dying to know what had happened last night—*before* she'd heard him singing.

She prayed Buck would make up something to tell her father, any excuse for her not coming home. Sooner or later she would have to tend to placating him herself; she couldn't rely on Buck forever. But for now, it was necessary to watch Pendergast like a hawk. If her suspicions were true and he wasn't a schoolteacher after all, he was bound to slip up.

And even if he didn't slip up on his own, he was bound to catch hell when those readers were discovered missing. She practically rubbed her hands in glee at the thought. Where finances were involved, Beasley wouldn't care who had actually been responsible for the theft, he would just want to have someone to blame. Pendergast was doomed.

But she would have to keep her wits about her. Last night she'd almost let the man kiss her—for no reason other than some silly little dream she'd had! Never in her life had Cecilia considered herself fickle, and now, with the enemy at her gate, was not the time to start behaving like a complete ninny.

The front door opened and closed, and Cecilia braced herself. *What if this was Pendergast?* She was alone in the house, except for Mrs. Baker, who couldn't hear anything anyway. What if he tried to corner her like he had last night?

Footsteps sounded in the kitchen doorway and Cecilia jumped with a startled intake of breath. Dolly stared at her oddly, then sniffed, raised her head proudly and continued on in.

Cecilia sighed. Of course it wasn't Pendergast! Why would a schoolteacher be home before midmorning?

Besides, as she watched Dolly pointedly ignoring her, she realized she had other problems to tackle. It seemed just about everyone in town had a beef against her. She walked to the small table and picked up the wrapped package from Beasley's that Dolly had put there.

"What's this?" she asked, attempting to break the silence between them. Dolly hadn't spoken a word to her since fleeing from Pendergast's bedroom the night before.

"Yeast."

And that, Cecilia gathered, was all Dolly intended to say about that. "Are you going to bake something?" she persisted.

Dolly continued to ignore her, but made an abundance of noise as she gathered things she would need. "Bread."

A wave of dread went through Cecilia. Given the positioning of her little room, baking bread in the oven meant she baked, too. "Is there anything I can do to help?" she asked, trying to keep her voice chipper.

The lighthearted tone appeared to be her friend's undoing. Suddenly, Dolly's shoulders sagged, then trembled, and she clasped a hand over her mouth. She shook her head as she leaned over the sink, and Cecilia could tell by the way the muscles in her jaw clenched and twitched that she was in the final throes of fighting back tears.

"Dolly, what is it?" she asked, scurrying over. She put an arm around Dolly's shoulders, but the woman shrugged it away. "Is it me? What have I done?"

Red faced, chest heaving, Dolly turned on her. "*Done?*" she asked, her voice steely. She dashed an errant tear from her cheek. "I think you know, Cecilia."

Cecilia stared at her, stupefied. "If it's about last night—"

A sharp accusatory laugh erupted from Dolly's chest.

"I know it looked strange," Cecilia said, but Dolly stopped her by holding a hand toward her, palm out. "I can explain," Cecilia insisted. "Well, most of it."

"Don't," Dolly said. "I'm going to have to tell your father the next time I see him, Cecilia. I don't think you ought to stay here."

A flush suffused Cecilia's cheeks. She was being thrown out. Thrown out. Just like yesterday, when Pendergast tossed her out of the schoolhouse. How the mighty had fallen.

"You can't, Dolly," she pleaded. "It wasn't how it looked. And you know how my poor father would react. It would kill him, or else he would kill me."

Dolly's mouth remained set in a firm, taut line. And then Cecilia detected a quiver. And then another. And then a cry erupted, a sad little moan. Dolly barely made it to one of the woven-backed chairs around the table before she collapsed.

"Oh, Cecilia," she wailed, "you wouldn't understand!"

At this rate, Cecilia feared she never would. She hurried over and put a comforting hand on Dolly's shoulder. "You must explain to me what is wrong. Maybe there's something I can do to set things right again."

Dolly's head shook to and fro. "You're so pretty and young, you'll think I'm foolish."

"For what?" asked Cecilia, astonished.

"For hoping that . . ." She let the sentence trail off, leaving Cecilia still mystified. "And then, seeing you together . . ."

Slowly, understanding dawned. Somehow, Dolly must have sensed that there was something going on between her and Pendergast. Of course, there *wasn't,* nothing besides animosity, nothing at all. What a horrible misconception!

"Oh, no, Dolly, you're wrong." As Dolly's eyes peered at her in hope, Cecilia shook her head decisively. "I have no interest in him whatsoever, nor he in me. Not the kind you mean, anyway."

She didn't know what to say next, but she felt in her heart of hearts it was her duty to dissuade Dolly from pinning her hopes on Pendergast. True, he was a bachelor, of a marriageable age and arguably attractive after a fashion, but Cecilia had serious misgivings about his character. Overall, they knew very little about this man. Also, if she had her way, he would soon be a man with no means of employment.

But before she could speak further, Dolly said, "That's not true, Cecilia. Perhaps you don't like him, but he's been flirting with you for five years."

"Five years!" Cecilia said, astonished again. "But Mr. Pendergast just got here a few days ago!"

Dolly gaped at her. "Mr. Pendergast? What has he to do with any of this?"

"But that's who you mean, isn't it?" Cecilia asked, perplexed. "Who else—"

An unbelievable possibility occurred to Cecilia, cutting her sentence short. She felt herself go pale as the blood drained from her cheeks. "Dolly, you can't mean . . ."

Fresh tears spilled freely down Dolly's face, and she nodded miserably. "Yes!" she cried.

"But you can't possibly. . ." She hardly knew how to put it into words.

Dolly did it for her. "It's Buck! I love him terribly!"

How else? Cecilia stared at her friend in horror. And disbelief. "Buck?" she asked, unable to keep the amazement out of her voice. "Buck McDeere?"

"When I saw you two together, Cecilia, I felt something die inside me," Dolly said, wiping her eyes with a wrinkled soggy handkerchief.

"But, Dolly," Cecilia said, still trying to cope with her friend's initial pronouncement, "Buck?"

"You're just a snob, Cecilia," Dolly said harshly. "You think he's unsuitable because he works for your father!" Cecilia took offense at those words. True, she had her faults, but this wasn't one of them. "You're wrong, Dolly. I wouldn't condemn a man for doing honest work. But, think. When you saw him last night, he was passed-out drunk!"

Dolly shot her an accusing glare. "That obviously didn't deter you from playing fast and loose with him while he was vulnerable."

Cecilia's mouth popped open in astonishment. "He fell on top of me!" she defended. "Truly, Dolly, that's absolutely all there was to it."

Suddenly, Dolly's eyes cleared. For a moment she gazed doubtfully at Cecilia, as if the news was too good to be true. "Honestly?" she asked, blinking.

"I swear it," Cecilia said. "But nevertheless . . . Buck? Dolly, he drinks, and goodness knows what else. He spends half his life at Grady's."

Dolly smiled radiantly, as if Cecilia's words had conjured the image of a saint for her. "You're wrong, Cecilia. No one is a lost cause. I'm sure, deep inside, Buck McDeere has it in him to be a great man, if someone would just set him straight."

Cecilia released a frustrated breath. "I'm not certain about that. . . ."

"I know what you're really thinking." Dolly looked at her sharply and sniffed. "You think I'm too old."

"The thought never entered my mind." Which was the truth. Cecilia had been too stunned to think things through even that far. "But now that you mention it, wouldn't you prefer someone more...mature?"

Dolly lifted her chin proudly. "I'm not yet thirty, after all, and Buck is nearly twenty-four. If our sexes were reversed, no one would blink an eye at the difference."

Everything she said was true. Still, Cecilia had serious misgivings. She was so used to thinking of Buck as a clown, or a pest, like a fly persistently buzzing around that needed to be swatted away. Considering him as a serious marriage partner—for anyone—was a stretch. But especially one for Dolly, who always seemed overly concerned with appearances and having things done properly.

What couldn't be denied was that Dolly was still young, and pretty, and had endured four lonely years of widowhood. She deserved love in her life, but men, good ones, were scarce—at least in Annsboro, which hadn't become the boomtown people like Lysander Beasley had hoped. And so Buck had become a serious prospect by default, especially since lately he was coming by more often to see Cecilia.

"I suppose I can see where he might be molded into marriage material," Cecilia allowed grudgingly, feeling half-responsible for the catastrophe.

Dolly shook her head emphatically. "I wouldn't want to change him."

"You'd take him as he is?" If so, Dolly had gone bug crazy.

"Well..."

Cecilia breathed a sigh of relief. At least her friend hadn't gone completely over the edge. Oh, but what a mess. She had no idea what Buck thought of Dolly—if he thought of her at all. But what difference did any of this make to her? She was about to be packed off to the ranch, never to gossip again, except on the occasional revival day. It was too pathetic.

And then, miraculously, an idea occurred to her through the murk of her despair. If she played her cards carefully, she just might hold disaster at bay for a precious while.

"Oh, how terrible," she gasped, sounding an alarming note.

Dolly's eyes snapped open wide. "What is it?"

Cecilia worried her lip to calculated effect. "Oh, nothing."

"Yes, it is so something," Dolly said. "Is it about Buck?"

Cecilia spoke her next words carefully. "I feel so sympathetic to your plight, Dolly. But unfortunately, once I go home, Buck probably won't come to town so much. Really, I'll be helpless to give you a hand."

Dolly straightened alertly.

"I might hint to him about you," Cecilia reasoned, "but I'm sure you wouldn't want him to know the extent of your feelings. Not before you know his."

"Oh, no." Dolly looked horrified at the thought. "He can't find out what I just told you!"

"Hmm." She wrinkled her brows thoughtfully. "With me back at home, this might be hard to maneuver."

"Oh, Cecilia!" Dolly's eyes were pleading, the set of her shoulders contrite. "If you'll just do this one thing, I swear I'll never tell your father about last night. I was only going to because... I was jealous."

Cecilia felt a pang of guilt for manipulating her friend this way. If her livelihood and her liberty weren't at stake, she wouldn't have stooped to such conniving. "If you had just asked me, you would have known there was nothing to be jealous of."

Dolly's face reddened with shame. "It was foolish of me, but I was afraid you would laugh if I told you how I felt about Buck."

Cecilia swallowed. "Not at all."

"Then you'll do your best to bring Buck around?" Dolly asked.

"Of course."

Dolly clapped her hands together. "I want to make a new dress, and I saw the sweetest little pattern at Beasley's! I've got the perfect material for it upstairs—I'll get it and show you."

She flew out of her chair and bounded up the stairs, leaving Cecilia still sitting in a stupor. How on earth was she going to manage to get Buck to fall in love with Dolly? She chewed her lip in deep thought. If she didn't manage to succeed, she wondered, would Dolly exact some kind of revenge?

She would have to get busy—both on Buck and on Pendergast. Because if she didn't bring Buck around, she might well end up on the ranch anyway. And then she'd never be able to oust the suspicious schoolteacher from his job!

Ten-year-old Beatrice Beasley sat on the topmost schoolhouse stair, waiting for her teacher. Two nut brown braids fell over her yellow checked pinafore, neat as you please. Generous freckles dotted her face and hands, made darker by a summer exposed to the sun. Nevertheless, she held her hands primly in her lap atop her schoolbook. Her big brown eyes, magnified by round spectacles, were focused adoringly on Mr. Pendergast, who was just shutting the building for the day.

At her feet was her dog, Mr. Wiggles, an old yellow hound that was treated by the entire town as if he was a queen's precious lapdog. The faithful animal roamed Annsboro all day until it was time to fetch his mistress home from school. Though the dog was sometimes known to be troublesome, Lysander Beasley, who because of his social status was always fearful his daughter was at risk of abduction, wouldn't allow a word to be spoken against the animal.

Catching sight of Bea and her hound, Jake let out an exasperated sigh. The child tormented him. Just seeing her bespectacled little face made him go clammy with fear. Of all the children in school, Lysander Beasley's daughter was the smartest. Smarter than her teacher, which gave Jake nightmares. Sometimes he imagined that even Mr. Wiggles could see right through his ruse.

The trouble was, he'd only finished seven years of schooling himself. When his father had had the ranch, Jake couldn't be spared once he was grown enough to work. Then, when his family had lost their farm due to Otis Darby's greed, he'd had to work even harder trying to do enough odd jobs to keep him and his mother going.

Burnet Dobbs had saved their lives by offering him the deputy job. It didn't offer much as far as pay went, but it gave him a sense that he was working for right, for justice. Sending Otis Darby up the river had been one of the high points of his life, like vindicating his father's death. But that had been before justice had backfired on him.

The upshot was that he hadn't ever expected to step inside a school again, except maybe for a town meeting. Now he was forced to dredge up memories of lessons he'd learned nearly twenty years ago. The school had few books, just enough math primers to go around. Jake spent a lot of the day on spelling, because the school did boast a new dictionary. Besides, he'd always been a good speller.

Saturday, when Jake had first arrived, Beasley had touted some newly bought readers, but Jake hadn't been paying attention, and now he didn't see them. For lack of any other inspiration, he'd brought out one of Pendergast's books, *Dancehall Gunfight*, and read it aloud today. Perhaps it wasn't great literature, but the children's faces had been rapt as he'd read the story of Two-step Pete, desperado turned federal marshal, and Willa the dance hall girl. Some of the girls had even cried at the point when Willa thought Two-step Pete had been fatally wounded.

Bea Beasley had cried. And now, as she looked at him as lovingly as Willa had gazed at Pete, Jake felt a shiver go down his spine. If the kid used her noggin, she'd have no trouble figuring out he was an impostor. All she had to do was tell her daddy that the new schoolteacher wasn't up to snuff—and just like that, he'd be out of a job. Maybe he should be thankful for her schoolgirl crush, he reasoned. Better she see him as a hero than a deputy turned ranch hand doing a poor imitation of a teacher.

He smiled at Bea, put his hat on his head and hurried down the stairs. Bea fell into step beside him with Mr. Wiggles right at her heels.

"Are you going to read us more about Pete and Willa tomorrow, Mr. Pendergast?"

"I suppose so," he said. "Do you like that story?"

"Oh, yes! I'm going to ask my father if I can grow up to be a dance hall girl, just like Willa."

"Don't do that!" he said too hastily. Imagining what Lysander Beasley would think of that book put him in a panic. Mr. Wiggles growled and Jake stared at Bea's surprised face. "Uh, I mean . . . stories lose their magic when you tell other people about them."

Bea looked shocked. "They do?"

"Absolutely." Jake winced at how easily the silly lie had jumped to his lips. Nevertheless, he breathed easier when he saw she was falling for the line. "You have to keep them to yourself." Lord, he prayed that would make the pesky kid keep her lip buttoned!

"Oh." Bea appeared worried. Probably thinking about all the stories she'd demystified through the years, Jake guessed.

Just then, he caught sight of Cecilia and Buck across the street, in front of the defunct blacksmith's shop. Cecilia had the ranch hand practically pinned against the storefront and appeared to be working him over about something or other. Jake felt his spine stiffen at the sight of the two of them together. Undoubtedly, it meant more trouble brewing.

Didn't Buck ever go home?

Without thinking, Jake veered so that he was walking straight toward the blacksmith shop. Bea and her dog did the same. He just couldn't shake that kid.

"Aw, Cecilia, why?" Buck's expression was petulant.

"Because, Dolly's one of the best cooks in town. Why, Mr. Walters *pays* to eat there!"

"I know, but . . . but isn't it more fun to walk around and talk on the street?"

Cecilia put her hands on her hips, took one step forward and glared at him crossly. "I'll thank you to show the decency to at least pretend to care about my reputation."

"What reputation?"

"Precisely," Cecilia snapped. Trying to convince Buck to visit her at Dolly's was harder than she'd thought it would be. Even the promise of better chow wasn't bringing him around. "I won't have a reputation left if you continue to chase me around the great outdoors like you do. So you can either come for a nice sit-down dinner at Dolly's or just leave me alone entirely."

He took on a kicked-puppy appearance, leaned against the blacksmith's wall and stubbed his toe in the dirt. "But Dolly's so—"

"It's no wonder you're intimidated by her," Cecilia broke in. "I've always thought she was the most beautiful woman in the county."

"Dolly?" Buck asked, astonished.

"And the funniest." As if to demonstrate, Cecilia looked at the empty September sky and chuckled merrily.

"What is it?"

Cecilia shook her head. "Oh, I was just thinking of this story Dolly told me the other day." She put a hand to her mouth. "But I forgot. You were in it."

"Dolly was talking about me?" He cocked his head first in surprise, then in wonder.

"She talks about you all the time." This, at least, was the horrible truth. Now that the matter was out in the open, Dolly used every free moment to drag details about Buck out of Cecilia.

"Really?" Buck rubbed his chin thoughtfully and glanced around, as if Dolly was going to pop around the corner of the building any second now.

"Only in passing, of course," Cecilia said, her heart tripping a little faster. She almost had him. "But I do think I've heard her say that you were a good-looking man." She looked up again, squinting in thought. She could practically feel Buck's curiosity awaiting her next words. "Yes, I do believe 'good-looking' is exactly how she phrased it. Or was it 'handsome'?"

"Me?" Buck asked, his bug-eyed look indicating he considered the idea absurd. Still, he was holding his breath.

"Or maybe she was referring to Mr. Pendergast."

"Pendergast! Why—"

"Oh, I can't remember," Cecilia interrupted, waving her hand as if to dismiss the whole dull topic. Five more minutes, and Buck would be planted at Dolly's dinner table for the next week.

"Well," Buck said, peering over her shoulder with narrowed eyes, "speak of the devil."

Cecilia twisted to follow Buck's gaze. Pendergast and Bea Beasley were striding toward them two abreast, Pendergast with the strangest, most determined look on his face.

Her heart sank. This was the last thing she needed! If not the devil, he was her own personal demon at this moment.

Nosy Pendergast *would* show up just when she was managing to make some headway with Buck. Now all her hard-planted information about poor Dolly would be forgotten, and she'd have to wait until Buck came to town again and start from scratch. And if Dolly became impatient, there was no telling what she would do.

This time next week, Cecilia could well imagine herself back on the ranch, bored, bored, bored. And all because Pendergast couldn't mind his own business.

From his angle, Jake didn't know why the two were frowning at him so vehemently, but he could hazard a guess. Obviously he was busting up an intimate discussion. He didn't stop to think why that should annoy him. It just did. If only to be perverse, he decided to stick around. Maybe he could intimidate the ham-fisted cowpoke all the way back to the ranch.

"Howdy," he said. "To put it in your own language."

Cecilia's lip curled up in a halfhearted attempt at a smile. "What are you doing here?"

"Yeah," Buck said belligerently. "We're talking."

"A private conversation on a public street?" Jake asked, amused and intrigued by the way Buck appeared to be sizing him up, almost as if they were rivals. But why would he do that? Jake looked at Cecilia. Could she have said something to Buck that would have made him jealous?

Although at first she met his gaze defiantly, color soon rose in her cheeks. "Yes, this is private," she said.

"I guess that means we should go," Bea said, tugging at Jake's sleeve cuff.

"Wait just a minute," Jake drawled, a smile touching his lips. He stepped closer, enjoying Cecilia's disquiet. "You mean you're just going to send me away, just like that?"

His voice dripped with hurt, a lover's pain, and Cecilia looked at him more anxiously as she crept backward, away from him. "What are you talking about?"

"Well, I thought that after the other night..."

"What happened the other night!" Buck exclaimed, his face immediately red and explosive.

"Don't you remember?" Jake teased. "You were there."

"Why, you—"

Buck burst forward, but Cecilia shot out a restraining arm. "Buck, down."

"If he took advantage of you..." he growled warningly.

"Oh, for heaven's sake," Cecilia said with an exasperated sigh. "What's gotten into you two? You're behaving as though this were the Dark Ages."

"Well, certainly," Jake said, smiling at Buck. "After all, when a lady enters a man's bedroom, people are bound to make a fuss."

"Bedroom!" Bea cried, her eyes bugging to the rims of her glasses.

"Cici, is that true?" Buck demanded.

"I was carrying your inebriated body, you fool," Cecilia said. She turned on Pendergast, her eyes flashing angrily. "As for you, what kind of teacher goes around knowingly spreading lies like that? Why, if this story *got back to Mr. Beasley,*" she said pointedly, darting a meaningful glance at Bea, "he just might have your job."

Bea shook her head emphatically as she spoke to her hero. "I would never say anything bad about *you*, Mr. Pendergast. Or Miss Summertree. I swear."

Jake patted the girl's head.

"I still want to know what happened," Buck insisted.

Cecilia huffed out a sigh. "Nothing, absolutely nothing," she said, her voice squeaking with frustration. As he continued to stare at her, his innocent face veiled with confusion, Cecilia rolled her eyes. "Go home, Buck."

"But—"

"I'll explain later," Cecilia said firmly.

His shoulders rounded with defeat, Buck looked from her to Pendergast and then back to her. "I don't like to leave you like this—"

"I'll be fine." She extended a hand and warmly squeezed his arm. Jake could barely swallow as she bestowed her warmest smile on the dim cowboy. "Thank you for walking with me, Buck."

Buck, hardly believing his luck in her change in tone, blinked, then puffed up his chest in response. He shot Jake a warning glance. "If you need me—" he said to Cecilia.

"I'll let you know," she said obligingly.

He gave Jake a final smug glare and swaggered away toward the saloon, where his roan mare was tethered. Cecilia watched him until he was out of earshot, then turned on Pendergast.

"I don't know what you're up to, Pendergast," she said angrily, moving in on him, "but I do know that it's not going to work."

He stood firm and forced his mouth into a grin. "You don't honestly have feelings for that cowhand, do you?"

She threw a glance to Buck, then crossed her arms. "What if I do? Is that your business?"

"I leave that up to you." He stepped forward and spoke in a low voice. "Is it?"

Her eyes widened as he came closer to her, and she bit her lower lip anxiously. Suddenly, she threw another glance over her shoulder, but Buck was already mounted and heading out to the north.

"Buck is an old friend," she said evasively, still not willing to back down.

Jake guessed that his first hunch was correct—Cecilia was keeping the cowboy at arm's length because she didn't like him but didn't want to hurt his feelings by saying so. Besides, in country like this, as isolated as folks were, having people available to talk to was a luxury you didn't throw away lightly. The fact that Cecilia wasn't actually considering Buck as a potential husband made him inordinately happy.

Not that it truly mattered, he thought. But Cecilia was a cute thing, and he was going to be in town for a good solid spell. Female companionship wasn't something to throw away lightly, either.

"I'm glad you're just friends," he said.

"I didn't say that," Cecilia corrected. "He's been coming to town regularly since I opened the school early last month."

"But you aren't in charge of the school anymore."

She narrowed her eyes on him. "No, I'm not. At the moment," she said, attempting to look down her nose at him, which was difficult, since he was a foot taller.

He admired her backbone. Wrongheaded though she was, he couldn't blame Cecilia for trying to hold on to what was hers. He himself had made the mistake of running once, and since then he'd been playing the role of mouse in a cat-and-mouse chase. He couldn't allow himself to forget that Cecilia had her own agenda, but that didn't mean they had to be enemies. Or that he couldn't enjoy being her antagonist.

"If he was really your sweetheart, you would have gone back to the ranch like a shot." Jake moved almost imperceptibly closer. "Wouldn't that be more convenient, so you could see each other more often?"

Cecilia's throat worked visibly as she swallowed a dry gulp of air. She didn't like the predatory glint in Pendergast's eye. Or the quivery feeling in her stomach.

She glanced down to his vest. It wasn't buttoned all the way to the top, and without that comical effect, she saw that his chest was quite expansive—not burly, but wide and lean. Catlike. And his arms, encased though they were in a starchy white cotton shirt, up close seemed as sculpted and muscled as those on the men at the ranch. Physically, she'd underestimated him, which was not a smart thing to do, she realized, when a person was two of you.

"I'm glad he's not your sweetheart," he said, his voice a low, husky drawl.

Somewhere in the distant recesses of her mind, warning bells sounded. But for now, all her attention was held by those deep brown eyes. They came nearer and nearer, until she was completely captivated.

"Why?" she asked.

He smiled, and Cecilia's heart hammered against her breastbone with heavy uneven thuds.

"Can't you guess?"

In a last-ditch effort to save herself, Cecilia took a step backward and felt her shoulders bump against the corner

beam of the blacksmith shop. Surely he wouldn't do anything, not right here, not on the street!

"No," she whispered, and shook her head, although that
was a lie. She could guess what he meant, but for the life of
her she couldn't have found the spit to voice it. Her mouth
was bone-dry.

His eyes darkened further, which Cecilia hadn't thought
possible, and suddenly, one of his hands clamped down on
her arm. "I'll show you," he said.

With two firm tugs and a dizzying twirl, Cecilia found
herself in a shaded area around the corner, out of sight of
any of the other buildings, and held firmly in those arms
whose strength she'd so underestimated.

"How did you do that?" she said breathlessly.

"You know what they say, teacher." Dark eyes glistened.
"Where there's a will..."

The raspy words were cut off as his mouth descended on
hers. Cecilia let out a surprised gasp, although she had been
anticipating just this for a full minute that now seemed like
a lifetime. He pressed his lips to hers gently, and she snaked
her arms up his chest and around his neck.

Cecilia lifted onto her toes at the same time that Pendergast drew her body nearer to his. As a result, she found
herself more intimately entwined with a man than she had
ever been in her life. When his tongue parted her lips and
delved inside her mouth, she nearly fainted with a mixture
of dismay and pleasure. Surely, what he was doing wasn't
right—no lady would stand for it, especially in broad daylight. Cecilia would have slapped him...if only she wasn't
holding on to his strong shoulders for dear life.

Her breath came out in a little moan, and Pendergast
smiled. Slowly, he pulled back, and Cecilia unwound herself from him in a daze. She was sure her face was beet red,
but she couldn't look away. Those eyes still mesmerized her.

Pendergast lifted one dark eyebrow. "That's why," he
said, dusting his hands together. With a wink, but without

another word, he turned and ambled around the corner, out of Cecilia's sight.

Why what? In a daze she stared at the point where he had disappeared. Somehow during the past few minutes she'd completely forgotten the question—perhaps because the answer itself had been so fascinating....

Chapter Five

Bea Beasley's eyeglasses were nearly popping out of their frames. The girl clasped Cecilia's hand—a steadying gesture, Cecilia was embarrassed to admit, she desperately needed.

"He kissed you!" the child cried dreamily. "Oh, Miss Summertree, how romantic!"

Still woozy-headed, Cecilia lifted a hand to her lips. So that's what kissing was supposed to be like, she realized with awe. After the fumbling attempts made by other men, she'd always wondered why everyone always made such a big deal of such a messy exchange.

"Miss Summertree? Miss Summertree?"

Bea gave her a shake, then exclaimed, "It's just like in the books! You're pale and your pulse is fluttering wildly, madly. Oh, it's all so thrilling I could just die!"

Cecilia focused on Bea's rapturous face and frowned. Wildly, madly? She shook her free wrist, trying to tamp down her own absurd rapture. The last thing she needed at this desperate juncture in time was to fall wildly, madly over anybody—especially Eugene Pendergast, her archenemy.

In good time, her senses returned to normal and a healthy rage started coursing through her veins. That low-down viper had kissed her on purpose! And not because he couldn't help himself, the usual male excuse, but because he wanted to exercise his smug superiority. What galled her most was that she had just stood there and allowed him to bend her around like clay. For heaven's sakes, she'd practically wilted in his arms. She must have lost her mind.

Clara would doubtless have a mouthful of platitudes for this situation.

Still in a state of exaltation, Bea stared at the point in space where Pendergast had disappeared. The precocious girl sincerely believed there was a special place reserved for educators on Mount Olympus, and it was obvious that she thought she had witnessed something tantamount to the coupling of the gods. Now Cecilia had to figure out a way to keep her quiet. All she needed would be for news of the kiss to spread around town, on top of all her other troubles!

"Now the two of you can get married," Bea said enthusiastically, "and we'll have *two* teachers."

Over my dead body, Cecilia thought heatedly.

"Mr. Pendergast is so handsome. Just like Two-step Pete. Don't you think so, Miss Summertree?"

Since she didn't know who Two-step Pete was, Cecilia could only nod. Refuting would only put Bea on the defensive, and she knew from exasperating experience that once that kid got in an argumentative mood, there was no winning.

"But I don't think you look a bit like Willa, Miss Summertree," the child prattled on, "your hair's not red enough."

Her hair wasn't red at all, but that, apparently, was beside the point. "Who is Willa?" Cecilia asked distractedly, her mind whirring at a frightening speed to think of some way to keep Bea from blabbing about this incident to her father.

"Willa's a dance hall girl. She wears fancier clothes than you do, too, I'm afraid. Her dresses are always of the finest satins, and very alluring to the male eye. But I'm sure Mr. Pendergast doesn't mind your clothes too much, since you are supposed to be a lady, although it's only fair to tell you that men always seem to prefer women who reveal a graceful show of ankle every now and again, no matter how respectable they are.''

Bea and her books! ''Beatrice, where are you picking up these ideas? I can't believe your father lets you read trash. What's the name of this story?'' Maybe she could use a little blackmail for leverage....

The girl poked out her chin proudly. ''The name of the book is *Dancehall Gunfight,* and it is *not* trash, either. It's literature, because Mr. Pendergast is reading it to us.''

Now this was interesting. Cecilia felt a little surge of hope. ''Mr. Pendergast is reading a book called *Dancehall Gunfight* to you in school?''

Bea nodded. ''He's not finished with it yet, even though he read it all afternoon. He said he'd bring in more of his own books, too.''

Cecilia pursed her lips thoughtfully, gleefully visualizing the brand spanking-new-readers tucked neatly beneath the schoolhouse steps. ''What ever happened to the Gibson readers?''

Bea shrugged. ''I think Mr. Pendergast is a more progressive sort of educator.''

Cecilia swallowed a sigh of frustration. He had this kid hoodwinked, all right. Since when did upstanding Eastern-educated teachers choose material as attention-grabbing as saloon girls in low-cut satin dresses? Something about this Pendergast character wasn't right.

And yet, reading one measly book wasn't likely to get Pendergast fired. Even the missing readers might not do the trick. She needed more....

Bea's earnest little face looked curiously into hers. ''Is there anything wrong, Miss Summertree? They say sometimes that love makes women scatterbrained.''

Cecilia smirked. As if she was actually in love with Pendergast!

Then, out of the blue, a possible solution to her problem occurred to her. If she could stomach it. "Quite the opposite, Bea. Love makes women *curious*."

"What are you curious about?"

"Mr. Pendergast," Cecilia said, going in for the pitch. "You see, Bea, I've known Mr. Pendergast such a short time. Why, you've been around him more than I have!"

"I have?" This fact seemed to amaze Bea—and make her realize her own importance, which is exactly what Cecilia wanted.

"Of course, because you spend so much time with him at school. Well, I just bet you could tell me loads of things about Mr. Pendergast that I'd never be able to find out on my own."

Bea's brow wrinkled. "Like what?"

"Well . . . like what he says in school. And what he reads to you children. A person's literary tastes are very important, you know."

"Oh, yes!"

"In fact, Beatrice Beasley, you could be a big help to me, if every few days you would tell me about Mr. Pendergast."

"You mean, spy on Mr. Pendergast?" The child reacted to the suggestion as if it was the vilest form of treachery.

"Well . . ." Cecilia decided to appeal to the child's romantic sensibilities. "Yes, but in a good way. You wouldn't want Mr. Pendergast to grow old and lonely and bitter, completely unloved, would you?"

"But aren't *you* in love with Mr. Pendergast?"

Hmph. Cecilia swallowed her disgust and smiled. "Almost, but a woman shouldn't cast her lot with a man she knows nothing about. That's where you come in, Bea."

"I see," Bea said. "It wouldn't really be spying, it would be more like ensuring Mr. Pendergast won't turn into a heartless old geezer, like Ebenezer Scrooge, or someone like that."

"What a horrible thought!"

"I would be *helping* Mr. Pendergast," Bea said, gaining enthusiasm for the plan. No doubt she would find the role of go-between in this little drama romantic in itself.

"That's right, and you would be doing me a great service, as well," Cecilia said with a wink. "We women of the world have to stick together."

Bea beamed.

"And Bea, the most important thing of all is never to tell anyone what we're doing. The first rule of spying—I mean *helping*—is secrecy."

"I swear I won't tell a soul!" Bea said in a rush, then amended, "except maybe Mr. Wiggles."

Cecilia looked at the yellow hound, who at the sound of his name was wagging his tail eagerly. "I guess we can trust Mr. Wiggles," she lied. That dog had always made her nervous.

She and Bea sealed their bargain with a sober handshake, agreed to a clandestine meeting later in the week and emerged from the shadows of the old building into the afternoon sunlight. Bea clearly relished her new cloak-and-dagger persona, and moved furtively from tree to tree as she made her way home. Cecilia only hoped she relished her role enough to keep quiet, and decided a few candy bribes might be in order to reinforce the importance of this point.

Cecilia sighed as she headed for home. Dolly would no doubt want to know where she had disappeared to; maybe love actually did make women curious. Given that her meeting with Buck had been cut short, she would just have to fabricate some encouraging news for her friend. Even so, Dolly would not be satisfied until Cecilia produced Buck in the flesh as a willing suitor. And in anticipation of her failure to do so, she had probably designed some terrible task for Cecilia to do, like churning butter. Her back ached just thinking about it.

Not to mention, she would have to spend another evening across the dinner table from Pendergast—this time with the memory of that kiss fresh in her mind. It was too humiliating.

All this, just so she could live with some iota of dignity, on her own terms, as a lady. Not for the first time, she was struck by the tragic irony of her plight. *By the time I actually am in a position to be a lady,* she thought sadly, *I'll have spent so long lying and laboring that I'll have forgotten how to be one!*

Rosalyn Pendergast sat on the edge of her mahogany bed, straining to comprehend the words on the page in front of her. ... *regret to inform you of your brother's untimely departure from this life...* That one shocking phrase summed up the whole of Mr. Jake Reed's letter.

And yet the man wrote in such vague language, he posed more questions than he answered. How had Eugene—timid, bookish Eugene—become involved in a "barroom fracas"? Mr. Reed didn't say. Nor did he say whether there had been a proper burial. And what of her brother's possessions? Rosalyn was sure Eugene had more things than the forty-seven dollars Mr. Reed had sent along.

No, none of this made sense. And yet, even as the tears for her only brother spilled down her cheeks, Rosalyn had to admit that it wasn't entirely unexpected. Hadn't she begged Eugene not to leave, fearing just this sort of calamity? But her dear, foolish brother had insisted that Texas was just the place he was looking for. It would make a new man of him, he'd said.

She'd even begged him to reconsider the precise destination he had in mind. Annsboro, Texas ... the frontier ... it was so remote! And all they knew of the place was from a short description written to Gene from Chadwick Watkins, an old college acquaintance who had become superintendent of schools in that area. Galveston, Rosalyn had suggested, was also in Texas, yet it had some of the niceties available, too. But he'd insisted he'd wanted something dif-

ferent, something rugged, as though a change in geography
would transform his whole personality.

Poor, poor Gene. Perhaps she'd stifled him, because he
was her only relation besides Aunt Patrice. Though Rosalyn gave lessons that earned a little money, Eugene had felt
obligated to support her. He'd been trapped, saddled with
a spinster sister, relegated to living with his old fretful aunt.
And this, his one attempt to free himself, had failed miserably.

Rosalyn slowly stood and walked to the bureau to get a
fresh handkerchief. In the small mirror on the wall, she
caught a glimpse of her wretched appearance. Her fair skin
was mottled, almost scarlet in places from her weeping, and
her brown eyes were bloodshot and red-rimmed. Hair that
had been so carefully combed and tucked back earlier now
threatened mutiny, breaking free of its confining pins. She
would have to put herself together before she talked to her
aunt. The sad news would probably cause Patrice to take to
her bed for at least a month.

And yet, though the lady would never say so, Aunt Patrice would probably consider Eugene's death a just end to
such a foolhardy expedition. Their aunt had been most vo-
cal in her disapproval of Eugene's plan, especially when she
discovered that Rosalyn was supposed to follow him to
Annsboro once he was settled. Ingrates, she called them, for
abandoning the very person who had taken them in as pen-
niless orphans, reared and educated them.

Rosalyn had agreed—it was terrible of them to leave dear
old Patrice after all she had done for them. But the elderly
lady firmly refused to join them on their adventure, even
when Rosalyn had practically begged her. Patrice had lived
in Philadelphia for over sixty years, in this very house, and
she wasn't going to budge now. Especially not to travel to
heathen country.

Yes, Rosalyn had agreed, what Eugene and she were
planning was heartless. Beastly. Ungrateful.

She could hardly wait to go!

She went red with shame just thinking about how she'd secretly yearned for the moment she could board a train and say goodbye to Philadelphia and this stuffy old house. For months she'd been dreaming about it. Freedom. Eugene felt stifled? He, at least, was a man!

He wasn't forever expected to accompany Patrice on her tedious round of calls to the same people every week, or tend Patrice through her imaginary aches and afflictions, or to sit endlessly in the claustrophobic parlor, sewing or reading while the noisy mantel clock ticked away the long, insufferable hours. Rosalyn's only moments of freedom came as she walked to and from the few lessons she gave to people's children—Latin and French and mathematics for girls. The rest of her hours were diligently and dutifully accounted for. She loved her aunt dearly, almost as much as she loved her brother, but oh, she'd staked all her hopes on escaping this place!

Now escape was impossible. That was what Mr. Jake Reed had truly conveyed to her.

Again she blushed at her selfish, unseemly thoughts. Poor Eugene! Of course, that was the biggest loss of all. Except...

Well, at least *he* had seen something of the world. And from the moment he had heard his loose connection to Chadwick Watkins might help him attain the position in Annsboro, Eugene had had a hope to cling to. He'd been walking on air for months in anticipation, happier than she'd ever seen him at the prospect of leaving everything behind—he'd seemed a wholly different person from the one she had known for twenty-nine years. Maybe Texas *would* have given him a new identity.

Rosalyn looked in the mirror just in time to see her face go pale again. *A new identity?*

She rushed back to the bed and plucked the letter off the eyelet coverlet. It said so little—only that Eugene was dead. Jake Reed gave no details, no dying words to comfort a grieving sister. The way he skimmed over the event made it seem so unreal....

No, that was ridiculous. She was being foolish. And yet, Mr. Reed's letter was so vague. She would have to write to this Jake Reed....

No, she thought, that would be especially foolish. If Eugene was dead, Mr. Reed would think her a lunatic for not believing his first letter. Besides, if foul play was involved, who could she trust—a complete stranger Eugene had met in a saloon?

She quickly did some math in her head. On top of the forty-seven dollars Jake Reed had sent, she had nearly thirty dollars of her own saved, not to mention whatever she could get for bits of jewelry that had no sentimental value to her. That would be more than enough money to get her to Texas!

For one riotous moment, her life seemed to explode with possibilities. But what would she tell her aunt? Patrice would think she'd lost her mind. After all, she had no proof that Eugene was still alive—to the contrary, all she had was an eyewitness account that he wasn't. Using that as evidence that her brother was still living would sound like the most twisted kind of logic.

And perhaps it was. She paced the room and stopped to give herself another good look in the mirror. The face that stared back at her was that of a thirty-one-year-old woman. A spinster. Nothing anchored her to this city, really. But she was a lady, and ladies just didn't run off to the frontier. The idea was absurd! How would she even know how to start looking for Eugene? She'd never taken a trip farther west than Pittsburgh, and that was traveling with Aunt Patrice.

If it had been in her to slump, Rosalyn would have at that moment. She walked back to her bed where the horrid letter still lay, taunting her. Something about all this just didn't seem right to her. If she wasn't going to Texas, and she wasn't going to confront Mr. Jake Reed, she had to at least do her best to investigate in the only way she knew how.

Her back rigid with determination, she walked over to the small escritoire by the window, brought out a sheet of paper and dipped her old pen. In her elegant practiced hand she began to write to the one person she hoped would know of her brother's fate.

Dear Mr. Watkins...

It was strange, indeed, if something had happened to Eugene, that she hadn't heard from his old college acquaintance before now. Eugene had given her Watkins's address, just in case of an emergency.

Which this might or might not be.... She decided not to tell Mr. Watkins of her suspicions. It would just be a nice friendly letter, an older sister asking a man to look after her brother. One that the man would feel bound to answer—she hoped with news of whether Eugene had ever arrived in Annsboro.

"Today we spelled."

"Hmm," Cecilia said. She and Beatrice stood by the water pump to the side of the school for their fourth meeting in almost two weeks. Beside them, Mr. Wiggles was stretched out beneath a mesquite tree. If anyone happened to see them, it would seem perfectly natural that Cecilia was fetching herself a pitcherful of water.

"What else?" she asked Bea.

"That's all."

Cecilia took in this information with amazement. Pendergast had the darnedest ways of teaching that she'd ever heard of. A whole day of spelling?

Of course, what else was he to do? Bea, with much prodding from Cecilia, had let slip to her father about the absence of readers at school, and Lysander Beasley had marched down to the school to investigate. When he learned that Pendergast didn't know where they were, he'd almost hit the roof. About town, speculation was high that one—or all—of the older boys had taken them as a prank, but even if the blame was being misplaced, it still left Pendergast with nothing to do all day.

Except spell, she thought with an evil grin.

Bea tossed her thick braids proudly. "Of course, I'm the best speller in the class. I won five spelling bees in a row, so Mr. Pendergast let me ask the questions for the rest of the day."

Cecilia didn't like the sound of that. It wouldn't do to have Pendergast muscling in on her source. "Of course you're the best speller, Bea. You always were," she said, stroking the child's ego. She brought out the stick candy she had purchased at Beasley's that very afternoon. "Before I forget, here's something for you. You know how much I appreciate what you're doing, don't you?"

Bea took the candy and inspected it. "I guess it must take women longer to fall in love in real life than it does in books."

"Much longer," Cecilia said. She couldn't afford to have Bea let up her vigilant watch just yet.

"Well . . . if that's so, do you think we could devise a different form of appreciation?"

This request took Cecilia by surprise. "What do you mean?"

Bea grew bolder. "For instance, it might not be a bad idea if you varied the candy a little. It wouldn't do any harm to bring licorice every once in a while, instead of the same old peppermint time after time. Since my father owns the store, I know for a fact that they're the same price."

Cecilia crossed her arms and looked at Bea with a new caution. What a little operator she was turning into! Still, Cecilia knew she herself wasn't much of a role model. And Bea had her over a barrel. "Okay, okay, you'll get your licorice," she said.

Bea's face paled and the little girl nodded her head, indicating that someone was approaching. Cecilia didn't have to turn to know it was Pendergast. His reflection showed in Bea's glasses.

"Mr. Pendergast," she said, turning.

Bea began to edge away from them. "I . . . I guess I'll be going."

Before trotting off toward her father's store, she sent Jake a wink, making him feel somewhat relieved. She'd persuaded Cecilia to bring licorice, then.

"I just love talking to Bea," Cecilia said cheerfully, as if that explained the reason she was here.

Jake wondered how fast she'd change her tune if she found that her spy was a turncoat. After each meeting with Cecilia, Bea reported back to him, then presented him with most of whatever candy she'd garnered. Jake in turn parceled out the candy to his class in return for some semblance of obedience. So far the setup was working out quite nicely for everyone—with Bea, of course, coming out slightly ahead—except some of the older boys had insisted they preferred licorice to peppermint. Hence the change.

"I guess you must like talking to her, since you come so far out of your way to do it," Jake said.

"But you see, I was just passing by and decided to fetch some water." The excuse sounded lame even to her own ears, especially when she looked down at the pitcher she'd been hauling around. Empty. She quickly began pumping the handle to fill it.

Pendergast stopped her arm in mid-pump by placing a firm hand over hers. But it wasn't so much his touch as his words that made her freeze. "I know what you're doing, Miss Summertree."

"You do?" A chill went down Cecilia's spine. Had he found the readers? Had Bea snitched about their secret meetings?

"Indeed I do," he said in his suspicious drawl, a broad smile on his face, "and I think I should warn you against it."

"And just what do you think I'm doing?"

"Falling in love with me, of course."

Cecilia's jaw dropped open, but words failed her. She pulled her hand free.

Jake let out a smug chuckle. He didn't mind playing Pendergast one bit when he was able to annoy Cecilia.

"I can assure you, Mr. Pendergast, I am not falling in love with you!"

"Then may I ask why you're following me around all the time?"

"Following you!" Cecilia huffed. "Where did you come up with that absurd idea?"

Jake rubbed his jaw thoughtfully. "Maybe the day I noticed you peeking around the corner of Beasley's when I went in to buy some tooth powder."

"I just happened to be there!" Cecilia protested.

"And then, at church last Sunday, I noticed that you switched seats to get a little nearer to me."

Cecilia rolled her eyes. "That's because I accidentally sat down next to Mr. Whitman, whom I cannot abide. It's trying enough to sit through that long service without someone snoring in my ear the whole way!"

"Come now, Miss Summertree," Jake cajoled.

"I am *not* in love with you!" Cecilia blushed furiously at the position she was in, which of course made it appear that she was lying. She let out an exasperated sigh. At least the man didn't know what she was really up to. "I'm not in love with you," she repeated, and like the poor madman who jumps up and down swearing he's not insane, she knew she sounded less than convincing.

"Isn't it a coincidence that you took a job at Mrs. Hudspeth's boardinghouse when I arrived in town?"

"Not when you consider that I had just lost my other job when you came to town, which was no coincidence at all."

"Your father's ranch would be much more comfortable for you, wouldn't it?"

"Not that my comfort is any of your business," Cecilia said snappishly, "but I hate ranches. I prefer to be near people."

He grinned. "Especially certain people?"

Cecilia gritted her teeth in annoyance. "For the last time, I swear you mean nothing to me."

"I think the lady protests too much, as the old saying goes." At least, Jake hoped that was how it went. He felt nervous, as though he'd just spoken a foreign language off the cuff. Now he had to wait to see if it translated.

What could she say that would convince him? Cecilia wondered. Having Pendergast start spouting Shakespeare at this late date wasn't a good sign, either. She felt her shoulders sag with hopelessness. It seemed that nothing was working out for her these days.

Still smiling, he sidled nearer and leaned leisurely against the pump. "I'll admit, I was bowled over by you at first, Cecilia. You don't mind if I call you Cecilia, do you?"

"I wish you wouldn't," Cecilia mumbled. Was there no deterring this man?

"Cecilia . . ." He looked dreamily off into space. "It has a downright persnickety sound to it."

"What!" Cecilia couldn't believe what she was hearing. "Well, I beg your pardon, *Eugene!*"

He grinned triumphantly. "By all means, call me Eugene, Cecilia. I want us to be friends."

"Friends, ha! I'd rather be friends with a sidewinder."

He frowned with concern. "But I'm afraid friends is all we can be. As I was saying, at first I was flattered by your obviously amorous intentions, until I realized you were just a young thing, and probably not ready for a deep, mature love."

Cecilia saw red. "I'm almost nineteen. And when I go looking for a deep, mature love, Pendergast, you can believe I won't be knocking on your door to find it."

"No, I would think you would be more the type to leave notes."

"I would never—"

He leaned closer still and said conspiratorially, "Or maybe you'd just send Bea to tell me."

So that was it! Bea had obviously let on to Pendergast what she was doing and had spilled the ridiculous business about her being a woman in love. Well, no harm done, as long as Pendergast didn't find out she was spying on him so she could get him tossed out of his job. She didn't want him to change his behavior. In the end, she was going to have the last laugh.

"Tell me something," Pendergast asked, "do those little scorch marks you always put on my shirts have any special significance?"

Cecilia bit back a hoot. Those little scorch marks meant she couldn't iron worth a flip. "My mind wanders," she said through clenched teeth. To have to stand here while this man insinuated that she was sending him little love messages through the laundry was almost unbearable.

"Ah, I see." He winked at her—as though her mind was wandering because of *him*.

She wished she could slap his smug grin clear off his face. Instead she said, "Just out of curiosity, Pendergast, why are you warning me from falling in love with you? You haven't left an abandoned family back East, have you?"

That would be too good to be true!

"Good heavens, no," he said. "I told you. You're a child, if not in years, then emotionally. It's obvious you're not ready for a real man."

"And I suppose *you're* a real man!"

"Judging from your reaction to our innocent little kiss, it's obvious that you think so."

Outrage seared through every vein in her body, chased furiously by bewilderment. That kiss was supposed to have been *innocent?*

"I can see by your silence that you agree with me," Pendergast said. "Which is for the best, I can assure you. I wouldn't want you getting your hopes up."

Cecilia was sure she would explode with rage if she heard any more, but she had to ask, "Hopes?"

Jake chuckled. The woman was about to burst. Looping a thumb into the pocket of his strangling vest, he opined, "You little ladies think one tiny kiss means everything. What you don't understand, Cecilia sweetheart, is that men are sort of like trees. There are saplings who can be bent to your will, and then there are mighty oaks, which don't bend at all, and take a lot longer to chop down."

Why was she listening to this drivel? Cecilia lifted her chin haughtily and leveled a withering gaze on him. "Believe me, Pendergast, I wouldn't take an ax to you if you were the last tree on earth and I was about to freeze to death!"

With a final huff of dismay, Cecilia turned and stomped off down the road toward the boardinghouse. Jake laughed out loud at her retreat, just to annoy her even more. And then he sighed. Much as he enjoyed sparring with the county's worst laundress, there was no denying the relief he felt to have survived another encounter. Insisting that she was in love with him had been a good strategy. He wanted to devil her any way he could—especially since he had more than a hunch she had had a hand in the disappearance of those schoolbooks.

He worked the pump handle until a stream of cool water spewed forth. Annsboro was as dry as the devil's tongue on Judgment Day. Looking around and seeing no one, Jake undid his collar button and dipped his entire head beneath the spigot. Lord, he couldn't remember early October being this hot—just his luck that it would be steamy when he was stuck wearing some Yankee's winter suits. Probably by the time it actually turned cold enough to make them bearable, he wouldn't even be in Annsboro anymore.

At least, he hoped that was the case.

Jake stared down the road at Cecilia and felt a pang of regret. Another time, in different circumstances, maybe he would have carried on an earnest flirtation with her, instead of the two-fisted brawl they were involved in. But then, it was hard to say. He'd been on the lam so long now it seemed years since he'd sparked a decent woman. And now, he reminded himself firmly as he went into the school to collect his things, was no different—except that now, instead of running, he was temporarily stuck.

Stuck living with a woman who hated his guts.

He should never have kissed her. He'd thought that would put an end to the attraction to Cecilia, like scratching an itch. But just the opposite was true. He felt himself doing just what he'd accused her of—seeking her out, watching her furtively, waiting to talk to her again. To kiss her again.

Well, the next time he felt that urge, he was just going to think of Otis Darby and Will Gunter instead of a pert little blonde. That should effectively quash his desires—as well as remind him that he was only in Annsboro killing time until the moment he could move in for the kill.

This time next week, he decided. One more week of cooling his heels, and then his time in Annsboro would be a memory.

Chapter Six

Cecilia was at the boiling point as she neared Dolly's. Mighty oak, ha! If Pendergast was a mighty oak then she was...exhausted. This business of getting her old job back was taking more effort than she had expected.

"Cecilia!"

Cecilia looked up and saw Beasley almost upon her, his face crimson from bustling through town during the heat of the day. Somehow witnessing his exertion made her feel momentarily less tired herself. At any rate, maybe he would have good news for her—or bad news for Pendergast, which was the same thing.

"Still no sign of those books?" she asked him the moment the man came within earshot.

He pulled a handkerchief out of his pocket and mopped his brow. "No, I was just on the way to the schoolhouse to see if they had turned up."

Good. Cecilia felt only the tiniest bit of remorse for her evil deed. "I was just talking to Mr. Pendergast, and do you know, he didn't mention it? I'm afraid he doesn't even seem worried about those beautiful new books."

"Two years it took to raise that money." Beasley shook his head mournfully.

She didn't give a hang about the money. "You'd think a schoolteacher would be more concerned with supplies than that man is."

Beasley's mustache drooped with his lips into a frown, and he looped his thumbs in his suspenders. "What are you saying, Cecilia, that Pendergast isn't up to snuff?"

"Well..." She let the word hang doubtfully in the sticky air.

"He came with the very best credentials," Beasley said, standing behind his imported schoolteacher from the East.

Cecilia proceeded with caution. "But you know, Mr. Beasley, sometimes practical experience can be just as important."

He squinted at the schoolhouse for a second, the trace of suspicion in his eyes more resembling that of a horse trader fearing he's just been rooked than that of a town elder concerned for education. Finally, he shook his head, coming to a firm decision on the matter. "Bea likes him."

Cecilia's heart sank. "Bea?"

"Girl can't stop talking about him. Which reminds me, I've got to tell Pendergast how much Bea just said she likes these new spelling days of his. Good afternoon, Cecilia."

He smiled dismissively and bustled past her, leaving Cecilia heartsick in the street behind him. Wonderful—just wonderful! What was she paying Bea all that candy for if the girl was going to sabotage her efforts by praising the man to the heavens? She might have to rethink expending her efforts on that girl.

In fact, she might have to devise a whole new strategy, Cecilia decided with a sigh, continuing on toward the boardinghouse.

She couldn't wait to get to her stinky little room and rest until dinner. Because Cecilia was truly abysmal in the kitchen, Dolly usually allowed her an hour of peace before the evening meal. Then she was called in to set the table, then came dinner, which she was forced to endure sitting across from Pendergast, and then came more work getting the kitchen cleaned. How had Lupe, a tiny little slip of a girl, managed? Now Cecilia understood what motives would drive a girl to marriage.

As that thought crossed her mind, she heard shouts coming from the boardinghouse. And the voices sounded like Buck's and Dolly's.

Cecilia picked up speed, fast, taking the porch stairs two at a time. Earlier she'd seen Buck coming up the street and had slipped out of the house to go meet Bea. Until just this moment, she'd forgotten all about him.

Buck came crashing out the front door, almost slamming into her. "Gosh darn it all, Cici!" he cried. "That friend of yours is the most nagging, mean-spirited woman I ever bumped up against!"

She didn't like the sound of Buck's having "bumped up against" Dolly, whatever that meant. "That wasn't you yelling at her, was it?" Cecilia asked futilely. Unless Fanny Baker's voice had dropped an octave since breakfast, who else could it have been?

"Every time I come over, she's telling me I ought to dress better, or not eat with my hands so much, or talk different. How's a man not supposed to cuss with a woman like that annoying him all the time?"

This was so unfair! All her life Cecilia had been regaled with stories of women making foolish marriages that they regretted for the rest of their lives. According to Clara, it happened all the time. But when she herself tried to arrange such a disaster, the Fates conspired against her.

"Buck, have you ever thought just once of being nice to Dolly? Maybe bringing her flowers?"

"Why should I? It's you I come to see, but you always disappear and then I get trapped by that...woman." He stepped closer. "I don't know, Cici. I sometimes get the feeling you're avoiding me."

"Nonsense," she lied guiltily. "But I just don't see why you can't wait in Dolly's parlor and carry on a civil conversation. You can really be quite charming, you know."

"I can?"

"Well...Dolly says so." This, exasperatingly enough, was the truth. The pair couldn't sit in a room ten minutes at a stretch without having a blowup, but usually an hour after every visit, Dolly would forgive Buck all his uncouthness and return to her prior state of unquestioning smittenness.

"Huh," Buck said, obviously as confounded by Dolly's admiration of him as Cecilia herself was. "Well, I'll try to come by next week, then. Will you be here?"

"Of course," Cecilia answered. She'd nip out and go to Beasley's while Buck was there. She smiled and sent him on his way, then went inside to face Dolly, who, predictably, was in hysterics in the kitchen.

"I don't know why I bother with that man!" Dolly cried between sobs. "Oh, Cecilia, you must think me a terrible fool!"

Cecilia waited for her to choke down a few more tears before commenting, "Really, Dolly, if you like Buck—"

"I don't! I swear I don't!"

"But if you do, don't you think you should make an effort to be a little more accepting of who he is? You can't expect Buck McDeere to turn into the man that Jubal Hudspeth was. At least, not overnight."

Dolly blew her nose and thought this over. "No, I suppose not."

"You just need to give Buck time."

"Oh, it's so easy for you to give advice! You've got men fawning all over you," Dolly complained.

This was news to Cecilia. "Who?"

"Cecilia, please," Dolly said dismissively. "You can't tell me you haven't noticed the way he dotes on you."

"You mean Buck? But I've told you—"

"No, not Buck," Dolly said testily. "Mr. Pendergast!"

Cecilia howled at the very idea. "The man wants me to drop dead."

"He can't take his eyes off of you."

Cecilia smirked. "Most of the time those eyes have daggers in them."

"He hangs on your every word at dinner."

"So he can twist around what I say and use it against me later."

"He laughs when you make a joke."

"That's because he's a fool. He laughs at everything."

Dolly sniffed. "He never laughs at my jokes."

"Well..." Not knowing how else to respond, Cecilia shrugged. "It's just not true, Dolly. Mr. Pendergast and I are nothing but enemies. Do you think I'm working like a slave here so I can capture some Yankee schoolteacher's fancy?"

In a motherly fashion that never failed to make Cecilia cringe, Dolly put a hand over one of hers on the table and said softly, "I would think you'd want to capture *some* man's attention, Cecilia."

"Not Pendergast's, I don't," she insisted.

"But if you take that attitude, how are you ever going to get yourself married?"

Nothing exasperated Cecilia faster than Dolly when she decided to be condescending about having experienced wedded bliss...unless it was Clara when she spent hours warning Cecilia against the innumerable no-accounts just waiting to weasel her into the obligatory bad marriage.

All Cecilia wanted was a measure of independence—and she hadn't found a man yet who would give that to her, or who would be worth giving it up for.

She stood up abruptly. "I don't care about being married. I just don't want to have to live on a ranch!"

She escaped to her little room, cursing herself for being in such a peevish mood. But how else should she be when she was surrounded by such conflict? First she had to deal with Pendergast, including making sure that Bea Beasley had enough candy to keep her eyes open and her mouth shut, which wasn't even working. The girl was chatting up the schoolteacher to her father, of all people! And with Buck and Dolly to contend with, along with more manual labor than she'd ever hoped to do in her entire life...well, it was too much.

And now Dolly was saying that Pendergast was actually in love with her! It was absurd, especially when he had just been accusing *her* of being in love with him.

As she lay on her back, looking at the ceiling above her bed, a wonderfully optimistic thought occurred to her. Maybe it was Pendergast who was protesting too much... maybe he was just trying to deflect his own feelings by teasing her. Or maybe he had secretly hoped that she *had* fallen in love with him, and that after a little ribbing she would blurt out a confession!

She tried not to think about the little zip of satisfaction she felt at the thought of the smarmy schoolteacher falling in love with her. The man was impossible! And in spite of the way he shamelessly brownnosed Beasley, Dolly and everyone else in town besides her, sometimes Cecilia would catch a glimpse of his face when no one else was looking, and his face in repose was cold and taciturn—and wary. Underneath the thin veneer of civility lay a man with more than his share of raw, rough edges. Pendergast was hardly a prize.

So why was her heart beating like crazy at the off chance that he might have developed a crush on her?

Now that she thought about it, didn't Pendergast's little observations—as though he'd been watching her every movement—indicate a loverlike attention to detail? Like those scorch marks he'd mentioned. He'd probably been mooning over the marks for weeks now, trying to read some romantic meaning into them, like tea leaves. Cecilia chortled with glee at the image. Poor pathetic man.

You can catch more flies with honey...

For the first time in her life, one of Clara's clichés struck her as potentially useful. She felt her spirits lifting. The possibility of Pendergast's being in love with her, even just a little, changed everything. Now she would have the upper hand, even if it was a dry, cracked, dishwater-soaked hand.

Open hostility had not intimidated the man. The stolen schoolbooks had only resulted so far in what Beasley obviously thought were innovative teaching techniques. Perhaps it was time to try a little charm.

Cecilia's best day dress was muslin with an adorable violet print that brought out the deep blue of her eyes. The scalloped neck dipped just enough to show a glimpse of her collarbone, which, Cecilia noted ruefully, was poking out a little more these days. The bodice fitted her slender figure like a second skin, and the skirt rounded the soft curves of her hips and thighs before flaring gracefully. With a modest bustle in back it looked quite sharp—just right for day wear in New Orleans, where she had brought it back from.

For Annsboro, however, it seemed just on the verge of overdoing it. Not to mention, the material was thick and stiff, and uncomfortably hot. Dolly had laced her up this morning with more than her usual rigor, with the overall effect that, by the time the dress was on, Cecilia felt like a human sausage packed into a violet-sprigged skin.

Nevertheless, an inspection in the mirror assured her that the end result was worth her pains. She looked clean and fresh and stylish, and for the first time in weeks she actually felt pretty. Uncomfortable, but pretty.

"It's a dream," Dolly said wistfully as she beheld Cecilia. Then a frown puckered her lips. "But Cecilia, you can't wear that today!"

"Why not?"

"It's so dusty out. That beautiful dress will get dirty."

As if I have to worry about washing my own clothes for once, Cecilia thought. "Don't worry, Dolly," she consoled her friend, "I'll be careful. And I'm not going far."

Just to the schoolhouse, where she was sure Pendergast would be. School let out at noon on Saturdays, and at twelve-thirty, he would be closing up shop. Perfect.

If she could just get him to open up to her a little bit, she thought on the way over, and learn something damning about his past. Or if she could snoop around his classroom for something she could use to damage his reputation with Beasley...

The schoolhouse door was wide open when Cecilia arrived, a fact that brought a smile to her lips. Pendergast was there. Lysander Beasley, who always overestimated Annsboro's potential, even when it came to the criminal element, insisted that the school be locked. Especially now that he thought there had been an actual honest-to-goodness theft.

Before entering the schoolroom, Cecilia rapped lightly on the open door, sucked in her stomach and held her head at its best angle to maximize the tableau effect for her victim. Pendergast looked up, and standing, nearly knocked over his chair. So far so good.

"Miss Summert—" As if getting a good second glance at her, he cut himself off and took a deep breath. "Cecilia."

Cecilia smiled brightly. "Hello, Pendergast."

Slowly, Jake took in every inch of the woman walking toward him. He couldn't help it. In her pretty figure-hugging dress she was the most beautiful female he'd laid eyes on since...well, since maybe forever. And when she stopped just on the other side of his desk, he could smell the light scent of flowers. Was it soap? Perfume? He breathed in and felt nearly light-headed. He had the strangest urge to take her into his arms and kiss her rosy lips....

In an instant, the image of a white-haired man and his father-in-law popped into his head. *Remember Gunter and Darby,* a little voice said. *They tried to kill you...soon you'll have revenge.* If he could just keep his head on straight. If he tripped up and it came out that he was masquerading as the town's schoolteacher, people all over the area would be spreading his name.

But Cecilia was so tempting, so beautiful, like a single exotic flower blooming in his barren life. And the adoring way she was smiling at him made him feel...

Suspicious.

Purposefully, he sank back down into his chair and folded his arms skeptically across his chest. Thank God he hadn't completely lost his good sense. Something was up. Cecilia wouldn't have squeezed herself into her best dress just to come show him, her sworn enemy, her dimples. Now he just had to figure out what her devious motive for today was.

"What are you doing here?" he asked.

Her blue eyes widened innocently at his change in demeanor. "Why, I was just passing through, so I thought I would take a minute to visit my old stomping ground."

He stared at her evenly, put on guard even more by this silly explanation. Much as he was enjoying her eye-pleasing display, Jake knew the only thing Cecilia Summertree wanted from him was a resignation. Which she wasn't about to get, no matter how pretty and sweet she was. She might want this job, but his life depended on it.

Cecilia shifted uncomfortably as Pendergast continued to stare at her with those hard brown eyes of his. That was another odd thing about Pendergast. When he looked at her, it wasn't with the playful indulgence or breezy interest she'd experienced with men of his class from New Orleans and Memphis. His gaze was too keen, too fathomless, as though he could see right into her soul if he looked long enough. And given the shady way she'd been playing people lately, she'd much rather he look at her dress than her soul.

Anyway, why didn't he say something? Suddenly, an answer occurred to her. "I keep forgetting you're a—from the North. Stomping grounds means..." She bit her lip. What exactly would be the Yankee translation?

Jake rolled his eyes. "I think I know what stomping grounds means."

That flat voice. Somehow, Pendergast didn't seem as won over by her charm as she expected him to be. He hadn't even mentioned how nice she looked. In fact, she was beginning to doubt Dolly's hypothesis altogether. He didn't appear to be the least bit in love with her!

She decided to take a stab at wheedling her way into his confidence. Shoving aside a battered old geography book, she daintily perched herself on the edge of the desk. Casting her eyes downward, she said demurely, "I'm afraid I have a confession to make, Pend—Eugene."

Jake raised an eyebrow inquisitively. He couldn't wait to hear this.

"It's just..." She let out a light breathy sigh. "I'm ashamed of myself for not being as much a help to you as I could have been."

"I've managed all right," Jake said.

Cecilia thought for a moment. The man wasn't bending like a sapling, that was for sure. "But you must admit I could have been more...neighborly."

Her eyelashes fluttered gracefully before Jake found himself looking into her willfully guileless blue eyes. He barked out a laugh. "So could the rattlesnakes, Miss Summertree, but I'm glad they weren't."

Cecilia hopped off the desk and faced the man down, hands on her hips. "If you aren't the vilest—" She sputtered in anger. "You're lower than a rattlesnake yourself!"

"And you're a pretty little piece of work," Jake said, rising from his chair. He didn't know what her game was, but he was going to find out right this minute. Circling around the desk, he caught hold of her arms. "What made you put on that fetching little dress and come over here?"

"Get your hands off me—"

"And don't tell me you came over to apologize for not being helpful enough, because we both know that's not true."

Cecilia tugged and tugged, but Pendergast was surprisingly strong and kept an iron grip on her arms. She felt short of breath, both from Dolly's lacing job and from Pendergast's sneak attack, and attempted to take several steadying gulps of air. "All right," she admitted finally, only wanting to get away from his hard, mesmerizing gaze, "I came to spy on you."

"That's more like it." Abruptly, he let go of her arms. "And just what were you expecting to find—that I'd turned your precious school into a gambling house?"

"No." Cecilia rubbed her arms where his fingers had dug into them. She wasn't so much a fool that she was actually going to tell him the truth. "I . . . I just wondered if you'd started work for the harvest pageant." That sounded like a reasonable explanation.

Jake combed a hand through his hair. Along with the missing schoolbooks, Beasley had been buzzing about this harvest pageant, which was supposed to take place in a few weeks, at the end of October. Bea, too, had been pestering him. Jake hadn't paid talk of it much mind, since he planned to be long gone by then.

"I haven't given it much thought yet," he answered truthfully.

Cecilia's eyes widened in surprise. "You hadn't?"

"Is it a big to-do?"

"Why, it's practically the event of the year," Cecilia answered. "In fact, it *is* the event of the year. There's a big picnic, and the children put on a play in front of the school, and then there's dancing afterward."

He found it hard to believe that Cecilia could really get excited about such a small-time wingding, but this town *was* hard up for entertainment. In fact, Jake felt a little guilty for giving the pageant short shrift. He might be gone, but he would leave behind a whole town with no play to watch. It didn't seem quite right, especially given the way the people there had taken him in. Under false pretenses, of course, but . . .

"A pageant, huh?" he asked.

"The plays are almost always about the Pilgrims . . . and they're usually pretty bad, if you want to know the truth."

Hearing her description, Jake felt a little more confident. He could handle bad. Only Bea hadn't mentioned anything about Pilgrims . . .

"I could help you," Cecilia suggested.

So could Bea. He certainly didn't want Cecilia poking her nose into his schoolroom all the time. "I think I can manage."

There was only one word to describe the look on Cecilia's face. *Crestfallen*. The pretty young woman looked utterly, completely dejected.

Suddenly, he found himself wanting to console her. After all, just as soon as he left town, which was going to be soon enough, she could have her old job back. Of course, he couldn't tell her that.

Then again, what would be the harm in letting her help, just a little?

Her eyes downcast, she said in a voice laced with self-pity, "Very well…if you don't want my help, then I guess there's nothing to say." She turned to leave, shooting him one last sad-eyed glance.

Jake sighed. "We'd have to meet in the evenings," he said.

Her face lit up immediately. "Here?" she asked.

"Not here," Jake said.

Her brows knit together worriedly and her gaze swept about the room. "Why not?"

Good question. "Where does the pageant usually take place?"

She thought for a moment. "Outside."

"Then that's where we can meet."

Cecilia paused, considering his offer. It was better than nothing, she supposed. "All right. We can start this evening if you like."

"Tomorrow," he said.

Why was he putting her off? Cecilia wondered. Dolly had to be wrong about Pendergast's attraction to her. This would be a Saturday night, beneath a full harvest moon—a man in love would take advantage of that.

She tried not to think too hard about why Pendergast's not being in love with her should depress her. He was agreeing to let her help with the pageant, and that way she would be able to be around him, snooping; she was getting what she wanted.

"You've got yourself a deal," she said.

Chapter Seven

That night, for the first time since coming to Annsboro, Jake panicked. As he lay in bed, tossing and turning from the heat, he couldn't help worrying about what Cecilia's sudden visit to the schoolhouse had meant. Moreover, why had she come all dolled up? The woman had a trick up her pretty little sleeve, and not knowing exactly what it was made him very nervous.

She was on to him.

That could be the only explanation. She'd always suspected that he was a fraud, and now, by hook or by crook, she had found herself some evidence to prove it. But how? Maybe through Bea. Jake knew he shouldn't have trusted that kid. Probably in a little while, when his guard was down, the two of them would confront him with what they knew. Or maybe they would expose him publicly....

At the harvest dance! Of course. Cecilia was setting him up for that event. Or maybe she was just hoping to.... That's why she wanted to nose around his classroom. Which she would have plenty of time to do, now that he'd taken her up on her offer to "help him out."

Damn, damn, damn. Was he ever going to get a break?

Jake swung his long legs to the floor and reached over to grab his pants from the bedpost. He pulled them on and stuffed his feet into a pair of boots, cursing his luck. Of all the one-horse towns in Texas that probably needed teachers, he would get stuck in the one that had a busybody woman already entrenched in the schoolhouse.

And that busybody would have to have the bluest eyes he'd ever seen, and a lilting feminine voice that stayed on his mind hours after he talked to her. Jake never thought he'd find a woman who would make him regret having to leave a place. His life had been so consumed with dodging Darby that he had given up hope of ever having the kind of domestic life other men enjoyed. But Cecilia, for all her prickliness, made him dream about what it would be like to have a house, with a woman working alongside him…in her figure-hugging dress with the pretty violets all over it.

Shaking his head, Jake let out a cross between a laugh and a sigh of regret. Cecilia Summertree of the Summertree ranch would have nothing to do with him—especially if she knew who he really was. She was a rich rancher's daughter and he was the son of a sharecropper. All he had to show for his life so far was unfulfilled dreams, and it wasn't likely that a woman like Cecilia, with her relatively privileged background and New Orleans schooling, would be very impressed with those.

Especially when the only way she probably thought of him at all was in terms of putting him out of a job.

There was nothing for it but to sneak out to the schoolhouse and clear out anything that would look suspicious to the academic eye. Like Pendergast's books. Bea had said that Cecilia had been particularly interested in the content of the books he read, which probably meant that he shouldn't be reading them. But hell, what else was there to do in a hot school building all day?

He'd have to worry about that later, he thought as he began a slow creep down the stairs. Right now the most important thing was to cover his tracks.

Cecilia ached from being cinched in like a prize mare for half the day. It was another hot night, and because Dolly's lacing job had left her feeling maimed, she just couldn't get comfortable on her thin mattress. She sat up and stretched, then stood and scooted around the bed to her window.

There was no breeze to push air through the house, much less through her room, but she opened her window as far as it would go and stuck her head out into the night. Not a cloud was in sight—only a bright yellow moon and a few million stars. Cecilia sighed and draped her arms over the sill.

Why did she feel so restless? All day she hadn't been able to shake Pendergast's hard gaze from her memory, or the way he had held her, as though he was prepared to shake the truth about her visit to the schoolhouse from her.

Never in her life had a man elicited so many reactions from her. Normally she felt sure about herself and how to handle situations, but it seemed that since Pendergast came to town, she'd been on edge, apt to blurt out inappropriate statements, and overall not her usual self. At night at the boardinghouse, or sometimes when she walked too near the schoolhouse, her heart would trip erratically and she wouldn't know what to do with her hands.

In short, she was making a fool of herself over a man. But she didn't know how to stop, unless she could get the man out of her life. For good.

At that moment, she saw a figure moving in the darkness. She hung farther out the window and squinted into the night. Pendergast! She couldn't believe it. Why was he running around in the middle of the night? When her eyes adjusted to the darkness, she saw that his shirt wasn't even tucked into his trousers properly. Apparently, he'd awakened with an uncommon urge to visit Grady's. Men and their liquor!

At least, she hoped liquor was what he was venturing out for....

Yet oddly enough, when he came to the main road, he didn't head for Grady's, but turned left, toward the schoolhouse. Now this was interesting.

In a flash, Cecilia threw an old work dress over her nightgown and pushed on a pair of boots. She was almost through the kitchen when she stopped. It would be just her luck if someone was to see her leaving the house in the middle of the night. She crept back to her room and, seeing no alternative, began to climb through the window. It was a squeeze, but she finally managed to pop out the other side and dropped about five feet to the ground.

Pendergast had to be heading for the school, and in that case, Cecilia planned to take a more roundabout, shadowed route to get there. There was no use risking someone's seeing her on the main road, especially him. Whatever Pendergast was up to, she wanted to catch him at it redhanded.

Upstairs, drawn to her window by the fat yellow moon shining through it, Dolly peered out into the beautiful night. But weren't all nights beautiful to a woman in love? She smiled, thinking of Buck and wondering where he was, and if he was looking at the moon, too.

Then she frowned. Buck was probably at Grady's.

Drinking, she hoped.

A loud thud sounded somewhere below, and moments later, Dolly watched Cecilia whip around the corner and head off into the night at a sprint. She held her body slightly bent as she ran, as if she was afraid of being seen. That girl! Now where would Cecilia go in the middle of the night?

The only possible answer came to Dolly almost instantaneously, and she lifted a hand to her mouth in horror as a vision of Cecilia running off to a clandestine meeting with Buck came to her mind. Who else could it be? Pendergast would be the only other candidate for an illicit rendezvous, but Cecilia swore she hated the man. Moreover, lately Cecilia had seemed to become more and more annoyed each time Dolly mentioned Buck.

Probably now that another woman wanted him, Cecilia was seeing what a good man Buck McDeere truly was.

Oh, what a deceitful pair! For weeks Cecilia had insisted she felt nothing for Buck, and Dolly, being the kind, trusting soul that she was, had believed her. Of course she should have known better. What woman wouldn't be in love with Buck?

Dolly cried bitter tears as she bustled toward her armoire, picked out her nicest dress and hurriedly pulled it over her head. What a horrible thing it was to be betrayed, and by one's best friend! A woman she had taken in, sheltered under her own roof...employed!

Furthermore, Cecilia had been running off in the direction of the school, a fact that made Dolly pale with mortification. Even if Cecilia was going to steal her beau, she ought at least to have better taste than to choose a public building as her trysting place.

Why, Dolly had donated money in Jubal's memory just last year to have the school painted!

By the time she was out the front door and was marching down the main road—unlike Cecilia, *she* had nothing to be ashamed of!—Dolly had worked up such a rage that for the first time in her life she feared she would do bodily harm to someone. She dearly hoped she ran into Cecilia first, and not Buck.

Poor Buck. Men were such fickle creatures, so easily led on.

First he saw Pendergast moving stealthily down the road with his shirt hanging out of his pants. Then, a few minutes later, Dolly appeared, tearful, indignant and barely dressed herself, following him.

Buck sat atop his horse and rubbed his stubbled jaw thoughtfully. He'd been headed back to the ranch, but now he found himself unable to move. Even with a good bit of rotgut liquor in his stomach, he was as clearheaded as ever; besides, it didn't take a genius to figure out what was going on here. That Yankee schoolteacher had taken advantage of Dolly, and now he was trying to skip out on her.

Buck's blood boiled. Not that he really cared for Dolly…and why should he? The woman never let up! Even so, she deserved better than to be used like she was no better than the women who worked over at Grady's. And by that darn schoolteacher, too—the one Cici was always so riled up about.

Oh, she said she hated him but he didn't buy it. Cici couldn't pull the wool over his eyes. He'd seen it a million times, or at least once or twice. Just because a man like Pendergast talked different and wore nice clothes and came from the East, women couldn't get enough of him.

Poor Dolly. All these weeks she'd been nagging at him, she was probably trying to turn him into another Pendergast. Well, what did Pendergast have that he didn't? Just a tight suit and a better job, was all. He didn't even sound all that educated, truth to tell. Leastways, not any more than most folks. Fact was, the man hardly sounded like a Yankee, and what was the point of falling in love with a Yankee if he didn't even talk like one?

Buck weaved in his saddle, trying to imagine the little drama that was about to take place in the schoolhouse. Poor Dolly. She really wasn't that bad. At times during the past few weeks he'd kind of thought she maybe had a yen for him. And Cici was always saying how Dolly thought he was funny, or good-looking. In fact, now that he thought about it, he imagined Dolly probably actually liked *him* more than she did Pendergast. She probably just didn't realize it yet. Women always got mixed up when it came to love.

That damned Pendergast. Buck hoped Dolly didn't do anything foolish, like convince the man he ought to marry her or something like that. A refined upstanding woman like Dolly shouldn't have to beg for a man's undying love. Especially not when she owned the biggest house in town, and was the best cook, and was pretty, to boot. Why, come to think of it, he'd almost swear that Dolly was at least as pretty as Cici.

His blood was boiling, all right. He had half a mind to show Pendergast how Southern gentlemen behaved, but damn it if he hadn't gone and left his rifle back at the ranch. Well, hell, he was at least as big as Pendergast. He could take the man bare-handed. Especially when he was good and mad.

Especially when Dolly Hudspeth's honor was at stake!

He nicked his spurs against his mare's flanks and streaked down the road at a gallop. The world was a blur, but he could still see Dolly. Poor Dolly. Coming up behind her, he sawed on the reins and came to a jerky stop that nearly sent him flying over the saddle horn.

"I'll get him for you, sweetheart," he drawled as his horse pawed the ground menacingly. "I'll show him how we treat men who abuse a woman's honor in this part of the world!"

Dolly looked up in shock. "Buck!" When she noticed the state he was in, her surprise quickly turned to anger. "Drunk, no less! You're a fine one to be talking about *my* honor, when you're about to—"

Her words were incoherent garble to Buck, but the word *honor* caught his attention. "I'll show that Pendergast how to treat a woman of honor!"

"Pendergast?" She darted a tearful glance toward the schoolhouse. "But I thought—"

Just at that moment, Pendergast appeared on the front steps of the school with a bundle in his arms. He was about to turn to lock the building when, glancing around stealthily, he noticed Buck and Dolly. The schoolteacher looked guilty, as if he wanted to crawl under a rock.

Which is just where he belonged, Buck thought with rage as he swung down to the ground. Dolly clung fiercely to his arm. His dear, sweet little Dolly.

"Come on out and fight, Pendergast!" he cried.

Pendergast froze in his tracks as Buck came forward. Coward.

"He *is* out, fool," Dolly hissed, digging her heels into the sand to impede Buck's progress.

"Well..." Buck puzzled the situation through for a moment. "Just come fight, then!"

Buck, Dolly realized, was as strong as an ox. As he dragged her along, she also began to suspect that she might have misjudged the situation.

Cecilia darted out from the shadows behind a stand of spindly cedars as Buck had almost reached the stairs. "What's happening?" she cried, skidding to a stop.

"This coward's going to get what's coming to him," Buck said, and before Cecilia could join Dolly in restraining him, he broke free and hauled Pendergast off the stairs. Books flew out of Pendergast's arms, landing on the stairs and sandy ground below.

Jake didn't know what was going on, but every survival instinct he'd honed during his life kicked in at once, and as he and Buck fell in a heap to the ground, he gave as good as he got. Physically, Buck was the bigger man, but Jake at least was sober.

"Buck, you must stop this!" Dolly hopped uselessly up and down as the men pummeled each other.

"For heaven's sake!" Cecilia muttered. She had just picked out a leg to grab on to to stop this insanity when something else caught her eye. *Dancehall Gunfight.*

And lying near that book were at least ten others like it. All had illustrations on their covers of various action scenes. As the men brawled on the ground, Cecilia quickly flipped through some of them, amused by their florid language and raucous pictures. She remembered Bea's one comment about the book Pendergast had read to them and smiled. He did look a little like Two-step Pete.

One thing was certain—judging from this sample, Eugene Pendergast certainly had an interesting idea of what was appropriate reading material for children. But why on earth had Pendergast ventured out in the middle of the night to get the books out of the schoolhouse?

"Cecilia, you've got to make them stop!" Dolly cried. "Oh, Buck, be careful!"

Absorbed in trying to find a picture of Willa the dance hall girl, Cecilia crossed over to the pump, poured a bucket of water and returned with it. "Hold this," she told Dolly as she handed her the book. Then, aiming the bucket to best hit both men's faces, she dumped the water on her target.

"Hey!" Buck cried, holding Pendergast's collar in one fist. "That ain't fair!"

Jake shook his head in disgust. "I didn't throw the water, you mutton head."

Buck looked up at Cecilia and Dolly staring down at him. The water had apparently sobered him somewhat. "What are you doing here, Cici?" he asked.

"I could ask the same thing," she replied.

Dolly pushed past her and dropped to her knees in the fresh mud. "Oh, my darling," she cooed, cradling Buck's head. "You've hurt yourself."

"Dolly," Buck murmured lovingly, burying his face in her soft muslin-covered chest. "I was just trying to protect your honor."

"Oh, dear, what will make you feel better?"

Buck reached into his back pocket and produced a flask of hooch. "This will."

Shaking his head, Jake moved away from the action and leaned back against the school's porch steps to catch his breath. What a mess this had turned into! His books were scattered all over creation. As he picked up the ones nearest him, something caught his eye. The moonlight filtering through the boards next to him revealed something beneath the steps. Something that looked like books.

A quick duck into the crawl space confirmed his suspicions. Jake grabbed one of the readers, pushed himself up from the dirt and stumbled over to the pump, trying to assess the damage to his person. As far as he could tell, he would come out of this with only a few bruises and aches. Worse by far than any physical harm was the fact that Cecilia was thumbing through Pendergast's books with keen interest. When she saw him moving toward the pump, she was right on his heels.

"You look fine!" she said in astonishment.

"Thank you. What did you expect?" Jake worked the pump and splashed water over his face and arms.

"I expected Buck would probably beat the thunder out of you."

Jake smiled. "Yeah, I could tell you were real concerned."

It was amazing that the man could laugh about it—most men would still be spitting mad. Cecilia looked into his face with renewed curiosity. Though she hadn't been paying close attention to the fight, it seemed Pendergast had stood his own quite well—and Buck was considered one of the most formidable brawlers in the county. Even more so when he'd had a few.

"Seems you managed to protect yourself pretty well for someone so...bookish." She gingerly held up *Dancehall Gunfight.*

The inane cover of the cheap little book mocked him as effectively as Cecilia's blue eyes did. "Humorous story, isn't it?" Jake said.

Her triumphant smile reached from ear to ear; she held the book by her fingertips, as if it was distasteful. "I bet Lysander Beasley will be interested to see what the youth of Annsboro have been consuming."

With a smile equally broad, Jake produced with a flourish the barely used Gibson reader he'd retrieved. "You mean, as opposed to consuming this?"

Her jaw hung slack in surprise. "Why...it's one of the missing readers!"

"Apparently so."

Under his sharp gaze, Cecilia fidgeted for a moment. Then, composing herself, she exclaimed, "Those boys and their pranks!"

Jake smirked. "So you think it was the older ones, hmm?"

"Of course," she said nervously. She leaned against the pump and crossed her arms. "You know, now that I think about it, Tommy Beck even locked Bea under those porch steps once."

"The porch steps?" Jake took a step closer to her, so that she was pinned between him and the well. "And just why did you jump to the conclusion that that's where they were hidden?"

Her mouth snapped open, then closed. Even in the moonlight, he could see her face darken in a deep blush. He had her. "I sure don't think Beasley would consider reading some fun little stories nearly as offensive as playing fast and loose with school property."

Her jaw set stubbornly. "It's your word against mine."

"And who do you think they'll believe?" he asked, placing a hand on the stones to either side of her waist.

Pendergast, naturally. "I don't care who everyone believes!" she said defiantly. "I still say you're a curious excuse for a schoolteacher."

"Curious, how?" he asked, enjoying the way the moonlight made her blue eyes look sparkly and dark.

"First, you're a Yankee, but you don't sound like one. And you're a schoolteacher with an odd sense of what's appropriate for your students to do all day. And you sure as hell don't fight like a schoolteacher, and I know you don't kiss like one!"

As her own ears registered what she'd just blurted out, her lips pressed shut and her cheeks reddened even more.

Lord, she was pretty. He remembered how she looked this afternoon in her fancy dress, but she looked just as inviting tonight in her work clothes. He leaned closer to her, breathing the sweet female scent of her hair and getting himself more wound up than was wise.

"How are schoolteachers supposed to kiss, Cecilia?"

"Not like you," she said, looking straight into his chest.

"Well, you're a teacher," he said. His heart pounded heavily as he pulled her toward him. "Show me how it's supposed to be done."

Her breath caught just before he kissed her, a little sound that aroused him more than he would have thought possible. This time when their lips met, she snaked her arms around his neck and pulled him down to her, just like he'd imagined her doing on the many sleepless nights he had lain awake thinking of her. It was as if she, too, had anticipated this moment....

They were both brought back to earth by the sound of Dolly, who was still kneeling in the mud across the yard from them.

"Cecilia?"

Startled, Cecilia looked at Pendergast through glazed eyes. He was grinning at her. Like he'd just won a second victory for the evening. She stepped back in horror. "I must have lost my mind!"

"Or maybe you just don't know your own mind," Jake said, loving the sweet confusion on her face. "Women sometimes don't, I hear."

"Oh, if that wasn't the most—"

"Yes," he said, interrupting, "and you were enjoying every second of it."

God help her, she was, and Pendergast knew it. Cecilia looked down and felt her herself blush from head to toe. Pendergast laughed softly and lifted her chin, as though about to kiss her again.

"Cecilia?" Dolly called into the darkness. "I think I might need help with Buck."

Cecilia pulled away from Pendergast and threw him an accusing look. But what could she accuse him of? She hadn't even thought to duck away from his kiss.

"I won't say anything if you won't," he said.

"About the kiss?" she asked, shocked. As if she wanted *that* spread all over town!

"No, about the books."

Well, there was simply no question about that! Backfired. Another plan had backfired, this time so completely that she hardly knew what had gone wrong. Or what to do next.

Making no promises, she turned and marched over to where Buck was lurching up from the ground. Pendergast was right behind her, she was glad to note, because it looked as if it was going to take all of them to maneuver the ranch hand back to the boardinghouse. She shook her head, remembering the time she and Pendergast had carried Buck before.

"I'll take one arm, you take the other," she directed Pendergast.

"Maybe we can lift him onto his horse," he suggested.

She had to admit it would be easier. They hoisted Buck to standing and began stumbling toward the horse.

Dolly was completely useless. "Poor Buck," she said fretfully as they heaved his inert body. "I fear he's a tad inebriated."

Hearing his name, Buck came out of his stupor long enough to say, "I ain't too drunk, Dolly. I was just worried about your honor."

"Dear Buck." Dolly smiled tenderly at him. "Please don't say ain't."

Luckily, Buck passed out or Jake feared they would have had another brawl on their hands.

He glanced over at Cecilia as he took the reins to lead the horse, but she was pointedly not looking in his direction. He remembered their kiss and felt desire surge through him all over again. He should have been happy—finding those readers meant he could breathe easy for a while. If she tried to devil him again, he could snitch on her to Beasley.

He had her.

But after that kiss, he feared she also had him.

Chapter Eight

Early Sunday morning, just when it was beginning to seem that summer might last until Christmas, autumn blew into Annsboro with one blustery gust. And that same wind, Jake decided, would be at his back as he blew out of town.

He'd waited too long already. And after last night, he feared Cecilia would be hot to figure out some new way to expose him.

He had cried sick while the others were bustling off to church, and now he dashed about the empty boarding-house snatching things to take with him. He would keep Pendergast's clothes, which finally matched the weather, his gun, a few things from Dolly's larder and the little flask of whiskey Dolly had hidden there. All this basically added up to the clothes on his back, which was fine with him. It was best to travel light.

He looked out his second-story window at the deserted town, then noted Buck's horse tethered by the shade tree to the side of the house. Dolly had dragged a woebegone-looking Buck, who'd spent the night folded onto the parlor settee, off to services this morning. Poor man. All he was going to receive for his holiness today was a stolen horse.

But at least Jake could count on his leaving being the answer to someone's prayers. He could just imagine Cecilia jumping for joy the minute she discovered he was gone for good. She would have her coveted job back, and her precious room, and she probably wouldn't have to launder another shirt as long as she lived.

The thought of Cecilia's happiness at seeing the back of him made him smile wistfully. Because of her, he would have almost wanted to stay in Annsboro. Almost. He liked her spirit—but that same spirit was exactly why he needed to hightail it out of town as quickly as possible.

After last night, there was no telling what Cecilia would do next to get rid of him. In spite of the sweet way she kissed, he knew she wasn't about to surrender her ultimate goal. The woman had the tenacity of a snapping turtle; once she sank her teeth into something, nothing could shake her loose.

Maybe even the way she had responded to that kiss had been just another tactic of hers. Who knew? The woman had him so off-balance he couldn't be sure. He remembered the way she'd laced her hands behind his neck and pressed herself against him, and he groaned in response. Good thing he was leaving—much more of that kind of treatment and she would have him under her thumb.

No, that wasn't true. He was already completely under her spell. For weeks his thoughts of Gunter and Darby had been completely usurped by his dreams of Cecilia. And, of course, his worry that she would finally figure out a way to prove he was a fraud.

He shook his head in awe. Perhaps he was the only man in Annsboro who could truly appreciate Cecilia Summertree. For over a year he'd been on the run, dodging bullets and staying up nights wondering whether he'd live to see daylight again. Lying low in this peaceful small town was supposed to be a rest for him, a relief, but his time around Cecilia had been as stressful as dodging Darby and Gunter.

In fact, Cecilia's campaign against him had been so successful that leaving town would almost seem like a relief. He was fairly certain, at least, that Gunter wasn't out there looking for him. He estimated Otis Darby's ranch to be about a two-day ride to the south, and he intended to go there straight off and face his enemy down. The man would probably think he was seeing a ghost, but that could work to Jake's advantage.

Trouble was, if Gunter had rejoined his father-in-law, traveling to Darby's ranch meant it was going to be two against one. For a moment Jake considered enlisting his old mentor Burnet Dobbs in his cause, but then he dropped that idea just as fast. He'd gone it alone this long, he might as well finish it up by himself, as well. He did have the element of surprise in his favor.

He crept quickly and stealthily down the stairs, then slowly opened the door. He still had some time before the church service was finished, but he didn't want to draw attention to himself as he rode out on Buck's horse.

As he stepped out onto Dolly's porch, prepared to dash over to the animal and sneak out of town, Jake heard Lysander Beasley call his name.

"Pendergast! Look what I have for you!"

Oh, hell. Of all the times . . .

Jake looked up to see Beasley and another well-dressed man approaching through Dolly's yard. As they came closer, Jake hurriedly took in physical details for clues as to the stranger's identity. The man wore a bowler hat, and his build was slight; perhaps to compensate, he sported a thick bushy mustache and fussy muttonchop whiskers. This was not a person from around here. Overall, the closer the man came, his hand already thrust outward for a hearty shake, the more his appearance made Jake nervous.

But not nearly as nervous as Jake's appearance seemed to be making *him*. His hand still extended, the man's expectant smile froze, then disappeared altogether, replaced by a narrow-eyed look of confusion. "Pendergast?"

Not knowing how else to respond, Jake clasped that hand and pumped it for all he was worth. His skin prickled with dread as he mentally relived his early-morning conversation with the real Pendergast over and over for clues that might reveal who this man was. But Pendergast had mostly talked about himself; besides, they'd both been drunk. Stupidly, Jake realized now, he had never considered that Pendergast actually knew anyone in Texas; the man had seemed such a fish out of water. Unfortunately, this person's voice had no trace of an accent that Jake would recognize, so it was impossible to say where Pendergast had met him.

The stranger finally retrieved his hand and stepped back to get a better look at him. Jake turned his profile to the man, hoping avoiding eye contact would fool him. Maybe he really hadn't known Pendergast that well. . . .

"Well, well!" Jake said jovially to Beasley. "This *is* a wonderful surprise!" Just when he'd been about to get out of town for good, too!

Beasley beamed a red-cheeked smile. "Man showed up on my doorstep right before church asking about you. I thought we'd probably find you at the school."

"I was just on my way," Jake lied.

"Us, too," Beasley said. "I felt I had to offer our friend a cup of coffee, however, which is why we're late. Cold morning and all."

"Yes, finally." Jake felt his throat growing drier and tighter the longer the stranger remained silent. Who was he and why wasn't he telling Beasley that Jake was an impostor? Maybe, Jake thought, grasping at any hope, he really looked more like Pendergast than he remembered. After all, Gunter had been confused. . . .

"You certainly have changed!" the man exclaimed, dashing Jake's desperate hopes.

"I . . . yes, I have," Jake said. What was the point in denying it? Pendergast *was* a completely different person now, as this man was certain to figure out in mere moments. He screwed up his courage and looked the stranger straight in the eye. "So have you."

"I have?" The man, who had been squinting curiously, now stepped back in amazement.

"The whiskers," Jake guessed. No man, not even this one, would bother with such a troublesome-looking appearance for long.

The stranger laughed and rubbed his hand thoughtfully along his cheek. "Do they make me look more like a sport?"

More like a lapdog, Jake thought, but agreed, "Absolutely, old man," and clapped the fellow on the back.

"How do you like Annsboro, Eugene?"

Jake nodded and smiled, nodded and smiled. "Fine, fine." In spite of the brisk temperature, he could feel nervous beads of sweat popping out on his brow. He reached into his pants pocket for a handkerchief but felt only Buck's whiskey flask.

If only he'd left five minutes earlier!

Beasley chuckled to fill the lengthening silence. "Watkins here was saying you had quite a reputation for oration at your university, Pendergast."

Watkins!

"And I was telling Watkins that pretty soon we'll have a university out here...."

Watkins. The smile that Jake had so carefully frozen on melted. This was worse than he could have imagined. Pendergast and Watkins had been school chums, then; there was no way on earth he could keep his disguise going for more than a few minutes more.

His stomach flip-flopped anxiously as he thought of the repercussions of this stranger's visit. The citizens of Annsboro would run him out of town. Word of his subterfuge would spread. Within days, Darby and Gunter would be able to sniff out his trail and the chase would begin again.

Jake felt sick, literally sick. What would he say to Cecilia, to everyone? Could he get down to Darby's ranch before word broke? The jumble of thoughts made him feel dizzy.

Suddenly, a possible solution to his dilemma occurred to him. Maybe Watkins had a bad memory, or bad eyesight.

Surely this man would not stay in Annsboro indefinitely, which meant that all Jake needed to do was avoid contact with him as much as possible. And the best way to do that was to put himself out of commission.

Beasley stopped rambling in mid-sentence, his expression suddenly filled with concern. "Say, Pendergast . . . are you all right?"

Jake lifted a hand to his realistically sweaty brow. "I . . . I . . ." Knees, waist, shoulders and neck went limp, then collapsed to the porch steps in turn.

"Pendergast?" Watkins said.

"Pendergast!" cried Beasley. The two men lunged forward too late to catch his fall.

Not a bad faint, if Jake did say so himself.

"We were just standing there, and then he fainted!"

Lysander Beasley had repeated his version of the incident about ten times by the time Jake was finally hauled up the stairs and into his own bed, where he immediately turned, deliriously, onto his stomach, stuffing gun, flask and two pears beneath the mattress while everyone was turned to listen to Beasley's retelling of his meeting with Watkins.

Watkins—he couldn't believe his bad luck. Foolishly, he'd stopped worrying about such a person when it became clear that there was no one in town named Watkins. He never dreamed the man, who it turned out was the superintendent of schools in the area, would make a surprise appearance.

At each retelling, Beasley inflated the details of the story to heighten the drama of Jake's having passed out cold on Dolly's porch. Which suited Jake just fine. The sicker everyone thought he was, the less strange they would think it was when Watkins got around to mentioning the fact that he looked suspiciously unlike the fellow he went to the university with. Jake's biggest blessing so far seemed to be the fact that Watkins was apparently a closemouthed type.

There was a racket of someone taking the steps two at a time, then Cecilia whisked into the room. Apparently, she'd just heard the good news.

"What's the matter with him?" she demanded, displacing a hovering Dolly from his bedside and slapping her hand against his temple to check his temperature.

"He felt feverish to me," Dolly informed her.

"Feels fine to me," Cecilia said flatly.

Dolly was still fretting. "Oh, he told me he was sick before church! I should have stayed with him."

"Hmph." Cecilia removed her hand and said nothing for a moment. "Should he be lying on his stomach?"

"I tried to turn him, but he kept flopping back over." Dolly clucked her tongue. "I suppose if he feels like lying on his back, he'll turn himself."

Not a chance. Jake wasn't about to let Watkins get another good look at his face, even if he had to suffocate to death by having his face smashed into a pillow. He would have loved to have seen Cecilia's expression, to gauge what she thought of this whole business, but he didn't risk peeking.

Of course, her eager, breathless voice had spoken for itself—the sicker he was, the better. He felt her hands moving along his limbs in a quick examination.

"Doesn't feel like anything's broken," she said with disappointment. "Where's Dr. Parker?"

"Mrs. Landers out to the east is having a baby. I've sent Walters after him," Beasley said.

"A baby! That could take forever," Cecilia muttered.

But then, when it came to finding out whether her nemesis was truly at death's door, Jake doubted whether any doctor could have been speedy enough for Cecilia.

All afternoon, Cecilia kept up her bedside vigil. Something suspicious was going on here, and she didn't intend to budge until she figured out what it was. Despite Dolly's observations, Cecilia had seen no evidence of a fever, nor did Pendergast appear to have a head wound.

And why would a man faint away right on Dolly's porch? It wasn't even hot outside anymore!

All morning she'd been praying for divine intervention on her behalf, and now it looked like she might have gotten it. Oh, she would admit when she'd first heard about his illness she had felt a moment of worry...but anyone with half a brain could tell this man wasn't sick!

Certainly judging by his kiss last night, he was just fine. Perhaps it had made *her* feel feverish and fitful, but when it was all over he had looked as smug and happy as ever.

Which was why this was all so strange. After the debacle with the schoolbooks, she would have thought he really had the upper hand, so why this subterfuge? And again, why had he been wandering around in the middle of the night in the first place? And if he was sick—which he wasn't—why had he been out on Dolly's porch when he could have been in bed?

The long quiet hours were punctuated by Chadwick Watkins wandering into the sickroom, staring at Pendergast's back, then wandering out again, shaking his head. After the second time this happened, Cecilia began to suspect that perhaps Pendergast's ailment had something to do with Watkins's arrival. But how could that be? According to Watkins, he and Pendergast had been university acquaintances together in Pennsylvania. Their loose association had been the reason Pendergast had heard about the teaching position in Annsboro.

On his third time around, she was ready for him.

"Mr. Watkins, I'm curious," she said. "Why do you keep looking at Mr. Pendergast and shaking your head?"

He came forward, rubbing his muttonchops thoughtfully. Personally, the man had always given Cecilia the willies.

"It's just, when I first saw Pendergast today, something seemed odd to me."

Cecilia, who was tugging a quilt over Pendergast's shoulder, stopped in mid-motion. "How do you mean, odd?"

"Well..." He spent a few moments more rubbing at his facial hair. Truly, Cecilia thought, the man got on her nerves. "Mind you, we were not what I would call more than casual acquaintances, really, but *I* remembered Eugene Pendergast as being a slightly smaller man."

"As small as yourself?" Cecilia blurted out, then instantly regretted her rash words.

Watkins puffed himself up and regarded her with disdain. "No," he corrected her. "But slighter of build than this man."

This man seemed a peculiarly objective choice of words to describe an old friend. "Couldn't he have grown since then?"

"Oh, I'm not saying that couldn't very well be the case," Watkins put in quickly. "Absolutely. At least, there has to be some explanation..."

"You mean for the change in build," Cecilia asked, "or is there something more?"

Pendergast moaned in his sleep, and his whole body began shaking in an alarming manner. *Faker,* Cecilia thought with disgust as she watched the elaborate convulsions die down.

Once the room was quiet again, Watkins explained in a low voice, "I must say, I did not socialize with Pendergast overly much, yet...this man doesn't sound quite like the Pendergast I knew, either. Eugene's voice was not so deep."

"But if a man grows, his voice is apt to change," Cecilia said, playing devil's advocate. Watkins was a fool. Besides, if anyone was going to expose the schoolteacher, it was going to be her.

"Oh, I'm not saying this man *isn't* Pendergast," Watkins said quickly. "It's just the build and the voice and..."

"*And?*" Cecilia prompted.

"Well, this man has a definite accent."

"Mr. Pendergast's parents were from Alabama."

"I never knew that," Watkins said. "But then, as I said, we were only what I would call friends of friends."

Cecilia smiled. What a dense fool this man was—unwittingly sitting on a bombshell and shying away from admitting it! "Besides, Mr. Pendergast has been in Texas for a month now. He's bound to have picked up a trace of our speech," she said.

"You're absolutely right. Believe me, I'm sure the fault is all with my poor memory. And yet..."

"Is there some other physical characteristic that's bothering you, Mr. Watkins?" Cecilia asked with some irritation. If he had some conclusive evidence, she wished he'd just spit it out.

The man hesitated. "I'm sure it's only me..."

"You might as well come out with it," Cecilia said.

"It's rather hard to explain. Something about the eyes."

A chill went down Cecilia's spine. Those eyes, dark as coals; she'd always suspected they weren't the eyes of a mild-mannered schoolteacher. She swallowed against the dryness in her mouth. "The passage of time can harden a man about the eyes, I've always found."

Watkins nodded energetically. "I'm certain you're right, Miss Summertree. It's silly of me, standing here casting suspicion when I only saw Mr. Pendergast for a short moment."

"And he's an old friend!" Cecilia scolded.

She felt elated. If what Watkins was saying was correct, this man not only wasn't even a schoolteacher, he wasn't a Pendergast, either! It was too good to be true.

It was perfect. Now she only had to wait for medical confirmation. When Dr. Parker arrived and gave his diagnosis that nothing at all was wrong with Pendergast, she would be able to gather up Watkins and Parker, march over to Beasley's and tell the old blowhard that she had been right about the schoolteacher all along. And if the store-keeper had any decency, he would offer her old job back then and there. She would be vindicated at last.

She hoped Watkins didn't go straight to Beasley and muck up all her plans. She didn't want Beasley getting suspicious before she had the chance to expose the school-teacher. This would be the talk of the town for years to come, and she wanted to make sure her own heroic role was duly noted.

Dolly swept through the bedroom door, followed by Dr. Parker. Finally! The old bearded doctor pulled a chair up to the bed, grabbed the covers and tossed them to the bottom of the bed.

Dolly gasped. "Cecilia, you'll have to leave."

"He's got his clothes on," Cecilia said. She hated when Dolly, ever mindful of having once been a married woman, said things like this. "Besides, I've been sitting here forever and might have some important observations for the doctor."

Her words effectively shut Dolly up, though Dr. Parker regarded her skeptically. "*Did* you observe anything?" he asked.

Cecilia shrugged. "Not really."

"Tremors?" Watkins cued her from the back of the room.

"Oh, that's right," she said. That had completely slipped her mind. "He was convulsing." *Faking* convulsing, she might have added.

As if to demonstrate, Pendergast moaned and shook again.

Cecilia didn't miss Watkins's silent creep out of the sick-room, but she was too concerned with Parker's diagnosis to waylay him.

The doctor *hmmed* with his jaw jutted dramatically forward, then poked and prodded at the patient for what seemed like hours. He lifted one droopy eyelid with his thumb and stared into one of those dark eyes, then felt Pendergast's forehead as Cecilia and Dolly had done periodically since he'd fainted.

"Can you tell what's the matter with him?" Dolly asked.

Nothing, Cecilia wanted to say. But she knew Dr. Parker never left a house without making a thorough examination, no matter how pointless. Besides, the more pains he took, the more conclusive the evidence would be when she announced the man was a fraud.

After pondering the matter a bit longer, Parker finally announced, "This is quite serious—a delirium led on by a fever caused by the sudden change in climate conditions."

"What?" She hadn't expected anything so elaborate to come out of the doctor's mouth—not when there was so obviously nothing wrong with the man.

Parker shook his head gravely. "He might be bedridden for some time. It could be dangerous to him if he tried to get up too early."

Oh, for heaven's sake! If that old sawbones couldn't tell that Pendergast was a faker, it was definitely time to hang up his little black bag.

She was about to tell him so, too, when Dolly interceded. "Cecilia, don't you think you should go downstairs and clean the kitchen? You've hardly left this room for hours and it's nearly time to start on dinner."

Cecilia went down to the kitchen and fumed as she listened to Dolly showing the doctor out of the house. Mindful of not wanting to lose her job, she picked up a rag when she heard Dolly coming and started wiping it over the table.

"Poor Mr. Pendergast!" Dolly cried.

Cecilia could hardly stand it. "Why are people here so gullible when it comes to that man?"

Dolly looked appalled. "Cecilia, how uncharitable. You heard the doctor. And Mr. Watkins was quite distressed!"

Watkins! Belatedly, she remembered that he at least might still back her up. Mumbling a lame excuse about needing to buy something at Beasley's, she dashed out of the house and hotfooted it down to the mercantile. The men who held court on a various assortment of stools and barrels at the front of the store fell silent as she walked in. In the center of them stood Beasley.

"I need to talk to you," she told the shopkeeper without further ado. "About Pendergast."

"I hope he's all right!" Beasley said with alarm.

Cecilia rolled her eyes toward the ceiling. "Well, of course he is."

"I was just telling the folks here about what happened, then Dr. Parker came by—"

Cecilia clucked her tongue in disgust. "Dr. Parker doesn't know beans."

Several of the gathered company laughed, but not Beasley. He sputtered indignantly. "He's a fine doctor! Came from Baton Rouge eight years ago."

"Pendergast is a faker," she said. "Just ask Watkins—he'll tell you the truth."

Beasley crossed his arms over his chest and poked his gut out. "Watkins rode out ten minutes ago. And he didn't say anything about Pendergast being a faker to me."

Cecilia's mouth parted in surprise. "He just left?" And he hadn't said anything to Beasley about Pendergast? "That can't be! Where did he go?"

"Abilene. Said he could post a letter there before evening."

Oh, of all the luck! Cecilia let out a sigh of frustration. This meant she was on her own. As usual. "Well, before he left he told me that Pendergast doesn't even look like he used to."

Beasley barked out a laugh. "'Course not—it's been eight years or more since he's seen the man."

"But it was more than that..."

She winced as a patronizing smile bent Beasley's lips. "Now, Cecilia, honey. You aren't trying to tell me that this man isn't a schoolteacher again, are you?"

"But he's not!" she declared.

He stepped forward and put a fatherly arm around Cecilia's shoulder. "I thought we'd gotten beyond this. He's a very talented educator from Philadelphia. He's got the most impressive credentials of any teacher in all of West Texas."

"But Watkins said—"

"*I* was there when the two of them met, Cecilia," Beasley assured her. "Watkins recognized Pendergast right away."

"But why would a man just faint like that?" Cecilia asked doggedly. "He was fine last night!"

Beasley shrugged at the mysteries of human health. "Right before he passed out, the man looked clammy and green. I saw it with my own eyes!"

"He's faking, I know it," Cecilia insisted. "He's been faking about being a schoolteacher, and now he's faking this mysterious ailment of his. And if Watkins is right, then his name probably isn't even Pendergast!"

Her rising hysteria met with chuckles and hoots from Beasley's cronies. "Better get a rope," one man joked.

"If I was to lie about my name, I'd sure think up something better than Eugene," said another.

Cecilia sent them all a withering glare. Naturally, these tobacco-chewing chowderheads would miss the point completely. "I'm telling you, the man's taking us for a hayride."

Beasley clucked his tongue disapprovingly. "I'm surprised at you, Cecilia. I thought you had more decency than to try to sabotage a man when he's helpless."

"He's about as helpless as a bobcat!" Cecilia said.

"Dr. Parker told all of us that the schoolteacher was in a delirium, and now you're over here trying to take away his livelihood."

She could tell by the nods and frowns around her that Beasley was winning the war of public opinion. At this point it was the men against the woman. She felt her shoulders sag in defeat. Why did Pendergast have such an easy touch with these people? she wondered in frustration.

Beasley pushed her toward the door. "Now you go on back to Dolly's and look after things there, Cecilia. And if you get any real evidence—I mean written proof—that this man isn't the upstanding schoolteacher we in Annsboro all think he is, then you come straight to me, young lady.''

Before she knew what was what, Cecilia found herself out on the sidewalk again. As she started trudging toward home, Beasley called after her, "But be ready to go back to school just in case Pendergast doesn't get better by tomorrow. Will you do that?''

Cecilia turned, her lips pursed in displeasure. She was supposed to *fill in* for Pendergast while he lay about in bed all day? It was too infuriating!

Nevertheless, it wasn't an offer she could refuse. When she did finally get Pendergast booted out of that schoolhouse, she wanted to be on Beasley's good side. "Of course," she said, gritting her teeth into what she hoped was a pleasant smile. "I'd be delighted to.''

This time Jake was being more careful. He should have known better than to think he could slip out of town in broad daylight. This time he was waiting until three in the morning.

Slowly, he edged down the staircase in his stocking feet, boots in hand. He felt stiff as a board from lying flat all day long, but at least he was somewhat rested up for his journey. With Dolly and Cecilia watching him like hawks the entire day, all he had been able to do was sleep. Fitfully.

He didn't trust that Cecilia. He didn't know what had happened when she'd left the boardinghouse today, but one thing was certain—she was good and steamed when she came back. More than once he'd considered just getting it over with and explaining everything to her. Why not? He knew he'd be heading out as soon as he was sure everyone was in their beds asleep. That way Cecilia could leave him alone, secure in the knowledge that she would be queen of the anthill once he was gone.

Only, considering what he'd put her through in the past weeks, he doubted she would keep such a revelation to herself. He nearly laughed out loud just thinking how improbable that was. Face it, she would want to parade him around in chains for crimes to Cecilia, crowing all the while to the world that she was right all along.

It was amazing. The woman wanted his head on a platter, but for all that, he would miss her. And this house, he thought as he stopped for a short moment in the hallway, his ear straining to hear any movement. His time here hadn't been as peaceful as he'd hoped, but it had been a home, with people around all the time to talk to and three squares a day. And Cecilia to annoy, or flirt with—mostly it added up to the same thing.

He couldn't go back to the old ways now, which was why it was more important than ever to put his little game of chase with Gunter and Darby behind him. He'd never have a normal life again until he had gotten rid of them, never be able to settle down and start that ranch he'd always dreamed of. Even hiding out under an alias in a tiny town like this one had been a headache. It was either them or him, now or never.

The front door hinges were blessedly silent as he let himself out. Jake took a deep breath of the dry nippy air and smiled. Good traveling weather. Good conditions for settling an old score.

Chapter Nine

The long open wagon pulled by three old plugs lurched slowly down the rutted road. At the reins beside Jake was a silent, skinny man who nonetheless had the biggest potbelly Jake had ever seen, and behind him were six women who wouldn't shut up. Maybe he should have walked, Jake thought for the hundredth time. Better yet, maybe he should have stolen a horse.

Of course, Buck's horse hadn't been tethered in front of Dolly's when he left. And when he thought about stealing someone else's horse, he just couldn't bring himself to turn thief. Not only would that probably put somebody on his tail, it would have undoubtedly awakened someone. And if caught, how would he have explained himself—that in his "delirium," he'd decided to go out for a moonlit ride?

He had been lucky to come across a farmer who had given him a ride to Buffalo Gap, where he had found this would-be stagecoach bound for Fredericksburg, which was all he could afford, anyway. Teaching in Annsboro hadn't exactly made him a millionaire.

The only seat available was shotgun, and that was fine with him. But that had been hours ago, when he was still fresh as a daisy, comparatively. Now he was tired and hungry and anxious.

How long before he could jump off this infernal buggy and set off for Darby's ranch? He kept his eyes on the horizon, looking for a landmark. He'd never traveled this road before, barely even knew it existed. Now that his backbone felt as though it was a nail someone had tried to pound into a rock, he knew why.

Also on his mind was what the people in Annsboro had thought when they discovered him missing this morning. Cecilia, no doubt, was triumphant. Right now she was probably in his schoolroom, telling the class about history's famous deceivers—Judas Iscariot, Benedict Arnold and now Eugene Pendergast, who she had known all along was a fake and a fraud.

He shook his head thinking about it. He might just as well have stolen a horse. It couldn't have harmed his reputation in Annsboro any more than his sneaking out silently in the night, especially with Cecilia in charge of the town's history.

Really, it wasn't such a bad place. Not much to do there, but then he hadn't stuck around for the harvest shindig. Too bad. He wasn't usually too wild about these affairs, but he would have liked the chance to dance with Cecilia, to hold her in his arms for a good long time, out there under the stars.

But that wasn't likely to happen now. He probably wouldn't even live to tell the tale of his showdown with Darby, but on the off chance he did, the good people of Annsboro weren't going to welcome him with open arms. In fact, Lysander Beasley would probably want to have him shot on sight if Jake so much as stepped foot near the place.

And what cause would he ever have to return there, anyway?

"You say you're a schoolteacher?" The driver didn't look away from the bony backs of the horses as he spoke.

"Yeah."

Jake didn't see the point in giving up his alias just yet. He'd rather have Lysander Beasley after him than Will Gunter. And it wasn't probable that telling the driver would do much damage, anyway. The man couldn't keep a con-

versation going for more than a few minutes at a time, and
then it was mostly to go over what you'd already told him.

After a few more minutes hunched over the reins in
thought, the man asked, "In Annsboro, you said?"

"That's right."

The man slowly moved his head up and down in understanding. Was there anything this fellow didn't do slowly?

Behind them, two matronly women had been gabbing
without cease since leaving Buffalo Gap, about mutual acquaintances, about their husbands and what they did, about
various mundane things like planting and cooking and sewing. You'd think they had never had a soul to talk to before. One of the women—Mrs. Randall, he thought she had
said—was a stout farm wife, and the other spoke in Ger-
man-accented English, which wasn't surprising, since the
wagon was headed for Fredericksburg. What was surprising was that after so many hours of chattering either woman
had any spit left to keep talking.

Even so, they had nothing on their companions, four
older girls, probably around thirteen, who wouldn't shut up
and on top of that spoke nothing but German in loud, high-
pitched girlish voices punctuated every so often with giggles. The four of them had varying degrees of blond hair,
but it was done identically in simple braids down their
backs, and they all wore the same blue dress, dark stock-
ings and black boots. Were they sisters, the daughters of the
German woman? Jake couldn't say. Nor could he imagine
what the hell they were talking about that was so funny.

He avoided looking at them, because doing so seemed to
set off more peals of laughter, which left him staring straight
ahead and brooding. This would surely have to go down as
the longest day in his life.

"You got business down south?" the driver asked. This,
at last, was a brand-new question.

But Jake could only shrug in return. Really, he would
have loved to have talked to the man, yet he couldn't. On
top of not wanting to leave tracks, he feared he was revert-

ing to his old self already. As the wagon crept farther away from Annsboro, his more gregarious Pendergast persona was being shucked off like an old skin. Jake remembered now that, before Annsboro, he'd always been a man of few words, a man who preferred living on the range to in town. Independent.

Funny, those characteristics never struck him as so lonesome before, but that's how he felt now. Hollow inside, or as if he wasn't rooted properly. Cecilia's pretty face flitted through his mind, and he shut his eyes, hoping to keep her there. But she disappeared, elusive as ever, and when he opened them again, his eyes beheld a landscape as unfamiliar and barren as before.

He couldn't remember needing a woman this way, or this feeling of not wanting to leave someone. More than once he had thought of turning around, going back. But back to what? Just because he felt like a lovesick puppy didn't mean she did, too. In fact, he doubted Cecilia's layers of pride would allow her to surrender herself so completely to another person…but he would like to have been the man who found out for sure whether this was the case.

Go back, his gut told him. Maybe life had something in store for him beyond avenging all the past wrongs Darby and Gunter had done him. He even wondered whether, by hunting down Darby as that man had hunted him, he wasn't stooping to his level. He pondered this for a moment, allowing himself a brief dream of putting aside bitterness in favor of hearth and home and long peaceful winter nights with Cecilia in his bed.

Yet he still had a voice inside telling him to push on, to get revenge. Or was that simply the sound of the high-pitched voices of six women yammering in his ear? He sighed in frustration.

"Long trip," the driver said.

It was when you had horses that would lose a race with a slug.

"Fredericksburg's a far piece. We're still probably closer to Buffalo Gap than where you're going, even."

Great.

"Where *are* you going?" the man asked.

Jake remained silent, his eyes trained on the road ahead of him. This was one piece of information he wasn't going to divulge, or even lie about, no matter how many times the man returned to it.

From behind them, he heard a noise. In a flash, his hand felt for the gun at his belt and he twisted in his seat, his narrow-eyed gaze sweeping over the countryside they'd just covered.

Nothing. Must have been a rabbit or something.

The tension that had gathered so quickly seeped out in a long exhaled breath. The girls, their blue eyes wide and lips parted in surprise at the speed with which he'd whipped around in their direction, looked at him for a moment of blessed silence and then burst into fresh peals of laughter. They were already chattering again in their foreign tongue when Jake turned to face forward, grimacing.

"Jumpy there, ain't you?" the driver noted.

Well, who wouldn't be? Maybe Pendergast—the real Pendergast—had been right. He should have chucked it all and gone somewhere like Philadelphia, to civilization. He didn't know much about that place, but it had to be more relaxing than where he was now, or had been for the past month, or his entire life before that. Sometimes he felt he hadn't had a good night's sleep since way back before his father had died, back on his tiny family farm.

It wasn't as if he really wanted that much. Just a house, some land, a chance to live in peace without having two crazy men on his tail. He tried to imagine such a place, how it would be if he finally did get it. He could just visualize the little house, the pasture dotted with livestock, a little garden plot that could be worked by his wife.

His *wife?* Jake shook his head. Now where had that thought come from?

Of course he knew exactly where, because in the few moments of fantasizing he'd allowed himself, he'd had a very clear view of the woman—silky blond hair, blue eyes, pretty crimson lips . . .

He nearly hooted at the very idea. Cecilia Summertree picking turnips. That was a fantasy, all right.

"Damnation!" the driver cried, spinning in his seat even as he whipped the reins on the horses' backs.

Startled from his ridiculous daydream, Jake was a second behind the man in hearing the horses of the two riders already bearing down on them. The wagon jerked as the wagon horses responded to command, and when Jake turned and looked over the heads of the six terrified women, he saw what surely seemed like doom—the two riders, wearing hats and with faces covered, were nearly flanking them.

One of the girls caught sight of the gun in one man's hand. *"Bandits!"* The women erupted into a chorus of shrieks.

Bandits, all right, and they were aiming to take out the driver and Jake. As he drew his Colt revolver and cocked it, he barked orders at the women behind him. "Down! Get down!"

All at once, the women dived for the wagon bed. The driver had a rifle, but he was slow on the uptake, and Jake, worried about the dark man who was riding along his side of the wagon, was too busy trying to take him out to see to the other man.

A shot was fired, and Jake was half-surprised when he wasn't hit. He took aim at the dark-haired man and got one off on him. The man was thrown from his horse and fell to the ground as the wagon horses again leapt forward and started charging down the path for all they were worth. One down! Jake thought eagerly, his blood pounding faster than the rhythm of hoofbeats. Then he felt something slump against him.

He pivoted. The driver, pale, clutching his shoulder but still holding the reins, had fallen against him. Jake pushed the man down lower and turned his attention to the second rider. In the briefest moment, beneath hat brim and over a brown bandanna, pale blue eyes squinted up at him.

It couldn't be! But those eyes, so icy, they could only belong to one person. Gunter!

What was he doing here? Did Darby have his son-in-law out robbing stages now?

He ducked down and pulled his hat brim low as he took aim. The jolting movement of the wagon made accuracy impossible, but Jake gave it his best shot.

An explosion of gunfire cracked through the air. Gunter was thrown back in his saddle, but a smile of satisfaction never got the chance to reach Jake's lips. White-hot pain seared through him and he buckled. It felt as though his insides had just been tossed over the side of the wagon. He managed to keep a slippery, shaky grip on his revolver until he could check on Gunter.

His Appaloosa horse galloped away, off down a hill, out of Jake's sight. Gunter was listing, but alive.

Jake didn't know how much longer the same description would apply to him. He felt nauseous and dizzy. "Stop!" he yelled. "Stop the wagon!"

The pounding of hooves and wagon wheels against the hard dry earth sounded like thunder in his ears. And there was that other noise, too, he realized—that symphony of female voices behind him, crying and comforting each other. In spite of the cold air, he felt hot. Feverish. Even after another shouted command to stop the wagon, the racket continued.

He looked beside him and saw the lifeless slumped form of the driver. How long had the horses been running on their own? No wonder the women were panicked! He grabbed the reins in his hands, and using his weight as he fell backward on the seat, reined in the frightened animals.

The stiff wagon rattled, bumped and lurched for what seemed like forever before the world became still again. Eerily still. Jake tried to open his eyes and focus on the clear blue afternoon sky over his head. Blue, he thought groggily. Cecilia's eyes were that color blue...

Muffled crying came from behind him, and then high voices. Jake couldn't make out the sounds until one of them cried, "The schoolteacher! He's still alive!"

His eyes blinked rapidly, and he tried to focus on the large matronly face of Mrs. Randall looming above him. "Mr. Penderfloss! Where are you hurt?"

Jake swallowed and then winced at the effort. "Pendergast," he corrected. A voice had issued from his throat. That was bound to be a good sign. He tried to continue. "Annsboro. I have to get back to Annsboro."

"It's his side," the woman told her German companion, ignoring his murmurings. Jake felt a hand pulling on his shirt, and it felt as though the woman were peeling the skin off him. He groaned in agony.

"What ees he sayink?" another voice asked.

"He's saying he's from Annsboro," the matron translated. "We've got to get him to a doctor. Girls, give us a hand!"

Jake couldn't imagine so much misery could be involved in being dragged the few feet where they laid him out in the bed of the wagon. The pain that burst through him was so intense that for a moment his vision blacked out and he was left only hearing what the women were saying around him as they went about his torture.

"There's bound to be a doctor in Buffalo Gap."

Oh, no... Jake thought of the long hours it had taken them to travel this far. Surely they wouldn't go back! Surely... He willed himself to look up, to face these women and let them know what was what. Didn't they realize he was a dying man?

When he finally was able to see, he discovered four pairs of blue-eyed blond-haired girls peering down at him, like curious little angels in plain blue dresses. At least they weren't giggling.

He tried to speak, but only one word came to his lips. "Cecilia."

As he felt himself slipping away, he wondered at his choice of last words. Maybe it was all that blond hair. Or maybe it was because he knew what he would most regret about dying right now. He'd never get that dance.

Bea Beasley propped her chin on her chubby hand and sighed. "I miss Mr. Pendergast, don't you?" Beneath her, lying across the first step of the schoolhouse, Mr. Wiggles sighed in agreement.

But Cecilia was the one who had been asked the question. "Mmm," she mumbled distractedly.

Bea regarded her with watery eyes. "Oh, you're so brave, Miss Summertree! It makes me want to cry when I think that I'm the only one who knows how heartbroken you are."

Cecilia harrumphed a response. In all honesty, she wasn't sure what tag to put on the crazy jumble of feelings inside her. Pendergast had been gone for over two days now, and the truth was she was still stunned.

His disappearance had created quite a stir. Half the town—Beasley's half—felt that the lying Yankee must have absconded with funds they hadn't discovered missing yet. The other half, a contingent led by Dolly and Dr. Parker, maintained that Pendergast had stumbled out of town in his delirium, and was who knows where by now. Dolly had even tried to drum up enthusiasm for a search party, but Buck had dissuaded her. As far as he was concerned, the schoolteacher could wander right into the Gulf of Mexico.

Cecilia withheld her opinion. More compelling to her than where Pendergast had gone was how she felt about his leaving. First there was disappointment. People weren't cheering her in the streets for having figured out he was a fraud, after all. And being reinstated in the schoolhouse wasn't quite the coup she'd anticipated. Pendergast's sneaking out in the night had deprived her of a decisive victory.

And then there was an odd restlessness to cope with, which she put down to boredom. Annoying as the man had been, he had at least given her something to focus her attention on. She had tried these past two days to throw herself into planning the school pageant, but she was finding it difficult to get too excited about Pilgrims just now.

"Maybe in his delirium," Bea conjectured aloud, because of course she had sided against her father on this point, "maybe Mr. Pendergast will wander into a Quaker community, like the hero did in *The Gun-toting Peacemaker*."

Cecilia was beginning to think she would have to read some of Pendergast's books, which were still stacked next to her bed. From Bea's descriptions, they sounded as if they might keep her from brooding.

"Of course, that doesn't do *you* any good," Bea added. "Because most likely Pendergast would fall in love with a Quaker woman, and where does that leave you? You'll still be here, getting older and sadder, pining away for your lost lover until you become so eccentric that the town considers you a freak."

"Thanks, Bea."

"Oh!" The little girl seemed to sense she might have said something inappropriate. "I hope you didn't think I meant anything against you, Miss Summertree, when I said that I missed Mr. Pendergast," Bea assured her.

"No offense taken," Cecilia replied. In spite of Bea's inflated estimation of the tragedy of Pendergast, the little girl did seem to be the only person in town who was sympathetic to her loss-of-Pendergast malaise.

After a moment of silence, Bea stubbed her toe along the runner board of the stair. "You know what?"

"What?" For a moment it seemed as if the girl might have a secret to tell about Pendergast. "I don't want to be Priscilla this year."

Cecilia first felt disappointment that they were only talking about that stupid pageant, and then her eyes widened in surprise. Ever since she was five, Bea Beasley had played Priscilla Mullins in the school harvest pageant. The little girl must be depressed!

"Oh, Bea, you don't want to give up your prize role! Mr. Pendergast would want you to have it."

Bea sighed long and hard. "Well, of course. Naturally I still want to be the lead. But this year I want to be Dolly Madison."

"Dolly Madison wasn't a Pilgrim," Cecilia told her.

Bea rolled her eyes. "I *know* that. I think this year we should do the burning of the White House. Mr. Pendergast said we could."

Great. Cecilia wished the man had consulted her before making all sorts of promises to Bea on the eve of his disappearance. Now she was going to have to deal with this. Of course, when it came to the pageant, Bea always got what Bea wanted. *The burning of the White House?* How on earth were they going to manage that?

"I'd better go home," Cecilia said, making no commitment to the little girl's idea. She pushed herself off the stairs and started walking.

Bea and Mr. Wiggles tagged alongside her. "And my father said he would donate any materials the school needs for the pageant."

"How generous," Cecilia said.

"As long as I get to be Dolly Madison," Bea stipulated.

Cecilia gritted her teeth. She'd forgotten that being able to enjoy being strong-armed by a ten-year-old was a requirement for the teaching position in Annsboro. Honestly, there were times when she wondered if it had even been worth campaigning against Pendergast to get her old job back. Working at Dolly's was easy once she had gotten used to the physical aspect of it, and it was less of a headache.

"I'm sure we can work something out," Cecilia said.

"Oh, good! Miss Summertree, you're almost as good a teacher as Mr. Pendergast was!"

"Thanks."

"I mean it! Can I go tell my father about the pageant?"

Cecilia nodded, and Bea and her yellow dog streaked off down the street, leaving her in their dust. As she neared Dolly's, the pageant problem retreated to the recesses of her mind, and she thought again of Pendergast.

It was strange not having him in the boardinghouse anymore. The conversation always flagged at dinner now—once speculation about Pendergast's vanishing had run its course. She missed his dark mischievous eyes watching her over the table sometimes. And at night, in her spacious room, when she lay in the soft down bed that he had lain in for so many nights, still breathing the rough scent of him that lingered on the pillow her head rested on, it was practically impossible to sleep for all the questions that would run through her mind.

Who was he really, and where had he gone? She couldn't stop thinking of the times he had kissed her, the way his arms felt wrapped around her waist, pinning her to him. Did he remember these things, or had she just been one among hundreds of passing flirtations in his life?

Oh, it was terrible the way he had been able to manipulate her. The man was insufferable, frustrating and infuriating. She was a thousand times better off now that he was gone, and she had her old job back, secure until Beasley managed to find another teacher who would suit his overblown needs. Maybe she would even try to get a teaching certificate herself, Cecilia thought. Her father might be willing to ship her off to the teacher's college, if he thought it would keep her out of trouble.

Before Pendergast had entered the picture, she had only cared about the job because it kept her away from the ranch, in town, where there were lots of people. Now that Pendergast was gone, it was clearer than ever that town was pretty boring, too. And there were so many annoying people to deal with!

As if to underscore her thoughts, she noticed Buck's horse outside the boardinghouse. She headed inside, hoping to find something to eat before dinner in the kitchen; unfortunately, Buck and Dolly were holding court there.

"Hi, Cecilia." Buck spared her only the briefest of glances. Ever since last Saturday night in front of the schoolhouse, Buck had said barely two words to her, though he did seem to puff himself up to show her what a marvelous masculine opportunity she had passed on. And the name Cici was strictly a thing of the past. He only had eyes for Dolly now—wide, surprised eyes, as if he didn't know what had hit him.

Dolly, however, was all benevolence again. And why shouldn't she be? Cecilia thought churlishly. The man of her dreams had fallen head over heels in love with her. Everything had worked out fine for Dolly.

Of course, things had worked out fine for herself, too, Cecilia thought dismissively, what with the job, and the room, and... She sighed. All told, a job and a room were better than nothing. Those things had certainly seemed important to her a week ago.

There was water in a pitcher by the sink, and she poured herself a tall glass.

"Long day?" Dolly asked her.

Cecilia grunted in reply.

"Maybe you should take a nap," her friend suggested, watching her face anxiously.

"Oh, I'm not tired." Cecilia sighed. She didn't know what she wanted to do. Tiresome as they were, at least Buck and Dolly were adult company after a day with rowdy children. "Don't mind me," she said.

Dolly sent a secretive little smile across the table to Buck.

"What is it?" Cecilia asked.

"Oh, nothing," Dolly replied. Then she smiled again.

Oh, she hated it when Dolly did this to her! "What?" she insisted.

"It's just that I was telling Buck a little theory of mine."

Cecilia wasn't sure she wanted to hear this, but she couldn't help asking, "What theory?"

"That you're in love with Pendergast."

"What!" Cecilia nearly choked on a slurp of water. Hearing this kind of talk from Bea was one thing—she had lied to Bea, after all—but where had Dolly picked up such a notion?

"Well, you certainly have been in a bad mood since he left," Dolly explained.

"Think you'd be happy, getting what you wanted and all," Buck said derisively.

"I am happy!" Cecilia snapped.

"Oh, you poor thing, you don't have to put on a brave face for us." Dolly lowered her voice. "Besides, Cecilia, that night by the schoolhouse, I *saw* what you two were doing by the well."

Cecilia's face paled even as Buck's reddened. "What were they doing?" The anger in his voice indicated he might rethink the search party idea.

"Oh, for heaven's sake!" Cecilia said. "It was just a little kiss."

Dolly's eyebrows lifted dramatically.

"It's not as if I asked him to!" Cecilia protested.

"Cecilia," Dolly lectured, "you *followed* him out there." She said this as if she herself hadn't done the exact same thing—but after Buck, of all people.

"Hell," Buck said, "Cecilia's been trailing after Pendergast for weeks. The slicker probably thought she was easy game."

Cecilia couldn't believe her ears. Was this what people were saying about her? "I was attempting to prove to everyone that Pendergast wasn't who he said he was!"

"By kissing him?" Buck asked.

"I didn't want to kiss him," Cecilia said. Buck and Dolly laughed at her, and Cecilia could feel herself redden. "Besides, I was right about him, wasn't I?"

Dolly shook her head sadly. "Poor Mr. Pendergast. I know he's just out there wandering like a vagabond, a poor lost soul."

Cecilia huffed in outrage. "That's ridiculous! He's probably in another town, pretending to be *their* schoolteacher."

"Now why would he want to do that?"

This was a sound question. Hard as she tried, Cecilia couldn't figure out what Pendergast's game was.

Buck snickered. "Maybe so he can spark *their* old schoolteacher."

Cecilia's spine stiffened. She couldn't believe Buck—the man who until four nights ago was willing to pledge undying love to her—was treating her so shabbily. So much for the Dooley Hodges tradition in this town!

She looked over and saw Buck's hand covering Dolly's across the table and suddenly felt like the odd man out. She decided to go up to her room before the two of them actually started billing and cooing right there in front of her.

"I think maybe I'll go up and rest, after all."

They smiled at her patiently as she trudged away, feeling lonelier and more restless than ever.

"And I'm glad he's gone!" Cecilia hollered behind her, just to make sure they didn't cling to the notion she was carrying a torch.

Seeing her large inviting room should have given her a little lift, but it didn't. When she looked at the fluffy bed that would have been so relaxing to flop onto, she remembered that it still smelled of Pendergast, and that lying in it would remind her of his stirring up feelings inside her that were the very opposite of relaxing. And when she moved toward the rocking chair, she saw Pendergast's little valise was still sitting beneath it.

The contents of that black bag were no mystery to her. She had sifted through the old clothes and little stack of letters more times than she wanted to count. Dolly had also looked through his things—although, unlike her scrupulous friend, Cecilia had torn into those letters the first moment no one was looking, relieved when she learned that the Rosalyn Pendergast who had written them was only an old spinster sister.

Unfortunately, nothing else in the letters pointed to a contradiction in Pendergast's story. But why had he never mentioned his sister? And why, unless one were to believe Dolly's foolish hypothesis about his wandering about the countryside in some kind of fever-induced trance, why would a man who had carried these letters all the way across six states leave them in a boardinghouse room as if they meant no more to him than the soiled shirt they were buried beneath?

It was suspicious. But she and Pendergast had never spoken on personal topics, so it wasn't so strange that she knew nothing of his sister. And perhaps he had simply forgotten the letters.

Now she wished she had asked him more about himself. Not only would it have been the only way to discern whether his leaving the letters had any special significance, but she also found her mind inexplicably craving information about the man. In moments of repose, questions would pop into her mind. Who were his parents? What kind of house had he grown up in? Had he ever had a sweetheart? That last preyed most on her mind, aside from the question that inevitably recurred no matter how futile she told herself it was to ask—who was Pendergast really?

Perhaps she would never know. Letting loose another long sigh, she scooted the rocking chair over to the window. She was not going to read those letters again, she promised herself. There was no point to it.

But her fingers itched to leaf through them one more time, to search for clues she already was aware weren't to be found. Reluctantly, but drawn as if by a magnet, she reached down and opened the bag, pushed aside the white shirt and picked up the lavender envelopes.

She knew what was in them, so what would be the harm in looking at them again?

Just as she was untying the neat little ribbon around the envelopes, a commotion started coming from the direction of Beasley's. Diverted from her pointless snooping, Cecilia leaned forward and peered out the window toward the general store, where a long rickety wagon had just pulled up. Two women and a handful of girls surrounded the vehicle so that Cecilia couldn't tell what was going on. She tried leaning her upper body farther through the window to see past the obstructions.

Suddenly, Bea Beasley broke through the crowd of people by the store and began running down the street, followed of course by her dog, who was barking even as his mistress yelled out like the town crier. "Mrs. Hudspeth! Miss Summertree!" she hollered over and over as she sped toward the house.

Cecilia heard the front porch door beneath her window open and bang closed, then Dolly and Buck appeared below. Dolly shaded her eyes with her cupped hand as Bea, winded, with brown braids frizzling out of their tight confines, finally delivered her big news.

"Mr. Pendergast is back!"

Cecilia was so taken off guard at first that she felt her knees buckle and feared she would drop right out of the window onto Buck's head. Her sudden intake of breath—signaling equal parts happiness and horror—was enough to make the other three spot her.

"Miss Summertree!" With the sun glinting off her glasses Bea shouted joyously again, "Mr. Pendergast is back!"

"I don't believe it," Cecilia mumbled to herself, trying to still her heart's hammering. Why on earth would that man come back here?

Bea was too jubilant to pay Cecilia's shock much mind. "He's back," she raved, "and he's an honest-to-goodness hero!"

Chapter Ten

Beasley was elated. He himself drove the wagon up to Dolly's boardinghouse and oversaw the procedure of hauling Pendergast up to the schoolteacher's bedroom—which now took on the appearance of a sacred shrine. Everyone in town wanted to come see the citizen of Annsboro who had risked his life to save two women and four German schoolgirls from vicious bandits.

And, Dolly insisted several times in a very adamant voice, the man had been half-delirious already when he'd done the heroic deed!

Cecilia would have been more indignant at this newest bit of chicanery if initial word on Pendergast's condition hadn't been so dire. She had to push through the gathered crowd at her bedroom door and swat away the four adoring blond girls just to get a look at him, and even then two stout women were standing guard on either side of the bed.

Cecilia ignored their disapproving glances and looked down at her old adversary, stunned. His normally dark skin was waxy and pale, and judging by the size of the bandage wrapped around his middle, she couldn't believe the man was still alive at all.

He certainly wasn't faking this time.

She dropped down on the bed, feeling drained, and heard one of the women who had brought Pendergast back to town make a clucking noise. Dolly rushed over to assure the woman Cecilia's presence at the hero's side was all right.

"Mrs. Randall, they're almost sweethearts," Dolly whispered to the woman, then sent Cecilia an encouraging little smile. Really, she was going to have to set Dolly straight on this matter.

"Don't worry, Cecilia," Dolly continued, "they say the doctor said his condition looks worse than it is."

It looked very bad.

"Just a flesh wound, really," the matron announced. "That's what the doctor in Buffalo Gap said. He gave him a draft of laudanum for the pain."

Cecilia shook her head. "I don't understand . . . why did he come back here?"

"He kept saying 'Annsboro' over and over, so we decided we owed it to the man to bring him. He saved our lives."

The room fell silent as once again they were treated to the whole story of the slow wagon to Fredericksburg, the two bandits, Pendergast's heroic defense of the six women and the way he had killed one desperado and routed the other. Mrs. Randall's voice shook with emotion, and the girls wept fresh tears as she recalled the way their savior, wounded and in excruciating pain, had even managed to stop the crazed horses after their driver had died.

Even Cecilia was awestruck. Though a string of questions a mile long ticked through her mind, she couldn't help but feel a welling of pride for what this man had done.

Beasley, the man who for two days straight had not been able to get the words *Yankee thief* off his lips, proclaimed loudly, "I always said the man had an outstanding character."

Dolly nodded. "He has tidy habits, too."

A regular saint, Cecilia thought grudgingly. Though, as she looked down on his strong jaw, dark with stubble, and those lips that had kissed her so passionately, if not completely sincerely, she had to admit she would have been sad never to have seen him again. Very sad... but not devastated, she assured herself, feeling somehow buoyed by the distinction. The fear that had pierced through her heart when she'd heard he'd been shot was now safely hidden away in the recesses of her memory.

"Well, I suppose the man needs his rest," Beasley announced, and he and Dolly proceeded to herd the people downstairs.

"I hope you'll all stay for dinner," Dolly told the visiting women. "I'm sure there's plenty of room for you here to stay the night, too. I have a room off my kit—" Dolly stopped in mid-sentence, looking at Cecilia. "Oh, I forgot, that's *your* room."

Cecilia fought the resentment she felt at being tossed out again—and then to have even her little room promised away! Oh, well. *He did save those four German schoolgirls,* she reminded herself with a sigh. "I suppose I'll find somewhere else to sleep," she told Dolly.

"You're such a dear," Dolly said as she directed the women and girls out of the room. She stopped at the door. "You won't mind watching him through dinner, will you?"

"Not at all," Cecilia assured her. She intended to keep an even closer eye on him this time.

"I figured not." Dolly sent her a sly wink, then looked conspiratorially from her to Pendergast and back again. "I just know you must be so happy he's back!"

Cecilia grumbled in reply, but stood her post through dinner and a good deal longer, leaving the sickroom only for time enough to eat something in the kitchen and take a brisk walk in the cool night air. She attempted to clear her thoughts of the conflicting feelings she had, yet her mind clung like a burr to the center of her confusion—Pendergast.

Did no one else think it strange that their mild-mannered schoolteacher had turned sharpshooter overnight? And why in tarnation had the man bought a cheap seat on a wagon going to Fredericksburg? Was that where he was really from? If so, why would he have wanted to come back to Annsboro? If someone was offering *her* a free wagon ride to anywhere, there were a lot better places she could think of to go!

She couldn't wait until she would be able to ask him…not that she expected him to be truthful. But after two days of fretting and boredom, she had to admit that she was even looking forward to hearing what lies he had to offer. In fact, she just wanted to talk to him, to see those dark eyes looking at her once more.

When she returned, Dolly was at Pendergast's side, but gladly relinquished the post to her friend. It made perfect sense that she would have night duty, Cecilia decided, since she had no bed to sleep in. She pushed aside the little straight-backed chair that had somehow been designated for the nurse and pulled the big rocker next to the bed.

Pendergast lay across the bed, his body positioned at a slight angle to accommodate his height. He still had a sickly pallor that she found a little frightening. But the more she looked at Pendergast, whose strong, muscled arms lay over the bedcovers—which only covered him from mid-chest down—the more she felt reassured that he would pull through. It didn't seem possible that something could sap the life out of anyone that impressively built.

Yet a bullet very nearly had. Her eye caught sight of something black and glistening next to the bed. She reached down and picked up a Colt revolver, measuring its heavy weight in her hand. Suddenly she shuddered.

She wasn't prissy when it came to guns. But it occurred to her suddenly that mysterious Mr. Pendergast might be something a little more sinister than a mere fraud. What if he wasn't a hero at all, but an outlaw?

Once again, Cecilia took in the dark face, the set jaw, the long, lean, muscular body. Then she remembered those eyes again, and felt her pulse in her wrist jump in alarm. Maybe the bandits attacking the wagon hadn't been a coincidence at all! Maybe he knew the man he'd killed and the one he'd wounded—maybe they were the reason he'd had to sneak out of Annsboro in the middle of the night in the first place.

She swallowed hard against the dryness in her throat. She couldn't help remembering the times he'd kissed her... and she'd responded so enthusiastically! She burned with fresh embarrassment, and curiosity, and held tighter to the gun.

One thing was certain—Pendergast wasn't going to slip out tonight.

Jake woke up to the feeling of cold steel against his ribs and pushed himself up suddenly. Pain burned through his middle, and he collapsed against the downy pillow, gritting his teeth.

If he was lying in feathers, he assured himself, chances were Gunter wasn't anywhere nearby.

He swallowed, looking up at the ceiling, trying to get his bearings without putting much physical effort into it. It was morning. The soft bed felt as if it was his old bed at Dolly's. Although that possibility just seemed too good to be true, the familiar weight and feel of the bedcovers seemed to confirm it. How had he gotten here? Bits and snatches of the previous day ran through his mind; the wagon, the bandits, the gunfire. After that it was all pain.

There was a flowery smell in the air, a scent that was reminiscent of the best part of Dolly's... Cecilia.

He turned his head and saw the crown of a silky blond head and smiled. Cecilia was sprawled in the most uncomfortable-looking position he'd ever seen. She was sitting in the rocking chair, which was tilted so far forward it probably looked as if it was on tiptoe, but her torso and arms were flung against the mattress of his bed. One hand cradled her head; the other gently gripped his revolver. In sleep she wore the sweetest secretive smile, even though she was poking a gun at him.

Jake closed his eyes and slowly gave thanks to whoever up there was looking out for him. By some miracle, he'd made it to the right place.

Risking the pain it would cause, Jake reached over and gingerly disconnected the gun from her hand. Just as he had dislodged her last finger, she stirred and looked up suddenly, her blue eyes wide and wary in the morning light.

"You're awake!" she cried.

"Nothing a man enjoys more than awakening to the snuggly feeling of steel against his ribs," Jake quipped. "Unless it's seeing a beautiful woman in his bed."

That beautiful woman sat up so fast she nearly sent her rocking chair flying out from under her. Two dark stains appeared on her cheeks. "I was just watching you."

Jake laughed as forcefully as he thought was healthy. "Yes, you looked very attentive."

She crossed her arms, sat back and rocked badtemperedly. "Fine thanks I get for all the concern I've expended on you."

He lifted an eyebrow in surprise. "Were you worried, sweetheart?"

"Don't call me that!" she snapped, tilting her chin up. "Yes. If it makes you feel better, I was worried you might try to sneak off again."

He hadn't forgotten how pretty she was, he thought, as he took in her pale skin and bow mouth and those beautiful blue eyes, but memory couldn't compare to being with her in the flesh.

"Just seeing you makes me feel better, Cecilia," he said.

"Well, it shouldn't, because I intend to see you don't get away with whatever you're trying to pull over on this town."

"And just what would that be?" he asked, hoping the playfulness in his voice would belie the worry he felt. Had she figured out something? Had he talked in his sleep, or left something incriminating behind?

"Just—" She looked down at her hand, and her eyes flew open in alarm. "Where's the gun?"

Jake pulled the Colt from under the covers. "You mean this?" he asked innocently.

"How—"

He chuckled. "You've got some lessons to learn about staying alert."

Her eyes narrowed on him suspiciously. "Yes, and I bet you could teach me a thing or two."

Uh-oh. It sounded as if her suspicions were coming closer to the actual truth now. "Well...the first thing would be not to doze off."

Her lips pursed into a frown. "Don't try to be cute. I know who you are, Pendergast."

Jake froze. Great. He would finally get discovered when he was laid up sick in bed with a hole in him the size of Nebraska! "All right," he challenged, "who am I?"

Their stubborn, wary gazes locked and held. Cecilia broke first, then she groaned in frustration. "Oh, I don't know!"

"Not much better at bluffing than you are at staying on the lookout, are you?"

She started rocking again—rocking in a choppy staccato rhythm and shooting him a skeptical gaze. "Judging from the way you reacted when I said I did know, though, I'd say you must be something pretty bad."

Jake hooted. "Cecilia, if I was as dangerous a character as you say, it wouldn't be likely that I would put up with your needling. Especially when I'm armed and you're not."

She gasped in outrage. "Is that a threat?"

He frowned. "No."

The room was silent for a moment as Jake watched Cecilia looking out the window. She seemed to be plotting something under that adorable mop of blond hair. Her lips turned up in a devious smile.

"Who's Rosalyn?" she asked, turning quickly to watch his reaction to her sudden question.

Rosalyn? Rosalyn? Jake's mind whirred muzzily, trying to find his connection to the familiar name. The letters!

He grimaced, as though somehow the sound of the woman's name caused him pain. Maybe it would divert Cecilia's attention from how long it had taken him to remember. "Rosalyn is my sister."

"Why were you going to Fredericksburg?"

"I had some business there."

"What kind?"

He sent her a flat stare. "Personal business."

"Personal business so urgent you couldn't wait for daylight to leave?"

Jake rolled his eyes, but his heart was thumping nervously. She wasn't going to drop the issue this time. "Just tell me this," he asked her, "have you managed to convince the whole town I'm a desperate character?"

"Ha!" she cried.

What did that mean?

"All I want to know is, why were you so eager to get back here?"

That was an easy one; he wouldn't even have to lie. A broad smile pulled across his lips. "I wanted to dance with you."

She stared disbelievingly at him, her lips parted in surprise. At least he'd managed to catch her off guard again. "I mean it," she insisted. "I'm curious to know why, since you'd gone to so much trouble to sneak away, you'd come back."

Jake blinked solemnly and ignored her probing. "Which do you prefer, waltzes? Reels?"

"Don't change the subject."

"Jigs? Mexican hat dances?"

"Waltzes," she said with some irritation. "Now tell me the truth."

"I just did." The rocking chair stilled, and as their gazes met, color appeared again in her cheeks. He grinned. "You're beautiful when you blush, Cecilia."

"I think that gunshot wound must somehow have affected your brain, Pendergast!"

"Maybe it just made me see what's important."

"Dancing?" She let out a scoffing sneer. "It's not likely you'll be doing that anytime soon."

"Oh, well." Jake raised his hands off the covers in a helpless gesture. "At least the desire to seems to have gotten me back where I wanted to be."

Cecilia jumped up in outrage. "Yes, back in *my* room!"

He laughed.

"It's not funny. And while you're on the mend, I'm supposed to be doing all your work on top of mine!"

"So tell Beasley you won't do it."

"You know I can't do that."

"Why not?"

"Because I want Beasley on my side once I've gotten you drummed out of town for good."

"And he's on my side now?" This sounded promising.

"Ha!"

She kept saying that—*ha*. What did it mean? Jake had the eerie feeling that something was happening that he hadn't even guessed at yet.

"Town change much while I was gone?"

Cecilia scowled. "Annsboro? It won't change if it's here for a century!"

"No courthouse yet?"

To his surprise, Cecilia let out a laugh of recognition and walked closer to him. "No. And in case you were wondering, Beasley's drug emporium hasn't appeared, either."

Jake reached out and captured her hand. The gesture cost him a smarting pain, but it was worth it to feel her soft skin against his, to trace her slender fingers. "I thought about your laugh, too, that day I left."

She tugged gently to retrieve her hand, but he didn't let go. Her expression was confused and—amazing though it seemed—bashful. Cecilia, bashful. He felt a surge of desire for her that surprised him, given the fact that his lower half was already in a different kind of agony.

"Oh, for heaven's sake," she said, but the exclamation lacked its usual bite. "I suppose this is just another one of your tactics to throw me off track."

"I'm beginning to think that's impossible."

"There! So you admit that's what you were doing those other times."

Jake was perplexed. "What other times?"

She bit her lip and looked away shyly. "You know..." She glanced back at him and rolled her eyes. "At the blacksmith shop. Then the other night by the well..."

Understanding finally dawned. "You mean when I kissed you?"

"Yes! Don't tell me you'd forgotten."

Oh, no. "Did you brood about that kiss the whole time I was gone?" he teased.

"Absolutely not!" Cecilia protested, horrified. "I've hardly thought of it at all, except to remind myself how conniving and sneaky you are."

"For kissing you?"

"For trying to manipulate my affections to throw me off your scent," she corrected with a pert tilt of her chin.

"Obviously that plan backfired."

She snatched her hand away and leaned it on her hip. "What does that mean?"

He shrugged. "Just that kissing me has obviously made you more attentive than ever. Rather than scaring you away, you seem to be coming back for more."

"That's not true!"

"So why did I have the pleasure of waking up with you in my bed this morning?"

She sputtered helplessly for a moment before finding words. "I told you, I was just trying to—"

"Oh, I know what you *told* me."

"It's the truth," she insisted.

"Then I'll tell you the truth, Cecilia." He made sure that he was looking straight into the clear blue pools of her eyes as he carefully spoke his next words. "I never wanted to kiss a woman like I wanted to kiss you that night by the schoolhouse. And if we'd been somewhere else, and alone, I probably wouldn't have stopped with a kiss."

Her jaw popped open in sheer astonishment at his words. "Wh-what . . . You mean . . ."

Nodding, he grinned at her, enjoying the idea of having finally shocked Cecilia into complete incoherence. All traces of color drained from her face, and for a moment she merely weaved speechlessly in front of him. If he could have managed it, he would have taken her into his arms right that moment.

Into the heated tension in the silent room burst Dolly, washed and dressed for the day. "Good morning!" she chirped to Jake. "You look so much better."

Jake smiled affably. "Thanks to you, Dolly, and I guess to Cecilia here."

Dolly looked at her friend and frowned. "Cecilia? Are you all right?"

Cecilia stilled and snapped her jaw shut again. "Mmm," she mumbled.

"Poor thing!" Dolly cried. "She probably didn't get much sleep at all. But of course, how could she? She didn't have a bed!"

Jake frowned. "What happened to it?"

"The girls are in it."

"Girls?"

"The ones who brought you." Dolly put her hands on her hips. "Didn't Cecilia tell you what a hero you are here now?"

Ha! Jake thought. That's what Cecilia had been so upset about. He looked up and saw her still standing where she had been when Dolly came in.

"You saved a whole wagonload of people, if you don't remember!" Dolly informed him proudly. "And they brought you here, where we plan to treat you like a king until you're all better."

Jake beamed a smile at her. "It was no more than anyone else would do."

"Still and all, we haven't had such a show of heroism from one of our citizens since . . . well, since the Indian raid!

You'll be written up in the history books, isn't that right, Cecilia? Cecilia?'' Dolly looked over at her friend again. ''Cecilia, I think you should go out for a morning constitutional. You look feverish yourself!''

Wordlessly, Cecilia moved toward the door. She looked back at Jake once, opened her mouth to speak, then closed it again and silently slipped from the room.

''Now what could be the matter with her?'' Dolly wondered mockingly. She sent Jake a meaningful little grin. ''She's been in a state ever since you disappeared.''

Jake watched Cecilia disappear through the hallway, wishing he could jump out of bed and follow her. Maybe he'd been too forward. He didn't want to scare her away.

Of course, given that he'd just had a run-in with the man who was trying to kill him, that might not be a bad thing. He could only stay now until he was sure he was mended enough to go after Darby again. His attraction to Cecilia had tugged him all the way back to the safe haven of Annsboro, but if Gunter had recognized him during their brief shootout, how much longer would Annsboro be safe?

Her limbs felt quivery and weak. *Because I slept in a rocking chair,* she assured herself.

Because you're falling for a man who might be a desperado! a little voice corrected.

That was just not possible! Cecilia took a deep, healthy breath of air and exhaled slowly. She was being ridiculous again. Pendergast was *not* an outlaw, and she certainly did *not* have feelings for him, other than disdain.

A vision of that revolver flashed through her mind, however, chased by a fleeting memory of those eyes searing right through her as he said, ''I probably wouldn't have stopped with a kiss.'' Those were not the words of a gentleman. And that Colt wasn't exactly a dueling pistol.

She began to quake all over again. Maybe he *was* an outlaw. And he guessed she knew he was one. That's why he had come back—to make sure she kept her mouth shut. That's what that gun was for!

She stumbled forward a few steps to the road in front of Dolly's property and looked out over the town. She had to teach school today, yet her thoughts were such a jumble she didn't know how she was going to rally for the task. Her chest was pounding so hard that she could only breathe in little puffs. Was Pendergast really just biding his time until he got better so he could do her in?

Or had he been telling the truth when he said he had come back to dance with her? That didn't seem likely, and yet . . . his eyes had looked at her with such raw desire that she felt she hadn't even known the meaning of the word until now. In fact, she knew she hadn't. No man had ever said he wanted her so bluntly.

And she'd never responded so mutely! But how could a person put words to the terrifying feeling those dark eyes of his caused her to have? If Dolly hadn't come in when she had, Cecilia feared she might have done something she would have regretted forever, like crawling right into that bed—the whole way this time.

Dangerous? Even if the man wasn't an outlaw, the wanting he stirred in her was very dangerous. Being just on the verge of getting everything she had been working for was no time to do exactly what Clara had always warned her against—namely, fall for the wrong man.

How had Dolly known? She'd just been teasing her the day before about falling in love with Mr. Pendergast, and she was right! Only Cecilia didn't know whether *love* was the correct word. Pendergast himself had certainly never used that term. He'd pinned her with his gaze just like she'd seen men eyeballing the women from Grady's—only his look said that she would be much more of a challenge.

She reeled toward a shady tree nearby and leaned against it for support. Who else could have guessed what feelings she had for this man? And what would everyone say about her once it came out that he wasn't a hero at all, but a desperado, maybe even a bandit himself!

Oh, how could she have been so foolish! She couldn't believe, after eighteen years of being sensible and so satisfyingly self-absorbed, she'd allowed her thoughts to focus on a shady character who was bound to ruin her reputation beyond repair. Beasley would never allow an outlaw's moll to teach school. And if her father found out she had feelings for such a man, he'd snatch her back so fast her head would spin. Then she would spend the rest of her life hearing Clara clucking her tongue and telling her she should have listened. . . .

She pushed herself away from the tree. She couldn't just stand here, panicking! She had to do something to protect herself. Just because she had feelings for Pendergast didn't mean her situation was irredeemable—it just meant she needed more desperately than ever to get the man out of town.

Fleetly she headed off down the street, ignoring the hellos of people going about their business. On the way to Beasley's she passed Bea walking the other way.

"Miss Summertree? Aren't we having school today?" the little girl asked, her voice anxious at the thought of missing school.

"Yes!" Cecilia tried to think fast. "But I need to see your father about something, so Bea, you'll have to take charge of the class."

Behind her glasses, the girl's eyes seemed to magnify a hundred times, and a big smile broke out across her face. "Oh, boy!" she cried, skipping off to try out her new role.

Cecilia hurried on until she reached the general store. Mindful of what had happened the last time she was here, she tried to gather her wits before storming in making accusations. Nevertheless, surely Beasley would want to know that there was a potentially dangerous person in their town.

When she pushed open the door, there was a biddable smile on her face, and she nodded a friendly good morning to the three men who had already stopped by to congregate for the morning.

Beasley was behind the counter, working on his account book, by the looks of it. "Something the matter at the schoolhouse, Cecilia?"

"Not a thing," Cecilia answered. "I'm just on my way over there. But first I thought I should tell you about Pendergast."

His eyes immediately looked up from his ledger. "Nothing wrong, I hope."

"I don't know..."

"Well, land's sake, girl, what is it? I was just gonna tell Bert here on his way to Abilene to stop by the newspaper office there and see if he can get someone out here to write about Pendergast." He snapped his suspenders proudly, as if the newspaper article was a done deal.

"Mr. Beasley, I have a suspicious feeling about Mr. Pendergast."

There were chuckles behind her, and Cecilia struggled not to turn a glare on the men.

Beasley gesticulated impatiently with his hands. "Oh, no, not this again. What's the matter now? We know you don't think he's a schoolteacher."

"No," Cecilia agreed, "I think he's a criminal."

All three men behind her broke out laughing, and unable to keep her resolution, Cecilia threw them a disparaging glance. "Don't you see?" she asked urgently. "Our mild-mannered Mr. Pendergast sneaked out in the night, armed, and defended himself when he was attacked, and now crawled back here to hide."

"Hide? What do you think he's hiding from?" Beasley said.

"I don't know," Cecilia answered, reddening at the snickers that met the admission. "You're all just too busy fancying a hero in your midst to see Pendergast for what he really is."

"What's that?" one of the men asked.

"A vicious outlaw."

Hoots of laughter echoed off the wooden rafters of the store. "That's right," the man named Bert joked, "we got Jesse James teaching school right here in Annsboro."

"Maybe he's just not famous," Cecilia explained. "Have you seen that pistol he's got?"

Beasley shook his head patronizingly at her. "Lots of men carry guns, Cecilia."

"Even Yankees," one agreed.

"They were sure carrying them twenty-five years ago!" one older fellow said, and the rest of them laughed along.

"Then why was he sneaking off to Fredericksburg?" Cecilia asked.

With a sigh of pure exasperation, Beasley snapped, "How should I know! The man was delirious, he probably didn't know where he was going himself."

"I doubt that very much," Cecilia said.

"You doubt because you want the man gone," Beasley scolded. "You have since he got here. First you tried to cast suspicion on him, then you wanted to turn us against him while he was sick, and now you want to deprive the man of his glory. You weren't saying the fellow was an outlaw the other day, when your old job was secure."

The others were nodding in agreement, which infuriated Cecilia. Did the whole town think she was that selfish and mean-spirited? In that moment, she realized she could run around town for the rest of her life wailing doom like Cassandra and no one would believe her. They were all on Pendergast's side.

"If you want to do this town a favor," Beasley instructed unctuously, "you'd best go back to that school and mind that this year's pageant is the best ever."

Cecilia screwed her lips into a pout. Success was always the best revenge, but how successful could a piddly little pageant be? She doubted she could plan one so good it would get rid of Pendergast. But perhaps a good showing might make these small-minded people regret booting her out of her job when Pendergast was finally unmasked, which of course he would be eventually. She clung to that assurance for all she was worth.

At any rate, working on the infernal play would at least give her something to focus her energies on. The more she concentrated on Dolly Madison, the less time she would have to think about Pendergast.

"Someday, you'll see I was right," she vowed.

She turned from the store with a flourish and a proud toss of the head, then stomped back across town to the school. There was no doubt that her situation was desperate, especially when she stepped inside her classroom and found it completely empty. What had happened to the children?

Not wanting to be held responsible for the disappearance of every child in Annsboro, she quickly ran back out, trying furiously to figure out where they had all gone. She had left Bea in charge, she reminded herself. If she was Bea, where would she hold class?

That was an easy one!

She fumed all the way back to Dolly's, up the stairs and into Pendergast's room, where the man was savoring his role of hero surrounded by adoring children, giving them a heartfelt dramatic reading from *The Gun-toting Peacemaker*. He looked up when she appeared in the doorway and flashed her a devilish grin.

"Something wrong, Cecilia?"

Chapter Eleven

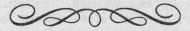

"I think our patient is fooling us," the old doctor said with a wink.

"I see." Rosalyn peeked through the doorway of her aunt's bedroom. Her aunt was intently focused on the conversation taking place in the hall concerning her "condition."

Dr. Fitzhugh patted Rosalyn gently on the shoulder, then let out a long hacking cough. The old man's health couldn't have been better than many of his patients'. "Sometimes unexpected events—like what happened to your poor brother, God bless him—can make people take to their beds without any symptoms."

"I see." Bad as the news about her brother had been, however, cagey Aunt Patrice hadn't taken to her bed until Rosalyn announced, days later, that she was thinking of going to Texas herself. She had only told her aunt that she merely wanted to see the place Gene was buried, but even so, the woman had collapsed in a weeks-long swoon. Rosalyn had spent the intervening time waiting on her aunt, ushering her aunt's many friends into her sickroom, and dashing out only occasionally to give lessons.

More than ever, Rosalyn feared she would be stuck in this rut forever—and never be able to find out what had happened to Eugene. Mr. Watkins had never written her back, and she was considering setting out on her own. She'd even pawned a ruby ring that had been her grandmother's to raise enough money for the journey so that she could leave whenever she wanted; the only thing stopping her was the niggling fear that she would be setting out on a fool's journey.

And, of course, her aunt. But now the doctor seemed to be telling her that Patrice was fine. "Are you sure that my aunt is quite well?" Rosalyn asked. "Her heart—"

The doctor's laugh was a sad wheezing sound. "I've known Patrice Pendergast since she was in short skirts, and believe you me, she has the constitution of an ox."

In as low a voice as could still be audible, Rosalyn asked, "Would she be able to stay by herself for a while?"

In the next room, her aunt launched into a suspiciously robust fit of coughing.

"Are you going somewhere, Rosalyn?" the doctor asked, surprised. And why shouldn't he be? She had never been anywhere in her life!

"Well, yes. To Texas," she explained, clearing her throat anxiously. "Just for a few weeks. Or a month or two." What was the use in lying? She stepped closer and said in a whisper, "Perhaps longer. It has to do with my brother." She looked toward her aunt's door and felt herself vacillating. "But I don't suppose I have to go at all . . ."

"Ah." Dr. Fitzhugh again wore his grave professional expression. "I should think your aunt would be absolutely fine. In fact, it would probably be good for her. If I know Patrice, without you here to wait on her, she would probably be out of bed like a shot to go calling on friends."

His words made Rosalyn feel infinitely better, yet she hesitated. This house had been her entire life; in a way, caring for her aunt's quirks and illnesses gave her a purpose in life. What would it be like to set out on her own, in a strange place? The prospect terrified her and excited her at the same time.

She was showing the doctor out just as the postman came by with a letter. She took the white envelope from him with a smile, then noticed her name written in an unfamiliar hand. Her heart leapt into her throat as soon as she saw the postmark—Abilene, Texas, which was also where Jake Reed had sent his correspondence from. This was the letter she'd been waiting for—it had to be!

"Not bad news?" the doctor asked, concerned.

"No," she assured him, though she felt no such confidence. She feared opening the letter and finding a note of condolence.

But once she got up to her room and read Chadwick Watkins's strange account of his recent visit to her brother, describing him as mysteriously "much changed," she felt, for the first time, trust in her instincts. Something horrible was going on in that little town called Annsboro, and more likely than not it involved Jake Reed.

Her journey to Texas couldn't be put off a moment longer.

The afternoon before the pageant, Dolly's house was bustling with activity as food was prepared and washing and ironing done. Cecilia was itching to get over to the schoolhouse to make last-minute preparations, but she'd promised Dolly she would help her get dressed.

Buck, Dolly had confided to Cecilia just this morning, had finally proposed.

Finally... after two measly weeks? And not only that, but Dolly hinted that they might not even wait through an engagement, but marry right away.

"Unbelievable!" Cecilia grumbled to herself as she hastily unpegged a chemise from the line and dropped it into the basket at her feet. Mr. Wiggles came up to sniff at the item she had tossed, and she shooed him away. Troublesome dog! He seemed unusually frisky today; Bea was probably too busy rehearsing her part to play with her dog.

Cecilia still had a million things to do. Dolly's dress, which hung on the line, needed to be ironed. She would have to be especially careful with it, given that Dolly considered

this a special night—the night her wedding would be announced. The bright white would show the slightest scorch
or stain, and Dolly would be sure to inspect the garment
carefully.

As soon as she could possibly dress, she would have to run
over to the school and give the children last-minute instructions. She was fairly certain Bea would do well, but those
older boys always made her nervous.

In the end, she would probably have no time for herself,
she thought with resigned self-pity. Her violet dress was laid
out on her bed in readiness, but there would be no time for
the leisurely bathing and preening she was used to before
parties. No, it would be rush, rush, rush—she would be
lucky if Dolly even took time out to lace her up.

Mr. Wiggles growled and Cecilia threw a glance his way.
What she saw made her eyes bug in horror. The dog, having decided that if Cecilia wouldn't rise to the bait, then the
clothesline made an adequate substitute for a playmate, had
his teeth firmly sunk into Dolly's white dress!

Cecilia gasped and stood rooted to the spot, her eyes
pinned on the frisky dog. When the hound shook his head
in mock play—as if to snap the dress in two—she knew she
had to take action. Slowly, she approached the dog, cooing
in a soothing voice. Thinking she was playing at stalking
him, Mr. Wiggles growled more menacingly.

Cecilia smiled anxiously. "There, there, Mr. Wiggles. You
don't want to eat that old dress, now do you?"

The dog bared his fangs, confirming that his incisors had
ripped two tooth-size holes in the fine white linen. Cecilia's
heart sank. She looked around for something to distract the
pooch, and quickly picked up a stick. Taking a gamble, she
waved it for a second, then tossed it beyond the clothesline.

Mr. Wiggles, his teeth still embedded in Dolly's dress,
hesitated, looking first at where the stick had landed, then
nervously at Cecilia poised to grab the dress once he had let
go of it. It was decision time, and his tail wagged anxiously. Finally, he compromised. With a mighty yank, he

pulled the dress from the line and went dashing after the stick, with Dolly's dress waving behind him like a battle flag.

But more than the visual display, Cecilia's attention was captured by the sound the fabric had made as the dog tore it from the line—the sound of two tiny holes becoming two great big undisguisable ones. She scampered after him, and when she was close enough, dived for the dress. Thus attacked, Mr. Wiggles mounted an aggressive defense and began tugging her toward the open fields.

"Let go, you mongrel!"

The dog growled ferociously as yet another few inches of Dolly's dress was lost.

"Cecilia! Cecilia!" The voice Cecilia most dreaded hearing shrieked at her from a second-story window. "What is that in his mouth?"

Cecilia gritted her teeth but tried to keep her voice chipper. "Don't worry about a thing, Dolly!"

Another voice joined in from the next window—a laughing, mocking voice. "Write to us when you get where you're going, Cecilia!"

Pendergast! It would just figure that man would have to be witnessing this latest indignity.

After a moment's scrutiny, Dolly finally sized up the situation completely. "Oh, my heavens!"

No, your dress, Cecilia thought in distress as her friend disappeared.

"Hold tight," Pendergast cried out, "sounds like help's on the way."

Wasn't he supposed to be sick? Cecilia thought in irritation. Since his return, Pendergast had been shut up tight in that room of his, coming out only recently for a few meals. He'd even refused to talk to the newspaperman Beasley brought in from Abilene. Everyone thought it was wonderful that their town boasted such a modest hero, and Beasley had naturally used the opportunity to tell the newspaperman more about himself and that drugstore. Cecilia felt like the only rational person in the world; she knew the man was hiding from something. But of course he *would* poke his head out of his shell just in time to catch her at her worst!

Oh, this was terrible. In a moment, Dolly would come running outside and discover that her beautiful white party dress was just a sad linen carcass of its former self. How would she ever set this to rights?

True, it wasn't entirely Cecilia's fault that Bea Beasley's dog ate the dratted dress. But she was sure Dolly would exact repayment... somehow. And it wasn't long before the price of her hapless laundering accident was made clear to her.

"You look beautiful, Dolly," Cecilia said a half hour later, trying to keep the despondency out of her voice.

Pirouetting in front of the standing mirror by her bed, Dolly inspected herself from all angles. Cecilia's violet dress, the only nice dress she possessed in town, perfectly set off Dolly's slim figure, and the bright color made her peachy complexion fairly glow. Normally Cecilia wouldn't have even minded making the loan, except...

What in heaven's name was *she* going to wear? "You're such a dear to offer it to me," Dolly said.

"Of course you should wear it," Cecilia said absently as she mentally tallied up the contents of her wardrobe. Work dresses, discolored and scorched by her own handiwork, made up most of her belongings. She had a yellow muslin summer dress, but it was years old and the wrong weight.

Cecilia suppressed the mighty sigh building within her breast. There was only one social event in Annsboro all year long, and she was going to arrive at it looking as plain as a stump.

Dolly twirled prettily. "Buck is sure to be impressed seeing me in this."

"I'm sure he will," she answered in a dejected monotone. This was supposed to be her big night to shine as the schoolteacher, and already she was off to a bad start. "I'd better get ready myself."

Before she could leave the room, Dolly caught her by the arm and singsonged conspiratorially, "I talked to a certain someone today who's very interested in dancing with you."

"Not Mr. Walters!" Cecilia cried. This was all she needed to hear. "That man can turn a girl's toes into bruised stumps faster—"

"Mr. Pendergast," Dolly corrected.

Cecilia's eyes flew open. "He's not supposed to be out wandering around yet!"

"I was there today when Dr. Parker pronounced him fit to work, and Mr. Pendergast asked him, 'But am I fit to waltz?'" Dolly giggled. "Isn't that sweet? I think he might like you!"

Cecilia gaped at Dolly—and managed to suppress the urge to rip her dress right off her friend's back. She had been avoiding that man as much as possible, which of course didn't necessarily mean that she had been successful in not thinking about him. The man had haunted her thoughts every waking moment. She'd been devoutly hoping not to see him at the pageant. Or the dance afterward.

In her room she brought out the yellow dress and set it in the place of honor across the bed, where the violet dress had lain, for inspection. Biting her lip, she tried to look at the situation objectively. Actually, nothing was terribly wrong with this dress. It simply lacked . . . sparkle.

The very idea made her scoff. What need did she have to sparkle, especially at a little school pageant? Pendergast immediately came to mind, but the thought that she should fall into a slump because she wouldn't be able to impress a desperado made her all the more determined not to care whether he looked twice at her. And she certainly didn't care if the man never asked her to dance.

But the tripping of her heartbeat made her admit—at least to herself—that all her suspicion and careful avoidance of the man had come to nothing.

As she peeled herself out of one dress and into another, she thought of how little she knew about Pendergast—little more, in fact, than she had known that first day Lysander Beasley had introduced him. The only difference now was that her heart flopped in her chest whenever she caught sight of that hard, dark gaze of his, and she found herself daydreaming of each and every time he had taken her into his arms, cataloging each sensory detail and guiltily hoping for another incident to add to her memory.

Each time she saw him, she felt more ridiculous for the tension that started building deep inside her as she looked into those eyes, or caught herself gazing at the broad expanse of his chest and at his strong arms.

Cecilia shivered. The truly terrible thing was, she craved having those arms around her yet again, no matter who he was.

Blankets and festive-colored tablecloths dotted the schoolyard, and on them women in their best Sunday dresses spread themselves and their picnic suppers around them to watch the pageant.

The show Cecilia had helped the children prepare was blessedly short. Four kerosene lanterns lit the schoolhouse steps, behind which was draped the banner of the burning White House. Beatrice Beasley, dressed in an empire-waisted gown, her hair done up in ringlets and dusted with twice-sifted cake flour, narrated the audience through the War of 1812 up to the moment when the redcoats burned Washington. The older boys, sporting red-dyed newspaper hats, relished their roles as the evil British, and nearly tripped Bea up by sneaking around behind her.

"You're not supposed to come out yet, Tommy!" Bea snapped at a tall blond-headed youth who was standing behind her with a lit match.

The audience laughed, momentarily flustering Bea.

"Go ahead, Tommy, the dang picture's been on fire for ten minutes now anyway!" a man in the audience yelled. Several others hooted their agreement. Most of the men were anxious to get this part of the evening over with so they could get down to the important business of drinking and dancing.

Lysander Beasley bustled to the head of the crowd. "Please, please," he entreated with an officious frown.

"Ahem!" Bea cleared her throat loudly and, with a backward scowl at a grinning Tommy, continued the story of chaos in the nation's capital.

When the redcoats finally did get their chance, they were met with exuberant boos and hisses. The boys came running out with crude torches, and the audience gasped in surprise. The redcoats circled around Bea several times, causing her to display some very true-to-life anxiety.

Cecilia watched nervously as the teenage boys pestered Bea. Bea had hated rehearsing this part and had insisted that the torches would completely overpower the show. But watching the rapt faces of her audience, even Bea had to admit that including the pyrotechnics had been a wise choice. In the waning light of evening, the kerosene lanterns and the torches lent the scene an eerie feeling of authenticity.

Then, suddenly, from somewhere in the audience, a cry went up. "Fire! The White House is on fire!"

Cecilia rolled her eyes. Of course it was—that was the whole point! When women started jumping to their feet in alarm, however, she looked over to the side and caught sight of the muslin in flames. "Water!" she cried to a handful of ranch hands next to the pump. "Get water over here!"

Their surprised eyes summed up the situation in a second and they snapped to action, manning the pump furiously to fill the two buckets available. Meanwhile, mothers ran to retrieve the children near the fire. Given the lack of rain they had suffered through for the past two months, the school building was doomed unless the flames could be doused quickly.

Cecilia, watching in horror as the White House went up in flames for real, grabbed Dolly's picnic blanket from the ground in front of her and started running forward. She heard her friend gasp as all her carefully prepared food and drink went flying, but she didn't stop to assess the damage. Holding the blanket as wide as she could manage, she dashed up the schoolhouse steps and started beating the blanket against the flames. Smoke billowed out toward her, and her lungs, unprepared for the assault, filled up quickly. She coughed and soon felt herself being dragged back by a pair of strong arms. Through watery eyes, she saw Pendergast's concern only fleetingly before he pushed her away.

"Do you want to get yourself killed?" he yelled at her. He took the blanket from her and dashed up the stairs.

"Do you?" she yelled back.

She ran forward again, this time aiming her shawl at the remaining embers. The thin material was completely insubstantial, but she just couldn't stand aside and do nothing! This schoolhouse meant as much to her, if not more, than to the children who received their lessons there every day. More, certainly, than it did to Pendergast.

He glanced over at her, his smoke-smudged face creased in annoyance. "Get back, Cecilia!"

"No!" she called.

Behind her, a man ran up and tossed a bucket of water onto the muslin—and her. She stood for a moment in shock, her bare arms streaked and dripping, then stepped away before the next cascade of water was aimed at the wall.

At the bottom of the steps, Pendergast smiled at her, his white teeth gleaming against his smoke-darkened skin. "I told you to step back."

Before Cecilia could spit out the retort on the tip of her tongue, Dolly hustled forward and pushed her aside. "Oh, Mr. Pendergast, how brave you are! You saved the schoolhouse!"

"Here, here," seconded Lysander Beasley, who stepped up to pat the man on the back. "Ladies and gentlemen, Eugene Pendergast has done it again!"

The audience, most of whom were still standing from all the excitement, applauded and cheered and whistled.

Pendergast had saved the schoolhouse? Cecilia thought heatedly. She glanced at the men who had quickly drawn the water to douse the flames—and even they were applauding the man.

"It's all right, folks," he said, taking over Cecilia's duties effortlessly. "Now that the fire's out, Beatrice will tell you how they took care of fires seventy years ago."

Beatrice, her ringlets looking slightly frazzled from the ordeal, which altogether had not lasted more than a couple of minutes, stepped up to her place with some trepidation. As her shaky voice continued the narrative, smaller boys, representing the beleaguered American forces, saved the day with pantomimed buckets of water.

"Careful you don't hit Cecilia with that water!" jeered Jim Brennan, one of the Summertree hands. He looked at Cecilia with mock surprise. "Oh, never mind—here she is!"

"Very funny," Cecilia muttered. Leave it to Pendergast to rouse himself from his sickbed to steal her thunder!

Behind Bea, girls in mobcaps helped put out the fake flames. The first mural was then pulled down, revealing the muslin rendering of the present-day White House. It was scorched, but otherwise surprisingly intact. The whole cast squished together on the steps to sing a patriotic song for their finale.

Much clapping ensued, and Bea descended to the kerosene footlights to take her bow. A smattering of the other girls and boys joined her, but most ran restlessly out to play a rowdy game of tag before being rounded up by their relatives to eat.

As Cecilia made her way through the crowd all the talk was about the fire. But in spite of that calamity—or more likely, because of it—several people were exclaiming that "Pendergast put on the best pageant ever!"

Back at the boardinghouse, she rifled through her remaining dresses in dismay. She could only thank heavens it was dark out; perhaps no one would notice that the cotton dress she picked out with the striped sleeves and skirt was practically threadbare.

She took off her yellow dress and went to the washbasin, which she had filled with water when she came in. No amount of scrubbing seemed to get the soot off her arms and neck—especially the smell. After ten minutes of trying, however, she dried herself and slipped the clean dress over her head.

At least the striped pattern and scooped neckline set off her figure, she thought as she started fastening the multitude of tiny pearl buttons up the front. Once that was done, she took a bottle of amber liquid from her washbasin table and dabbed the rose scent on her wrists. Still smelling smoke, she dashed some behind her ears for good measure.

The sound of old Charlie Moore's fiddle was already coming from the schoolhouse when she stepped outside again, and it was joined by Toby Clark's harmonica by the time she reached the clearing where the picnic baskets were being gathered up. Cecilia scurried toward Dolly and Buck, hoping to get a nibble of chicken. The request for food, however, was met by a sour purse from her friend.

"Chicken? Cecilia, all the chicken we had went flying when you grabbed up my blanket during the fire! Poor Buck said it looked as though I'd used sand for batter."

Buck frowned in greeting. "You sure weren't using your head when you went running headlong into that fire, Cecilia."

"My head just wasn't thinking about your stomach," she retorted more sharply than she'd intended. But honestly, it seemed, if men weren't in love with you, they could hardly spare a civil word! "Anyway, maybe I can get some grub off the men from the ranch."

Dolly laughed haughtily. "Those scroungers? I bet they've already picked every bone in the schoolyard."

Cecilia's stomach growled in protest. Wonderful. "Well, maybe I can rustle up a cup of water. That is, if everyone hasn't sucked the well dry."

She trudged off toward the well. It was dark, so she had to squint to see the faces belonging to the voices who called out greetings to her—and snide comments about getting drenched. No one was telling *her* that she had put on the best pageant ever!

The well was happily deserted, and Cecilia drew herself some water and looked out over the crowd. The kerosene lanterns that had provided illumination for the pageant were now doing duty in the clearing that had been designated as the dance floor. A few couples had already gathered in their light to twirl to a spirited waltz. In spite of herself, Cecilia tapped her foot and looked about anxiously for Pendergast, but the man had disappeared.

"So here you are!"

The deep voice caused Cecilia to choke on the swallow of water she was taking from the dipper. She turned, coughing, and looked squarely into the disapproving eyes of Silas Summertree.

"D-Daddy?" she said, trying to catch an even breath. She'd been so consumed in looking for Pendergast that she'd completely forgotten about her father, who had obviously just arrived.

Silas Summertree was not a towering man by any stretch of the imagination. The crown of his head only topped Cecilia's by a few inches, with one marked difference. Whereas Cecilia had a cascade of golden blond hair, Silas's head was as smooth as an eggshell. The most striking similarity between them was the brilliant blue eyes they shared, which so often mirrored each other in affection, irritation and stubbornness.

"Well, I'm glad to know you can still recognize your own father," he said gruffly. "I see you so seldom I thought you might have forgotten."

"Oh, for heaven's sake," Cecilia huffed, giving her father a quick hug. "I just couldn't get away."

"Humph." Silas scowled and reached into the breast pocket of his jacket for a cigar. "Couldn't, or wouldn't?" he asked, lighting a match and taking a tug on the tobacco.

The sweet scent never failed to remind Cecilia of home. She smiled warmly, feeling nostalgic. "*Couldn't.* Dolly needed me. Didn't Buck tell you?"

"Buck!" Her father barked out the name. "He hasn't talked about anything in weeks except for Mrs. Hudspeth. I promised them they could get married at the ranch Sunday."

"Sunday!" Cecilia cried in dismay. "That's so fast it's almost shameful!"

"Nothing shameful about getting married," he retorted brusquely. "You might ought to try it sometime."

Cecilia rolled her eyes. "And marry who? Mr. Walters?"

Her father stepped forward and wagged a finger in her face. "That's your problem—you're too picky!"

"Clara says you can't be too picky."

"That woman!" He rolled his eyes in frustration. "I left her at home, baking for the wedding."

"Clara hates things like this," Cecilia reminded him. "She thinks dancing is hazardous to people's good sense."

As if for the first time, her father looked her over from head to toe and frowned. "Good Lord, what are you wearing?"

"A dress," she replied.

"It's a mess!" he cried, appalled that his own daughter should be seen in such a rag.

Cecilia scowled at his unknowingly insulting her prowess with the wash.

"I think it's time you come back to the ranch," he said.

"Oh, no." Cecilia moaned.

"Now don't get up on your high horse, Cecilia. I had a friend over last week who owns a ranch outside San Antonio. Good-looking fellow. You could have some new clothes made up and—"

She clucked her tongue. "Daddy, you know how I feel about ranchers."

"Then why in thunder don't you find someone else to marry?"

"I told you, there *isn't* anybody."

His eyes opened, as if an idea occurred to him. "What about that new schoolteacher fellow? You must have seen him around here quite a bit."

"What about him?" Cecilia asked suspiciously. If Buck was shooting off his mouth at the ranch...

"I hear he's quite a good-looking fellow," her father expounded, "and a hero, to boot. Saved a whole wagonload of women from bandits." He craned his short neck to view the crowd. "What happened to all those Germans, anyway?"

"They went back to Fredericksburg." Thank goodness. Pendergast was hard enough to stomach without his own fawning throng.

"When I arrived here tonight I heard this schoolteacher fellow practically put out the fire by himself!" her father added.

"That's not true," she said. "*I* helped, too."

"Is that why you smell so peculiar!" her father cried in relief, but he was too involved in this new idea about the schoolteacher to concern himself with her reaction. "Seems like he'd be a smart fellow, too—just the type for you."

"Hardly," Cecilia said.

Her father perched on his toes and craned his neck to glance around the crowd. "Where is the man—what's his name, Pender... Pender..."

"Pendergast!" Cecilia said through clenched teeth.

"That's it! In fact, the more I hear about him, the more I like him." He stopped his search and glanced at her with interest. "This Pender-whoozit isn't why you haven't been home, is he?"

"No!" she cried emphatically. "Daddy, you don't know what you're saying. Pendergast isn't at all marriageable material. If you knew more about him—"

"About who?"

Together, she and her father turned toward the sound of the deep voice behind them. And there he was, Pendergast, grinning like mad. "Here we are at the well again," he joked.

Cecilia opened her mouth to make a tart reply, but before she could speak, he thrust his hand out toward her father. "You must be Silas Summertree. My name's Eugene Pendergast."

Her father, who was at least a head shorter, took his hand and shook it vigorously. "Well!" he said, impressed so far.

"You don't travel in this part of the country for long without hearing about the Summertree ranch," Pendergast said.

Silas Summertree ate up the shameless flattery and gave as good in return. "You've created quite a stir yourself in your short time here. Well, I was just telling my daughter here that you and she—"

"What are you doing here, Pendergast?" Cecilia interrupted before her father could embarrass her completely.

"Don't you remember?" he said, his eyes sparkling.

A waltz was playing in the distance. Cecilia stared at him for a moment, mesmerized by his gaze, tempted by the prospect of being swept up in his arms. God knows she wanted to...

"No," she lied, telling herself to have a little backbone.

"I told your daughter that I came all the way back to Annsboro just to dance with her, and now is the perfect opportunity."

Her father beamed with pleasure. "So that's it!" he exclaimed, turning a scolding voice on her. "You *have* been cultivating a little romance for yourself here in town."

"I have not!" Cecilia cried, horrified.

Pendergast winked at her. "Everyone's bound to find out sometime, sweetheart."

The blood drained from her face. Why was he saying these things in front of her father? She'd never hear the end of it!

Of course, maybe that's precisely why he was saying these things in front of her father....

"You're sick," she told him, "you can't dance."

He extended his hand for her to take, his eyes glistening challengingly. "Try me."

When Cecilia hesitated, Silas moved forward to join their hands together. "By all means, you young people go dance your hearts out."

"But—"

It was too late. Tugged toward the dance floor—dance dirt was a more apt description—by Pendergast, and pushed in the same direction by her father, Cecilia felt helpless against the forceful tide pulling her into the arms of this dark stranger.

Chapter Twelve

"Buttering up my father will get you nowhere," Cecilia said icily as she attempted to shuffle her feet to the tune being played. One firm hand held her waist, pulling her close to him. Too close. All this time she had been trying to avoid him, and now she was in his arms, with the approving gazes of her father and the whole town pinned on her.

Pendergast, his eyes almost a glistening black in the weak light, smiled down lazily at her. "But maybe it will convince you I'm not a complete villain."

She laughed bitingly. "Heavens, no. To everyone here you're practically a living legend."

"To everyone except you?"

"Except me," she agreed.

"What am I to you?"

"A headache."

"Maybe if you got to know me a little better, you'd change your opinion."

"Isn't bamboozling an entire town enough for you?" she asked impatiently. "Do you have to make a fool of me, too?"

"You're the one I care most about."

She sent him a cynical look. "Care most about getting out of your hair, you mean."

"I certainly couldn't get you out of my mind."

The way he was looking at her made her suspect that maybe he was telling the truth. Her heartbeat sped at a pace that was out of sync with the gentle refrain of the song. Did he really care for her, even after all she had done to sabotage him?

"And from what I've heard, you were having a hard time forgetting about me while I was gone."

That Dolly! "Of course I was—nobody would talk about anything else!"

He laughed lightly, and leaned closer to whisper, "Dolly insists you were pining."

She noted that his grip firmed so they were locked into a closer stance. "Pining!" she said, thinking for the first time that that was exactly the word for how she had felt. But it wouldn't do to let him know that. "In case you haven't noticed, I haven't darkened your door much lately."

"You've been avoiding me."

"That's right."

"Because you're afraid you care for me."

"That's ridiculous." She attempted to push away from the solid wall of his chest.

He held her tight, and a smile played across his lips. "Then why do you blush like crazy every time we look at each other across Dolly's table?"

"Who says I do?" Cecilia snapped.

"You're blushing now."

Lord help her, she was. This man had her all turned around. She knew he wasn't who he said he was, but the mystery of his identity just served to attract her to him all the more. She had tried to get rid of him, but that always backfired. Attempting not to think about him this past week had also failed. The only thing she'd been successful at was not letting herself be caught alone with the man—yet here she was, dancing way too close to him, in full view of everybody. And loving it....

Mostly. Suspicion was a hard thing to part with. "You accused me once before of falling in love with you."

"And you see, I was right."

She grunted in frustration as he twirled her in a tight little circle. "For a man who was at death's door just last week, you certainly are light on your feet."

"Thank you." He sent her a mock bow. "I owe my resiliency to you."

"To me?"

"Looking forward to this dance was the reason behind my speedy recovery."

"Lucky that masked man didn't shoot you in the foot."

"I would have found a way."

"Are you so determined to win me over?"

He bent closer. "Are you so determined to resist?"

"I...I—" Was she? Their faces were inches apart; with only the slightest of movements he could have captured her lips in a kiss. She half expected him to, but instead of trying again to push away, she waited expectantly, watching what he would do.

It felt as though time was suspended. If her feet were moving at all, she wasn't aware of it, and if the fiddle and mouth harp were playing, she didn't hear them. She couldn't tell whether every citizen in Annsboro was at this moment observing Pendergast seducing her right there in front of the schoolhouse, and witnessing that she didn't seem to mind his forwardness one tiny bit....

"I have an announcement to make!"

The loud voice of her father broke through the sensual fog in Cecilia's brain, and she turned her head to where he stood, not ten feet away. She attempted to pull away from Pendergast's grip, but he held her fast.

The crowd quieted for her father, and suddenly she noticed Dolly standing next to him, looking extremely pretty in Cecilia's dress, with Buck shuffling his feet behind her. "Now I'm sure you've all heard about the upcoming nuptials between Buck and Dolly," Summertree began.

"Dolly ain't exactly kept it a secret!"

Everyone laughed, especially when Dolly's cheeks turned bright pink.

"It's gonna take place day after tomorrow at the Summertree ranch, at two o'clock. Now I expect to see every face here tonight at the ranch on Sunday."

"Especially Buck's!" somebody yelled from the back of the crowd, and everyone laughed and clapped.

"Let's have a dance for Buck and Dolly!" Silas suggested.

Chin poised over his fiddle, Charlie looked at Toby, and by some silent arrangement, the two of them burst into a raucous reel.

Cecilia felt jolted by the change in tempo—she had expected another romantic song for the lovebirds, not the lively tune that sounded in her ears. She attempted to move, and realized Pendergast was still holding her as if they were dancing intimately and slow. She dared a glance into those eyes, and found herself being drawn once again into the desire she read in them.

"I'm afraid we're out of pace with the rest of the world," she told him, tugging to free her right hand, which was clasped within his rough larger one.

"Would you like to walk for a bit?"

The question tantalized her. She envisioned them, arm in arm, strolling down a field, maybe out by Dolly's house, just them and the stars and the moonlight. Perhaps they would stop, and he would take her in his arms, even closer than they were now, and he would finally kiss her again.

And if we were alone, I probably wouldn't have stopped with a kiss.

Mustering the strength of ten Cecilias, she freed herself from his embrace. "No," she said.

"Talk?"

Her face felt feverish, and now that she was on her own, her legs seemed as if they might not be able to hold her. She had to calm down, to think, to spend some time alone. Alone, by herself!

Unfortunately, this was not a night for solitude. She looked across the crowd, and her stomach grumbled, reminding her that she had missed most of the picnic grazing while changing her clothes. "I'm hungry," she told him.

His eyebrows lifted high into his forehead. "Hungry?" Apparently, food wasn't uppermost in his thoughts at the moment.

"Uh-huh." Suddenly, she thought of a way to finagle some time to herself to simmer down. "If you could manage to find something, I'm sure we could find a secluded spot to talk..."

A smile spread across his face. "One dinner, coming up." He sent her a little salute, spun and went off in search of eats.

For her part, Cecilia turned and sped quickly in the opposite direction. But she didn't make it far.

"Hey, Cecilia, long time no see!"

Jim Brennan, a rangy fellow with a shock of red hair who had been working for her father since Cecilia could remember, spotted her racing through the crowd. He captured her arm and swung her around in a playful jig. "You've become a regular city girl, Cici."

Cecilia laughed with the spry ranch hand, who she could tell was already lightly sauced. Just seeing him settled her thoughts as effectively as any lonely brooding would have. "I don't suppose Clara packed enough for leftovers, did she?"

"C'mon over. There's sure to be plenty of vittles wandering somewheres about. I guess Clara knew you'd be coming."

They ambled over to the center of a group of hands from the ranch. Cecilia had forgotten how she missed the camaraderie of the men who lived and worked on the ranch with her. The ragtag bunch of men, who were uncomfortable socializing anywhere outside of a campfire or Grady's saloon, clapped her on the back and greeted her with loud protests that she'd gone and gotten too big for her britches.

"And don't forget, I can still remember when you wore britches!" Abel Scott yelled over the other men.

Cecilia blushed. "Abe, you've been hitting the hooch, haven't you?"

He held up an unlabeled bottle of rotgut and smiled. "Want some?"

"Have you forgotten? I'm supposed to be a lady." She postured her body into an elegant, nose-upturned tableau for the men, who laughed appreciatively. It was a relief to be around people she could act silly with and not care, and a bigger relief to get her mind off Pendergast, though her eyes turned often to scan the crowd in search of him.

"What happened, Cici, did Buck throw you over for Dolly?"

Cecilia leaned against a tree and laughed lightly. This was one point on which she could honestly lose gracefully. "He threw me over, all right. Don't I look brokenhearted?"

Jim regarded her with a dead-on gaze. "Judging from what I saw of your dancing just now, I'd say you look like your heart's set on someone else entirely."

She immediately felt her skin redden in a telltale blush and pushed herself away from the tree. "Can't a girl go to a dance once a year and actually try to enjoy herself without people spreading rumors?"

Old Pitt Wilson spat out some tobacco juice and smiled broadly. "Last time I danced with a woman that close, we ended up married by the next afternoon.

"You're lucky Clara wasn't here to see you, Cici. She'd be all over you trying to find out something wrong with this new fellow you're in love with."

"I'm not in love with him," Cecilia said. A few men laughed chidingly, which only made her flush all the more. "I'm not," she insisted.

"She might be telling the truth," Hank guessed. "I only saw the schoolteacher making googly eyes at her. Could be that he's the one in love!"

"Some man in love!" Cecilia said with a scoff. "He said he'd get me something to eat, but he's certainly taking his time."

"Probably because he's in a daze," Pitt conjectured. "I reckon you probably didn't notice, Cici, seeing's how you was so busy trying not to look lovesick, but that fiddler wasn't playing a waltz."

The men cracked up all over again, and Cecilia folded her arms across her chest, quickly tiring of all the ribbing. So much for camaraderie, she thought. So much for settling her conflicting thoughts. "Don't you all have anything better to do than poke fun at people's dancing?"

"Heck, no, that's what we come here for!"

Other men cackled in assent. But if they truly came for the dramatics—official and otherwise—their evening hadn't even begun to warm up yet. When Cecilia turned casually to look for Pendergast, she saw him coming toward her ... on the heels of her father.

Her very angry-looking father. "Cecilia Summertree, you've got some explaining to do!"

Behind him, Pendergast, holding up a piece of chocolate cake in one hand, shrugged innocently as if he had absolutely no idea what her father was so worked up about. But Cecilia was skeptical. The man must have done something to make her father this furious.

"What is it?" she asked in a soothing voice, taking her father's arm.

He shrugged away and bobbed on his toes, his arms akimbo. "Don't play the innocent with me, Cecilia. I know all about what you've been up to!"

Suddenly, Cecilia felt very alone. Pendergast, no matter how he'd instigated all of this, was shut out of the argument now by her father's turned back. And the semicircle of men from the ranch, knowing the temper of Silas Summertree all too well, backed in unison until they were a safe distance away.

Cecilia sighed to herself as she stood nose to nose with him. "What did I do this time?"

"You've shamed yourself, and me, for the last time!"

Having Pendergast see her father upbraid her this way was too humiliating. "Daddy, please keep your voice down."

Using a slightly lower tone, he wagged a finger in her face and raged, "I knew better than to let you out on your own again, after New Orleans. And your aunts in Memphis warned me that you would seek out any kind of trouble that didn't come to you first."

Cecilia couldn't help glancing at Pendergast. His eyes were cast down, staring intently at the icing on the chocolate cake he'd brought. She smirked. Secretly, he was savoring every moment.

"But never in my life," Silas continued, "*never* would I have thought you would pull a stunt like this."

"Oh, for heaven's sake!" Cecilia huffed, anxious to get this battle over with. "What have I done now?"

Her father lifted his chin imperiously. "You have shamed the family name!"

Cecilia rolled her eyes in exasperation. "Again? How?"

"I've just heard that you've been working at Dolly's."

Was that all? After the big buildup, she'd been expecting something much worse.

Her gaze darted toward Pendergast again. He shuffled his foot in the dirt—a sure sign of culpability. "What if I have?"

Her father colored a fresh shade of crimson and fairly shook with rage. "I'll tell you what! No daughter of mine is going to run around town working like a mule—"

"You always said work was good," Cecilia protested.

"*Ladies'* work!" he yelled. "I didn't send you to a finishing school in New Orleans so you could come back and do people's wash!"

"I'd think you'd be proud that I was earning my keep."

"There are plenty of things to do around the ranch," her father said, "as you'll have ample opportunity to find out."

The blood drained from her face. That was her worst nightmare. The ranch was nearly an hour's ride from town. What would she do there, and how would she ever get her job back? Worse, she would never see Dolly or Pendergast or—

She looked up at Pendergast as understanding began to dawn. Pendergast. She'd told him that buttering up her father would do no good—but oh, it obviously had! He'd led her on just until he'd had the opportunity to talk to him. What a little idiot she'd been!

And what a patient schemer he was. Right up until the moment they'd been dancing, he had probably been trying to gauge what the quickest way to get her out of town was. Instead of food, he'd probably set off immediately in search of her father. And she'd been mooning around like a lovesick puppy—just like Jim, Pitt and all the others said!

The humiliation of it all almost made her want to give up the fight. Almost.

"I can't go back to the ranch," she said, more to Pendergast actually than to her father.

Nevertheless, it was her father who answered. "Yes, you can. Tomorrow I'll send Buck to town to pick you up, and you will come back to the ranch, for good."

It was like a death sentence. And Pendergast was still standing mutely behind her father, the smug executioner.

Suddenly her anger was at a boiling point. "All right, Father, since I don't have a choice." She couldn't blame her father too much, since she'd known all along he'd be furious if he found out the circumstances under which she'd been staying in town. She stepped past him and narrowed her eyes angrily at Pendergast, a worthier target for her wrath. "Don't think I'll forget this. Or forgive. Ever."

Pendergast's eyes widened, confused. "You don't think I..." He shrugged haplessly and attempted a smile. "I just brought you a piece of cake." He held out the chocolate wedge as though it would solve all her problems.

But the last thing Cecilia wanted was a peace offering from this man, this snake who had been using her, duping her. She looked at the mouth-watering cake again and became even angrier when she felt her stomach rumble. Putting her heart's need for revenge over her stomach, she snatched the napkin and cake out of Pendergast's hand.

"Maybe it will make you feel better," he said in a lame attempt to soothe her temper.

Her eyes glistened. "I know exactly what will make me feel better, Pendergast."

He raised his eyebrows with interest, but curiosity turned to panic in his eyes as he watched the cake arc its way through the air. With the giddy energy of someone who knows she's making a scene but is beyond caring, Cecilia aimed straight at the bridge of his nose and smiled joyfully as the cake hit its target with a satisfying *splat*. Pendergast stepped back, wiping the hard sugary icing from his face with the backs of his hands.

When he blinked at her in surprise, the whites of his eyes shone through the icing like a second-rate actor's in a minstrel show. Cecilia almost laughed. Almost.

"Don't you dare double-cross me again, Pendergast," she warned. "Don't even cross my path, do you understand? I never want to see you, ever!"

Jake decided a quick stop by the water pump was in order to wash up. Luckily, the clearing was empty of people, so no one was there to remark on the cake he'd gotten in the kisser.

As he left the lights of the party behind, his legs fell into a faster walk, and then a run. He wasn't certain what had gotten her so riled up, but he couldn't allow Cecilia to leave town thinking the worst of him.

This crazy mix-up would have to happen just when things were going so well between them!

The house was dark when he trotted up the porch steps; from the tiny entrance hall he could just see a glow of light

coming from Cecilia's little room behind the kitchen. Like
a moth, he swerved through the darkened rooms toward that
light, taking note of the hodgepodge of sounds he heard.
Bangs. Curses. Sniffles.

He slowed as he approached her open doorway. Inside the
tiny room, which was lit only by one flickering tallow candle, Cecilia had been throwing all her worldly goods into the
tiny valise that rested on her bed. Her eyes were red, her
cheeks tearstained. She wasn't one to suffer in silence, either. As his frame filled up the doorway, she let out a last
muttered curse.

"Damn." Without having to look up, Cecilia knew Pendergast was there. She sank down next to her travel bag,
about as close as she'd ever come to feeling utterly de-
feated. "Why'd you have to follow me?" she asked petulantly.

"Why did you run away?"

"You know why!"

Jake stepped carefully toward the bed. "If you think I
had anything to do with whatever angered your father,
you're wrong."

"Ha!" Cecilia snapped. "You started planning the day
you blew into town. For weeks you've been sweet-talking
me, haven't you, just so you could get me where you
wanted—on a ranch twenty miles away!"

He had suspected she thought something along these
lines, and given the messed-up way they had gone about
getting to know one another, he was hardly surprised that
she would be suspicious of him. Tonight, however, as they
danced, he had begun to hope they had moved beyond that.
She could have at least given him the benefit of a doubt.

"Is that really what you think? That all along I've just
been trying to get rid of you?"

"Think?" Cecilia scoffed. "I know!" She'd had the same
objective in mind for him!

Pendergast stepped forward, clamped his hands on to
both her arms and pulled her to her feet. There wasn't much

space to maneuver in the little room—just a couple of feet between the bed and the washbasin—and Cecilia found herself smack up against his chest. Releasing his hold only enough that he could tilt her chin up with one hand, he looked into her eyes. His coal dark gaze was intense.

"Why would I want to do that?" Jake asked, his voice dropping low. His lightly stubbled jaw worked from side to side with tension. For the first time, he wished he was truly Uncle Thelmer, who would have known exactly what to say to a woman. He searched for pretty words that would win Cecilia over without putting his pride on the line, but none came to him.

She smirked as another tear welled precariously in the corner of one eye. "That's an easy one. Ever since you came here, I've been nothing but trouble for you."

"You've troubled me, all right." He pulled her closer still, until he could smell the sweet scent of her hair. "You've deviled my thoughts, day and night. When I left, I felt you tugging me back the whole time."

The space between them seemed to disappear without either of them moving a muscle. Cecilia's breath caught in her throat. What magic had closed the distance? Not quite able to trust this sudden change in her adversary, she pulled back but remained locked fast in his arms. In defiance of his superior strength, she turned her profile to him.

"How can I trust you?" she asked.

A shudder rippled through her body when she felt a soft husky whisper in her ear. "The same way I know I can trust you, even though you've had me figured out for weeks now."

Her head snapped back and beheld mischief mixed with desire dancing in his eyes. He was admitting he wasn't who he said he was! As her eyes focused in on his, her hands held fast to his strong shoulders. "You're wrong. I don't know who you are at all."

The words, every syllable laced with wonder, shocked her even as they issued from her lips; shocked her because she had to confess that though she knew very little about this man, his presence had shaken the very foundation of her world.

"Don't you?" he countered, his head dipping down to impart little nips to her neck.

Her nails dug into the crisp ironed fabric of his shirt. "I don't know your name, Pendergast."

His throat emitted a chuckle and his hands moved down to encircle her waist. "You just said it."

Cecilia clutched to the last shreds of her skepticism. "Your *real* name," she said. As he bent lower to kiss the little valley where her collarbone dipped down, her head lolled backward. His lips were doing powerful things to her, and she strained to keep a grip on her sanity. "And I don't know where you came from...." She gasped as she felt the topmost button of her dress pop loose from its confinement. Swallowing hard against the parched feeling in her throat, she continued, "I don't know what you do...."

Except that he was doing wonderful things to her now. One by one the little round buttons came undone and the skin below was thoroughly lathed and tended. The tedious job of fastening those buttons always took aeons; never in her wildest dreams had she imagined that unfastening them could be such a pleasurable task. Her hands moved from his shoulders, roving over the short cropped hair at the nape of his neck. She tried in vain to steady the uneven tripping of her heart.

Jake nuzzled against the ridge of her camisole. Leaving Cecilia standing, he swung around to sit on the edge of her bed, his eyes remaining at eye level with the soft swells of her breasts. When he looked up into her face, the blue pools of her eyes were shimmering with new depths of emotion, and the desire he saw there made him find words, ones that came from the depths of his soul.

"I think you do know me, Cecilia," he said, his voice a rasp. "Same as I know you."

She shook her head, but there was a glint of understanding in her expression.

"You know that I've fallen for you when every gut instinct told me you were trouble," he insisted. "Isn't that how you feel?" He pushed the top of her camisole aside and traced the ridge of her breast.

She let out a soft moan and her fingers played through his hair. The feel of her hands nearly drove him wild. "Yes, you're trouble," she said, her voice surprisingly low and raspy. "You're a liar."

"You're beautiful," he whispered.

"You're low-down and mean." She leaned forward and rubbed her lips across his temple. "You have a wicked sense of humor."

He grinned. "You make me want to do wicked things."

Cecilia shook her head. He was shrugging off every doubt she had about him as if none of them mattered, and as he traced a pathway over the center of her stomach through her sheer undergarments, she began to ignore her doubts about that, as well. He was right; against all her better instincts, she wanted him. Only...

She licked her dry lips. "I know I shouldn't trust you. You told my father—"

"Cecilia," he interrupted in a whisper, dragging her onto his lap. His mouth once again caressed the tender skin of her neck. "Why would I want your father to take away the person I care most about having near me?"

For a long, agonizing moment, their gazes met and held. He cared for her... the words, spoken in such hushed reverence, repeated again and again in her mind, and created a combination of joy and fear and desire inside her that she had never experienced before. A heat from deep inside her started radiating outward until she felt as though every inch of her skin was on fire.

He cared for her....

"Pendergast." The only name she knew him by came unbidden to her tongue, and when he looked up, she smiled in affirmation. "I didn't want to leave you," she admitted. "That's why I was crying."

She was crying now, Jake realized, and he kissed the stray tear away. She turned her head toward him and their lips met in an explosion of feeling. Cecilia opened her mouth to his, and their tongues intertwined with pent-up relish. Within moments, the camisole was unlaced, the corset beneath unhooked and pushed away. Freed, Cecilia arched needfully against Pendergast—although needing just what, she wasn't sure. When she found herself lying halfway beneath him on the mattress, however, she welcomed the weight against her lower body.

Suddenly, she wanted to touch him as he was touching her. Her hands moved boldly to unbutton his shirt, though anxious fingers trembled as they worked, revealing a solid muscled chest liberally dusted with dark hair. Candlelight danced across the bronzed skin, and she angled her head to discover the taste and texture of him. His hands skimmed down her back as she explored, pushing her clothes away until she was completely exposed from the waist up. And with little effort and less resistance from her, he began doing away with the rest of her garments, as well....

"You're beautiful," he said, his voice a deep caress as he gazed at her naked body. Cecilia was speechless, but felt none of the shame she suspected she should feel. She was too overwhelmed with longing to care about modesty.

She reached up her arms to encircle his neck and brought his head down to hers. As they kissed, she experimented moving against him, tentatively at first, and then more aggressively. Her hands skimmed the firm corded tendons in his neck, the broad musculature of his shoulders and chest, tapering down to the jagged violence of his gunshot wound's scar. White heat built up in her core until it was almost painful; she longed for friction, for release, and her hands traveled down his body in search of both. They got as far as Pendergast's belt buckle when suddenly he groaned.

"Cecilia, you don't..." Jake gritted his teeth as he felt the last of his restraint slipping away. "I want you. Do you understand?"

She nodded and hugged herself tightly against his chest. "Oh, yes... I need you."

Control snapped as the words he'd longed to hear reached his ears. Leaving Cecilia only long enough to dispose of his clothes and boots, he returned to her feeling more aroused than he could ever remember. And yet he knew that for Cecilia's sake, he needed to go slow. He eased his body on top of hers gingerly, and the feel of her soft skin came close to driving him mad, especially when she arched against him, testing.

Cecilia gasped as she felt the evidence of his arousal brush against her thigh, and her eyes flew open and met his reassuring gaze. "Trust me," he whispered, his husky voice underscored with an urgency that made her blush. It was the same urgency she herself felt.

Trust me....

She swallowed hard, knowing they were both on the brink of something irrevocable. Her whole body ached with need, but still she knew what he meant. He wouldn't blame her for turning away from him, painful though it would be. Pendergast was still a mystery to her, as were the intimacies between men and women, yet she realized she had never wanted anything as forcefully and deeply as she wanted him now. Maybe she never would.

She looked into his eyes again, strange and dark in the flickering candlelight, and saw longing and tenderness mixed in equal parts. She had only to say the words, or to say no.

Cecilia hesitated only long enough to lift her lips to his for a brief kiss.

"I trust you," she whispered, surrendering herself to his embrace.

Chapter Thirteen

Cecilia's eyes blinked open and she quickly assessed her surroundings. The faint noise she heard outside was coming from the schoolhouse. The party hadn't broken up yet. The candle had flickered out, probably from a cold breeze coming through her window, which would explain the inky blackness of the room, now lit only by what moonlight filtered through her flimsy curtains. And the two-hundred-pound weight on top of her...

That was Pendergast!

She listened to his soft snoring and felt herself blush to the tips of her toes. Starting from his head, which was cradled in the crook of her shoulder, Pendergast was completely sprawled over her like the world's heaviest, sweatiest coverlet; there hardly seemed a square inch of her that wasn't touching his bare skin. But then, there wasn't a square inch of her that this man hadn't felt, tasted or, at the very least, thoroughly inspected.

Mortified. She was completely mortified.

Vague snatches from the evening came to mind—the fire, the dance, her fight with her father. But what happened after Pendergast came into her bedroom was all crystal clear in her mind, and very specific. Every moan, every touch, the sharp stab of pain and the flood tide of sweeter feeling that came afterward—these things she would never forget. Not if she lived to be as old as Fanny Baker's grandmother.

Pendergast sighed softly in his sleep, and his lips curved up in a lazy, satisfied little smile. Cecilia forced her entire body to be still, which wasn't hard, since most of her circulation had been cut off anyway. She didn't want to face Pendergast just yet—or ever, for that matter. Unfortunately, extricating herself without waking him might be a tad difficult.

She stared out her tiny window, her mind working fast. What was she going to do? What would she say? She'd never felt so ashamed of herself! Pendergast had said only that he cared for her, and she had lapped up those paltry words like a starving kitten being offered a saucer of cream, without even stopping to examine her feelings on the matter for more than a few seconds. After all, having built up silly fantasies about a mysterious stranger was one thing. Waking up with the deadweight of a possible desperado on her chest was quite another.

Where was he from? What if he truly was some sort of desperate character—a murderer, even! What did that make her?

Good lord, she had entered this room as innocent as a lamb, and now she was no better than a murderer's floozy!

She didn't bother to keep her voice down. "Pendergast, wake up!" She punched him on the arm.

With a catlike swiftness that scared the hell out of her—and heightened her worst fear—Pendergast raised up on his elbows and sent her a razor-sharp glance. He was instantly alert, as though he was accustomed to watching his back. Cecilia's stomach clenched with dread.

"Who are you, Pendergast?"

He stared at her for a moment suspiciously, then let out a relieved rush of breath and collapsed against her again. "Oh, it's just you."

Just her? Very nice. Tender.

She slapped him. "Get off of me, you big galoot! Do you think I'm made of granite?"

He nuzzled his head against her chest and let out something between a groan and a purr. "Mmm...not at all, sweetheart."

When his lips made contact with a tight bud of sensitive pink flesh, the resulting sensation was like a warning bell clanging through her system. With every ounce of strength she had, she pushed against his chest with all her might until they were both sitting up on the bed facing each other in shocked silence.

Finally, his lips tilted up in a grin. "You're full of surprises."

She let out a mirthless laugh as she lifted a sheet to cover her nakedness. "I'm not interested in surprises anymore, Pendergast. I want to know who you are."

Jake thought quickly, but his mind was still fuzzy in the aftermath of their lovemaking. In the few minutes he had dozed off, Cecilia seemed to have worked herself up into a lather. He wanted nothing more than to pull her back down onto the mattress for a leisurely encore, but that apparently wasn't going to happen. Instead, she was looking for answers—ones he wasn't sure she was in a state to receive with good grace.

A sudden wave of guilt struck him with the force of a blow. He had asked her to trust him, and she had—but now he realized he had done nothing to earn her trust. Nothing at all. He had come to her, a jumble of half-truths and partial lies, and she had accepted him. The realization was humbling. What would she think now if he confessed he was a man on the run, an impostor who wasn't above using a dead man's identity?

That she would scamper directly to her daddy and Lysander Beasley was a distinct possibility, but that alone didn't keep him from blurting out the truth. There was also the fact that she would simply reject him, Jake Reed, man of little mystery and many faults.

"Who are you?" Cecilia repeated, her voice growing more urgent. "I want your name, Pendergast."

That much, he could tell her. "It's not Pendergast. It's Reed. Jake Reed."

"Jake Reed?" She looked as if she wouldn't have been any more surprised if he had said he was Grover Cleveland. "What kind of a name is that!"

To say she didn't sound impressed was putting it mildly. "Just mine."

"Jake Reed," she said again, then she looked into his eyes for confirmation. "Jacob?"

He nodded. Somehow, just telling her his real name made him feel more naked than the fact that he wasn't wearing a stitch.

Back on that wagon to Fredericksburg he had thought he'd realized that something was more important than getting even with Gunter and Darby, and maybe that was so. But seeing Cecilia now, looking at him with all her trust and vulnerability, Jake knew that while they were still out there—and if Gunter recognized him they might still be hunting him even now—he had no right to involve her in his life.

Too late, he said to himself with scorn. But it wasn't too late to shield her from the whole ugly story. Or to keep himself from making promises he might not be able to follow through on.

"Are you a teacher?"

"I can't say," Jake admitted reluctantly.

"I know you're not from Philadelphia. Where are you from?"

He met her eyes, then looked away and shrugged noncommittally. "Around."

Cecilia blew out a frustrated breath. After a moment of silence, she asked, "Did you kill a man?"

Jake leveled an even stare at her. "No," he said. *But that doesn't mean I'm not planning on it.* Seeing the hurt look in her beautiful blue eyes, he wanted to tell her the truth, but he couldn't bring himself to do it. She wanted him to be a different kind of man than who he was; and who he was was a man still in a heap of trouble.

"What happened to the real Pendergast?" she asked.

"I told you, Cecilia, I'm not a murderer." He lifted a brow at her. "Is there anything else you'd like to know?"

Anything else? She still felt she had so many questions rattling around in her head she couldn't possibly ask them all in one evening. "Tomorrow I'm going back to my father's ranch. When will I see you?"

He felt an ache deep in his chest, and it wasn't from a gunshot. "I'm not sure." If he left tomorrow, he might could be back by the middle of the next week. But that was only if luck was on his side. If things didn't work out his way, he might never be back. He might never see Cecilia again.

"You'll come to Dolly's wedding on Sunday," she said.

Jake looked into her heartbreaking blue eyes. Lord, what had he done?

"Surely, you will," she repeated.

He doubted it was physically possible to make it down to Darby's ranch and back again by Sunday, even if he left right now. Even if he was a bird and could fly the whole way.

Disappointment registered in Cecilia's eyes. Disappointment, and a hint of regret. He would say anything to get that look off her face. "I'll be there." He would find a way to buy a horse tomorrow, he thought, justifying his stay to himself. He wasn't going to put his faith in another wagon.

Tentatively, she smiled, then looked around the room. "It won't be like this," she said. "I mean, there will be lots of people around. But we could dance again."

That was good enough for him. It would have to be. "Sounds like heaven."

There was a pause, and Cecilia sent him a nervous glance. "So when are you going to tell me this big secret you're carrying around?"

Trying to change the mood in the little room, Jake reached down to the floor, picked up his pants and started to pull them on. One or the other of them needed to get back to that schoolhouse, or Cecilia's father might not let him live to see Sunday.

"I can promise you one thing," he said.

Her expression sharpened to acute interest. "What?"

"When the time's right, you'll be the first person I'll tell."

Not knowing who he was right now was obviously about to drive Cecilia mad. "I can't wait that long!" she cried. "How can I go back to the ranch not knowing who you are, or whether..." Her voice broke off.

Jake's heart felt as though it had flipped over in his chest. She was worried this all meant nothing to him. It might have helped if he could have told her how long it had been since he'd felt anything for a woman, apart from the kind of lust that could be satisfied as easily as thirst could be quenched, but he couldn't.

Instead, he reached over and chucked her under the chin. She shot him a look that was half resentment, half reluctantly lovelorn. "I'll be there Sunday, Cecilia. I promise you that."

Clara clucked her tongue mournfully as she stuck another pin into Dolly's wedding dress. "This is bad business," she muttered. The diminutive woman hadn't stopped shaking her head for two days straight, ever since she had heard Buck had found himself a bride. "Bad."

"Ouch!" Dolly cried as one of Clara's hemming weapons grazed her.

Cecilia gazed at the elaborate dress of creamy silk almost without seeing it at all. So far, she'd managed to smile and nod and mumble appropriate words to describe the bridal gown, but now that Dolly was actually in the thing, she felt as if her mind was miles away.

Or maybe she'd simply lost her mind altogether. What else could explain the horrible, horrible thing she had done?

Jake Reed! She repeated the name to herself for the millionth time in one day, as if that would give her a better idea of who he was, or whether he was lying when he promised to see her again. Oh, she was a fool to believe anything he said. For all she knew, the man wasn't even in Annsboro now; he'd sneaked off once before without a word. And what could be the nature of his "personal business" in Fredericksburg?

Since Friday night, her emotions had been so erratic she felt dizzy from all their highs and lows. One minute she was dreaming up all sorts of wonderful possibilities concerning the man's identity. Was he wealthy—an eccentric millionaire playing at being a schoolteacher? That fanciful notion had lasted for all of two minutes. Regardless of what rosy scenario she dreamed up, the next moment she would be convinced that the man was simply what she had suspected right along, and that he had used her, and now that she'd given him what he wanted he was going to discard her, which made her seethe with anger and humiliation.

If only she'd listened to Clara's warnings!

"Well, what do you think?" Dolly asked when Clara finished pinning and buttoning. With the wedding less than twelve hours away, Dolly wanted to make sure her old dress still fit her as it had when she was eighteen.

Cecilia stuffed one of the cookies she'd stolen from the larder into her mouth. Good food always raised her spirits, especially when it was supposed to be off-limits. "Beautiful," she declared, swallowing a sand tart.

Dolly blushed. "Do you really think Buck won't mind that I'm reusing this dress?"

Though it crossed her mind to tell Dolly that Buck probably wouldn't give two hoots what she wore as long as she said "I do," Cecilia decided this might not be too flattering. She shook her head.

"It would seem a waste not to wear it," Dolly said, "since it still fits. And it's hardly yellowed a bit."

Fortunately, Clara made a last-ditch attempt to compensate for Cecilia's lack of enthusiasm. The short, stout woman stepped back to assess her handiwork, straight pins sticking out of her tight raven black bun. With hands on her hips, she declared, "It's going to be the most beautiful dress Annsboro's ever seen! Again!" In the silence that followed, she delivered a scowl to Cecilia.

Cecilia sat up straighter and tried to get into the spirit of things. But she felt so gloomy and alone; she couldn't talk with Dolly about what she'd done, and she absolutely couldn't mention her indiscretion to Clara, who had raised her on stories of fallen women and disastrous marriages that had been "forced."

A mental image of her father poking his old Confederate carbine into Pendergast's back popped into her head, but that scenario was too humiliating to endure.

She tried again to focus on the dress. "Buck won't think a thing except that you look lovely," she said. Dolly was extremely pretty in the old-fashioned gown with its fitted bodice and wide skirt. The sleeves were tight and the neck dipped into a demure V. But more than the finery made Dolly glow with beauty. Her friend radiated happiness, which was the exact opposite of how Cecilia felt.

She popped another sand tart into her mouth and chewed glumly.

"Cici, wipe those crumbs from your mouth and stop stealing the wedding food!" Clara scolded. The robust woman scurried over and took control of the plate Cecilia had secreted away from the pantry. "You're going to get as fat as a pregnant woman!"

Heat suffused Cecilia's cheeks. A flash of memory—one of heat and bare skin and the sweet smell of sweat—overtook her. Her stomach clenched. This was a possibility she'd been trying to keep at bay ever since Friday night.

"I was just hungry," she said defensively. Oh, she had been a fool. What would happen if she never saw this Jake

Reed character again? What if she was carrying an outlaw's child?

Clara nodded curtly. "That's what happens when you push your dinner around your plate instead of eating it."

True, Cecilia hadn't had much of an appetite lately. Everything, even food, was a distraction from the activity she was most interested in—brooding.

"I know a secret," Dolly said, looking furtively at Cecilia, then winking a Clara.

Cecilia leaned forward in her chair, her stomach turning with dread. Could Dolly possibly have figured it out—or worse, did everyone know? Maybe they could tell just by looking at her. Clara had always said you could tell fancy women by the way they walked—did that go for her now, too? Beads of sweat popped out on her brow and she automatically reached for the plate of cookies that was no longer there.

"What do you know?" she asked.

"Cecilia's in love," Dolly announced to Clara.

Cecilia let the word sink in, then sank back in her chair with relief.

"With who?" Clara asked, her eagle eyes examining Cecilia for signs. "That teacher fellow?"

"Mr. Pendergast."

"I am not in love with Eugene Pendergast." That, at least, was one thing she could be sure of.

"She used to hate him," Dolly said. "But he's been smitten with her since he first came to town. I could tell right away they were bound to be a couple. He couldn't keep his eyes off of her."

"He was just nervous because he knew I could see through him."

"Oh, Cecilia," Dolly chided, "are you still plucking on that same old string?"

"It's true!"

"Love and hate," Clara said, the very idea sending her into another bout of tongue clucking, "they're just different sides of the same wooden nickel. The coin is still worth-less."

"I don't even care if I never see him again." Which was a distinct possibility. Sure, he'd promised to see her tomor-row, but how could she take the word of a man who wouldn't even tell her what he did for a living?

Dolly and Clara shook their heads, bestowing looks of loving pity on her. "How many times did I say that about my poor dear Buck?" Dolly asked wistfully. "And now look at me."

She smiled a blushing, new-bride smile, as if she had achieved the woman's dream.

A knock sounded at the door just before Silas Summer-tree's head peeked into the room. "Well," he said, beam-ing paternally, "don't you look beautiful!"

Dolly preened with delight. "Thank you. I hope Buck thinks so."

Cecilia let out an impatient sigh.

"What's the matter, Cecilia," her father joked, "are you jealous of your friend?"

"Oh, for heaven's sake!" she exclaimed, almost at the end of her rope.

"I'll bet Cecilia's beau proposes any day now," Dolly as-sured the father.

Cecilia bit her tongue. If these people knew the truth—what kind of man Jake Reed was and how he had treated her—they would be apoplectic.

"So the schoolteacher is the one who's finally captured my little girl's heart!" he exclaimed, his voice booming.

Cecilia cringed. "We know nothing about him!"

Silas chuckled. "Nothing except he's brought a bloom to your cheeks."

Was the man insane? She'd been bleary-eyed and pale from sleeplessness for days! And since she'd come back, she was cross and weepy by turns. The only thing she did with gusto was work, because it helped to have something to fo-cus on to pass away the miserable days.

And since when did her father care about blooming cheeks? "I thought you cared more about his income than whether I was blooming or not."

His smile faded without disappearing completely. "What did I do to raise such a pretty little cynic?" he asked. "Of course I care about his situation, but he seems a fine upstanding fellow."

"A hero," Dolly chimed.

Cecilia frowned. "I bet we never see him again."

The three faces stared at her in astonishment. Too late, she realized her slip of the tongue.

"Why not?" Silas asked. "He's still the schoolteacher, isn't he?"

"Didn't he say he would come to my wedding?" Dolly demanded, appalled by the possibility that someone might not attend.

"Well, of course he *said* he would come."

Clara's eyes narrowed on her. "Did you have a lovers' quarrel?"

"We are not lovers!" she squealed.

The three of them laughed. "He'll be here," Dolly said. "I'll bet coming to my wedding puts ideas into his head."

"Perhaps we'll hear wedding bells twice before the year is out," her father conjectured happily. "As long as you don't smash another cake in his face."

"Pendergast? Never heard of him."

Rosalyn sighed heavily as the man across from her hid himself once again behind his newspaper. She was just outside Abilene, her last stop, and no one on her whole journey had heard of either Eugene or Jake Reed by name. Surprisingly, a few people had mentioned hearing of Annsboro's schoolteacher—but the heroic deed they described in connection with this man hardly seemed something her brother would be capable of. Not that he wasn't brave, but Eugene had never owned a gun. She doubted that he could have saved a wagonload of women single-handedly!

Which left her with only one certainty. Something very strange was going on in that little town.

It seemed she would just have to wait until Annsboro to find out for herself all the answers to the questions Watkins's letter had created in her mind. Was Eugene truly very ill—and "much changed," as Watkins had described? Or, more likely, was someone pretending to be Eugene? If so, she was almost certain that someone was Jake Reed.

She leaned back against her seat and looked out the window at the ocean of yellow grassland unfurling in all directions. How did people live out here, especially ladies? She'd had some trouble relating to the rough-hewn people she had met thus far on her journey, though she held quite a bit of admiration for anyone who could survive in such an odd, rugged country.

Rosalyn smiled. Even though she couldn't imagine what she would possibly do here, she couldn't help liking the place. She wondered if Eugene had liked it, too... or if perhaps he still did.

That puzzling question brought her thoughts back into line. She needed to start devising a plan. Once she arrived in Annsboro, should she attempt to furtively examine the town for signs of her brother, or should she announce right away who she was? From what she'd learned, the town sounded so small that it shouldn't prove too difficult to get to the bottom of the situation. Sometime this day, she would have her answers.

"Excuse me, ma'am?"

Startled, Rosalyn looked up to see a man wearing rough denim pants, a faded blue work shirt and a black hat gripping her seat to steady himself against the rhythmic pitching of the train. She looked questioningly into his sky blue eyes and noticed that the workman—or was this a cowboy?—had a very strong, distinctive face.

"I couldn't help hearin' what you was asking that man across from you."

"Yes?" Rosalyn's heartbeat sped up considerably.

"I think I might be able to help you," he said.

In a moment, Rosalyn had flattened herself against the window to make room for the man. She patted the seat and he nodded, very politely, and sat down next to her. His long legs filled up the space between the facing seats. Really, he was very handsome—although Rosalyn, from her years of training in Aunt Patrice's parlor, couldn't keep her eyes from darting up at that black hat he still wore.

He noticed her glances and, ducking his head in embarrassment, mumbled, "'Scuse me, ma'am," and removed the offending hat.

Rosalyn swallowed a gasp. A jagged red scar slashed the man's temple, a recent wound, still swollen and grotesque to the eye. It appeared even angrier, perhaps, because in contrast the man's hair was so fair—so blond as to almost look white.

His cheeks reddened, and Rosalyn felt a bit ashamed of herself for staring so baldly—and for being such a stickler for convention in the first place. Eager to get to the subject that most concerned her, she said, "My name is Rosalyn Pendergast. Might you have heard of my brother, Eugene?"

His eyes registered confusion. "No... I'm afraid I've never heard of your brother, Miss Pendergast."

Rosalyn's chest suddenly deflated, and she realized she had been holding her breath.

"It's that other name you mentioned," the white-haired man continued. His startling blue eyes narrowed, and his voice took on a harsher tone. "Jake Reed. I heard of him often enough."

Finally! "Do you know if Mr. Reed lives in Annsboro?"

"Not the last I heard." His mouth set in a grim line again. "Why do you say that?"

Rosalyn searched through her beaded velvet satchel for Jake Reed's letter. She pulled it out and held it up for the man to see. "I have received correspondence from Mr. Reed saying that my brother, who was to be the teacher in Annsboro, died in a barroom fight in a town called Guthrie before ever reaching his destination.''

The man's expression froze. ''Is that so?''

Rosalyn nodded curtly. ''Then, weeks later, I received a letter stating that my brother was teaching in Annsboro, but was ill and looked quite different than he used to.''

The blue eyes shifted anxiously, and for the first time Rosalyn took note of their cold, icy appearance. This man was harder than he'd first appeared. He reached for the letter, but some gut reaction made Rosalyn hold it back. She stuffed the letter back into her satchel and snatched it closed.

''I intend to have words with whomever is masquerading as my brother,'' she said bitterly.

''Me, too,'' the white-haired man said, though his voice was almost inaudible. His eyes narrowed to slits.

Rosalyn shuddered at the man's cold gaze. Jake Reed must have done something very bad to be on the receiving end of so much hostility. But this stranger's appearance might have solved one of her problems, at least.

''If you're looking for him, too, then perhaps we should go together to Annsboro!''

Abruptly the man rose to his feet. ''Sorry,'' he said quickly.

''I've been told it's difficult to hire transportation,'' she explained, hoping to change his mind. It would be so much easier to have a man along.

Without another word, he shoved his hat onto his head and strode toward the adjoining car. Rosalyn twisted in her seat but refrained from calling after him. That wouldn't be very ladylike. She hadn't even asked his name, either.

Besides, she had a gut feeling that she would see the white-haired man again.

Chapter Fourteen

Fiddling with the ribbons hanging off her floppy-brimmed hat, Cecilia leaned against the front gate of the Summertree ranch and squinted anxiously down the road to town.

Where was Jake Reed? Most of the other guests for Dolly's wedding had arrived...except for him. Where was he?

Her father, Clara, Dolly and practically every guest who had come through these gates in the past hour—practically all of Annsboro—thought she was out here ostensibly greeting wedding guests so she could have a private tête-à-tête with Pendergast when he came riding up.

If he ever did come riding up, something Cecilia was beginning to think wouldn't happen. Was her worst fear about to be realized? It was nearly two o'clock!

A breeze gently whipped at the ruffles and flounces on her blue organza dress, a frothy creation that was perfect for a wedding. It was one of her older gowns, made for when she had first started being able to go to parties when she visited Memphis, or the few that took place around here. It wasn't to her taste now, but at least in such a girlish getup no one would be able to guess that she was actually a woman of rapidly dwindling honor.

A rickety wagon coming down the rutted road made her lift her eyes to the horizon. It wasn't Reed. Cecilia couldn't imagine who else had decided to show up; she crossed her arms against the chill in the air and watched the wagon's slow approach. When she noticed that it was a strange woman holding the reins of the scrawny pinto drawing the buckboard she walked forward to greet the vehicle, curious.

The closer the wagon came, the clearer it became to Cecilia that this woman did not belong to the dilapidated vehicle she commanded; her appearance was too refined, and her traveling suit, though travel-worn and dusty, was obviously of very high quality. The high neck of her black rawsilk dress was edged in lace, as were the cuffs of her sleeves, and the accompanying feathered hat perched on her head was simple but jaunty—though not particularly useful for blocking out the Texas afternoon sun.

Cecilia shook her head at the thought of an unexpected guest. She and Clara would have to ready another room, and given the fact that there was going to be a wedding in five minutes, when would they have time for that?

The woman sawed awkwardly at the pinto's reins. "Stop," she admonished the poor beast, then added a shaky, "wh-whoa, whoa, girl."

"Boy," Cecilia corrected her. She grabbed the bridle and steadied the horse. At close range, she noted the woman's hair, which had obviously been very neatly coiled and piled atop her perfectly shaped head at some point in the day, was coming unraveled and poking out from under her hat in untidy wisps.

The woman's high forehead squinched into vertical lines against the bright sun. "I beg your pardon, but is this the Summertree ranch?"

"You're just in time," Cecilia interrupted. "The wedding is going to start soon."

The woman shaded her eyes so she could see better. She and Cecilia took a moment to study one another, and Cecilia found herself straightening her shoulders self-consciously, much like she had when the headmistress of her New Orleans school had caught her slumping in her chair, or committing some similar atrocity against civilized behavior. Whoever this woman was—the even tones of her voice suggested she was not a Southerner—she was most certainly a lady.

Puzzlement showed in the visitor's travel-bleary eyes. "A wedding?"

Cecilia hesitated. "Yes, Dolly's wedding...you do know Dolly, don't you?"

"I'm afraid this is most awkward—but then, my entire trip has been rather odd," she added. "I had heard Annsboro was a small town, but I never expected to find it completely empty."

"That's because of the wedding," Cecilia explained. "Everyone's here at the ranch."

"Yes, the man in town said they would be."

Instantly alert, Cecilia let go of the pinto's reins. "Man? In town? Was it Pendergast?" she asked eagerly, stepping halfway up on the wagon.

The stranger's eyes widened in surprise. "Eugene?"

It *had* to have been Pendergast—*Reed,* Cecilia corrected herself quickly. But where was he? Why hadn't he followed this woman?

When finally the woman's question registered in her brain, she turned to her in shock. "Do you mean to say that you came here searching for Eugene Pendergast?" The real Eugene Pendergast, she reminded herself. She had almost forgotten that person existed.

"No—I mean yes." The woman shook her head in what Cecilia could only guess was acute confusion, then pulled out a handkerchief and dabbed gently at the tears that sprang to her eyes. "I've come to find out what happened to him."

Cecilia's swallow was an audible gulp. "Are you a relation?"

"My name is Rosalyn Pendergast," the woman said, her mouth smiling reflexively at the introduction, "his sister. I've come all the way from Philadelphia to find out what has become of him. Do you know him?"

Cecilia's stomach flip-flopped. This was Rosalyn, the woman whose letters she had read time and again, searching for clues to Pendergast's identity. And now Rosalyn herself was searching for clues.

An ominous fear suddenly gripped her. To clarify, she asked, "This man in town, was he tall, with dark brown hair and eyes?"

Rosalyn looked perplexed that the subject should so abruptly revert to the man who had given her directions. "Yes, very dark," she answered.

"And you didn't recognize him?" Cecilia probed.

Rosalyn shook her head. "No, but he was very kind. He said my brother wasn't there, but when I asked about another man named Jake Reed, he recognized the name and said I might find him here, at this ranch."

Only one man would recognize that name besides herself. Reed! "Why are you looking for Jake Reed?"

"Because he's a villain, a liar! Look at this!" The woman reached into a velvet bag, whipped out a letter and began waving it frantically inches away from Cecilia's nose.

"May I read it?" Cecilia asked, taking the letter.

At once, the handwriting startled Cecilia. The memory of the words *Mr. Pendergast* written across a blackboard went through her mind. As she rushed over the letter's contents, a horrible possibility chilled her. Had Reed actually murdered Rosalyn Pendergast's brother—the *real* Pendergast—before coming to Annsboro? He had probably written the letter in Annsboro, from Dolly's boardinghouse, where he was pretending to be Pendergast, fooling the lot of them, making her fall in love with him.

Love? Had she truly fallen in love with a cold-blooded killer? More to the point, could a man who had made love to her so tenderly actually be a murderer?

Cecilia felt sick. The suspicion had flitted through her mind once before, Friday night, but she had dismissed it quickly. Reed had assured her that he wasn't a murderer—and she, like a little idiot, had taken him at his word! Her silly girlish fantasies about a desperado now took on a darker, more deadly cast.

So, she had been right from the beginning. Her big mistake was only in thinking he was harmless for so long. Not until he had come back, hailed as a hero, had she suspected that he might be involved in something sinister. Foolishly, she had believed his profession of innocence, and allowed him to seduce her to get her out of the way.

The clearer his terrible betrayal became, the angrier she felt. And the more determined to let Jake Reed know that he couldn't get away with this. "Where is he?" she asked.

"Who?"

"The man from town."

"He was about to ride out when I left. But after we talked, he didn't follow me."

Small wonder. But why had Reed sent Rosalyn to the ranch—and where had he gone?

"I need to find the sheriff," Rosalyn said. "Is he here?"

"We don't have a sheriff," Cecilia informed her. For some reason, the idea of the law chasing Reed made her anxious.

Rosalyn's brow furrowed once again, this time with worry. "Then...there must be someone who will help me."

Cecilia thought fast. If a party was sent out after Reed now, there was no telling what the result would be. Rosalyn had some damning evidence against him, yet Cecilia still held out a hope in her heart—albeit it a slim, unraveling one—that her suspicions and the evidence were wrong. At any rate, she had to confront Reed herself to find out, and she needed to do it alone.

She would have to go after him, but first she needed to get rid of Rosalyn.

"I'll help you," Cecilia said quickly, giving the letter back. "We'd better go inside. I'm sure you need to rest, and to get something to drink."

Rosalyn's expression was one of sheer gratitude. "Yes, water."

The woman would need something stiffer than water by the time this situation was sorted out, Cecilia thought, leaping upon the buckboard to drive the pinto up the short path to the house herself. Her mind worked swiftly. One thing was certain. She didn't have time for a wedding.

She brought the horse around the back, then led Rosalyn up the small back stairway, pausing only to dart into the kitchen and pour a glass of water from the pitchers Clara had prepared. Furtively, they went up the back stairs.

Inside her bedroom, Cecilia said, "You're welcome to take a nap here, and I'll fetch you down after the ceremony's over. Then we'll be able to find someone to help us." The woman looked in dire need of that.

Rosalyn yawned daintily. "You're so kind, but I'll need to get back to Annsboro. There are so many things I still don't understand. Maybe if I saw the schoolhouse..."

Cecilia fluffed the coverlet, hoping her guest would take the hint and fall asleep. "We'll get this all sorted out, Miss Pendergast, you'll see," she said soothingly, and felt rewarded the moment Rosalyn's head hit the pillow.

Gathering her full skirts, she dashed down the hall. She threw open the door to the guest room and was greeted by a near-frantic Dolly, who was standing before a mirror in full wedding regalia, with Clara furiously buzzing around her.

"Is everyone waiting?" Dolly cried in alarm. "I thought I heard music!"

"No," Cecilia said. Dolly looked as if she was ready to run out the minute she heard the first piano strains, no matter whether she was dressed or not.

"Hold on," Clara admonished, trying to pin a tulle veil to the bride's head. "They can't have the wedding without you."

Dolly giggled. "I'm a bit nervous."

Cecilia ran over and gave her friend a brief but heartfelt hug. "Oh, Dolly, you're so beautiful. I just know you're going to be so happy."

"I hope so!" Dolly cried, but was kept from returning the embrace when Clara sank a hat pin into her scalp. "Ouch!"

"That ought to do it," the housekeeper said. "Should I tell them you're ready?"

Dolly gave her a wincing nod.

Cecilia would miss seeing two such good friends get married, but she didn't have a moment to spare. Even now it was a gamble as to whether she could catch up with Reed—she could only guess that he was heading south, toward Fredericksburg again.

The first strains of a wedding march were heard playing on Charlie's fiddle below, and Cecilia escorted Dolly out to the staircase. "Good luck," she said, watching until her friend had disappeared down the stairs.

She ducked farther down the hall. At her father's door she walked in and scanned the sparsely furnished bedroom until she saw Silas's trusted Spencer rifle propped against the bed stand and snatched it up.

She quickly dodged down the little stairwell and hit the back door running. The barn was in back of the house, requiring only a furtive sprint, and as she neared, she discovered a gold mine. It looked as though every horse in the county was assembled there; their number spilled out into the barnyard in various stages of harnessing. Cecilia picked out Jim's bay gelding, which, blessedly, was saddled. She tightened the girth, adjusted the stirrups to accommodate her shorter legs and hoisted herself up. Before she could think twice about such a rash action, she was galloping hell-for-leather for open pasture, due south.

He was making good time. The old black hack he had procured possessed more spunk than Jake would have expected. It was a lucky thing he'd found the animal as quickly as he did; he hadn't expected to make this journey for at least another day yet.

But that was before the woman he had least wanted—or expected—to see had driven into town, waylaying him on the way out to Cecilia's.

And the moment Rosalyn Pendergast had mentioned speaking to a certain white-haired man, he'd known the die was cast. He couldn't wait around a moment longer. Coming face-to-face with Pendergast's sister had been startling in itself. Knowing Gunter was on his way to Annsboro chilled his blood.

Jake stood up in his stirrups and turned, scoping out the area around him. His visual search revealed nothing suspicious, just sloping grassy pastures dotted with low live oak trees and bushes.

He faced forward again with a sigh of regret. It hadn't been easy to leave Annsboro, even knowing that Gunter was somewhere nearby. The thought of perhaps never seeing Cecilia again was almost unbearable. He'd almost given the Pendergast woman a message to deliver to Cecilia, but decided that would be a fruitless act. So he had put the idea out of his head, sent Rosalyn on to the Summertree ranch to get her out of harm's way, then had wasted little time coming to the conclusion that he had no choice but to move on.

Damn. He wondered whether Gunter had recognized him that day on the road to Fredericksburg. Probably, and he'd probably been hunting him down ever since. But that didn't explain why Gunter had been out robbing rickety wagons when he could have been sitting in cotton with his rich father-in-law a day's ride away.

The only thing that made sense to Jake was that the sooner he took care of Darby and Gunter for good, the sooner he could go back to straighten out the mess he was leaving behind in Annsboro. More specifically, the sooner he could return to Cecilia. He hoped he got that chance.

From somewhere behind him, a shot cracked through the silence. Jake spurred his horse toward a bush that would provide scant cover at best. His heart was beating as rapidly as a hummingbird's wings, and he held his breath, straining his ears for some clue as to what could be happening as he looked once more over the terrain. He didn't see anybody.

Then he heard the hoofbeats of an approaching rider galloping toward him. When he could finally focus on the sound, his eyes narrowed in the direction it was coming from. Every nerve tensed, he drew his gun in anticipation, and within moments the rider appeared. He'd been prepared for Gunter, for a battle, even for death. But not for this.

Cecilia!

Cecilia, garbed in an elaborate blue getup with ruffles and a floppy-brimmed hat to match, was thundering toward him, the yards of material in her skirt flying out behind her like a battle flag. Jake couldn't believe his eyes—especially when he saw the rifle she held in her arms.

He rested his revolver on his saddle horn and exhaled a sigh that was equal parts relief and annoyance. What was she doing here? Why had she been shooting?

She skidded to a stop not ten feet away from him, her horse lathered from its wild ride. "Hold it right there, Reed." Her lips pursing in a thin, determined line, she lifted the gun and aimed it straight at him. At the same time, she looked him over, obviously taking in the fact that he had changed back into the clothes that he hadn't worn since leaving Guthrie all those weeks ago.

"Cecilia, have you turned lunatic?"

She smirked. "No, I've finally wised up—right after talking to Rosalyn Pendergast."

Jake attempted to swallow his anger. Cecilia had every right to be mad as hell at him, but having her out here with Gunter on the loose scared the bejesus out of him. He urged his nag forward slowly, and Cecilia's eyes widened in alarm over the barrel of the gun.

"Stop right there!" she warned. A light breeze blew a flounce from her bodice to her chin and she shrugged it away. Her bent knuckle whitened as it tightened over the trigger. Jake suddenly found himself wondering nervously just how well Cecilia could handle that rifle, though it wasn't likely that even a child could miss from this short distance.

"I said stop," she ordered again.

Jake obliged her. For now. "I have a gun, too, you know."

"I'm fast, Reed."

"Not as fast as I am, sweetheart."

Though the endearment made her spitting mad, his tone, an assured drawl, got Cecilia's attention. She hadn't thought this through, but now she realized he did have a point. If he was a wanted man, he might very well be a quick draw. Sparing just a glance for the Colt revolver, she looked into those coal black eyes for some hint of his intention and saw an amusement in them that irritated her. "Do you think this is funny?"

"No, I was just thinking that I've never seen you looking more beautiful. What do they call that shade of blue?"

"Periwinkle," she replied hastily, "and don't think you can distract me by talking fashion. I want to know what you did with Pendergast."

"Nothing."

"Then where is he?"

"In a town called Guthrie, dead. Somebody else killed him by accident. They were aiming at me and missed."

"So you decided you'd run around pretending to be a dead man?"

Jake nodded. "I had to lie low."

One dark blond eyebrow shot up. "Why? Did you rob a bank . . . kill somebody? I want the truth this time!"

Jake sighed. He hadn't wanted to confront Cecilia with all this until his business with Gunter was finished. What good did it do her to know? But now he could see that she wasn't going to let him move on without some answers. The sooner he gave them to her, the sooner he could try to catch up with Darby and Gunter—and then come back to her. If he managed to come out of it all alive.

"Contrary to your hopes, I'm not a crook," he defended. "Those men responsible for Pendergast's death were after me, have been for years. One of them spoke to Rosalyn Pendergast on the train today, so he knows where I am. His father-in-law lives south of here—he's the head honcho. I intend to put both of them off my trail permanently."

Cecilia assessed the situation quickly. That meant one man was at their front and one at their back, and they were sandwiched in the middle. "Are you going to kill them?" she asked, her eyes intent on him.

"They're murderers themselves."

He didn't flinch to admit it, Cecilia thought. Didn't flinch, but didn't appear to relish his mission. Her body relaxed in the saddle. She'd been wrong about him, as had Rosalyn. "You're actually avenging Pendergast's death."

Jake bit back a laugh. "My motives aren't that noble, Cecilia. I'm going to save my life. It's either them or me."

"How long will you be gone?"

Jake shrugged regretfully. God, it was going to be hard to leave her again, even after seeing her only this briefly. He couldn't even promise that he would return, much less give her a day. And now he had to worry about getting her back to her ranch.

"Never mind," she said. "I'm going with you."

"Like hell you are," Jake replied. "You've got to go home—in fact, I don't want you riding out here alone, so I'm going to have to take you back myself."

"There's no time for that," Cecilia argued. "You said yourself that this man . . ."

"Gunter," Jake supplied.

"If he spoke to Rosalyn Pendergast, it's most likely he's somewhere hereabouts."

Dear God, why had she followed him? Cecilia was the last person he wanted out here. "You don't understand, Cecilia,'' he said, deciding to lay it on the line for her. ''This is dangerous. For you, too.''

''I *know* that,'' she said impatiently.

''I might not come back alive.''

She leveled one of those haughty looks. ''Precisely,'' she said coolly. ''But if you have me along, the odds for survival will be much better. I'm a good shot.''

''I'm sure that hoity-toity school in New Orleans taught you plenty about shoot-outs,'' Jake quipped.

A secretive smile appeared on her lips. ''I just might surprise you someday.''

This was a new one. In all his years, even his law years, he'd never met a woman to throw herself in danger's path with this much gusto. But then, Cecilia wasn't just any woman. He could never forget that, no matter how hard he tried. In fact, now that he thought about it, it might not be so bad having Cecilia along for company....

Jake gave himself a mental smack. ''Absolutely not.''

Her eyes shone steely blue. ''You can send me back or take me back, but I'm just going to turn and follow you whether you like it or not.''

''You're going home.'' If anything happened to Cecilia, he wouldn't be responsible for his actions.

Silently, she shook her head from side to side, uncompromising. She really was crazy enough to follow him, and that chilled him to the bone.

It also gave him no choice.

Rosalyn had never seen a town so empty.

She scanned the deserted main street and felt her heart begin a heavy erratic thudding in her breast. When she had seen Cecilia Summertree go riding off, she'd been certain she had ridden back to town. Now she suspected she'd been mistaken. Cecilia Summertree was not in Annsboro. Nor, it appeared, was anyone else.

No sooner had Rosalyn's head hit the pillow at the Summertree ranch than she'd pieced the whole mystery to-

gether. Miss Summertree had asked if the man Rosalyn saw
in town was Pendergast—as if she'd been waiting for him.
Then, when Rosalyn had shown her the letter from Jake
Reed, a man Miss Summertree said she had never heard of,
the girl's entire manner had changed. Unfortunately, Rosalyn had figured out too late that the lone man in town who
had given her the directions to the ranch had probably been
Reed; when she got up from the bed, she had seen Cecilia
racing down the road toward town.

Where was Miss Summertree now?

A cold, clammy feeling overtook her. Could it be that the
man named Reed had abducted the young woman she'd
spoken to? What a horrible thing that would be! She should
have impressed upon Miss Summertree what a dangerous
character this Jake Reed was.

Rosalyn began to regret that she had left the Summertree
ranch without speaking to anyone. Unless she found Miss
Summertree, not a soul here knew who she was.

At the far end of town was a large wooden building with
a sign that read Grady's above the door. Rosalyn, her eye
practiced from traveling through this odd state, guessed this
to be town's drinking establishment. Her first thought was
that she could use a drink herself. Her second was that
surely someone was inside the saloon, perhaps even a sober
someone who could give her advice.

Behind her, she heard the sound of hoofbeats. Relieved,
she turned on the hard wooden seat to get a glimpse of the
rider. Oh, she hoped it was Miss Summertree, or someone
who could help.

But when she looked around, she was startled to see the
white-haired man from the train. For a split second, they
simply stared at each other. As she caught the icy blue glint
in his eye, however, even from a distance of over a hundred
yards, Rosalyn's relief at encountering another human being was quickly replaced by an intense desire for solitude.
There was evil intent in those eyes.

The rider moved forward, and her heart started a tripping beat that sped up as the white-haired man closed the distance between them. In vain, she scoped out the emptied buildings around her, but there wasn't time to hide or even to try to run. Crying for help would be equally pointless. There was no one to hear.

All she really had time to do was send a quick prayer up to heaven before the stranger thundering toward her reached out and yanked her off the buckboard. Pain shot through her hip as she landed awkwardly against the saddle in front of him; her right arm felt as if it had been torn from its socket and ached where he had a lock on it still. Her heart hammered from unmitigated, blinding fear as the powerful horse beneath her galloped toward the open range.

"I can't get used to calling you Reed," Cecilia said over the bay's gracefully arched neck.

Nor was she accustomed to how Reed looked. After three hours of hard riding, she was still amazed at the transformation brought on by his trading in his brown suit for denim pants and a well-worn white work shirt. On top of his head was a gray felt hat that looked like it had been born there.

"So try Jake." They had stopped at a pond to water their horses and stretch their legs.

It was strange to think she'd known him for so long as Pendergast, a whimsical-sounding name that didn't fit the man she was beginning to know. While Pendergast had been offhand in manner, with a gentle mocking attitude, Jake Reed was wry, suspicious, always on the alert. His demeanor was a curious mixture of prey and predator, and the wary coldness in his eyes as they rode swiftly across the range nearly broke her heart.

Yet both men were one and the same, and equal in mystery. She knew nothing about Jake Reed, except what his present circumstances were—and those were pretty grim.

"Who are you really?" she asked as she stroked the bay's neck.

Jake broke his alert gaze from the horizon. "Do you really need to know right this minute?"

"Yes, I do," Cecilia said.

"'Cause we probably shouldn't have stopped even this long."

Cecilia took a steadying breath. "So far I've taken you at your word for a lot of things, but I'm not getting back on this horse until you tell me who the hell you are."

Jake stared into somber blue eyes that usually were so sparkling and felt a fresh pang of guilt. He'd dragged her into this mess because it was the only way he knew to watch over her, but having her here made him feel suddenly vulnerable. Whereas before he had been single-mindedly bent on finally getting revenge, seeing her riding alongside him, her face as tense as his own as she now shared the danger, made him feel defensive yet again.

It also made him realize that he owed her the truth.

He heaved a sigh and looked away across the grassy land, watching. "I spent most of my life in Redwood."

Her eyebrows knit together as she tried to remember the name. "That's south of here, right?"

"That's where we're headed, sweetheart."

"Oh." Cecilia continued to stare at him evenly, waiting for him to go on.

"I'm not a teacher." All this confession warranted, however, was a snicker. Jake took another breath, screwing up his courage to continue. In all the weeks he'd been on pins and needles trying to keep his identity from her, he had never been so filled with dread as now, worrying that she would despise the person he really was. "For a few years, I was the sheriff's deputy."

Cecilia's mouth flew open in shock. "You're the law?"

"Was. It wasn't much work, but the sheriff had offered it to me after my father died."

"That's so exciting!" she prodded encouragingly.

Jake's frown deepened. "Burnet Dobbs, a family friend, gave me an old badge from the bottom of a drawer somewhere, and as a result of doing what I thought was right, I ended up in a crazy situation where I was being hunted down like a jackrabbit. I wouldn't call that exciting."

Her lips puckered in thought, and Jake longed to take her into his arms and kiss her the way he had the other night, in her room, when they were alone. She was so sweet, so full of vitality... so eager to run headlong into trouble.

"I should have made you go home," he said.

"I'm glad you didn't." She made a stab at levity. "Besides, I told you, I would have hunted you down. Then you would have had three people to worry about."

He shook his head. "I should have told you who I really was before now. That way you might have known better than to follow me."

Smiling shyly, she sidled up close to him. "I gave myself to you when I didn't know who you were. Do you think I'd leave you now that I do know?" She put her palm against his chest tentatively, and he stepped back in response.

"Don't," he bit out, feeling his gut tighten uncomfortably. He focused his eyes across the expanse of land around them, trying desperately not to look into those blue eyes that could cause what little willpower he had to dissolve like so much sugar in water. As they'd been riding, he had resolved not to touch Cecilia until this whole mess was cleared up, even though every inch of him just wanted to take her into his arms.

"We need to get a move on," he said, ignoring the hurt in her eyes at having her flirtatiousness rebuffed.

"Fine," she said. Scowling, she led her horse a few feet away and mounted.

Cecilia brooded as they kicked their horses into a brisk lope and rode on. Jake Reed obviously considered her a millstone around his neck, which just plain made her mad. Why would a man want to go at something like this alone? Worse, why, after sharing her bed Friday night, would he pretend not to feel the powerful draw between them?

Finally, as they skirted an open field by hugging close to a line of trees, she came up close to him and said, "If you want my opinion—"

"I'll ask for it."

"I think you're pretending not to care for me just in case you get killed, so I won't grieve," she theorized. "But that's just plain silly. If you are killed, it won't make me feel any better to know that you didn't like me. If I'm going to grieve, I'd just as soon go all the way."

"That's the most twisted logic I've ever heard," Jake replied.

Cecilia shrugged casually. "Twisted logic's the best kind, didn't you know? Especially when dealing with someone who won't play straight with you."

Finally he smiled. "All right, sweetheart, I'll tell it to you straight. I'm selfish."

"How so?"

"Because I don't care if you cry over my carcass or not. But I sure as hell wouldn't want to go through the hell I would feel if something happened to you."

Perversely, her pulse did a little dance at his terse statement. "You don't have to worry about me. I can take care of myself."

"Good." He tossed her a tight smile and kicked his horse into a slightly faster gait.

Cecilia caught up with him quickly, but kept silent for a long stretch. Jake Reed wasn't a man who would open his heart to her all at once, but what he had revealed so far gave her hope in terms of how he felt about her.

She wondered what life would be with a man like Jake. In her imagination, she had no surroundings she could place him in, no context for their being together other than the time they had spent together in Annsboro. But Jake had only been pretending to belong there.

After they cantered around an isolated ranch house, Cecilia drew her horse up alongside his and slowed. "What are you going to do after this is all over?" she asked.

Jake kept scanning the horizon even as his mind scavenged hungrily on her question. Would it ever be over? He'd had so many plans once, but in the past two years, it had seemed all he could do just to hold down a job with some cow outfit or another for a few months.

"Will you stay in Redwood and become a deputy again?" she probed.

Jake nearly choked on her words. He doubted Cecilia would be much in agreement with his way of thinking on this matter, but it was best to get it out in the open. "I sort of hoped to get a job somewhere."

"A job?" Cecilia's forehead wrinkled lightly. "You mean, in a store?"

He shook his head.

"Where, then?" she persisted.

"On a ranch."

Cecilia drew in a swift breath. Of course, ranching was mostly what everyone did, but she was so used to thinking of this man as Pendergast, the hand-kissing schoolteacher! That, however, had been an act. Jake Reed wasn't a schoolteacher, or the mysterious desperado she had dreamed about, or a cold-blooded killer.

The bitter truth was, she'd gone and fallen for a would-be cowpuncher.

The horror of this discovery stunned her. She almost laughed, but instead heard herself asking, "Have you worked with cattle much?"

Jake nodded. "Since I left Redwood, that's what I've done. Sometimes, when I let myself dream about such things, I'd think about having a ranch of my own."

Cecilia nodded numbly. A ranch. Just when she'd finally thought she'd found a man she wanted to spend the rest of her life with, she discovered that he wanted to spend the rest of his life on a ranch! It was a good thing she hadn't made a complete fool of herself.

Then she remembered, she *had* made a complete fool of herself. It was too late to pretend she'd had a mere flirtation with this man. She'd been intimate with him; not only that, she had enjoyed it. But even the possible consequences of that union weren't what made her chase after him all this way. His pull on her was deeper than that. The plain fact of the matter was, she was stuck on the man.

She shook her head as they continued to plod along. His silence was wistful; hers, mournful. A ranch. This was bad. Very bad.

Chapter Fifteen

"A ranch!"

Cecilia wasn't sure how the exclamation had found its way out of her mouth, but it had been building up in her for hours, all during their long ride into evening and while they had choked down their Spartan dinner of stale biscuits, apples and water. It was bad enough to have lost her head over someone who was pretending to be something he wasn't, but when the something he actually was—or wanted to be—was a rancher, that made her error ten times as serious.

Her whole life had been geared toward one goal—finding a better life for herself than her mother had wound up with. And she had walked into the very trap she'd tried so hard to avoid!

Jake glared at her across their fireless makeshift camp beneath a live oak tree. "I never said anything against ranching, did I?"

"No, but you knew how I felt about it." Cecilia crossed her arms challengingly.

A belligerent silence settled between them. Finally, Jake looked away and muttered, "Forget it. We shouldn't be gabbing like this anyways."

"Heavens, no!" Cecilia rolled her eyes. "Mercy, I've never chattered so much in my entire life," she said, her voice dripping with sarcasm.

He shot her a quelling look and they lapsed into another wordless battle of wills. As he had all day long, Jake wavered between nearly overpowering desire and staunch determination not to start anything up again while they were on the chase. And fear. Anyone who said men weren't supposed to feel fear hadn't lived very long. He felt it now every time he looked at Cecilia and imagined anything happening to her, especially through fault of his own. When all this was settled, he swore he'd see to it that she was never in danger again.

"Still, you could have told me." Cecilia's sharp tone bit through the dark silent night, picking up the threads of argument where they had left off.

"When?" he asked. "When you were trying to have me booted out of town? I never told you I was a gentleman."

"But you pretended to be one! You never mentioned a word about *ranching*." She shuddered, as though the word was abhorrent to her.

And Jake guessed it was, though why he would never know. Cecilia could accuse him all she wanted of not being honest with her, but she wasn't exactly honest with herself, either.

He let out a chuckle. "Ranches are pretty nice places to be, you know."

She shot him a withering glance. "You sound like my father! He thinks a woman's place is on a ranch."

"And you disagree."

"Absolutely! I want to live in a big city."

Jake laughed. "I guess you decided to start small."

"Well, I *meant* to live in New Orleans," Cecilia replied huffily. "But that didn't work out so well."

Jake had forgotten about Miss Summertree's supposed misadventures in that city. "I heard they ran you out of town."

"Over nothing! I sneaked out one time."

"To meet a man?" Jake asked, unable to deny the twinge of jealousy he felt.

Through the darkness, he saw Cecilia's mouth turn down in a pout. "No...but could I help it if I just happened to run into a boy I knew, and then we just happened to run into the headmistress's husband?"

"So you were in the wrong place at the wrong time."

Cecilia shrugged her thin shoulders and smiled haplessly. "It didn't help matters that the wrong place just happened to be a gambling establishment."

"And things just snowballed from there," Jake guessed.

"I was snatched back to the ranch so fast I didn't know what hit me," Cecilia said. "You don't know how lucky I was to get that teaching position in dull old Annsboro."

Jake laughed. "So is that town not highfalutin enough for you?"

Cecilia leaned her elbows on her knees and rested her chin in her palm. "It's not that. It's just life here is so...boring."

"Where did your parents come from?"

"East Texas. They were one of the first families to settle around here. They had a successful farm, but Daddy was restless and wanted more land. So my poor mother had to follow him."

"Surely she didn't mind."

"Yes, she did." Cecilia's voice was dead serious. In response to his puzzled silence, she asked, "You remember that story about the Comanche raid?"

Jake thought back to his first dinner at the boarding-house. "The one where the little girl was taken captive," he recalled.

"Ann Summertree was my older sister."

Jake took in the information, saddened for her, for her whole family.

"That morning of the raid was the last time I saw my mother truly happy. She and I had been out walking, all the way out to a pond miles off where we had waded in the water. It was so hot, even in the morning, that we splashed each other until we were soaking.

"By the time we got back, it was all over. Our little house had been burned to the ground and Ann was gone. The family who lived just a little ways from us had a brother and the father murdered. Another man was killed, too. It was so horrifying—maybe even more so because I hadn't been there, I sometimes think. I was so young, I could only imagine..."

In the pale moonlight, Jake saw a tear streak down her cheek, which she didn't bother to wipe away. When another followed, he scooted across the ground and enfolded her in his arms. She gratefully buried her face in his chest and let out a long-pent-up sob.

"It's all right, Cecilia," he murmured.

She hiccuped lightly. "My mother never allowed us to talk about it, not even when they decided to name the town Annsboro, after Ann. All her life, she kept looking across that flat horizon, though, as if Ann would come running back home, still a little girl. She never stopped hoping."

Jake kissed the crown of her head softly, then her forehead. "Go ahead and cry," he said.

Still clinging to him, she stamped her heel on the ground in frustration. "I hate to cry." She sniffed. "But I suppose now you can see why I would rather be anywhere but here."

Jake thought for a long moment, torn inside. He'd never held a woman and spoken with her so openly before. Yet Cecilia's very words, telling him why she didn't want to live out here, argued for their separation. He wasn't sure he wanted to give her up, no matter how ill suited she proclaimed they were. He wasn't sure that he could.

"Still," he said, "I don't see where else you would fit in."

Cecilia looked at him, her eyes still wet and luminous in the dim light. In a split second, a little of her old sassiness returned. "I've spent a great deal of time in society, I'll have you know. And not just at school in New Orleans, either. I've stayed with my aunts in Memphis some, too."

"And hated every minute of it," Jake guessed.

Cecilia opened her mouth to deny it, but changed her mind when the image of her aunt Caroline's stuffy parlor in Memphis, full of knickknacks and gewgaws, came to mind. And then there was the endless round of calls to pay to people you really had nothing to say anything to, and dreadful dinners spent talking about such exciting topics as cotton prices and the bloodlines of people she had never heard of and couldn't care less about. And both of her aunts had considered her too rough around the edges to truly lavish much attention on. Cecilia always felt as though they were keeping her on a tether, lest she get loose and embarrass the family name.

"And I doubt it was much of a coincidence that you were tossed out of that place in New Orleans," Jake continued. "I'll wager that, somewhere in the back of your mind, you were relieved to come home."

"Ha!" She tossed her head, but she didn't contradict him.

Jake leaned as close to her as he dared, which was close enough to smell the soft, flowery scent of her. Memories of their time together cascaded through him. "You belong out here," he continued, leaning down to tenderly nuzzle the downy hair at her temple. "People accept you here just as you are."

How did he know? Cecilia wondered foggily. It was true, she had felt so out of place in Memphis and New Orleans....

"You've got a wild streak in you, Cecilia," Jake whispered into her ear, sending a thrill right down to her curled toes. "You try to hide it, but it always comes out in the end."

"Mmm," Cecilia purred as he nipped his way down her neck. Through a blanket of sensation, she gathered her wits enough to say, "You're wrong."

He responded by moving up to nibble at her ear. The only way she could stifle a moan was by allowing herself to brush her body against his chest. Like her father said, if you itched, sometimes it was best to go ahead and scratch....

"I only lose control—" She gasped as one of his hands moved up to massage her breast.

"Mmm-hmm?" he asked, his lips hovering over hers hungrily, taunting.

"Wh-when I'm angry," she said, turning away.

He put a hand to her chin and tilted her lips up to his. He was losing control, too, but after a long day of being strung tighter than barbed wire, he couldn't think of a more tantalizing way to unwind. "I've seen you lose control when you weren't angry," he whispered just before his lips dipped down to tease at hers.

Cecilia felt the stirrings of heat deep within her. She was heavy and weightless at the same time, limp in Jake's arms but so alive with desire that she thought she could pull trees out of the ground, roots and all. And if he didn't kiss her soon, she thought with rising frustration, she also felt strong enough to throw him to the ground and ravish *him*.

His mouth met hers in such a wild joining that she thought she would faint from lack of breath and the overwhelming sensations roiling within her. Tongues intertwined, hands explored and massaged and gave long-needed release to the tension that had been building between them. But still Cecilia wanted more, until finally she gave voice to the only word her muzzy senses could latch on to.

"Jake..."

At the sound of his name, the name she'd so recently said she would never get used to, Jake felt a strange triumph. Her high, husky voice worked on him like kerosene poured onto the flames of a campfire; desire leapt in him so fiercely that he could barely leash it as he lowered her to the blanket he'd laid out on the ground for her.

He began fumbling with the buttons of her dress with quaking fingers, and every inch of skin revealed by the task nearly drove him over the edge. Her head lolled as with one free hand he massaged the creamy skin of her neck and back, so smooth, glowing and pale in the moonlight.

Cecilia thought surely she would faint from the myriad sensations clashing through her, yet his slow prolonged movements were a sweet agony she couldn't deny herself. Finally, as she sloughed off the loose dress and turned to him only in a camisole and thin petticoat, she felt as if she had shed the last remnants of her self-control, as well.

He bestowed kisses on every exposed inch of flesh and made short work of both his and her remaining garments. When finally they lay beside each other, bare and exposed in their unchecked desire, Cecilia let out a sigh of awe at the powerful beauty of his masculine form. Never had she imagined that the mere sight of a man could move her to feel so much, to want so desperately.

He rose up and covered her with his body, stopping just short of joining them together. Though he longed to plunge into her moist heat, he had to see her, had to know that she yearned for him as much as he did for her. "Cecilia." Her name came out a barely audible groan, and when she looked up at him with eyes so moist with passion they were teary, his thin thread of control snapped.

He pushed inside her female warmth then, and in an explosion of feeling and fierce, blazing desire, they moved together to give and attain release. Cecilia never dreamed she could be so consumed with need, so fired by movement and sheer sensation. She strained against Jake and clung to him, blinded by the intense flames within her that spread to every place they touched and still continued to build at her very core until she thought they would burn out of control.

When finally they found completion in an explosion of blinding pleasure, they collapsed in each other's arms, passion-sated and slick with sweat. For a moment, the only sound in the night was that of their slowly steadying breaths, which at first were labored but gradually became soft sighs of contentment.

Content. That was how Cecilia felt. Despite the danger
around them, a light-headed giddiness pulsed through her.
There would be enough troubles tomorrow. For tonight,
moment-to-moment happiness would suffice.

Cecilia smelled the heavenly scent of brewing coffee and
stretched languorously. Every inch of her felt sated and
happy, and only a scant foggy moment passed before she
remembered why. A smile stretched across her slumbering
face as she purred happily and nestled once more beneath
the blanket.

"Time to get up."

At the sound of the gruff voice, Cecilia's eyelids swept
open to see Jake standing over her with a steaming tin cup
in his hands. She lifted to her elbows, trying to blot out his
frown and the hard cast she saw in those brown eyes. "Good
morning," she said, smiling seductively, shyly.

His frowned deepened and he held out the mug to her,
pointedly looking away from the peek of cleavage created by
the scant covering of the blanket. "Take it."

She did as he said, but just as quickly put the cup aside,
determined to chase away his sour mood. In a sneak attack, she snaked her arms around his neck and pulled him
on top of her. "Is that your way of saying good morning?"
she asked with a pout a second before her lips lifted to his
in a kiss.

Jake couldn't bring himself to pull away immediately.
Tasting Cecilia's sweet lips had to be the most wonderful
breakfast he could imagine, but there were long miles to be
covered today, and they needed to be on their way. Reluctantly, he pushed himself a safe distance away from her,
trying unsuccessfully to blot out memories of their long
night of passionate lovemaking.

She reached out and clamped a hand down on his arm
before he could move away. "Is something wrong, Jake?"

Jake's throat was so dry he could feel his Adam's apple straining to make the hike up his neck so he could swallow. "I—I think it would be best if we put last night behind us."

Cecilia reddened in confusion. None of this made sense to her, especially not with the sensual words he had whispered to her in the darkness still reverberating in her head. She sat up, careful to cover her nakedness with the blanket, and studied his granite-hard face for signs of any of the feeling he had revealed last night. There were none.

Awkwardly she cast her gaze to the ashes of the little fire he must have created this morning and mumbled, "I guess people don't do... things like that... in the morning."

Jake bit back bitter laughter. God knew, he wanted nothing more than to shuck off his clothes and jump under that blanket with her, but that was impossible. Now that he had had time to gather his wits, he realized that there was more than one reason to be hesitant. Gunter could be anywhere, and if he found them, Jake doubted the man would be too understanding of their need for privacy. There was also the problem of what could result from their exuberant couplings—what might have already.

But how could he explain this to Cecilia, who still seemed as eager to throw caution to the wind as she had last night?

Finally, he didn't try. "You need to get your clothes on," he instructed her instead.

Cecilia's face drained to a sickly white color. "Fine," she said indignantly. "But you're going to have to either make yourself useful and hand me my dress or do me an even bigger favor by making yourself scarce."

Jake stood and walked the few feet to fetch her dress. In the course of their late-night activity, apparently, they had traveled a ways. He smiled and handed the wrinkled blue garment to her. "I aim to please."

Her blue eyes were unblinking. "Then please go away." Practically speaking, there was nowhere to dress but a clump of scruffy bushes by the brown watering hole they had camped beside, and she had no intention of doing a mad naked dash over there.

Jake went to take care of the horses. He'd already led them over to the water this morning while Cecilia slept. Now he saddled them up, cursing himself as he worked. If he was more the kind of man Cecilia said she wanted, he would be able to articulate his reasons for not taking her into his arms and kissing the breath out of her this morning, like he wanted to. Lord, he'd lain next to her beneath that blanket for nearly an hour at dawn just looking at her sweet sleeping face. That she could doubt he wanted her, especially after last night, grated on his nerves.

He watched her make her way to the pond on wobbly morning legs, her dirty wrinkled dress unable to disguise her beauty. She tied her hair back simply at the nape of her neck, then proceeded to take a modest bath, washing her face and arms and even her feet before she pulled on her shoes.

"Wish I'd grabbed a pair of boots before I left," she said.

Jake suddenly looked away, as though he had been caught peeping at her, which annoyed Cecilia. What had happened during their short hours of sleep that would cause him to treat her like dirt?

Her blood working up to a rolling boil, Cecilia stomped back to the fire, folded the blanket, then tossed back the coffee in one hearty gulp. It tasted like mud, but she'd die before she let him see her wince.

"I'll take care of the bay," she said as she approached the horses. He was in the process of tightening the girth.

"I've about got it," he said dismissively.

Cecilia stood aside, stewing. Hadn't Clara warned her this would happen? *When a girl gets a reputation, men don't think they have to respect her anymore. They just take, take, take.*

Her chin lifted proudly a notch as she watched him finishing up. Did he truly not respect her? It seemed impossible—he'd been so tender, so loving. Yet there had to be some reason that girls were supposed to guard against situations like this, and Cecilia had a hunch she'd just discovered it. It cut deeper than the loss of reputation, or a scandal in the family. A man like Jake Reed could break your heart.

He *had* broken her heart, a fact that stunned her. How had she let it happen? Her whole life she'd been so careful not to fall in love, yet this time she had stumbled right into the trap, knowing this mysterious character wasn't who he claimed. Knowing she was attracted to him as she had been to no other man. And now he had taken what trust and love she had and crushed it beneath the heel of his boot.

Her face turned crimson with self-recrimination. Fool! Yet she knew if he asked her to repeat last night's folly, she would probably say yes in a heartbeat. More annoying still, it didn't appear likely that he would ask her to, now or ever, and she felt like crying like a baby because of it.

"Guess that's about it," Jake said, giving the horses a quick once-over.

Cecilia, her arms crossed, sashayed forward with a scowl. "I can saddle my own horse," she informed him.

"I know that," Jake retorted, edging away from her.

"I can also take a hint."

He looked at her. "What's that supposed to mean?"

She threw him a disbelieving glare. "I mean, you don't have to worry that I'll throw myself at you. I can keep my distance just as well as you can."

"Good." He started inspecting his bridle very closely.

Good? Cecilia nearly choked with rage. Did he think he could get away with that blunt a brush-off? If so, he had another think coming! She snatched her father's rifle off her saddle, checked to make sure it was loaded—and that Jake knew it was—and pointed it right at his chest.

"If you're going to be rude, you'd better find a more polite way to go about it," she said menacingly.

His dark eyes widened as he felt the barrel of her shotgun poke him. "What are you talking about?"

"I'm saying, even if you're through with me, you could have at least had the decency to pretend you weren't."

"But I'm not through with you," he said. The phrase, coming out of his mouth, irked her and she prodded him once more. Jake quickly explained, "We just can't...make love again."

Her face reddened with shame to hear him say the words aloud. "I couldn't agree more. We shouldn't have in the first place," she said, trying desperately to salvage some pride. "Or in the second place."

"Cecilia, we have a madman chasing us. He could have come upon us last night."

"I said I agreed with you, Jake." Did he have to rub salt in her wounds?

Jake heaved a heavy sigh and looked across the horizon. "Also," he added heavily, his voice a gruff mumble, "we really should get married."

Cecilia froze, half disbelieving what she'd heard. As his words slowly sank in, she lowered the rifle, completely stunned. "You mean, you want to marry me?"

Want to marry her? Jake couldn't believe she wasn't laughing in his face for having the audacity to suggest it. She might yet, he reminded himself, given how she so recently said she wanted nothing to do with someone who wanted something to do with a ranch. Warily, he nodded. "Yeah, I do."

It was like a miracle...a very reluctant miracle, judging by his tone of voice. Marriage. Mrs. Jake Reed. It hardly seemed real. Cecilia had received proposals before, but none that she had taken as seriously as this unlikely one. The way he'd spat it out at her still bothered her, though.

"I hope you don't feel obliged to ask me, Jake."

He let out an incredulous laugh. "Don't you think I should?"

"No, I don't," she said proudly.

"Well, you're wrong."

"I don't want you to put yourself out," she snapped.

Jake couldn't believe she was just sloughing off his offer of marriage. He reached out and took her arm, dragging her close. "I know you're not used to thinking about mundane, practical matters, Cecilia, but what we did last night has consequences."

Consequences. Cecilia's heart felt as though a crack as wide as the Grand Canyon had just rent it in two. "If you're worried about the wages of sin—"

"Aren't you?"

"I can take care of myself."

"But you're not going to," Jake told her flatly, backing up his words with an emphatic shake. "Not while I'm around."

She squirmed in his grasp, her eyes shooting daggers at him. "Your loving proposal has just about knocked me off my feet, Mr. Reed," she said in a high, lilting, sarcastic voice.

"I would think you'd be relieved."

Cecilia thought guiltily of the relief she did feel—that he still wanted her, not that he wanted to marry her. She was ashamed to say that she was perfectly willing to accept the former without demanding the latter. Nevertheless, not a word had he mentioned about love, which was something she absolutely required for marriage. How else could two people stand each other for a lifetime?

Love wasn't something her pride would allow her to beg for, however. "You're hardly the type of man I've been waiting my whole life for," she reminded him. As the spiteful words hit their target, Jake's hands fell from her arms.

Wasn't a woman supposed to be flattered when a man proposed? Jake wondered. For all he knew, Cecilia was happy and this was just her stubborn way of showing it. In which case, it looked like he might have a lifetime of swapping put-downs to look forward to. To show his willingness to put up with whatever she wanted to dish out, he took a conciliatory step forward.

His gesture was answered by the short, sharp crack of rifle fire. The black horse bolted away at a gallop, and Jake jerked Cecilia down to a crouch with him and they quickly scanned the open area. They were at the bottom of a slight incline; at the top was a stand of cedar trees. The only shelter they had was the clump of scrubby bushes near the pond.

"We've got to take cover!" Cecilia whispered. Before Jake could confer with her, she dashed toward the bushes, dodging a bullet as it whizzed by her.

Jake dived the last few feet to reach cover. "Are you crazy?" he yelled at her as she peeked over a branch. "Keep low."

She had her rifle poised for action while he was still fumbling. His heart pumping like mad, he spun the barrel of his Colt and checked his ammunition. Gunter! The thought filled him with dread, especially when he saw Cecilia kneeling as cool as a cucumber next to him.

"Put that thing down and get behind me," he instructed her, looking at the trees at the top of the incline. They were positioned like ducks in a barrel.

"Hide, you mean?" Cecilia asked.

"You don't know Gunter," Jake warned.

"Do you think he's alone?"

Jake said nothing. He hadn't been alone on the road to Fredericksburg, but this wasn't a guessing game.

It was a deadly game, with him and now Cecilia as both target and prize. Jake felt sick with dread, but kept his eye trained on the cedars. How long was Gunter willing to hold out? His adversary had already proven himself more watchful and patient than Jake would ever have guessed.

For endless minutes they sat crouched side by side, their eyes focused forward. Jake's heart beat like a tom-tom; beside him, he could almost feel Cecilia's alert tension. Neither party spoke until Jake finally made the first volley.

"Come on and show yourself, Gunter!" he hollered up the hill.

In answer, a bullet whizzed past his skull. Cold anger soared through Jake. "You missed me, Gunter!" Jake cried. "Come out and let's us fight this out one-on-one!"

Another shot cracked through the air.

"Damn!" Jake muttered. He glanced over to make sure Cecilia was okay. Her gaze was still intently watching the cedars. He thanked God she had a cool head, but wondered whether a weepy hysterical woman might be easier to deal with on some level. At least then he would feel as if he could protect her somehow.

Still, he had to try. "I've got a woman down here, Gunter. You've got no grudge against her."

Cecilia shook her head furiously. "Don't, Jake."

For a moment, the air was silent, until a loud, sinister chuckle reached their ears. "You and me both, Reed."

Cecilia and Jake exchanged startled looks, then watched as someone appeared from behind a tree. Someone female, and familiar. Recognizing the hostage's proud carriage right away, Cecilia let out a gasp.

"He's got Rosalyn Pendergast!" she exclaimed in a low angry voice.

How did that woman end up getting herself into this mess? Bile rose in Jake's throat, especially when he saw Gunter shove the lady forward, using her as cover. For as long as he could remember, he'd hated Gunter—but never so much as at this moment.

As the two came forward, with Gunter so close behind Miss Pendergast they were nearly in lockstep, Jake knew his odds for survival, and Cecilia's, had just shrunk exponentially. He would never get a bead on Gunter with the woman in the way, but using her as a shield Gunter could get close enough to blow him to kingdom come. And then what would happen to Cecilia, and the other lady?

Slowly, Cecilia started creeping away from him, toward the other edge of the bushes. "Stay still," Jake hissed at her.

"Don't mind me," she returned sharply.

Don't mind her? Nothing else had been on his mind for days now! He sent up a silent prayer that Cecilia didn't have some crazy notion in her head, like trying to make a run for their horses, or acting as decoy.

"Let the woman go!" Jake yelled. God, how had this happened? He'd been alone in this chase for so long, and now, at this critical juncture, he was saddled with the responsibility not for just one woman—which was frightening enough—but two. Pendergast's sister.

Gunter had gagged her with an old grimy handkerchief. Jake shuddered to think what else he had done to her. Now the villain laughed that sickening laugh of his again. In all these years, Jake had never heard that sound. Maybe Gunter was giddy with the prospect of triumph.

"Why don't you send your woman out, Reed, and then maybe I'll let this one go!"

Jake glanced over and saw Cecilia's jaw saw back and forth; her cheeks were stained with pent-up ire, but she was still holding that old Spencer up, which had to be painful since the rifle was so heavy. "She doesn't want to go," he answered, then added flippantly, "I don't think she trusts you, Gunter."

"Then come out yourself," Gunter shouted, "or I'll put a bullet through this one's head." He cocked his pistol and pressed the lead against Rosalyn Pendergast's temple. The woman's terrified eyes tortured Jake; her expression pleaded mercy to one man who had none, and begged rescue from Jake, who was helpless to aid her except by giving himself up. But what would happen to her once he was dead? What would happen to Cecilia?

He aimed his revolver, hoping against hope to get a miraculous shot at Gunter. It was the only way. The white hair beneath the man's black hat would make a clear target, but Gunter was careful to keep behind Rosalyn enough that Jake wouldn't be able to get a shot off without running considerable risk of shooting her, instead.

In the end, he decided that was a risk he would have to take. Every ounce of concentration he had was focused on that man's head. One shot. That would be his one chance before all hell broke loose.

For a moment, he caught a glimpse of hair and didn't hesitate. He cocked the Colt quickly—but not quickly enough. Gunter heard the sound and turned his pistol toward the bushes. In that second—the second before a shot cracked through the still breeze—Jake was sure he was a dead man.

He held fire, expecting a bullet to rip through his chest. But instead, an explosion of red burst through the air. Jake recoiled but watched the macabre display in amazement. At first he thought Rosalyn had been hit, because she jerked to the ground, but she only did so after being released from Gunter's fierce grasp. The white-haired man fell violently to the earth and writhed in unconscious reflexive jerks before becoming still. Forever still.

Jake looked at his cold weapon and then turned his gaze to Cecilia. Her eyes glittered with scant satisfaction and her mouth was turned down sourly.

"Got him," she said, lowering her rifle at last.

In the next moment, Rosalyn moaned. Jake thought perhaps she had been hit, too, but she lifted her hands and removed the gag from her mouth, turned and retched. Cecilia and Jake rose, still cautiously clutching their weapons, and approached the grisly scene.

When he came near, Jake reached out and held Rosalyn's upper arm steadily. He couldn't blame her for being ill; just glancing at his long-standing foe, he felt pretty close to sick himself. And he could well imagine that this wasn't the type of thing that a lady was likely to see too often in Philadelphia.

Chapter Sixteen

"Dead," Cecilia pronounced, examining Gunter's body without a drop of pity. "A clean shot."

Jake was still amazed. "I can't believe you did that."

"Told you I would surprise you." Cecilia shrugged, then dipped her head to rub her brow on her periwinkle sleeve. "I was at a better angle. Gunter heard your voice and was coming straight at you. Finally, I had an almost clear profile shot of him."

"I was afraid I was going to hit Miss Pendergast," Jake said.

"You probably would have," Cecilia concurred.

Rosalyn shuddered and groaned, then, still clutching her stomach, attempted to rise to her feet. "Oh, dear," she whispered.

"Are you all right?" Jake asked her.

She shook her head, and to Jake's surprise, slowly approached Gunter. Tentatively, as though the vile man might spring back to life, she poked his leg with her slender black boot. The limb moved stiffly, then fell still again. After taking a deep, shuddering breath, Rosalyn narrowed her eyes on the man's bloody head and spat.

"Bastard!" she said vehemently, spitting again. "Bastard!" She gave his leg another kick for good measure.

Jake took her arm. "He's dead," he assured her, attempting to pull her away from the gruesome sight. "He's gotten what he deserved."

A gravelly, guttural sound rose out of Rosalyn Pendergast's chest. "Never!" she cried. "Nothing could be terrible enough for the likes of him, not even if he'd been tarred and feathered, or drawn and quartered, boiled in oil, disemboweled—"

"Are you sure you're all right, ma'am?" Jake asked. He tossed Cecilia a worried glance.

Angry tears streaked down Rosalyn's cheeks and she looked at Jake almost apologetically. "You're Jake Reed, aren't you?"

He nodded.

"I feel so ashamed," she said. "I had begun to think that you killed my brother, and unknowingly I alerted this man of your whereabouts."

"I'm sorry about your brother, Miss Pendergast. And I'm sorry now I didn't tell you the truth right off," Jake said. Briefly, he explained the events that had led to his writing the letter to her.

Rosalyn shook her head. "Gunter told me what had happened in Guthrie—what he knew of it. I pieced the rest together."

"You must have been terrified," Cecilia said. Terror was the only thing she could imagine that must have gone through Rosalyn's mind when she realized she was her brother's killer's hostage. Surprised by how dry-eyed the woman was, Cecilia took her hand comfortingly in her own. "Did he . . . hurt you?" she asked quietly.

Rosalyn looked on the dead man with emotionless eyes. "If he had I would have killed him myself," she said.

Cecilia and Jake exchanged glances. "Thank God it's all over now," Cecilia said soothingly to Rosalyn. "We can go home, and you can be on your way back to Philadelphia soon."

"Philadelphia?" Rosalyn's eyes registered almost no recognition at the mention of her home. To Cecilia, it seemed almost as if the woman had completely forgotten about that city, which would make sense. After what she had been through, it probably seemed a million miles away.

"Nobody's going home yet."

Cecilia and Rosalyn looked up at Jake, who was staring across the horizon. The cold look had returned to his eyes.

"I don't know about you," Cecilia said, "but I could use a bath and a square meal."

Jake didn't crack a smile. "Then you'll have to wait until we get to Redwood."

"Redwood!" Cecilia cried. "That's another day's ride, and I want to go home!" She pointed emphatically to the north. "That way."

Jake's mouth was set in a grim line, and he slowly shook his head. "I'm sorry. Darby is still out there, waiting."

"Darby?" Rosalyn asked, startled. She darted her gaze between Cecilia and Jake, wanting to know whether there was another man somewhere who was going to snatch her unawares.

"Darby wasn't the one chasing you, Jake," Cecilia argued.

"But he's the one behind it all. Gunter was just his thug."

"Then you should send for the law."

Jake grimaced. "I used to be the law, which has never done me a damn bit of good."

"But if you just told them what Darby has done to—"

"What has he done?" Jake interrupted. "That's the trouble, Cecilia. Men like Darby don't do their dirty work themselves. The man kicked my family off our land and practically killed my father. Yet the only thing I was able to pin on him was horse thieving, and that didn't stick."

"You said he went to jail. Maybe that rehabilitated him."

Jake hooted with indignant laughter. "*Rehabilitated!* That's do-gooder blather. Most of the time jail makes men meaner."

"My father always says you only shoot something when it's coming at you," Cecilia tried to reason. "You said yourself that you haven't seen Darby in years."

"I know him, though. He's ruthless. He's Gunter's father-in-law, and while they were in jail together—because of me—they plotted my murder. I can't let him get off scot-free."

"But you aren't sure!" Cecilia cried in frustration. "You can't just hunt him down without any evidence."

Hearing that word, Jake wanted to spit the way Rosalyn had spat on Gunter's corpse. Evidence meant diddly. "You want to know what my evidence is?"

Cecilia's chin shot out stubbornly, but she didn't stop him.

"Being chased for over a year," Jake said. "My evidence is not having been able to live a decent life because I mostly suspected that the next day I would be dead. My evidence is a man getting shot in my place, and his sister abducted."

"By *Gunter!*" Cecilia insisted. "To get Darby you need the law on your side."

"Cecilia's right," Rosalyn said, nodding solemnly.

"No, she's as wrong as can be," Jake corrected, but he didn't know how to prove it. Cecilia could talk circles around him all she wanted; the only facts he had were those he felt in his gut. Darby had been the mastermind, and Jake wasn't about to let anybody get away with murder. "We're going on to Redwood. I'm sorry, Miss Pendergast."

Swayed by the sheer emotion in the man's face, Rosalyn changed her mind and nodded again. "Whatever you think is best."

Cecilia grunted in dismay. It would serve them both right if she turned her horse northward and galloped away. But she wasn't going to leave Jake; she wouldn't be able to rest not knowing whether he was okay.

"I'm not letting you out of my sight," she said.

"Oh, yes, you are," Jake replied. "Soon as we get close in, I'm sending you and Miss Pendergast into town. You can wait for me there."

This news swelled Cecilia to new heights of outrage. She was willing to back him up, even though she thought he was taking a rash course—and he was going to deny her even that! "*Wait* for you?" she repeated, aghast. "Wait for you to be killed, you mean?"

"I can see you have a lot of faith in me," Jake said.

His snide tone made her furious. How could he joke about the amount of faith she'd put in him? What did he think it had cost her to surrender herself to him, to ride out after him, to stay with him under fire? A wiser girl would have ridden straight home and waited until his vendetta was finished to decide whether she would have fallen in love with him.

But then, a wiser girl would have stayed home on the ranch in the first place, Cecilia thought with disgust, and done what Clara told her. Wiser girls were bores.

Attempting to put her rage aside, she said, "I had faith that you would see the sense in having a backup."

"It's only one-to-one now," Jake replied. "Those aren't such bad odds."

"But with me there the odds would be in your favor."

Jake shook his head slowly. The woman just didn't get it. "No, Cecilia. If you were there, chances are I'd be more worried about your safety than just getting the job done and getting out."

"I helped you just now, though," she argued, not about to budge an inch.

"Yeah, and I was scared to death for you the whole time. This is just between Darby and me."

Cecilia's face reddened. "I think you have a death wish."

Nothing could be further from the truth. Seeing her standing there in front of him, her head tilted at a petulant angle as she regarded him through accusing eyes, Jake knew he'd never had such a fierce desire to live. Cecilia had shown him just what there was to make a stand for. If her life was jeopardized, so was his reason for coming through the victor in his encounter with Darby.

Sensing tension in the air that perhaps had nothing to do with Darby and everything to do with the spark between the two of them, Rosalyn crept off to the place where they had made camp the night before.

Jake reached out to take Cecilia's arm, thinking maybe she could be swayed by a more physical approach, but she leaned away from his touch. It was hard to believe that just minutes ago he was telling Cecilia he wanted her to marry him, and harder still to believe this woman, who had spent the most incredibly passionate night of his life with him, couldn't understand why he would feel protective of her.

"I would rather die than see anything happen to you," he told her.

Her expression softened just a hair. "If we were together, both of us would be safer."

It was so tempting just to give in to her, to appease her, so that they could get on with their business and put this in the past. At least he'd be able to keep an eye on her if she was with him.

But that was the argument he had used in not taking her straight back to the ranch—before they'd run into Gunter and he'd realized how stupid he was for giving in to her. He never wanted to live through a scene like that one again.

"No."

She stepped forward, her eyes pleading with him. "You won't even consider it?"

He shook his head. "When we get to Redwood, I'll send you to town with Miss Pendergast. If you want to look after somebody, look after her."

Clearly, this was a secondary concern to Cecilia. She threw him a bitter look. "I don't want anything to do with a man who won't treat me as an equal, Jake Reed. If you don't respect me—"

Jake groaned in frustration. "This has nothing to do with respect. This isn't your battle to fight," he explained. "It has nothing to do with you."

Cecilia looked as though she wanted to scream, but she managed to restrain herself. Just barely. She cast her glance aside to make sure Rosalyn was out of hearing distance, then warned, "If you think I came all the way out here to play nursemaid to a Yankee woman while you get killed, you're wrong."

"Miss Pendergast is a lady," he said, deciding that this argument perhaps might sway her toward reason. "While you're playing nursemaid, you could take a few lessons from her. At least when it comes to being sensible."

She stared at him in shock, and Jake feared this might not have been a good thing to say, after all.

"Sensible!" Cecilia's face was beet red with rage. "If you think it's *sensible* to ride off by yourself to meet a man who's wanted you dead for all these years, be my guest!"

Shaking with rage, she stomped off toward their old camp, then, seeing Rosalyn, veered off in another direction to be alone. Part of Jake felt compelled to go after her, yet he stood stock-still, watching her go. If he went to her now, he would take her in his arms and tell her that he loved her and was scared to death of losing her. He would say again how much he wanted her to be his wife, to live with her and love her forever.

That's what he would have said, but maybe that wouldn't have been the best thing. Cecilia was attracted to a challenge, and adventure, and he'd given her those things. But she'd also made it clear that what he wanted to make out of his life once this adventure was over didn't appeal to her. Much as his heart ached to do it, to pressure her and make promises to her while she was keyed up and vulnerable like this would be wrong.

It could be that once this was all over, with the past behind him and a long, peaceful, uneventful future yawning ahead of them, on a ranch, Cecilia would want nothing to do with him. Cooler heads would prevail, and they could part company amicably.

He sighed. Lord, he was beginning to dread those peaceful days.

Rosalyn Pendergast bestowed a distasteful glance on the three blankets lining the fireside. "This is pleasantly rustic, isn't it?"

To Cecilia it looked like another night of tossing and turning on the rock-hard ground—only alone this time—and she wasn't looking forward to it. "Hope you've got a strong backbone," she warned.

"Oh, I'm not worried about that..." The older woman's voice trailed off meekly, and her eyes darted nervously around the campsite.

Cecilia looked around, as well, but nothing was amiss that she could tell. "What are you worried about, then?" she asked.

"Oh, I suppose it's nothing...."

Rosalyn Pendergast had spoken little during their long ride, and hadn't issued a word of complaint even though Cecilia knew she had to have wanted to stop and rest twice as much as Jake had suggested.

"If there's something that's bothering you, you'd better come out with it now," she told the woman.

"Well, it's just... I know this must sound terribly prudish... but, well, aren't these sleeping conditions a little *primitive?*"

Cecilia looked again at the three blankets and laughed. "I'd rustle up a feather mattress for you if I could," she returned. At least tonight, with Gunter out of the way, Jake had let them build a fire.

Rosalyn furtively eyed the clump of trees where Jake had disappeared in search of kindling, then cast a despairing glance at his designated blanket by the fire. Finally she turned back to Cecilia and said in a low voice, "I only meant that it seems a bit *improper.*"

Even stated so directly, it took Cecilia a few moments to catch her drift. Finally, understanding dawned. "Oh, you mean you don't want to sleep with Jake?"

Rosalyn blushed. "I suppose it's silly of me to think about such things."

Cecilia heard Jake's footsteps in the darkness and smiled wickedly. Silly? The only thing silly was that she hadn't thought of this before. "Oh, no," she said earnestly to Rosalyn as she rolled Jake's meager blanket into a tight little ball. "I am thoroughly ashamed that I didn't suggest it myself."

"I wouldn't want to inconvenience Mr. Reed...."

"Inconvenience me how, Miss Pendergast?" came a low wary voice from behind them.

Cecilia turned to Jake, her face a sober mask as she held out his bedroll. "We've decided it would be best if you slept elsewhere," she informed him.

"But what if something—" Jake stopped when he saw Rosalyn's eyes widen alertly. He didn't want to scare the wits out of her by talking about what might sneak up on them in the middle of the night. "You all would be without protection," he finished less ominously.

Rosalyn worried her brows as she contemplated Jake's argument.

By contrast, Cecilia was enjoying herself; after his telling her to take a lesson in ladylike behavior from Rosalyn, it pleased her no end to be able to appear the more prudent. "Please, Jake, it just wouldn't be right," she said demurely. "After all, we are ladies."

One black eyebrow shot up skeptically. "How far do you expect me to go?"

Rosalyn fidgeted beside them. "If it's too much trouble..."

"Far." Cecilia batted her eyelashes provocatively. "You know how we ladies cherish our privacy."

Jake scowled. Nevertheless, he wasn't going to argue the point of Cecilia's being a lady in front of a stranger—especially one who would probably be returning to Annsboro with them. Cecilia's reputation would no doubt have suffered enough without this woman being able to blab the actual truth around town.

"All right," he said, snatching the bedding from her with little grace. Last night had been more wonderful than he could ever have imagined, but tonight... Well, he could only hope riding hard had worn all the imagination out of him.

Cecilia smiled as she watched him trudge away, and even winked when he turned back once to look at her. "A little farther, if you don't mind," she instructed him primly.

She could hear his exasperation through the hundreds of feet of darkness that separated them. "Is this okay, your highness?" he hollered out to her after walking a little ways.

"Just try not to snore too loudly," Cecilia yelled back.

Rosalyn looked at her shyly. "You two are... going together, aren't you?"

"Ha!" Cecilia collapsed to her blanket and stretched out her legs. "Though I guess we're going to Redwood together."

Rosalyn, having stripped to a heavy cotton shift, sat erectly on her own blanket, which, along with an Appaloosa horse and all the accoutrements that went with it, they had stolen with relish from Gunter. She smiled wistfully into the low fire.

"It must be exciting to be involved with such a man," she announced suddenly.

"Annoying, is more like it," Cecilia replied. "Jake Reed is a tough piece of work."

"But so are you," Rosalyn blurted out, then, noting Cecilia's reaction, blushed at her own words. "I only meant, I admire your courage so much. You saved my life."

The addendum mollified Cecilia somewhat, though she shrugged off the compliment. "Jake would have killed Gunter with his bare hands before he would have allowed that monster to lay a hand on either of us."

"I was terrified," Rosalyn said. "But you! You never hesitated! And when it was over, I completely fell apart, while you were completely composed."

"I was as scared as I ever want to be," Cecilia said, embarrassed. Rosalyn made it sound as if her behavior was somehow unnatural. "The only difference between us was that I had a gun and you didn't."

"That wouldn't have done me any good!" Rosalyn said with a laugh. "I've never even held a gun. Can you believe that?"

"Never?" Cecilia asked, shocked.

"We don't keep one in my aunt's house in Philadelphia."

Even at her school in New Orleans, there had been an old Gatling mounted on the wall, a relic from the war. And Cecilia would have bet money that, if for some strange reason someone had laid siege to Miss Brubeck's finishing school, every last girl there would have known how to handle the repeating rifle. Cecilia herself had been nip and tuck with firearms ever since she could heave one shoulder high.

But Philadelphia was a long way from New Orleans, and probably another world entirely from Texas. Cecilia had dreamed so long of the life Rosalyn had, she had just assumed she would have been able to make herself fit in, given the opportunity. But Rosalyn was different from other women she had known, more guileless, earnest and genuinely refined. Jake was wrong; taking lessons from Rosalyn would be pointless. No one could teach natural grace like hers.

Pure envy surged through Cecilia even as she tried to duplicate Rosalyn's posture as she sat by the fire, her legs tucked neatly to her side and her hands clasped in her lap. Unfortunately, the urge to flop and stretch was strong in her.

She mentally dressed herself down for such a foolish notion. Why should anybody care about posture when they were in the middle of nowhere?

Cecilia shot a suspicious glance out in the darkness, but nary a sound did she hear from Jake. "I guess people are just different down here," she said, finally picking up the thread of Rosalyn's statement. "Guns mean the world to us."

"It seems so primitive, this obsession with protecting oneself," Rosalyn mused. "And yet, I find it exciting."

"Exciting?" Cecilia couldn't believe her ears. "After all you've been through, I would have thought you'd want to take the first train back to civilization!"

"But this *is* civilization," Rosalyn countered, adding effusively, "a burgeoning society with all the dynamics heightened. I find it thrilling."

Cecilia's jaw dropped in shock at the woman's characterization of what she had always considered to be, even on days when she was feeling generous, the edge of nowhere.

Rosalyn laughed, a trilly, tinkly sound. "I've surprised you. But it's true, though my poor brother died so brutally, I feel in a way that his mysterious death was his way of sending for me and showing me the wonder of this place he'd always wanted to be a part of."

"But surely you'll go back to Philadelphia," Cecilia said.

Rosalyn shook her head. "I can't imagine going back to such a humdrum little life after all I've been through here."

"But..." Cecilia wanted to scream with frustration. How could someone with so much that she wanted give it all up for so little? "You don't know what you're getting into."

"Perhaps not," Rosalyn admitted, "but I do know there's much to admire out here. Since coming to Texas, I've begun to realize what kind of person I want to be."

Cecilia hesitated to ask, but finally did. "What kind?"

"Someone like you."

Now Cecilia truly was flabbergasted. *"Me?"*

"Oh, yes," Rosalyn said, her eyes bright with admiration, "I would love to have your courage and skill."

So much adoration was enough to make a person self-conscious, but for a few seconds, Cecilia allowed herself to swell up with pride. She *had* kept her head in a sticky situation, and the shot she'd gotten off on Gunter couldn't have been better—or more timely.

Too bad they had sent Jake out of earshot. He needed to hear some of this.

With what scant humility she could muster, Cecilia replied, "I was trying to save my own life today, too."

"That's just what I think is so wonderful," Rosalyn continued. "You're so open, so honest."

Cecilia blushed, her pride deflating rapidly as she remembered how for weeks she had tried every devious way imaginable to get Jake out of town. She hadn't been very honest in that endeavor, or successful, either. "Don't go overboard," she said, shamefaced.

"And people take you seriously!" Rosalyn exclaimed, paying Cecilia's words no heed.

"They do?"

"Mr. Reed does."

This was news! "Since when?"

"Well . . . he listened to your argument about why you didn't think he should go after this Mr. Darby alone."

Cecilia grimaced. "And then he ignored it."

"I think you could change his mind, if you wanted to," Rosalyn said finally. "It's in his eyes that he respects what you say."

"I could talk till I'm blue in the face, and nothing would change," Cecilia argued. "There's no two ways about it. We're on our way to Redwood."

"And that displeases you?" Rosalyn guessed.

Cecilia sighed out a shaky breath. "Jake is simply walking into trouble."

"You love him, don't you?" Rosalyn asked gently.

Cecilia's head snapped up to give a tart reply, but in the face of Rosalyn's earnest, unyielding gaze, her cynicism collapsed. "Yes, I do," she admitted, hating to say it aloud but relieved to at the same time.

From the sound of it, Rosalyn's life—the kind of life Cecilia had coveted at least superficially for so long—was twice as confining as her own. And nothing compared to that freedom she had found in Jake's arms. Putting it all together, she decided maybe a rancher wasn't too far from what she wanted, after all.

"He only wants to protect you," Rosalyn said.

"I don't see why," Cecilia grumbled. "He should know by now what a good shot I am."

"He knows," Rosalyn countered, "but he can't help himself. He wants to protect you because he loves you."

The word *loves* shocked Cecilia. Jake, love her? He had never said a word about that. But perhaps in his own gruff way, not allowing her to put herself in danger was his way of showing her.

She lay back against her blanket, looked up at the stars and smiled. She could show that man a few things about love herself.

Chapter Seventeen

Jake's heart was breaking as he looked down the hillside to the town of Redwood. Home. It sure didn't feel like home now, but he suspected nowhere would, unless it was beside Cecilia.

Atop the bay, she wore a sober, unrevealing expression. Jake couldn't tell whether she was sad or angry or beyond caring, and he couldn't say which would have made him feel worse. They had barely spoken since their argument the day before, and now he feared he might never be able to tell her what she meant to him.

But maybe, he reminded himself, that was for the best.

Rosalyn, who seemed sadder than Cecilia at their parting, sniffed back a tear. "You'd better take this horse," she said, handing him the reins of the Appaloosa.

Jake looked at the animal, hesitant to ride into Darby's ranch on Gunter's horse.

"You said yourself he's faster than the black."

Finally, he nodded, and got down off his own mount. "Stay at the hotel in town," he told them, "and wait."

Cecilia looked up at him suddenly, her blue eyes wide and innocent. "Wait for what?"

Rosalyn put a hand on his arm. "We'll stay, and then, when you get back—"

"*If* you get back!" Cecilia interjected.

"—we'll go to the sheriff together and explain what happened to that awful Gunter man."

"And Darby." Cecilia shot Jake a resentful stare. "Or maybe we'll have a sad story to tell him about you instead."

"I don't want to hear it," he said.

"You won't."

They glared at each other from atop their mounts. This should have been an emotional farewell, Jake thought with frustration. But then again, maybe the animosity between them would make leaving her easier.

And maybe, just maybe, when he came back he could make her understand why he had to do this alone. That is, if she was still there waiting for him.

"Just lie low," he instructed again, more urgently this time. "Stay in the hotel."

Cecilia's lips were set in a stubborn line.

"We will," Rosalyn promised.

Why couldn't he have fallen for someone like Rosalyn? Jake thought briefly—a nice, biddable woman who cried and smiled encouragingly when a man was about to ride off to his death. Instead, he had to fall in love with Cecilia Summertree, a tough-as-nails beauty who was as uncompromising as he was.

Love. It was like a revelation, and he was stunned to think that, after all he'd been through, he had actually managed to fall in love at all. Not so long ago he'd decided that his prospects for ever finding anyone to share his life with were pretty small. But he had. Only now was rather late in the game to be realizing it—and looking at Cecilia, he knew it was a far sight too late to tell her. She didn't want to hear it, anyway.

"Don't worry about us," Rosalyn told him.

The advice almost made him laugh. How could he not worry when he didn't even know what he was going to find at the Darby ranch, and knowing he was leaving behind the person he most treasured in all the world? Life forced bitter trades, but this one was the hardest of all.

He had to say goodbye. Rosalyn smiled shakily at him and wiped her eyes delicately with an old scruffy handkerchief, but Cecilia looked dry-eyed and unfazed by their parting.

"So long, Reed," she said. "I hope you know what you're doing." *And what you're giving up,* her tone seemed to indicate.

Jake tapped his heels into the Appaloosa's flanks and rode off with Cecilia's words ringing in his ears.

Behind him, when he was fast becoming a speck on the horizon, Cecilia turned to Rosalyn, shaking her head. "You are the most shameless liar I have ever met." She cast her eyes to the heavens in a disbelieving scoff. "Crying, no less!"

Rosalyn smiled graciously and tipped her a bow. "He seemed so glum, Cecilia. You could have given him *some* hope, you know."

"I'm going to give him something better than hope," Cecilia retorted before they kicked their horses into a gallop down the long sloping hill toward town. "I'm going to give him help."

Sheriff Burnet Dobbs lived in a tidy wood frame house behind Redwood's small jail. A woman walking down the street with a basket of eggs on her arm pointed the way to Rosalyn and Cecilia, who immediately ran over and pounded on the door.

Moments later a towering man with gray hair and pale gray eyes appeared in the doorway. His surprised gaze took in the two women slowly, clearly not quite understanding why two such stylish yet bedraggled creatures had come to his house so early in the morning.

"Whooo-ee," he drawled, taking in their worn and dusty dresses—especially Cecilia's. "You two ladies look like you walked here clear over from Paris!"

"Not quite. We're from Annsboro," Cecilia said, getting right to the point. She was anxious not to lose any time. "We've come about Jake Reed."

The name got Burnet Dobbs's attention. "Jake?" he whispered. "I haven't heard from him in years."

"You've got to go after him, Sheriff, and round up all the extra men available—"

"Whoa, now," the sheriff said. Cecilia was practically hopping up and down in her panic. "Take it slow." He put his hands on her shoulders to calm her down.

As quickly as she could, Cecilia explained what had happened, who Rosalyn was and what Jake's mission was today. "Someone needs to help him!"

The sheriff's gray eyes registered alarm. "Killing Will Gunter is the best day's work anyone's done around here in years. But Darby . . ."

Cecilia shivered at the speculative glint in the man's eye. "Is it that bad?" She and Rosalyn exchanged worried glances.

"If Jake guns down Darby it will be cold-blooded murder."

"But the man is a bully!" Cecilia cried, jumping to Jake's defense. "You don't know what he's done to Jake! We've got to help him!"

The sheriff shook his head. "Otis Darby is a madman."

The word struck a chord of terror in Cecilia. The specter of a raving wild-haired lunatic jumped to her mind, and she felt instantly contrite for letting Jake go out there alone.

She only hoped now wasn't too late. She turned away, and the tears she had been holding at bay for so long sprang to her eyes.

"Wait a second."

"There's not a second to waste! Darby will kill him!"

"No, he won't," the sheriff said.

"You said yourself he's a madman," Rosalyn insisted, backing up Cecilia.

"He is, but he's also harmless. He's been off his head since getting out of jail."

"Harmless?" Cecilia asked.

"Since Darby learned of his daughter's death, he hardly knows who he is."

Harmless. Cecilia released a deep, heavy breath as her shoulders sagged with relief. For a moment she allowed herself to lean against the door, thanking providence, until she realized that the sheriff had turned into the hallway and was arming himself in preparation to set out for the Darby ranch. The alarmed look remained in his eye.

"What are you doing?" If he considered Darby harmless, then that rifle could only be in anticipation for a showdown... with Jake!

The sheriff grabbed a handful of cartridges from a box. "We've got to stop him. If Jake finally comes face-to-face with that man, he might shoot first and ask questions later."

"But he won't if he sees..." Cecilia suddenly remembered the determined look in Jake's eye when he left her. This whole trip had been about one thing—getting to Darby.

As her nerves kicked in, she sent up a silent prayer that Jake would use some restraint. "Can we get to him in time?"

"Maybe." The sheriff grabbed a rifle off a rack and opened the door. "Darby isn't living in his big ranch house anymore. Jake doesn't know that."

Cecilia followed the sheriff, then turned to Rosalyn on the small porch. "Will you be okay here?"

With an encouraging smile from Rosalyn, Cecilia ran toward the bay.

She shouldn't have left him. She shouldn't have left him. She should have sent Rosalyn into town and followed Jake on her own. Never, never should she have let him out of her sight. The reproach echoed over and over through her mind during the frantic ride to intercept Jake. Her nerves hummed with dull, persistent fear. Before she'd been worried that Jake would get himself killed. Now she was terrified that he was setting himself up for even more serious trouble.

The dogged set of Sheriff Dobbs's shoulders left no doubt in her mind that the man would send his own mother to the hoosegow if there was just cause. And no one would blame him for seeking recourse in this case if Jake managed to get his revenge. Especially since his revenge would apparently be misplaced.

The month and a half since Jake had first walked into the Annsboro schoolroom passed through her mind. She could hardly believe the man she knew was that same flippant, silly person, but the fact that he was made her care all the more for him. It was still a marvel to her that he could have successfully hidden his desperation from her for so long.

Cecilia galloped over the unfamiliar terrain with fear increasing in her heart. Every beat of their horses' hooves accentuated their mad race against time, and she prayed each homestead she saw in the distance would be the one they were headed for. But always they would pass the house up, or the gates, or the beaten path that seemed as though it would lead them to a ranch.

All the while, her insides were clenched with dread. What if Jake had already killed Darby before they could get to him? The sheriff, no matter what he thought of Jake, would certainly testify that Darby was a simpleton who had done nothing to provoke the attack—nothing that he hadn't already paid for with a jail sentence. And then it would be Jake who would be tried for murder. Tried and probably convicted.

She attempted to force the ugly scenario from her mind, but failed. What would she do if Jake was sent to jail? That answer, at least, was clear as crystal in her head. It would have seemed silly to her just a month ago, but now she knew without a doubt that she would wait for him, no matter how long it took. But most of the time judges weren't satisfied with jail time when it came to murderers....

Cecilia shuddered. She couldn't think about it. The only thing she was sure of was that she never should have left him, and once they caught up with him, she would never leave him again. She only hoped Jake would use his head until that time.

On and on they rode until all at once they cleared a rise and saw on the other side a shabby-looking two-story ranch house. The Appaloosa nibbled at the Johnsongrass in the yard. Sheriff Dobbs motioned for Cecilia to slow her horse, and pointed down the hill. Cecilia didn't want to stop until she found Jake, but she did as the sheriff said.

Beyond the house were stables and outbuildings, and farther away still, a small lone house of graying water-stained boards. It was that house that the sheriff's steely eyes were focused on.

"The overseer's house?"

Dobbs shook his head. "No overseer here for more than five years. That's where Darby lives now, 'cause it's smaller and easier to care for."

Heart hammering, Cecilia narrowed her gaze on the little house and the yard. Only barely could she make out two forms in front of the place.

"Look!" she cried.

One man was on his knees. The other had a gun pointed at the man's head.

The sheriff didn't look for long. Both of them spurred their horses into a gallop and sped down the hill as fast as they could. White, cold fear gripped Cecilia so fiercely that she couldn't see the world whizzing past her, but only followed the sound of the sheriff's mount in front of her. *Too late,* she thought, near hysteria. *I'm too late!*

The bay skidded to a stop and Cecilia jumped to the ground on wobbly legs. She felt sick as she turned to see what she was sure would be a scene more grisly than even Gunter's death had created. But what she actually saw was more heartbreaking.

The men were still positioned as she had seen them before, with Darby, his eyes wide with fright and confusion, kneeling in front of Jake. But the revolver that had seemed so threatening from a distance she could now see was held slack at Jake's side, and the expression on his dear face was simply stunned.

Cecilia looked on Jake's old adversary, an old withered man who was terrified by a stranger's appearance in his yard. His confused blue eyes recognized no one, not even when Sheriff Dobbs came forward to give him a hand to his feet.

"I haven't done anything," the old man pleaded in a desperate whisper. He clutched the sheriff's hand as if for mercy. "I did my time. That's all over now."

"That's right, Otis," the sheriff said in a kindly tone, as if speaking to a very young boy, "it's all over. Can you stand up?"

But the old fellow was too afraid to get out of his beseeching position. "I did my time," he insisted. "I have nothing you could want now."

"We only wanted to see how you were, Otis."

Jake's dark impassioned gaze met Cecilia's and she grasped his arm in support. "Oh, Jake," she said. "I was so worried. I didn't know what we'd find...."

"I would never have known him," Jake whispered. There was no venom in his tone now, only pity. "I barely recognized the ranch—everything's so different now."

He looked around, and Cecilia's eyes followed his gaze across the weathered buildings and overgrown scraggly grounds. Two skinny chickens were pecking at the yellow grass in front of the small house, heedless of the scene nearby.

After all these years, Jake felt pity for the man. In a way, Darby's condition was a worse reward for a lifetime of hate than even a bullet through the head would have been.

"He's destitute," Dobbs said to them in a low voice. "He hasn't been able to keep the place up."

Hearing the conspiratorial tone, Darby looked up sharply. "Do I know you?" he asked, his spindly limbs shaking when he noticed the star on the man's shirt. "I know! You're from the jail!"

"No, no," the sheriff said, soothing the terrified old man. "We only want to see how you are, and if you need any food."

"Food?" The man looked up at the sheriff gratefully. "I have no bread here."

"As far as I can tell, he's the only one on the whole place," Jake said, still shaking his head in disbelief. "This was once the finest ranch in the county. Now it's so empty and overgrown...."

This time when Darby looked up, he focused on something beyond Jake. Tears sprang to his old bloodshot eyes. "Eleanor," he said, mouthing the name more than actually speaking it. "Eleanor, my daughter!"

The three of them stared at each other in confusion, then turned to see Gunter's Appaloosa approaching. The old man stood and reached out as he walked to meet the horse. "How did you find her?" he asked as he rubbed the animal's muzzle. "My daughter raised this mare from a filly."

"Gunter must have taken him," the sheriff said in a quiet voice as they watched the man reunited with his horse. Dobbs walked forward a step and asked gently, "What do you call that horse, Otis?"

The bewildered expression returned to Darby's face. "I...I can't remember." He racked his brains for a few moments more, then, in a sudden change, asked, "May I keep her?"

The sheriff turned to Jake, as did Cecilia. The ownership of the horse was uncertain to all but him. Still half in shock at the scene around him, and the man he'd come to get even with, he said, "She's yours, Darby."

Darby smiled, a sad, nearly toothless smile. "Then I'll call you Eleanor," he whispered joyfully in the Appaloosa's ear. Then he said the name again, as if not quite remembering whether the name belonged to a horse, a woman or an angel. "Eleanor."

"A man loses his livelihood, then his pride, then his only loved one..." Burnet Dobbs sighed and shrugged. "That kind of shock is bound to change a man."

They were seated around the small table in the sheriff's kitchen, drinking strong black coffee. They had left Otis Darby at his ranch with promises to bring provisions. Being reunited with his daughter's horse seemed to have done a little good for the man, who had finally snapped to enough to recognize the sheriff. He'd even said he was certain he could come into town himself, since he had a good animal to ride.

Jake was still amazed at the transformation of his old adversary. "I nearly killed him, but when I looked into his eyes, I knew he wasn't quite right."

"It's a lucky thing you got close enough to see," Cecilia said.

Jake shook his head, chagrined by his own hotheadedness. "I went out there for the sole purpose of bringing Darby to his knees, begging forgiveness. That's why I got so close—so I could see the fear in his eyes. I'd waited so long for that moment, dreamed about it. Then, when it finally came..."

"You realized he'd stopped being your adversary long ago," Cecilia finished, covering his hand with hers.

"You have nothing to fear from that man," Dobbs said, shaking his head as he shoved his emptied cup forward on the table. "His daughter Eleanor's death while he was incarcerated had a terrible effect on him. When he got out, he didn't know what to do with himself. He had no money, and he discovered that before she took sick, his daughter had sold off all the livestock while he'd been in jail so she could live off the proceeds. Every time he came to town he looked worse and worse, and then finally we didn't see him at all for a couple of months.

"I went down to the ranch to check on him—mostly because I never trusted Will Gunter, who was also supposed to be living with Darby. But when I visited...oh, about a year and a half ago, Darby said Gunter had disappeared, and I could tell then that his mental state had deteriorated. After that, we've been bringing him food, but there's not a whole lot else to do for the man. He's given up."

"So he didn't know where Gunter had gone, and that he was chasing Jake?" Cecilia asked.

"Gunter was insane, too, only in a more violent way," the sheriff said seriously. "Darby had guessed that he had pushed farther west. If only I had known he was on your trail, maybe I could have helped, Jake."

Jake frowned. "I guess he'd clung to his hatred of me so he wouldn't have to think about losing his wife, and his crazy father-in-law." He remembered seeing the cold, manic look in Gunter's eye as he'd attempted to rob the wagon. "Or maybe he was just bad."

"He was a viper," Rosalyn said in an unrelenting tone. "Gunter deserved what he got."

"But Darby..." His voice trailed off for a moment. "I guess he probably paid for his crime more than was his due."

"And what now?" the sheriff asked Jake. "Are you thinking of staying in Redwood?"

"I don't know about that." Jake shrugged and glanced covertly at Cecilia. "Not much here for me now," he said. Everything he wanted was in Annsboro.

"Bet there are plenty of towns west that need lawmen," Dobbs said. "I could send word for you."

Jake shook his head. "To tell you the truth, I'm not sure what exactly my business is anymore," he admitted, "but I don't think it's the law." He was careful to keep from glancing toward Cecilia. They needed to have a talk about this someday soon—in private.

"Some people can wander so much they lose their bearings completely," the sheriff said. "Take care you don't let that happen to you."

"Don't worry," he assured his old colleague with a wink. "I might not have a good scheme for the rest of my life, but in the short term I know exactly what has to be done."

Cecilia held her breath, and felt Rosalyn's keen eyes on her.

"What's that?" Dobbs asked.

"These ladies have to be escorted home."

Chapter Eighteen

"More coffee, Miss Pendergast?"

Shaking her head, Rosalyn smiled at Jake and then sent a hapless shrug to Cecilia, who was standing away from the fire, sipping her morning brew in an uncharacteristically brooding manner. She was achy and cranky after another sleepless night spent tossing and turning on the cold, hard earth, thinking about the man who lay—at Rosalyn's insistence—a few hundred yards away.

She had thought his escorting them back to Annsboro was a good sign, but the man hadn't spoken two words to her the whole time.

"I think I'll walk a bit before we set out again," Rosalyn said, giving Cecilia a look that indicated she wasn't expected to join.

Somehow, since leaving Redwood, Jake just hadn't known how to talk to Cecilia. He worried she would reject him now that the excitement in their lives had died down and she was able to see him for what he was—a man without much money, no profession and no home as of yet to offer her. Not much of a deal, when you thought about it. Yet when he remembered how they made love together, how it was to be with her...

Jake approached Cecilia carefully but swiftly, knowing full well there was scant time for broaching what needed to be said. Rosalyn couldn't walk forever.

She turned away from him, her back stiff and proud, and he was filled with such tenderness that he couldn't help moving toward her, determined to let her know how he felt no matter how long it took, even if Rosalyn ended up strolling all the way to Arkansas. He placed his hands on her shoulders.

"Cecilia, we need to hash some things out here."

She turned, her expression expectant but leery.

"Namely, us," he explained hesitantly.

Cecilia scoffed even as her heart tripped a little faster. "You weren't so concerned about *us* when you went riding off hell-for-leather after Darby."

"I was only concerned about our future," Jake said.

"*Our* future?" Cecilia put her hands to her hips and tapped her foot in irritation. "How was I supposed to guess that, when for all I knew you were riding off to your doom?"

"You could have had a little trust in me," Jake said defensively.

"But I was only trying to help!" she explained heatedly.

They stared at each other in frustration. Jake had meant to take her into his arms and whisper in her ear all the wonderful things she had come to mean to him—love, a family, a future. Now all he could think about was his shortcomings, and how unsure the future truly was.

He sighed. His best strategy was cut to the chase, and Cecilia's impatient pout, which told him plainly that was all she had the heart for, spurred him on. Squaring his shoulders, he decided it was now or never.

"I think we ought to get married as soon as possible."

Wide blue eyes stared at him unblinkingly for a moment, then Cecilia's arms crossed, her chin jutted out, and the belligerent look he'd been expecting appeared in short order. Weren't women supposed to enjoy being proposed to? Jake wondered in amazement. "And no," he argued before she could, "I'm not saying this because I feel obliged."

"You could have fooled me," Cecilia said flatly.

"Just because of what I said before about consequences..." Jake stammered in frustration. "Well, hell,
aren't you concerned that you might be carrying my child?"

Cecilia felt a blush work its way right down to her toes.
How had she ever let herself be in this position? A woman
like Rosalyn would never find herself being proposed to this
way!

Still, she couldn't deny the truth in Jake's words, and she
answered him with a silent nod.

He kept at her. "Doesn't that tell you we should get married?"

"Maybe," she admitted.

His heart hammering in his chest, Jake took another step
forward and held her hands in his. "Why all this hesitation? Let's—"

Cecilia pulled away impatiently. "Wait a cotton-pickin'
minute," she interrupted, shaking her head. "I'm not going to marry just anyone, no matter what the circumstances. When I get married, it's going to be to someone...
well, special."

Jake shifted his stance with a heavy sigh. "Special, huh?"
He rubbed his chin thoughtfully. Wasn't what they had
special? Or was *special* just another word for rich?

Cecilia nodded curtly. "Someone who doesn't just care
for me..."

Jake's heart stopped beating. No one could care for her
more than he did, he was sure of that. But if she wanted
more than that...

"He would have to be someone who thinks I hung the
moon."

Jake smiled in relief. This was a specific he could handle.
"You did!" he swore. "The fool thing has your name written all over it." He leaned in closer. "Tonight I'll show
you."

So far, so good. Cecilia weighed her options for a moment. "And I also want someone who respects my opinion," she said, remembering their contentious argument

about his going after Darby alone, "and who won't send me away just because I disagree with him."

Jake made a show of crossing his heart. "I'll never make another move without your go-ahead." He took her into his arms and promised, "And I'm never letting you out of my sight again."

"Never?" Cecilia asked, her brows wrinkling as Jake became more and more carried away.

He nodded. "You'll be sick of me."

Cecilia laughed. "That wouldn't surprise me one bit."

Jake bowed. "Is there any other requirement I need to fulfill for you?"

"Just the proper proposal requirement," Cecilia said, trying to keep a straight face as Jake's expression screwed up quizzically. "For instance, I have noticed that you have no trouble playing the swain to Rosalyn...or should I say *Miss* Pendergast." She tossed her head petulantly.

"So..." Jake guessed slowly. "You would like to see a little more formality on my part."

The suggestion met with a pert toss of the head.

To her shock, Jake dropped down to one knee, took her right hand in one of his and used his free arm to clutch her legs so that she was effectively hobbled within his grasp. "Oh, Miss Summertree, if only I could tell you what your barbs and insults have meant to me," he began, his voice trembling dramatically.

Cecilia tugged at her hand, smarting at his sarcastic tone. She was willing to swallow her pride...to a point. But she'd given Jake the perfect opportunity to declare undying love and it appeared he wasn't going to take it. Frowning, she finally pulled hard enough to retrieve her hand, but in so doing, she was completely thrown off-balance. She swayed and tipped until she was just saved from falling rump first onto the ground by landing instead on Jake's bent knee.

"You planned that!" she sputtered in outrage.

Jake laughed outright. "No, but I wish I had. Unfortunately, I don't think anything involving the both of us will ever go according to plan."

He pulled her to him, and in spite of herself, Cecilia warmed to the raw emotion she saw in his dark eyes. His lips covering hers felt so right it was all she could do not to instantly melt against him. As it was, it took some coaxing on his part, and some sensuously whispered reminders of the pleasures they had shared together.

When he finally pulled away, she lay against his chest, breathless from their kiss but more alive than she could ever remember being. His heartbeat sounded in her ear, and she listened for a few moments to the wonderful quick rhythm that matched her own. They always reacted so strongly to each other, yet the connection between them had to be more than just a physical one—it just had to be.

For long minutes, neither of them spoke, but instead simply listened to the wind rustling through the grass and the sound of their own breathing. The world, after so long, seemed entirely peaceful. It felt perfect.

"I love you, Cecilia."

She looked up, her expression one of astonishment when Jake whispered again, as if in answer to her unspoken prayer, "I love you."

Surprise instantly turned to joy. "I can't believe you said that!" she cried.

He laughed. "Is that good?"

"Don't you know?" she asked. "I love you, too."

He brought her lips close to his own. "Then it's better than good," he said.

It was like a miracle, one that she had been beginning to doubt would ever happen. Two days ago she had sworn she would never beg for someone's love, but today she had been on the verge of doing just that ... or convincing herself she could live without it. Now she couldn't keep the unadulterated joy from her heart as they kissed again, this time with such tenderness it left her aching for more when he pulled away.

"I'm not sure what our life will be like," Jake began.

Our life sounded heavenly. "Happy, what else?"

Jake frowned. "Cecilia, I'm trying to be serious. As far as work goes, it will be a struggle. I might even have to leave for a while—"

"I thought you were never going to let me out of your sight."

Jake released a sigh. "You never hesitate to throw a man's words back at him, do you?" he asked.

"Not when I can use them to my advantage," Cecilia said coolly.

"Well, we'll have time to think it through," he conceded. His eyebrows raised speculatively. "If you're so concerned about our being parted, does that mean you've reached a decision?"

"Concerning what?"

"Marriage."

Cecilia's heart fluttered in hesitation for a scant second before she threw her arms around him once again, the momentum of which collapsed them both to the ground. "Yes!" she cried enthusiastically, then added, "when?"

Jake smiled with satisfaction. "As soon as we can scrounge up a preacher."

"Mr. Reed! Cecilia!"

Rosalyn, her skirts balled up in her fists, came dashing up from her lonely stroll and skidded to a stop not two feet away from them. Her eyes widened in dismay when she saw them sprawled on the ground, but she quickly recovered her composure—if not her breath.

"A rider!" she cried. She pointed out beyond a rolling hill. "He's headed this way!"

"Maybe he saw the smoke from our fire," Cecilia conjectured.

Jake sprang into action, kicking dirt over the dying coals as he unholstered his gun. "You all take cover," he instructed crisply.

Cecilia's lips turned down in a frown. "Jake..."

He looked up, his expression panicked by her and Rosalyn's inaction. "Didn't you hear me?" he said impatiently.

"But, Jake...why should anyone be after us now?"

Slowly, his tensed expression fell slack and the revolver dropped to his side. But he refused to completely relax. Old habits died hard.

"We don't know who this is," he said.

Cecilia picked up her father's rifle and waited until the approaching hoofbeats became louder and more insistent. The rider, who was galloping straight toward them, slowed as he came within better sight. Then, as he appeared to take in the number of people in their small camp, he again urged his horse into a gallop. A few hundred feet away, the stranger let out an exuberant, familiar cry.

"*Cici!*"

Jake and Rosalyn looked at Cecilia in surprise as a broad smile came instantly to her lips. "Buck!" she yelled, putting away her rifle and running forward to meet him.

Though she'd only been away for four days, it seemed ages since she'd seen Buck's familiar face. His horse came to a rearing stop and he slid off with as much joy as she felt. They embraced with a vigor that completely ignored the fact that he was a married man and she was, very unofficially, engaged.

"I'd about given up hope of finding you," he said.

"You've been looking for me?" she asked, surprised. She had known her father would be worried about her being gone, but it had never occurred to her that a search party would be sent out.

As if for the first time, Buck noticed the two people standing apart from them. He looked in confusion at Rosalyn, then at Jake.

"Pendergast!" he spat out. "You just wait—"

"I'm *Rosalyn* Pendergast," Rosalyn interrupted him, moving forward to offer her hand. Cecilia had to give her credit for anticipating this bit of confusion before she herself did.

Buck's bewildered gaze moved from Rosalyn to Jake and back again. "*Mrs.* Pendergast?"

"Miss," Rosalyn corrected.

"This is Jake Reed, Buck," Cecilia said. At his befuddled expression, she told him, "It would take to forever to explain."

Buck shook his head as he turned his attention to her. "That's not the only thing you have to explain, Cici. On the day you disappeared, the girls at Grady's said they heard gunfire, and then one of them saw a man abduct a woman—" His words were cut off as his startled eyes moved to Rosalyn again. "You?"

Rosalyn nodded.

His gaze returned to Cecilia. "Then you and Pend...I mean whoever this fellow is..."

"We went for a ride," Jake said jokingly.

Buck's lips turned down in a dogged frown. "Your father's not going to like this one bit, Cici," he said ominously. "He's already said that if Penderg—I mean, whoever this is—shows his face again, he'll have his hide."

Cecilia laughed. "Oh, Buck, it's all right. We're going to be married."

His eyes flew open as they darted between her and Jake. "You mean Dolly was actually right about you and... whoever this is?" he said, jabbing a thumb toward Jake.

"Absolutely," Cecilia confirmed.

Rosalyn let out a happy gasp. "Oh, Cecilia, I'm so happy for you!" She ran over and gave her new friend a brief hug and bestowed a smile on Jake. "I must admit, I was worried when I ran up and found you two rolling together on the ground."

Cecilia and Jake exchanged a giddy loverly glance.

Buck's face fell slack. "Guess you two will be getting hitched."

The rest of the day they rode and rode, picking up more members of the Summertree search party as the day passed. When they finally reached the ranch, they discovered Dolly, her boarders, the Beasleys, Parson Gibbons and several other townspeople had camped out at the ranch to offer Silas Summertree what solace they could. The small, tense group from the house came out to meet the raucous crew riding in, and the air was thick with relief and jubilation. Upon seeing Cecilia, Lysander Beasley, to his credit, actually threw his bowler in the air and let out a hearty whoop.

"You sure had us worried, miss!" cried Fanny Baker. "Especially your daddy."

Cecilia half dreaded seeing her father. Somehow, she had never dreamed that her disappearance would have caused so much heartache . . . and controversy. No one had been able to figure out if she had eloped, or whether another Summertree girl had tragically disappeared.

Her father met her with tears in his eyes. "Cecilia . . ." he said, his voice catching in his throat. "My daughter."

"Oh, Daddy," Cecilia said, throwing her arms around him happily. After all they had been through, this was the first time she had seen her small, hot-tempered father cry. "I'm back now."

He pushed his hat back on his smooth head and looked her over from tip to toe, as if to make sure no damage had been done. "I was so worried. And when they told me that Pendergast characte—"

Clearing his throat, Jake reluctantly stepped forward into Summertree's angry glare. "I'm Jake Reed, sir."

The people from town gasped in astonishment. "You're not Eugene W. Pendergast?" Lysander Beasley bustled forward to ask. His froglike eyes looked as if they might just pop out of his head.

"No, sir, I'm not," Jake admitted.

It took quite a while to explain who exactly Jake was to Beasley's satisfaction. They went indoors, and Cecilia's father sat dumbfounded through the whole story, as if he couldn't quite believe that even his muddle-prone daughter had gotten herself mixed up in a mess like this.

Clara had no such trouble. "Girls with independent notions always come to sorrow in the end."

"But you see," Cecilia assured the dining room full of people, "everything turned out just fine."

But the skeptical glare Clara sent toward Jake indicated that lady had yet to be convinced.

"Oh, boy!" Suddenly Bea Beasley ran forward, so excited that her glasses looked as though they might fall off their perch on her turned-up nose. She grabbed Jake's hand and looked up at him with more adoration than ever. "This was even more exciting than what happened to Pete and Willa!"

"Who are they?" Beasley asked his daughter indulgently.

"A gunfighter and a woman of ill repute," Bea announced loudly and dutifully. "Mr. Pen—I mean Mr. *Reed* taught us all about them at school."

"A woman of..." Beasley's jaw hung slack.

Jake blanched. "Bea, I don't think this is quite the time..."

The little girl's face screwed up in puzzlement. "They weren't bad people, Father. And they didn't kiss nearly as much as Mr. Reed and Miss Summertree."

Cecilia felt a red flush creep into her cheeks as all eyes in the room turned on her yet again.

"Only Pete and Willa's story was a lot happier," Bea added, unaware of the reaction around her, "because they ended up married."

Cecilia opened her mouth to speak, then failed as her father stepped forward. She had a feeling their audience was in for another famous Summertree scene.

At the last moment, Jake stepped between the father and daughter. "Actually," he said, quickly snaking an arm around Cecilia's waist and still finding himself nose to nose with her father, "before we came back, Cecilia promised to become my wife."

For an agonizing moment, the room was filled with stunned silence. Cecilia looked at one shocked face after another before her gaze finally alit on her father's eagle eyes looking into her own. Slowly, as he detected the depth of feeling he read in her pleading glance, a grin wide enough to match Jake's appeared on his face.

It was as if ten years of grieving disappeared from Silas Summertree in that one moment. The dark circles beneath his eyes were lost beneath the happiness that shone in them, and the careworn wrinkles in his forehead fell away.

He shoved his hand forward and pumped Jake's arm energetically. "Well, well!" he announced robustly, "I told them all along this was nothing but sweetheart shenanigans."

Everyone around them laughed and clapped. Cecilia couldn't believe that all the drama she'd been through was being reduced to the status of a lover's prank. "Oh, no, you don't understand," Cecilia told her father. "I told you, we were being chased by a madman!"

He reached forward and pinched her cheek. "Come, come. I knew you were in love when I saw you at the dance together."

Cecilia opened her mouth to deny it when she remembered what had happened when she left the dance. She *had* been in love all those weeks ago—it just took some people longer than others to get things straightened out. Especially when they weren't willing to admit who they truly were.

She turned to Jake. For years, she had dreamed of being something she wasn't, of living a life she wasn't by temperament suited to. But she knew now exactly who she was, and who she wanted to spend the rest of her life with, and, thanks in part to the loving reception the people around her had given them, and the pains they'd taken to find her, she knew where she wanted to spend that future.

On a ranch.

Jake sent her a tender wink and reminded her, "You promised you'd marry me as soon as we found a preacher, remember?"

She looked out among the group around them and sure enough, Parson Gibbons was staring right at her, with a smile that betrayed just the slightest hint of disapproval. "I certainly did," she said without hesitation. "Is it too late for a spur-of-the-moment wedding?"

Silas Summertree bellowed his approval. Cecilia couldn't remember seeing her father happier than he was now, surrounded by an entire town, with the prospect of having a new budding family around him.

Especially when Jake announced that he wanted to try his hand at ranching. What better place than right here on the Summertree ranch? Silas told Jake happily, extending an invitation to take over the running of the place in whatever capacity he would be happy with. Jake, though hesitant, seeing the need in the old man's eyes to keep the last of his family with him, decided they could work something out.

And at this decision, the sad old house itself seemed to brighten.

The only person more pleased with the arrangement than Silas was Dolly. "This is wonderful!" she exclaimed happily. "Buck's place on the ranch will be vacant once he moves into town."

Buck, though looking anything but jubilant, had a smile frozen on his face. "That's right. I'm gonna open up Jubal Hudspeth's blacksmith shop again."

"A town needs a blacksmith," Dolly said, beaming, to which Lysander Beasley nodded approvingly. "So you see, it's worked out perfectly!"

Perfect for everyone except the horses, Cecilia thought.

The wedding ceremony was short, with Cecilia's father giving her away and Rosalyn serving as an impromptu bridesmaid. Bea, fresh off of Dolly's wedding, adamantly insisted on being flower girl. That there was no aisle to march down, or even any flowers to hold, did not faze or discourage her.

After the wedding, Silas broke out his best wine and toasted the married pair, and Dolly came up to give Cecilia a choking hug. "Oh, Cecilia, I knew you'd be next."

"Thanks, Dolly."

Immediately, however, as Cecilia received a shy but heartfelt embrace from Cousin Lucinda, Dolly's mind again turned to business and her gaze, a mite peevish, landed on Jake. "Only now I've got an empty room on my hands! What's the town going to do for a schoolteacher?"

"That's a good question," Beasley said. "You don't know how hard it is to find well-qualified teachers like..." His voice trailed off as he looked at Jake and realized that his Philadelphia import hadn't been well qualified at all.

All eyes turned to Cecilia. "Oh, no," she protested, "I'm a married lady now. I'll have my hands full."

Beasley looked peeved by the domestic turn her dreams had taken.

"I can teach," Rosalyn announced. Her face was flushed, but her eyes glinted with determination.

"You?" Cecilia asked. "But don't you want to go back to Philadelphia? I thought for sure you'd change your mind about that."

"I'm staying," Rosalyn insisted. "So I might as well make myself useful."

And after talking to Rosalyn for five minutes, Lysander Beasley pronounced her more than worthy to be Annsboro's new interim schoolteacher.

It took a while for the newlyweds to extricate themselves from the crowd, but when they did, the sky was a brilliant blanket of stars above their heads. The night might have been the most beautiful one Cecilia had ever seen. Walking arm in arm with Jake, and stopping at leisure for long, slow kisses, only made it more dazzling.

"Would you have thought this morning we'd be married by tonight?" he whispered teasingly into her ear.

A little thrill zipped down Cecilia's spine. It seemed they had all the time in the world—and even that wouldn't be enough. "I was just waiting for you to get around to asking."

"That's right," Jake said, resting his forehead against hers, "put all the blame on me."

"Where it usually belongs," Cecilia said saucily.

He pulled her into his arms and kissed her like there was no tomorrow, and for a moment there wasn't—only now, on this dark night, with the two of them so thoroughly in love with each other they would be just as happy never to see daylight again.

"I feel like I could live on moonlight," Cecilia said, taking in a deep breath when their lips parted.

Jake placed another light kiss on the crown of her head. "If anyone should be able to, it's you," he said. "Your hair looks so luminous now, your eyes so deep blue, it looks as though you were made for night. Besides," he whispered, reminding her of her first request of that morning, "you surely had some good reason for hanging the moon up there."

Cecilia laughed lightly and laced her hands around the back of his neck. "You remembered," she said, pleased. "You told me you would show it to me tonight."

"There are more things than that I want to show you," he whispered intimately, pulling her close.

"You had better get started, then," Cecilia said, her eyes sparking with desire. "Time's a-wastin'."

And the kiss he answered with told her in no uncertain terms that he couldn't have agreed more.

*   *   *   *   *

RUGGED. SEXY. HEROIC.

OUTLAWS *and* **HEROES**

Stony Carlton—A lone wolf determined never to be tied down.

Gabriel Taylor—Accused and found guilty by small-town gossip.

Clay Barker—At Revenge Unlimited, he *is* the law.

JOAN JOHNSTON, DALLAS SCHULZE and **MALLORY RUSH**, three of romance fiction's biggest names, have created three unforgettable men—modern heroes who have the courage to fight for what is right....

OUTLAWS AND HEROES—available in September wherever Harlequin books are sold.

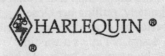

HARLEQUIN ®

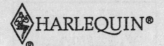

Harlequin® Historical

WOMEN OF THE WEST

Exciting stories of the old West and the women whose dreams
and passions shaped a new land!

Join Harlequin Historicals every month as we bring you
these unforgettable tales.

Don't miss any of our **Women of the West!**

OFFICIAL RULES

FLYAWAY VACATION SWEEPSTAKES 3449

NO PURCHASE OR OBLIGATION NECESSARY

Three Harlequin Reader Service 1995 shipments will contain respectively, coupons for entry into three different prize drawings, one for a trip for two to San Francisco, another for a trip for two to Las Vegas and the third for a trip for two to Orlando, Florida. To enter any drawing using an Entry Coupon, simply complete and mail according to directions.

There is no obligation to continue using the Reader Service to enter and be eligible for any prize drawing. You may also enter any drawing by hand printing the words "Flyaway Vacation," your name and address on a 3"x5" card and the destination of the prize you wish that entry to be considered for (i.e., San Francisco trip, Las Vegas trip or Orlando trip). Send your 3"x5" entries via first-class mail (limit: one entry per envelope) to: Flyaway Vacation Sweepstakes 3449, c/o Prize Destination you wish that entry to be considered for, P.O. Box 1315, Buffalo, NY 14269-1315, USA or P.O. Box 610, Fort Erie, Ontario L2A 5X3, Canada.

To be eligible for the San Francisco trip, entries must be received by 5/30/95; for the Las Vegas trip, 7/30/95; and for the Orlando trip, 9/30/95.

Winners will be determined in random drawings conducted under the supervision of D.L. Blair, Inc., an independent judging organization whose decisions are final, from among all eligible entries received for that drawing. San Francisco trip prize includes round-trip airfare for two, 4-day/3-night weekend accommodations at a first-class hotel, and $500 in cash (trip must be taken between 7/30/95—7/30/96, approximate prize value—$3,500); Las Vegas trip includes round-trip airfare for two, 4-day/3-night weekend accommodations at a first-class hotel, and $500 in cash (trip must be taken between 9/30/95—9/30/96, approximate prize value—$3,500); Orlando trip includes round-trip airfare for two, 4-day/3-night weekend accommodations at a first-class hotel, and $500 in cash (trip must be taken between 11/30/95—11/30/96, approximate prize value—$3,500). All travelers must sign and return a Release of Liability prior to travel. Hotel accommodations and flights are subject to accommodation and schedule availability. Sweepstakes open to residents of the U.S. (except Puerto Rico) and Canada, 18 years of age or older. Employees and immediate family members of Harlequin Enterprises, Ltd., D.L. Blair, Inc., their affiliates, subsidiaries and all other agencies, entities and persons connected with the use, marketing or conduct of this sweepstakes are not eligible. Odds of winning a prize are dependent upon the number of eligible entries received for that drawing. Prize drawing and winner notification for each drawing will occur no later than 15 days after deadline for entry eligibility for that drawing. Limit: one prize to an individual, family or organization. All applicable laws and regulations apply. Sweepstakes offer void wherever prohibited by law. Any litigation within the province of Quebec respecting the conduct and awarding of the prizes in this sweepstakes must be submitted to the Regies des loteries et Courses du Quebec. In order to win a prize, residents of Canada will be required to correctly answer a time-limited arithmetical skill-testing question. Value of prizes are in U.S. currency.

Winners will be obligated to sign and return an Affidavit of Eligibility within 30 days of notification. In the event of noncompliance within this time period, prize may not be awarded. If any prize or prize notification is returned as undeliverable, that prize will not be awarded. By acceptance of a prize, winner consents to use of his/her name, photograph or other likeness for purposes of advertising, trade and promotion on behalf of Harlequin Enterprises, Ltd., without further compensation, unless prohibited by law.

For the names of prizewinners (available after 12/31/95), send a self-addressed, stamped envelope to: Flyaway Vacation Sweepstakes 3449 Winners, P.O. Box 4200, Blair, NE 68009.

RVC KAL